FAIR LAUGHS
THE
MORN

Genevieve Gray

SUNSTONE
PRESS

SANTA FE
NEW MEXICO

First edition
Printed in the United States of America

Library of Congress Cataloging in Publication Data

Gray, Genevieve
      Fair laughs the morn / Genevieve Gray. -- 1st ed.
        p. cm.
      ISBN 0-86534-213-X : $14.95
      1. California--History--To 1846--Fiction. 2. Frontier and pioneer life--California--Fiction. 3. Women pioneers--California--Fiction.
I. Title.
PS3557.R29443F35   1994
813' .54--dc20   93-31048
                                         CIP

Published by Sunstone Press
         Post Office Box 2321
         Santa Fe, New Mexico 87504-2321 / USA
         (505) 988-4418 / FAX: (505) 988-1025
         orders only (800) 243-5644

ACKNOWLEDGEMENTS

The author wishes to thank Rev. Charles W. Polzer, S.J., specialist in history of the southwestern U.S., for his assistance with historical and liturgical details of the text; Mary Curnow and Beverly Anderson for their excellent editorial advice; Mary Clare Barteck, B.A., M.A., and Marguerite Pasquale, B.A., M.A., for their guidance regarding Roman Catholic worship and usage; Louise Kirkpatrick, R.N. and Beatrice Mason, R.N., for their help with medical details; Jean Dickens (ret.) formerly of Pima County Health Department for her expertise in community health practice; Frank Ott, B.A., M.Ed., and Mary Jo Wolfert, B.A., M.A., for Spanish language correction and assistance; John R. Gonzales of the California State Library and David Allen of UC Berkeley for their help with the roster.

The song lyric, "King David," is from page v of the preface in *Puro Mexicano*, Publications of the Texas Folklore Society Number XII, 1935, edited by J. Frank Dobie, Austin.

The roster at the back of the book is compiled from *Handbook for the Re-Enactment of the Juan Bautista de Anza Expedition 1775-6, 1975-6,* by Winston Elstob and Helen Shropshire (California Heritage Guides, 10 Custom House Plaza, Monterey CA 93940), and *Antepasados*, a publication of Los Californianos, v II, Bicentennial Issue.

FOREWORD

It could be said that a historical novel is a literary sandwich, with slices of "actually happened" plot structure enclosing romantic "might-have-happened" stuffing. Sometimes, of course, the "actually-happened" provides more genuine excitement per chapter than any "might-have-happened" the author could possibly invent. Such is the case with the Anza Expedition of 1775-1776, the historical episode which encloses the fictional "might-have-happened" of the literary sandwich which follows.

Locale of *Fair Laughs the Morn* is 18th century *Nueva España*, largest of Spain's colonies and already ancient as the story begins. More than twenty-five centuries have gone by since Cortés conquered the Aztec ruler, Montezuma; the Spanish Empire has since expanded to include half the known world. *Nueva España* is bounded on the east by the Mississippi River and on the west by the Pacific Ocean. The colony's resplendent capital is the great city of Mexico, the Paris of the western hemisphere.

By 1774, however, the splendor is fading. Spain has grown weak thanks, paradoxically, to her vast resources of gold and silver from the New World. Unlimited dependence upon this revenue has sapped its value so that while appearing to enjoy great wealth, she is severely straitened.

More virile nations, witnessing Spain's decline, have been quick to respond. Along the western coast of North America, Russian trappers are plundering the northern islands of seal and otter. English seafarers are probing for harbors from which they, like the Spanish, can trade with Hawaii and the Philippines.

Carlos III is an ambitious monarch who seeks—too late—to revive Spain's neglected commerce and protect her threatened lands. California is ripe for development but the area is difficult to reach by sea. The fragile hundred-foot ships are swept away by violent winds and tides, or they are becalmed for weeks in dense fogs. Braving the risks, the Spanish king has nevertheless sent Franciscan missionaries to establish settlements. By 1775, there are missions at San Diego, San Gabriel, San Buenaventura, San Luis Obispo, San Antonio de Padua, and at Monterey, San Carlos Borromeo.

Unfortunately, the natives, whom the padres are expected to convert and civilize are slow to accept Christianity and even slower to accept the discipline of agriculture. Sorely needed is the example of real farmers, husbandmen who plow and harvest, who milk cows each morning and go to church on Sunday, Needed even more urgently is a safe overland route from *Nueva España's* northern frontier to this earthly paradise called California. In Madrid, the monarch has allocated funds and appointed personnel to make such access a reality.

Thus in April 1775 an overland expedition of 250 mounted settlers — men , women and children — and a thousand head of livestock will leave the ancient frontier town of Horcacitas in northern Sonora. With them will travel pack animals to carry household goods and soldiers to protect the expedition from the uncertain friendship of natives they will meet along the way. The expedition will be led by Colonel Juan Bautista de Anza. With the loss of only one life, it will reach Mission San Gabriel on the California coast in January 1776.

So much for the "actually-happened" part of our literary sandwich. Mingled with the romantic "might-have-happened" stuffing are five of the novel's characters based upon actual historical figures: Colonel Anza, his bride Ana, his sergeant Juan Grijalva, the chaplain Padre Font, and the missionary Padre Garcés. All the rest are fictional.

All but one. Vasco Bellis (not his real name), was originally fashioned after a real expedition traveler. But as the story unfolded, Señor Bellis's character grew increasingly disreputable — infinitly worse than anything the research sources even remotely suggested. I wanted to remove him completely but the plot would thereupon have fallen apart. In the event, I kept him but changed his name, unwilling as I was to burden a modern California family, wherever its progeny might be, with so repugnant an ancestor.

For, of course, from what "actually" happened emerged "actual" pioneers who afterwards settled in many locations in California, raised their families and prospered. A complete roster with their ages and family affiliations appears at the back of the book. Today, 250 years later, their tjousands of descendants are among the oldest and most distinguished of America's families.

Genevieve Gray
Tucson, Arizona
1994

PROLOGUE   Convent of Santa Clara de Asís, Mexico
                                                                 April 1774

The nun's long face twisted with anger. "No!" she said sharply. "How many times must we go over it? Gabriella belongs here at the convent. Here she stays!" She whipped her robes to one side and seated herself behind the desk.

The bulky, graying priest standing beside the door nervously fingered the ruby-studded rosary hanging at his waist. Every month he journeyed the twelve miles from the city to visit his charge, María Gabriella Salgado. And every month his rich jewels and silk-lined cossack failed to secure him against the proud asceticism of his cousin Luz, abbess of the Convent of Santa Clara de Asís. Cousin Luz found it easy to bully him, and bully him she did.

The abbess was a deep-chested woman with bushy brows and eyes set too far apart for beauty. Her broad square face tapered to a narrow jaw full of big square teeth. Padre Mero thought she looked like a horse. An especially stubborn, spirited, resourceful and intelligent horse.

The abbess tossed the folds of her veil out of the way behind her shoulder, gathered the coins Padre had left on the desk for Gabriella's expenses and flung them into a small chest. To her family, the abbess was known as Luz, but to the archbishop in Mexico, she was María Augusta Cristina Valderia de la Tapiz. The name never failed to bring a satisfied smile to the old prelate's lips. He was proud of the convent of Santa Clara de Asís, with its reputation for saintly poverty, its distinguished sponsors, its school for young women of the better class.

Ordinarily the abbess was even-tempered, but earlier that afternoon the head gardener had discovered yet another crack in the crumbling wall of the sacristy. Her narrow lips tightened in frustration. The convent buildings had already fallen to ruin long before she was born, and now their very age precluded tearing them down: They were a monument, after all, to the illustrious age of Cortés.

A monument, perhaps, but the empire's riches were depleted long ago and funds were scarce. Convent repairs meant less money for the school and less assistance for the farm families, some of whom were scarcely able to survive from one year to the next. Not less money for the archbishop, however; the ever-increasing fees to Mother Church came first, and with each succeeding year they weighed more heavily.

Yes, Madre Valderia had her worries. And now in the middle of her busy afternoon, unannounced, came this vexing cousin of hers, "little Raoul", twiddling his gaudy beads and trying her patience with his disturbing plans for Gabriella.

At a soft knock on the door, she turned.

"Yes?"

An ancient serving woman appeared. "Refreshments for the padre are ready, Madrecita."

"Thank you, Lila." To her cousin, she said, "The refectory is deserted at this hour. We can talk there."

Padre Mero followed the abbess down the echoing marble- paved corridor. On the walls, portraits of Spain's royal family alternated with religious paintings and carvings of awesome beauty and great value. Wimpled nuns in their white robes and schoolgirls in their black petticoats stood aside to let Reverend Mother pass with her guest.

Many of the sisters and students greeted Padre with smiles and curtsies. Two young pupils, scarcely six years old, came running headlong down the hall. Madre Valderia clapped her hands and declared sharply, "No running in the halls! That's enough, Carmelita! Angela!"

With one swift arm, she scooped up the first child but the other escaped and collided with Padre Mero. Laughing, he swung her high. "Is this one Angela? Yes? Well, little angel, you'd better wait until you have your pretty white wings before you travel with such speed. It is lucky for you that you only ran into me. What if you had run into that marble column there? Your nose would be flat!"

"The girls have their schoolwork to do, Padre. Put the child down and come with me." Madre Valderia continued down the corridor to the refectory, just off the colonnaded patio.

At the entrance, Padre Mero paused. Across the courtyard, in the shaded portico opposite, he caught sight of Gabriella. She was seated with a group of girls busy with their embroidery hoops. Her tawny hair glowed among the somber school uniforms. As he watched, she rose and bent over a younger student, helping her. *She could be her mother's twin*, thought Padre. *More spirit, though, more fire. Far more.*

The priest followed Madre through a wide portal into a shadowed hall smelling faintly of stale bread. It was here that three hundred nuns, novices, students and convent staff took their meals each day. The room was majestic in scale and simplicity. Tables and benches were of unfinished lumber, worn with age. The cups and bowls, already set out for the evening meal, were of primitive ceramic, shaped and fired by Indian workers in the convent workshops. Each place was marked with a shiny apple grown in the convent's orchard and later there would be cheese from Santa Clara's famous dairy herd.

Each diner provided her own cutlery. Convent girls from wealthy homes, and some of the nuns, had spoons and forks of burnished silver whereas workers from the convent fields and orchards would eat with wooden spoons they had carved themselves.

Along the wall facing the entrance was a lectern raised several feet above the floor. Here, during meals, a nun read aloud from Scripture or from lives of the saints. Upon the wall hung a life-size crucifix, before which Padre Mero crossed himself and briefly bowed his head.

Madre Valderia waited beneath a narrow stained glass window where a table had been spread with cold meats, pastries, custards, fruit, and wine. Padre Mero sighed. All his life, he had wrestled with the sin of gluttony, a weakness well appreciated by his cousin Luz. More than once, he had arrived for his monthly visit resolved on some needed change for Gabriella only to be dissuaded over a sparkling glass of rare amontillado or an apple tart laced with cinnamon, fresh from the convent oven.

Today, once again, he had come with his charge's welfare in mind, and this time he was more determined than ever. Yet at the sight and smell of such fare, his mouth began to water, his breath to quicken, and his quest to fade in importance.

The abbess served a heaping plate of the choicest tidbits for her guest but Padre Mero ate sparingly. After a decent interval, he pushed away from the table and deliberately turned his back on temptation. "Now to Gabriella."

Madre Valderia's narrow lips twitched but she checked her anger. "It is a waste of time, Raoul, to keep going over this same question. She is only a child. Her place is here, where she is loved and valued for the little girl that she is."

"Fifteen years old is no longer a little girl, Luz. You yourself told me she became a woman three years ago."

— *And could have bitten off my tongue the moment I mentioned it*, thought Madre Valderia.

They had grown up together, she and Raoul. He was the motherless son of a wastrel uncle, taken by her father into a household crowded with brothers, sisters and cousins. From the beginning, she and Raoul had their love of God in common. But whereas she scorned her father's wealth and resolved to give of herself, he sought an easier path. After completing his training as a lay priest, he was summoned to serve as chaplain to the wealthy Costanza family. There he had stayed.

But Raoul's life was his affair; Gabriella's was hers. "We've been over the issue before. The answer is still no."

Padre Mero clasped his hands tightly in his lap to keep them still. "Gabriella's welfare is of importance to others besides yourself, Luz," he said gently. "Her legal status being what it is — "

"Gabriella's legal status is that she is an orphan, a ward of the Church. Her welfare has been entrusted to me."

"Hear me out. As Gabriella's confessor I understand, as you do, that she wishes to take her vows and become a nun, preferably here at Santa Clara de Asís. But the secret of her birth is no longer as safe as it once was."

"How can it not be safe? Gabriella thinks her red hair came from her mother who died soon after she was born. She has never known who her father is."

"I realize that," said Padre Mero. "She thinks her father was an unknown sweetheart of her mother's. And so it could have been. Carmen never named the father of her child, did she?"

"Not even when she realized she was dying. So who is there to know? Teresa, you, me."

"Earlier, yes. But Gabriella has grown into a very capable young woman, admired by the convent schoolgirls. They return to their families in the city and chatter about the orphan girl with red hair who is visited once a month by Padre Mero, chaplain of the Costanza family. She even went home for a week's visit with one of her schoolmates last year. There is much for gossips to wonder about."

"You see ghosts behind the door," scoffed Madre.

"Forgive me, Luz, you are mistaken. Only a few days ago, at the *paseo*, Doña Teresa was asked outright by a friend why her chaplain visits this girl every month."

"Raoul — " A pause. "Gabriella has readily admitted to her convent friends that the Costanza chaplain visits her because her mother was a maid in the Costanza household. So what of that? An unmarried household maid finds herself with child — that is not unusual."

" — And even for the family to show concern for the maid and her child, that is not unusual, either. But for the family's chaplain to oversee the child's welfare for *fifteen years*?" Padre Mero leaned toward the abbess and lowered his voice. "Especially when the child has hair the color of carrots and the son who disappeared fifteen years ago also had hair the color of carrots!" Reaching for his wineglass, he sipped. "Long memories are more common than one would think."

A pause.

"Tell me something," said the abbess. "Gómez forced her, didn't he?"

"I don't know. I suspect he did. If it had been otherwise, Carmen would have been the first to tell me."

Madre Valderia's jaw set in a grim line. "Gabriella must never, never suspect her father of such behavior! Never!"

"I sympathize wholeheartedly with your judgment on that score. But in the present matter, we must think of Doña Teresa and her sick husband. I always hoped that toward the end of his life, Don Eduardo's bitterness toward his son would abate. But it hasn't. The man is gravely ill, and if this escapade concerning Gómez came to light, the anger would kill him." A pause. "That, Luz, is why I have come, once again, to respectfully request that Gabriella be allowed to leave the convent."

"Pah!" Madre Valderia turned away impatiently. "Who would be likely to bring such news to a dying man? No. Gabriella is growing into an attractive young woman. Thus she needs more, not less, protection. You will grant that point, of course." Her glance was sour with resentment.

The wineglass in Padre Mero's hand began to tremble and he replaced it on the table. "You have always held me responsible for what happened. And, Luz, I swear to you by the Blessed Virgin I knew nothing of what had taken place until Doña Teresa told me. Carmen had gained weight and looked unwell. Doña Teresa questioned her."

The abbess rose. She moved to the window, opened the casement and gazed out over the well-tended garden. Ordinarily her careful eye would be checking the work of the gardeners, but now her thoughts were elsewhere.

"I've never believed you," she admitted. "I've never believed Teresa, either. Gómez was her favorite, her first-born. You expect me to suppose he told her nothing? That in confession he gave you not so much as a hint? Not even a guilty silence?"

"Before he left? He told me nothing."

"You knew what he was like. You told me yourself he was carousing with his friends from one end of the valley to the other."

"And for that very reason, I thought Carmen and the others were safe. Two, three dozen women we had about the palace at that time — nursemaids and bakery cooks and such. There were never any complaints of his unseemly behavior. Not from any of them." He paused. "And from Gabriella's mother, that sweet angel who had the most right to complain, there was never a word. Suddenly she stopped coming to morning mass with the family and the other servants. That was my first hint that something was wrong." He straightened. "But please, Luz, these events happened years ago. The matter of Gabriella is important now. Today. It must be settled."

"Very well, terminate your monthly visits. We can say to her that she is older now and no longer needs someone to counsel and guide her. — Which is quite true, you know. There is certainly no need to deprive the child of her home, as you propose to do."

" — Deprive her temporarily," qualified Padre Mero. "Later she would continue at the convent as though she had never left. Her plans would be interrupted briefly, that's all. It would be no worse for her than for the city girls who leave home to attend school here." He refolded his hands in his lap, cleared his throat and continued. "As I am sure you know, the friendship between the archbishop and Don Eduardo has always been close. Now with his illness, the archbishop comes to call more often than usual. Not long ago, I took the liberty of asking about the Church's position regarding novices. Girls who—"

Suddenly the abbess closed the window with more force than was necessary. Crisply, she interrupted, "Yes, I know all about the Church's position regarding novices."

A pause. Padre Mero began again, "According to the archbishop, the Church wants — "

Again Madre Valderia interrupted. "The Church wants nuns — needs nuns — but scorns candidates with no experience of the world. More than once I've had promising schoolgirls who wanted to become nuns but I sent them away. 'Church policy,' I told them. 'Go learn what life is like outside the convent and then come back.' And did they come back? Almost never. When they did, I wanted to weep. There they were at the gate with their babies, begging for food, for clothes, because the husband gambled and drank away everything they had. What a waste! And all because of church policy!"

"But Luz, it was the decision of the girl and her family that she marry," Padre Mero reminded her. "Their decision, that's the important thing. And perhaps it was God's decision too, don't you see? To take a girl like Gabriella who knows nothing but the convent and allow her to live out her life here safe and snug, what sort of decision for Christ is that? It's meaningless."

—*Or so the archbishop believes anyway*, thought the abbess rebelliously. "Raoul, the girl is a *bastard*!" she flared. "You blithely ignore that fact! Here she's safe. Outside the convent she'll fall victim to every lecherous rogue who drifts her way. You're mad to insist on this!"

"My dear Luz, you too are ignoring facts. The protection of the Costanza family will be readily available to her in the city. Far more readily available there than here."

The abbess drummed her fingers on the windowsill. It did not come easily to María Augusta Cristina Valderia de la Tapiz to lose an argument, but with the archbishop in the picture, she knew she was destined to lose this one.

She lowered herself heavily into a chair. A pause. A shrug of defeat. "Very well. You know what Gabriella can do, what kind of work is most congenial for her. Perhaps you can find an appropriate situation in the city."

Padre Mero cleared his throat. "Yes, under the circumstances, I seem to be the logical one to initiate an arrangement of this kind."

Madre Valderia eyed her cousin, suspicion dawning. "Could it be that you have already found such a situation?" she inquired sweetly.

"Well, yes," said Padre Mero, examining his fingernails. "I have given the matter some thought. There is a possibility of her joining the household of Avila Flores de Figuroa Beretta. Don Avila is an official at the court of the viceroy. This is a *gachupín* family with influential relatives in Madrid. They have a fine palace, Buena Suerte, located near the aquaduct on the avenue leading to Chapultepec."

"I see."

"There is a married son with children in Jamaica. Three daughters, two still living at home. The oldest daughter is married and lives in Vera Cruz with her husband's family."

"And I suppose Gabriella would be working in the scullery at Buena Suerte?"

"No, indeed, she will not! She would be the paid companion of the youngest daughter, Bonita, age sixteen. Don Avila has authorized me to offer Gabriella a salary of two pesos a month."

Madre Valderia's eyes widened. A real or two was the going rate for household servants. Two pesos was generous to the point of madness. A corner of her mouth lifted wryly. "This daughter, she is a witch, perhaps?"

Padre Mero smiled, and a dimple winked in his cheek. "She is a good Catholic. She is also said to be well-mannered and the most beautiful young lady in Mexico. Unfortunately, she is in poor health. Don Avila was especially interested to know that Gabriella has been studying with your *enfermera*, Sister Magdalena."

"Ah. In that direction she has the *don*, the gift of God. It's true. She is already an accomplished *yerbera*, more talented with remedies than Magdalena herself, I sometimes think."

Her glance came to rest on the padre, chubby hands clasped smugly over his paunch, a contented smirk gracing his lips. Reading him correctly, her mood hardened. "So, Cousin, your plans have turned out as you expected. She goes with you."

Madre rose abruptly, terminating the conversation.

As Padre Mero followed her from the refectory, she cast a final dark glance in his direction. "But it's too good, you know," she said. "Far too rosy a prospect. There's a thorn hiding in that lovely bouquet somewhere, mark my words."

CHAPTER 1   Convent of Santa Clara de Asís
                                                   April-May 1774

The sleeping patient on the examining table moaned softly. "Infected, is it?" asked Sister Magdalena, briskly drying her hands. "How bad?"

"Red streaks nearly to his knee." Her young assistant flexed the injured ankle and shook her head. The girl everyone called Gabriella was a slender, graceful young woman of medium height with strong, square hands. From the age of ten, she had worked in the convent's *botica*, preparing herbs, balms and syrups. But as she matured physically, her talent also blossomed. Sister Magdalena, finding herself short-handed the year before, brought her into the clinic.

The leathery old nun approached the examining table for a closer look at the wound. The patient was an eight-year-old boy, Pedrito, now drugged against the pain. He had stepped too near one of his father's smoking blacksmith tools and his flesh had been burned away, laying bare the bone. Clogging the bloody tissue was a suppurating mass of dried clay and cow dung, the remains of a poultice the boy's mother had applied to draw out the heat.

The injury had occurred three days before. Gabriella frowned. "If they'd brought him sooner, he'd be healing by now!"

"And if fish had knees, they could pray," Sister retorted crisply. Pedrito was not brought sooner because there was no one to bring him. Farm work demanded every able-bodied family member, a fact Gabriella knew as well as Sister Magdalena.

The boy roused.

"Ai, such a lazy one you are!" Gabriella teased him softly. She brushed his long hair clear of eyes still swollen from weeping. "You decided to wake up?"

She met his worried gaze and smiled. "We'll have a dressing on your ankle soon," she said. "Then your father will stop worrying. He is waiting for you in the courtyard."

Sister Magdalena finished her inspection. "Clean it with wine," she ordered. "Use the port. The old bottle. Then aloe and eggwhite. Have Rosalina make up a fresh batch. She knows how."

"She got it too thick last time."

"If it's not right, tell her." Veil flapping, Sister Magdalena departed to summon her next patient.

The boy watched sleepily as Gabriella plucked bits of clay and straw from the wound with tweezers. "I didn't mean to fall, Gabriella," he said. "It was an accident."

"I believe you, *hombre*. Nobody gets a burn like this on purpose."

"Can you fix it?"

"We'll do our best," Gabriella answered earnestly. "We'll ask God to help. You'd better ask God to help, too. Maybe with all of us together, we can fix it."

The office door stood ajar and Gabriella knocked softly.

"Yes?"

"You sent for me, Reverend Mother?"

"Yes, Gabriella. Come sit down. I have some news for you. I realize this is one of your days to help Sister Magdalena. What I have to say won't take long."

The girl closed the door behind her and sat opposite the desk.

"Gabriella, do you remember last year when I mentioned that you might have to leave the convent for two or three years before beginning your novitiate?"

Pause. "Yes. But then you also said I shouldn't worry about it, that I probably wouldn't need to leave."

"Yes, I did say that, didn't I? So I owe you an apology."

Gabriella tensed. "Has something gone wrong, Reverend Mother? Maybe the fee to join the order — ?"

"No-no. You mustn't worry about the fee. That's taken care of. It's only that you'll be gone for awhile." Madre's quick eyes flicked over the black school uniform. "By the time you get back, you'll be old enough to begin your novitiate. You'll like that, won't you?"

The spray of freckles across Gabriella's nose rearranged themselves as she smiled. "Yes, Madre."

"Very well, we'll count on that."

"But you say I'll have to go away?"

"Yes. I'm afraid there's no way to avoid it. My dear, we live a sheltered life here at Santa Clara. It's the same at any convent. In the city, outside in the world, there are ways of living, pleasures and luxuries we never see here. But there are also horrible things — brutality. Depravity, even."

"If it's so bad, then why must I leave?"

"Because it's important for you to experience the real world, to comprehend both the good and the bad, before you take vows that will close that world to you forever."

"But suppose I don't want to know what the world is like?"

Madre said firmly, "Your care has been entrusted to me by Mother Church, Gabriella. I must make decisions for you that are in your best interest. This is such a decision." Briefly she outlined the arrangments Padre Mero had made for her. "I explained to Padre that you are needed here for the next few weeks. April and May are busy months in the clinic." She shrugged. "We need you. So he has agreed to come for you at the end of May. It's best that way, I think. You will have time to get ready, perhaps stitch together a new frock to take along."

"But I'm too young to be sent away!" cried Gabriella, her dark eyes filled with fear. "Why must you shut me out? This is my home, here at the convent! Have I made you angry? Why are you sending me away?"

"Gabriella!" Madre's voice was sharp. "You haven't been listening. You aren't being punished. It isn't as though you were going to the city to stay. You'll be coming back."

"Other girls have left and said they were coming back, but they never did. We never saw them again! I'm not ready! Oh, Madre, please don't make me go!" Sobs erupted in her throat and emerged in a gale of weeping.

"Here now, this won't do!" exclaimed the abbess. She rose, rounded the desk and drew Gabriella into her arms. Stroking the auburn hair, she waited for the storm to subside. Then she said quietly, "Child, two or three months ago you said, 'Madre, I want to learn everything I can.' Do you remember saying just those words? The workmen were building a new retaining wall around the terrace and you were pestering them to find out how they did everything and why. Remember?"

Wrapped close in Madre's arms, head against the heavy shoulder, the girl nodded.

"Very well. Then last summer when I had you lance the boil on that old woman's neck — the Indian woman? — you said, 'Thank you, Reverend Mother, for letting me work in the clinic, because that way I can learn more.' Do you remember saying that?"

Again Gabriella nodded.

"And I asked you why it was that you wanted to learn so much. Gently the mother superior released the girl and held her at arm's length, searching her face. "And you said — what? What was it you said?"

Eyes averted, Gabriella murmured, "'So I can serve God.' 'So I can do better work for God.'" Her face burned with shame, for it had been the first and only lie she ever told Madre Valderia.

"Well, then," Madre said gently, "isn't this a way to learn more? Don't you think it might be a good thing for you to go to the city and live with this Figuroa family for awhile?"

Before sunrise next morning, everyone at Santa Clara, even the cooks, knew that Gabriella Salgado would be going to the city with Padre Mero. The days spun out their busy hours as they always had, and six weeks later, long before Gabriella was truly willing to leave, time had caught up with her.

On the day of her departure, the faint tinge of dawn found her already awake when the convent bells rang for matins. Their echo died away in the hills and a few novices silently rose, crossed themselves and murmured prayers to greet the coming day.

Gabriella identified their familiar shadows — Federica, Rosalina, Carmen and the others. Quickly the novices slipped into their modest habits and departed quietly so as not to disturb the schoolgirls still sleeping. In the corridor beyond the dormitory, the sound of their whispering footsteps faded in the chill night air.

That's the last time I'll hear that sound, thought Gabriella, and a hot cloud of dread engulfed her. Reverend Mother had said she must leave, so leave she would without whining. But *Santa Madre!* How she feared it!

Gabriella was six years old before she fully understood about her parents. In answer to her question, Padre Mero had gently explained, "Your mother was saintly, Gabriella, but she and your father were not married by a priest. You are an illegitimate child."

At that young age, Gabriella found little meaning in his words, and even less in his further advice: "'The hot blood of the mother scalds the daughter'," he warned her. "Remember, my child, that you will always be vulnerable to the sin of lust. Be on your guard."

"I don't understand, Padre."

"Good," he had said, gently touching her hand. "May the time never come when you do."

But the time had come, four years later when she was ten. One spring evening with the dormitory silent about her, she had dreamed of a dark spirit hovering above her — a warm, hungering presence whose touch made her breasts ache with yearning. In her lower abdomen, a slow series of contractions set her childish hips to thrusting gently. Her heart beat faster and she moaned. More quickly came the contractions until, gasping for breath, she felt her loins gripped in an overwhelming sensation unlike anything she had ever experienced before — pain? ecstasy? dismay? transfiguration? a sacred visitation of some kind?

Frantically, she threw back the bedclothes and looked about, staring. Her dormitory companions slept as though nothing had happened.

But what *had* happened? She had seen nothing, heard nothing but the surging of her own blood in her ears. When her breathing and pulse returned to normal, she lay sleepless, her thoughts a-swirl like sparks from a bonfire. Maybe Consuelo would know. She could ask her friend Consuelo anything without embarrassment or fear of betrayal.

But ask her what? Was it sinful, this feeling? Was it lust that she had experienced — the lust Padre Mero had talked about so long ago and had puzzled her ever since? She had never told Consuelo about Padre's warning. It was too shameful even to admit to her closest friend.

In the end, she locked her secret away, but her doubt haunted her. How could it be that the "hot blood of the mother had scalded the daughter" while the daughter was yet a child of ten? Until that terrifying night, Gabriella had assumed — as she assumed the sun would always rise — that she would someday become a nun. But above all else, a nun must be chaste. Could God be warning her, in the deep of the night, that the life of the convent was not for her? *You are a creature defiled!* — is that what God was saying to her? Was He turning her away?

The following day, Gabriella went about her work in a daze. If God had rejected her because of her parentage, would not a suitor do the same? In the great world outside the convent, she would need money to survive. Perhaps she should be learning something useful, something respectable that an unmarried orphan girl, alone in the world, could do to earn her way. She visited Sister Magdalena in the *botica*. If Reverend Mother would agree, would Sister Magdalena train her as a *yerbera*?

So the arrangement was made. Neither of the older women associated the child's request with her fever next day and her subsequent weight loss. Worried, Sister Magdalena ordered her new apprentice to the infirmary, where as a patient, the girl stared listlessly at the ceiling for two days. It was the first and only time Gabriella Salgado was ever ill.

She never confessed her experience to Padre Mero. But for months afterward, she spent furtive hours on her knees in the chapel begging Holy Mother to cleanse her taint, promising as penance to excel in every convent task assigned to her. She asked forgiveness not only for herself but for her dead mother, whom she now envisioned as a seductive coquette, a whore even, who probably deserved the suffering she endured.

And now, too soon, Gabriella was leaving the safety of Santa Clara for that hazardous wilderness known as "the world". In that unforgiving world, a young girl with no male relative to protect her was little more than sheep-eyed trash, fair game for any boy, rich or poor, seeking to take his first woman and thus prove himself a man. Convent schoolgirls weren't supposed to know men were capable of such brutishness. But at the clinic, an occasional raucus *paisana* would joke about hotblooded boys up to their usual tricks — referring to her own sons or brothers — and would even boast of their savage conquests!

Gabriella tossed restlessly on her straw mattress, then rose and struck a light to the candle beside her cot. Glow from the flame touched her almond eyes and dark lashes. Shadows flickered through the glossy red-gold of her hair tumbling over her shoulder.

"Couldn't sleep, eh?" asked a voice from the cot beside hers. "With your squirming all night, neither could I." Gabriella's friend Consuelo pushed free of her blankets and felt on the floor for her slippers.

"Sorry if I kept you awake," murmured Gabriella. "Let's go to the dayroom by the fire and sample that plum cake you made." She shrugged into her homespun robe, then led the way through the heavy door at the end of the dormitory.

"The cook let me into the kitchen yesterday to make it," said Consuelo. She carefully unwrapped a dark pudding-like confection, studded with cherries and nuts. "Are you sure you want to cut this? I made it for a journey gift."

"Of course I want to cut it! It will taste better here with you than beside a dusty road somewhere with Padre."

As Consuelo sliced, Gabriella's smile faded. "I'm going to miss everyone at the convent. You especially, Consuelo. We've been such good friends. You'll let me know when you're coming to the city to visit your parents?"

"I've already told you a dozen times, yes."

"Mmm," Gabriella nodded, chewing. "You've made a delicious cake and you said you never made a cake before."

Consuelo shrugged. "You're riding all the way to the city and you've never ridden a horse before."

"You're wrong! In the Easter fiesta last year I rode a pony."

"And fell off," Consuelo reminded her. "Whose idea was it for you to ride a horse to the city anyway? The Figuroas have three or four carriages; why didn't they send a carriage for you like the other families do?"

"I don't know. Anyway, I'm not riding a horse. I'm riding a mule. It looks like the twin of the big one Padre Mero rides all the time. Very tame and happy. Padre introduced us yesterday."

Consuelo stiffened. "*A mule*?! You were hired as a lady's companion, not as a servant to launder the family's underwear! And they expect you to ride *twelve miles* on this beast! *Santa Madre*, you'll be so sore!"

"Maybe not," said Gabriella, chewing contentedly. "I'm tougher than you think, probably. Anyway, there's nothing I can do about it. At first Don Avila told Padre he'd send six armed guards and a litter for me, but I guess he changed his mind."

"Changed his mind, did he?" sniffed Consuelo. "At home, my father and uncles know all about Don Avila Flores de Figuroa. If he changed his mind, that means he's been losing at cards again. He's a terrible gambler — drinks too much and then bets too much and loses money by the bucket."

Gabriella stared. "You're teasing. Consuelo, that can't be true."

"Oh, it's true, all right. But don't worry. For every bucket of money the old coyote loses, he has a hundred more from his plantations and silver mines. Not to mention the presents his rich relatives in Spain send him from time to time. The story Papa hears is that the old man's soft-hearted when it comes to his daughters, Bonita especially."

"The youngest," said Gabriella.

"The older one is Javiera. Javiera prays all the time." After a pause, Consuelo asked grimly, "Did Don Avila send any escort for you at all?"

"Padre Mero brought two guards with him. So on the trip back, there will be four of us. That's plenty, isn't it?"

Consuelo hesitated. Thieves along the road were a serious concern with travelers.

"Well, isn't it?" Gabriella asked again. "You travel to the city to visit your parents all the time and bandits never stop you. Last year, you took me with you, remember? And Padre makes the trip every month with no escort at all."

"That's different," said Consuelo. "When a convent schoolgirl goes home, half her family comes to fetch her. They look on it as a fiesta, except that all the men are armed. As for Padre, while he's on the road, you can be sure he hides his flashy jewelry. And with that big shovel hat he wears, a bandit can spot him for a priest a mile away. Outlaws usually stay away from the clergy. No desperado wants to be excommunicated because he robbed a priest."

Gabriella thought a moment, then shrugged. "If we run into trouble, the men will handle it."

At the fire, Consuelo warmed first one slippered foot, then the other as she nibbled at her cake. "Has Padre told you anything more about Bonita?"

"Not really. She's in poor health."

"What's wrong with her?" asked Consuelo.

"I thought you might know."

Consuelo shook her head. "The Figuroas are only friendly with people at the viceroy's court. Europeans. *Gachupín* families. I don't think they're a very happy family, though. My older brother used to know Alex de Figuroa before he moved to Jamaica. He owns a plantation, I think. But now Alex has nothing to do with his parents. His mother is a loud bossy woman, hard to please. But as for Bonita — "

"She's pretty, Padre said."

Consuelo brushed cake crumbs from her robe. "Before bedtime, Reverend Mother had you shut up in her office for over an hour. It hurts that old lady like anything, you know, your leaving. She's been hoping all these years you'd take her place someday."

If Consuelo had knocked her down, Gabriella could not have been more astonished. "What?" she said, dazed. "Take her place? What are you saying?"

"Holy Saints, Gabriella, don't be like that!" scolded Consuelo. "Don't pretend the thought never crossed your mind."

"Crossed *my* mind?! You're mad! Me, an orphan with no family? A schoolgirl fifteen years old?"

"All right," agreed Consuelo, "so you're a schoolgirl, fifteen years old. Country girls are married with children at that age."

Gabriella took a deep breath. "Consuelo, I don't know what's made you think that — "

But Consuelo pressed on. "It won't be long now before I'll be leaving the convent too, Gabriella. I'll go home and my parents will choose a husband for me, a husband with lots of money, naturally. Then I'll have ten babies and spend the rest of my life looking after children and servants and trying to keep my husband happy. I suppose it's as good a way as any to spend your life, but it seems stupid to me."

"That's no way to talk about — " Gabriella began hotly. "Your mother obviously didn't think it was stupid or she wouldn't have done it!"

Consuelo pleaded earnestly, "Oh, Gabriella, please don't be cross. This is so important! If you want to know the truth, I'm envious. Yes, envious of you. But do you think for a minute my parents would let me stay on at Santa Clara? I'm to be a wife and mother. That's it. I'm stuck. But it doesn't have to be like that for you! You should come back to Santa Clara, serve your novitiate and take your vows."

" — Which is exactly what I always hoped to do," said Gabriella, puzzled. "So what's the point of this discussion?"

"Well," admitted Consuelo lamely, "what *is* the point? How can I explain? Look, Gabriella. Once you get away from the convent, things are going to be different. You'll see. For one thing, you're pretty. My younger brother took one look at that red hair and now he's gone silly over 'Señorita Salgado'. In his letters, you're all he talks about."

Gabriella's eyes sparked with interest. "Really?"

"None of that!" commanded Consuelo. "You don't want my stupid brother; he's not good enough for you. The point I'm making is that you'll marry if you want to, wait and see. But your future here is better. You aren't like the other girls. You're a natural leader; no one — "

"Oh, Consuelo, for Heaven's sake!" said Gabriella in disgust.

Consuelo stood. "What I am telling you is the truth, Gabriella. You think no one at Santa Clara knows why Madre fought so long with Padre Mero to keep you here? Everyone knows, all right. If — "

Gabriella leaped to her feet. "Stop this!" she cried. "Remember, please, that we are not nuns. We are not even novices. We are schoolgirls, and this is nothing but silly schoolgirl talk!"

Consuelo shook her head. "No, Gabriella. Wait — "

"No. *You* wait! It would be a great honor for anyone to be appointed abbess of a convent like Santa Clara, and a tremendous responsibility. You have no idea how hard Reverend Mother works to keep this place going."

Consuelo murmured, "Without you, she'll work a lot harder."

Gabriella bit her lip, then said, "It's true I've always hoped someday I'd complete my vows and become her assistant. It's — it's what I hoped God intended for me to do. I dread leaving. I'll miss everybody, and especially Reverend Mother." She took a deep breath. "As for becoming abbess, Consuelo, I swear to you that Madre has never said one word to me — "

"Well, no, I guess not," interrupted Consuelo. "She's too clever to give away her plans like that. But there's that feeling between you two, a special kind of friendship. You can't deny that!"

"Of course I don't deny it. Remember, I wasn't born in a mansion in the city like you. My mother was a *lepero* woman who died the same day I was born, right here at the convent. This place is the only home I've ever known. And yes, of course, I have a special feeling for Madre Valderia; she's the only mother I ever had." Consuelo noticed, if Gabriella did not, that her voice trembled as she said it.

Without warning, the door leading to the corridor opened. Sister Anita, the dormitory matron, glowered over the candle in her hand. "What's this?"

"It's my last night in the convent, Sister," Gabriella explained, "and I couldn't sleep."

"Yes," agreed Sister Anita curtly. "It is indeed difficult to sleep as you sit gossiping and eating plum cake while others are praying. A Hail Mary for each of you and then to bed!"

Gabriella moved toward the table.

"Leave the cake where it is," ordered Sister Anita. "It will be here for you after early mass."

CHAPTER 2

The Journey
May 1774

Later that same morning, the four travelers made their way through the low scrub-covered hills toward the city. It was a pale blue morning, with flocks of wild ducks spraying up before them, indignant at being disturbed in their feeding.

Leaving had been hard for Gabriella, and the almond eyes under her broad-brimmed farmer's hat were still red with weeping. Saying goodby to Reverend Mother the evening before had been the most difficult time of all. "Please tell me it won't be for long, Madre!" she had begged tearfully. "I'll be so alone!"

Madre took Gabriella's hand in both of hers and murmured, "With God, you are never alone, child. Always remember that. Once, long ago, I felt abandoned and frightened as you do now. But God needed me to be strong, and he gave me strength. He has His own plan for you too, and He will guide and protect you, as He once guided and protected me." Briskly she patted Gabriella's hand. "Besides, you will have Padre Mero. If you find things difficult in the city, he will be there to advise you."

Gabriella mastered her tears but not her resentment. "It's his fault I'm having to go. Why can't he mind his own business?"

"That is precisely what he is doing. He promised your mother before she died that he would watch over you." Madre glanced at Gabriella's hair and smiled. "When Padre made that promise to her, I'm sure he little dreamed he'd have a second red-haired, freckled young lady to watch out for."

Gabriella's hands flew to her cheeks. "You said my freckles had faded!"

"So they had, two months ago. That was before you spent all one day in the hills looking for wild herbs."

"Am I all speckled?" cried Gabriella.

"More speckled than you were," said Madre. "If you want skin like magnolia petals, wear your bonnet. But now come, let's pray together." And the tall broad-shouldered abbess in her flowing robes and the slender auburn-haired schoolgirl in her black petticoats knelt together at the shrine in the corner of Madre's office. With arms entwined, they murmured, .."Hail, Holy Queen, mother of mercy..." "Pray for us, oh clement, oh loving, oh sweet Virgin Mary, oh Holy Mother of God..."

At the end, Reverend Mother, her head still bowed, put her arm around Gabriella's shoulders and prayed, "Blessed Holy Mother, who hath compassion on all our frailty, grant that the wings of heaven will shield and protect this darling girl, no matter where her path may lie."

They crossed themselves and rose. The familiar black eyes gazed down at Gabriella, and in their depths the girl read something she had never seen there before: deep, bone-searing weariness. "I shall pray daily for your return," said Madre huskily.

And now Gabriella, on the way to Mexico with her traveling companions, was haunted by that look. As Madre and the convent fell farther and farther behind, a hard knot of grief formed in her breast.

After an hour on the road, the brisk early-morning air brought color to Gabriella's cheeks and the priest asked a question that had been gnawing at him. "Young lady, I wish you would please tell me where you got that gray dress."

Gabriella read his uneasily furrowed brow and smiled. Ready to mount for the journey, she had appeared in a gray velvet traveling costume with a bonnet of gray plumes — quite a change from her drab convent uniform. Startled admiration shone in the alert, angular features of the slim young guard, Elias, and when presented he swept off his hat and bowed low.

Padre had never seen her in anything but her school uniform and thetransformation disturbed him. "Did Madre Valderia buy that outfit for you?"

"You know she didn't," Gabriella replied lightly. "Reverend Mother's extra money goes to the convent, not to me. Don't you think the gray velvet dress is pretty?"

"One might say so. Yes. But I don't recall leaving funds for anything of the sort."

"Consuelo's cousin in the city outgrew it. So Consuelo made it over for me."

"*Consuelo* made it over? What's this?"

"Sister Joaquina helped. She teaches us sewing. Consuelo is good at sewing. So am I. You should let me make you a cassock." She gestured. "One like that. Mine will fit better and last longer. And cost only half as much!"

"But my dear Gabriella, the convent girls are young women from families who *hire* seamstresses."

" — seamstresses who must be *supervised*. And to supervise them, you must understand what they're doing."

"Well. Quite a surprise. And all this time, I thought the sisters were teaching you to read and write."

"That, too."

"Ciphering? You can add and subtract. I've seen you."

"Of course."

"A relief. Have you any more surprises like the gray velvet creation?"

"Five. Almost six. Number six needs the sleeves sewn in. Ever since I told everyone I was leaving, they've worried about the clothes I'd need in the city. Consuelo's brother made a special trip to the convent for me. He brought boxes of family things I might be able to use — cloaks, fans, shawls, bonnets, gloves — things no one was wearing any more."

Padre remembered how important such trifles were to the womenfolk in the Costanza household where he served as chaplain. "Well," he concluded grudgingly, "I suppose it's best that you have them. — But not to wear on a trip through this wilderness with outlaws lurking behind every bush! In that velvet gown, you looked like a grandee's daughter with valuable jewels hidden in her luggage; — much too tempting."

Gabriella glanced down at her black wool rebozo, cotton stockings and much-laundered petticoats. Sighing, she agreed, "Yes, Padre, I'm sure you were right to make me change." She had been disappointed and so had the guard, Elias. His fond glance lingered only briefly before he returned to his work with the pack mules.

The road they followed was once a broad highway but was now riven with gullies and clogged with weeds. On either side, visible beyond the low hills, were abandoned fields and the occasional ruins of a hacienda with long-forgotten gardens growing rank with clematis and climbing roses.

After two hours in the saddle, Elias chose just such a spot for their first rest stop. His attention scarcely left Gabriella as she and Padre made a lively game of "restoring" the ruined estate to its original appearance of a century before.

Resuming their journey, Gabriella observed Elias' lithe form riding ahead of them and quickly averted her eyes. He was too attractive for comfort, and too gallant. She knew she looked unappealing in her ugly school uniform, yet he handed her about as though she were made of glass. His gentle glances sought her eyes and made her blush.

"It's surprising Elias hasn't married," Padre had murmured. "These country boys usually marry young. But I understand he is very loyal to his struggling parents on their farm." He had literally grown up at Buena Suerte and long ago dropped his country manners and speech. He was only twenty years old, but Don Avila had nevertheless named him acting chamberlain of the Figuroa household.

Gabriella could not believe it. Consuelo's family chamberlain was a gouty old man in braid-trimmed coat and knee pants. Elias, in his *vaquero's* hat, leather doublet and boots to his thighs, could have been supervisor at one of the great haciendas they passed. His role of authority fitted him easily enough, and his open features invited trust. But chamberlain?

One thing she *could* believe: He never tired. Consuelo had been right about the long ride. Already the underside of her right knee was rubbed raw by the hook on her sidesaddle and her bones ached from the unnatural sitting position on the mule's broad back. Furthermore, Elias' worried glances over his shoulder told her that he knew it.

The sun climbed high overhead. Just as she was hoping they would stop for lunch, Elias called to Padre, "We are coming to the cliff where we saw smoke from the campfire yesterday. For the next mile or two, we had better move a little faster." He signaled to Miguel, riding behind and leading the pack mules.

Then he checked the loads in his pistols and resumed his place at the front of their little column.

Dropping back briefly to ride beside Gabriella, Padre reassured her, "A good thing to remember about your convent garb, young lady, is that Madre Valderia has been very kind to many of these desperadoes and their families. Some of them would have starved but for her. No matter how much you wanted to wear your pretty velvet gown, it is wiser policy to advertise yourself as a student from the convent. At least, for now."

Gabriella's big mule objected to the faster gait and she kicked him smartly in the ribs to avoid falling behind. They were following a trail beside a shallow arroyo. Without slowing his mount, Elias turned in his saddle and signaled with his thumb. A dozen yards away loomed an escarpment fringed at the top with scrub oak and prickly pear. Silhouetted against the sky were two men looking down at them, each with a musket cradled in his arm.

Gabriella's scalp prickled with fear, but then she looked more closely. She had often helped distribute supplies to needy families in the convent courtyard, and she thought she recognized the smaller of the two men. Reverend Mother frequently complained that Mexico's poor had no way to earn a living. The great haciendas of a century ago hired armies of laborers but as the soil wore thin, the plantations were abandoned one by one. The small farmers working their own land received so little money for their harvests, it was scarcely worth the trouble of planting. No wonder there were thieves and cutthroats!

Elias set a brisk pace along the road, with Padre Mero and Gabriella following close behind and the older guard, Miguel, in the rear with the pack mules. After they passed the escarpment, Gabriella turned to look back. The two gunmen were gone.

Not long afterward, Elias halted the party for lunch beside a spring bubbling out of a rocky grotto surrounded by willows. When he helped Gabriella dismount, she could scarcely stand. She limped several steps as the circulation returned to her legs. But his firm support at her elbow made her uneasy; as soon as she could walk alone, he left her with Padre.

While Elias removed the saddles and hobbled the animals in a grassy swale downstream, Miguel located the lunch hamper among the baggage. Gabriella told Padre about the midnight feast with Consuelo, but when the hamper yielded no sign of a journey gift, he remarked wryly, "It looks as though Sister Anita exacted a severe penance."

Miguel grinned. "Small loss. Rita — that's my wife, the head cook at Buena Suerte. Yesterday she packed enough food for all of us. Yes, for those bandidos and their families too!"

The priest rattled off a blessing, after which a feast of beef, rolls and fruit was handed around and the guards retired.

In private, enjoying the restful murmur of the water and the deep shade of the grove, Padre cleared his throat and said, "Gabriella, Don Avila's household is one of the most distinguished in Mexico. I'm very pleased that I've been able to place you there."

"I'm pleased too, Padre," said Gabriella, wondering what was coming.

"I think you should be aware of something that is not generally known in the city."

She braced herself. City people with time on their hands loved to gossip, Padre most of all. She preferred the convent where everyone was too busy for gossip.

"Actually," Padre went on, "Don Avila represents wealth that is not his personally. Or at least not all of it. He is the youngest of several brothers. Most of them are dead but there are surviving widows and nephews in Madrid. The colonial properties of the Figuroa family in Mexico are extensive, but in addition he holds in trust several mines and plantations belonging to his wife's family, relatives of the queen. Don Avila bears a very heavy responsibility."

Only half listening, Gabriella said, "The one in the Figuroa family I want to meet is Javiera."

"The older girl. The novice. Yes. And due to take her final vows this winter, I understand. She seems to be a quiet girl, very reserved. Of course, she won't be at Buena Suerte when we arrive, but you will see her when she comes home for visits." He paused, kneading his hands thoughtfully. "Ah, there is a detail I didn't mention to Madre Valderia. I — well, I feel I should warn you about Doña Dolores."

"Bonita's mother?"

"Yes. She — "

"She's an old pirate."

"How did you know that?"

"Consuelo told me."

"Oh. Well. Yes, she's something of a tartar. Consuelo was right about that. I wanted you to be prepared."

"But what about Bonita, Padre? She's the one I've been hired to take care of and you still haven't told me what ails her. Actually, I needed to know yesterday. Sister Magdalena helped me pack a box of medicines and supplies, but we weren't sure if there was something special we should include. What's the matter with Bonita?"

Padre explained Bonita's illness as best he could. The longer Gabriella listened, the more puzzled she became. "No fever causing it, you say? No infection? Anyone else would start looking for the guilty party who bewitched her."

"Don Avila suspected the same thing. Two years ago, he sent to Italy for a *curandero* said to be Europe's foremost expert at counteracting the *mal ojo* and such. The man worked over Bonita for several days with his incense and lemons and whatnot. He pronounced her cured and went back to Sienna. Not long afterward the attacks began again."

"Perhaps it's a job for you, then."

"No-no!" Padre Mero shook his head firmly. "Exorcising demons is a specialty. Some priests are good at it, but not I. However if Bonita doesn't get better under your care, I might possibly counsel Don Avila to try such a priest. I know of one, as a matter of fact. Said to be quite successful."

"But what about me, Padre? I never heard of any disease like that. I won't know what treatment is best for her."

"Find out what's been done for her in the past," advised the priest. "Continue the treatment she's accustomed to. If she takes a turn for the worse, send word to me. There is a talented doctor from Seville in the city. We have called him to the Costanza household many times. You might suggest him to Don Avila but *only* if Bonita is very ill."

"Why *only?*"

"Don Avila doesn't want the gossip, you see. More than anything else, he wants a good marriage for Bonita. Outsiders mustn't know of her illness."

"'Let the buyer beware'?"

Padre said sternly, "Such matters are not for us to judge, Gabriella."

"Why not? Everyone else will."

"Will what? Judge? That is no concern of yours, what other people do. It is your first duty to keep this secret, regardless of how you feel about it privately. You must always bear this in mind. You and the servants who take care of Bonita, you are the only ones who are to know of her illness."

"*You* know."

"That's different." Padre frowned. "My dear, you must learn not to be saucy with priests. It's a bad habit you learned from Madre Valderia. I indulge you too much, I know, and I suspect she has indulged you too. But take care, young lady! A reputation for insolence can bring you grief."

"I apologize, Padre. I shouldn't have questioned what you said. I'm only thinking of the girls at the convent. From the way they talk, everyone in the city knows secrets about everyone else. I wonder how Don Avila plans to keep his secret about Bonita."

"He's managed to keep it so far."

I doubt it, thought Gabriella.

"You just hold to your part of the bargain, my dear," advised Padre, "and let Don Avila worry about his part."

Soon afterward they remounted and an hour later rounded the shoulder of a hill to discover the valley of Mexico, ringed by mountains, suddenly spread out before them. Irrigated farms and lakes formed bright patches of green and blue against the dun of the valley floor. In the distance sprawled the city, the spires and gilded domes of its many churches glowing in the sun. And to the east rose the giant snow-capped peak of Popocatepetl.

Padre Mero waved his arm. "Your new home," he announced. "What do you think of it?"

Only a year before, Gabriella had traveled this road in a carriage with Consuelo and her sisters, looking forward to a week's visit in the city. When the coachmen crested the hill, the girls were laughing over some foolish game and scarcely noticed the view.

But this trip was different: ahead lay not a few days' visit but months and possibly years in a city that could change her life. She gazed down on the Spaniards' gleaming bell towers standing where, three centuries before, the vast pyramids of the Aztecs challenged heaven with their might. This fabled city had seen the union of two colossal empires — one from the old world, one from the new — and the blood of both flowed in her veins.

She felt Elias' eyes upon her and glanced in his direction. His understanding gaze astonished her. He's *criollo* like me, she realized, and knows exactly what I'm thinking. She flushed, uncertain if she liked having her mind read so easily by a stranger.

Padre waited, smiling. "What do I think if it?" Gabriella repeated lightly. "I think it will be a very nice place to live, especially if I never have to ride a horse or a mule ever again!"

The sun was lowering in the western sky and Elias urged them on. By now, Gabriella had no feeling at all in her right leg. On one side of the road ahead, she glimpsed the roof of an inn and hoped Elias would stop. As they drew nearer, she changed her mind. The place was a rundown *cantina* from which drifted loud talk and raucous laughter. A ragged *lepero* rounded a corner of the structure, noticed them approaching, glared, and darted inside.

Elias liked the look of it even less than Gabriella. He reined his horse into a new position where he could more easily shield her. The shouts and drunken laughter from the tavern suddenly stilled and several reeling cutthroats, armed with swords and daggers, emerged one by one to stare at the riders. Nine? Ten? How many were there?

Gabriella's panic rose. Ragged men kept materializing from the *cantina* and from the thicket of trees immediately behind it.

A leader among the outlaws came forward. In a whining, insolent tone, he called out, "Padre! For the blood of the Most Blessed Savior, give us money for food. We are starving!"

Rude guffaws broke out among the men. Elias glanced back at Miguel, who had already perceived the threat and was hurrying along with the pack animals. Elias reached for the bridle of Gabriella's mule and pulled ahead along the road, leaving Padre and Miguel to deal with the derelicts.

Ominously quiet, they continued to emerge from the *cantina*. A dozen. Sixteen. Twenty.

Slowing his mule, Padre called out sternly to the men, "If you are starving, why have you wasted your money on *pulque* when you could have bought beef and beans? Why are you here carousing in the middle of the afternoon when you could be earning a real or two down in the city? The Holy Mother looks with a cold heart on sinners such as you!"

The leader, bearded and toothless with a cutlass hanging at his side, moved closer to Padre. His fellows moved forward behind him. He inspected Padre, his mount, his harness and baggage with a wicked smile. "The Holy Mother, she knows well enough there's no work in the city," he said, fingering the hilt of his sword. "So instead she sends us a fat priest with gold in his luggage. But see how generous we are, Padre? As well as gold, we could use that strong animal you're riding. But we're giving you a chance to buy us off. Come! Be a good fellow! Shake loose with a few coins for the poor!"

Only then did the other outlaws lift their voices. "Let's see the color of your money, Priest!" "If he's stingy, there's ways to change his mind!" "Going without a few meals wouldn't bother the priest, he's fat enough!"

Behind her, Gabriella heard the jeers change from teasing to ugly threats. Her throat closed with fear. There must have been thirty men, and more approaching through the grove behind the *cantina*. On every face was malevolence and in every hand a weapon — a few muskets and pistols as well as swords.

A clot of men dislodged itself from the larger group and hastened forward along the road toward Elias and Gabriella. Quickly, Elias handed Gabriella his quirt. "Stay behind me if you can. Don't let anyone touch your rein or bridle. Aim for the eyes. Strike as hard as you can."

He checked the loads in his pistols and loosened his sword in its scabbard. The approaching men scarcely paused.

And then as if from a signal, the outlaws attacked. Gabriella heard, behind them, first one and then a second report of a pistol — Miguel's? — and the scream of a victim. Bandits shouting in triumph were leading away one of the two pack mules. Both Miguel and Padre Mero laid about with angry blows, Miguel with the butt of his pistol and the priest with his quirt.

Five snarling desperadoes approached Elias.

"Stop where you are!" Elias shouted.

Instead, the men quickened their pace. Without hesitation, Elias shot their leader full in the face.

A man slain before her very eyes was something Gabriella had never experienced before. The victim fell, blood streaming from the splintered bone of his skull. She was galvanized with horror, but a tug on her reins brought her back. A kerchiefed bandit clearly intended to take her mount, and he was succeeding! She slashed at the villain's face, again and again, with all her strength.

Again, Elias' pistol roared. His ball shattered the arm of a nearby bandit but missed Gabriella's assailant.

The vagabond turned his back to her blows, which rained down with greater force than ever. "You damned wildcat!" he shouted, throwing up his arms. Instantly Elias seized the opening, spurred his horse into position, and plunged his sword into the man's naked ribs.

Behind Elias, another outlaw raised his dagger. With fury, Gabriella attacked this new threat with her quirt, slashing with all her might across his face. The villain's blade connected with Elias' horse, but the aim and force were deflected. Elias' mount leaped away with a long shallow gash along his flank.

"Elias!" cried Gabriella, pointing. "Look behind you!"

Fifteen feet away, a bandit stood carefully aiming at him with his musket. But Elias, having fired both his pistols, was powerless to stop him.

Suddenly from behind them on the road a shot rang out, and the marksman threw back his head and dropped his weapon. Cawing with pain, he doubled up on the ground. Miguel had managed to reload and fire when his help was most needed.

Three casualties in such quick succession discouraged the attackers. The remaining men drew back, brandishing their weapons and shouting threats. The captured pack mule, accompanied by half-a-dozen ragged men, was disappearing among the trees beyond the *cantina*.

Elias watched them, fuming. Retrieving the mule against such heavy odds was out of the question. Padre Mero and Miguel on their frightened mounts — Miguel hauling mightily at the balky remaining pack animal — closed ranks at last. With Elias and Gabriella, the little party retreated along the road toward the city.

Elias looked at Gabriella in awe. "You saved my life," he said, as though doubting it himself.

The skirmish had left her hands shaking and her lips trembling. "No. It was Miguel who fired. Miguel saved your life."

"Miguel didn't shoot the man with the dagger," insisted Elias. "The one who would have stabbed me in the back. You stopped him."

Wearily, Gabriella removed her big farmer's hat. Tears streamed down her face. Confused and exhausted, she wanted more than anything to be left alone to gather her wits.

And again Elias sensed her mood. Lightly he touched her hand, and without a word, left her and took his place at the head of the little column.

CHAPTER 3   Buena Suerte
                                                                 May 1774

Church bells were ringing vespers as the wearied travelers made their way through the city's outskirts. In the lavender sky overhead, drifts of pink cloud were all that remained of the departed sun. The perfume of mimosa, honeysuckle and tuberoses drifted from walled gardens lining the broad avenues.

Acknowledging the bells, Padre Mero crossed himself, but his concern was for the schoolgirl at his side. Long before the confrontation at the *cantina,* her eyes were sunken from exhaustion. Now she was wraithlike, head bowed under her rebozo. The neat black skirts of early morning were streaked with dust. The straight young shoulders drooped and the slender arms hung lifeless as sticks. Not long before, she had nearly slipped from the saddle. A quick response by Elias had prevented what might have been a nasty fall.

Suddenly the aqueduct loomed in the twilight. Padre asked hopefully, "The family won't insist on meeting Gabriella tonight, will they? It would be better if she could meet them tomorrow, after she has rested and feels stronger."

Elias shook his head. Regretfully, he said, "Tomorrow she will feel worse than she does now."

Gabriella moaned.

"I am sorry, Señorita, but it is true. As soon as we arrive, I will make arrangements for a hot bath for you. A good soak in hot water will ease your muscles so you can sleep."

Padre said crossly, "Don Avila first suggested a litter for her. A litter would have been better."

"Much better," agreed Elias. "For most people, learning to ride is not easy. Even strong men and boys ride only an hour at a time till they get used to the saddle. Even then they have sore muscles."

"You too?" said Padre. "When you were a boy, you had sore muscles? I can scarcely believe it."

"I never had sore muscles, but in the country, it is different. At the farm where my family lives, we all rode as soon as we could walk. All *paisano* children do." His white teeth glistened in a smile. "That is why Nueva España has the finest *vaqueros* in the world. Everyone says so. But for the Señorita here, it will be many days before she feels well again."

After a pause, Gabriella asked, "How much farther?"

"To Buena Suerte?" said Elias. "We have arrived. See just ahead? The big building on the left?"

"They have lit the torches for us," cried Padre, kicking up his mule. "Ah, for a hot cup of chocolate! Eh, Gabriella?"

The palace of Avila Flores de Figuroa Beretta was an awesome structure of masonry, three stories tall, with grilled windows along the ground floor. Torches flamed in iron brackets between the windows, and balconies outlined the floors above. Bas-reliefs of animals, flowers and arabesques decorated the facade.

Massive stone columns flanked the entrance to the courtyard, framing heavy wooden doors fifteen feet tall now open wide in greeting.

The travelers found the inner courtyard as bright as midday, lit from overhead galleries festooned with lanterns. It was an impressive sight. It would have been more so except that the paved courtyard with its heavy traffic of saddle horses and mule-drawn carts had not been cleaned in many days and an acrid stench assaulted the visitors' nostrils. Gabriella, already spent, retched and drew her rebozo close over her nose.

In a corner of the courtyard had been dumped what appeared to be household refuse. Perched on the gallery railings high above were several roosting *zopilotes*, the huge buzzard-like scavenger birds that citizens of the city depended on to clean the streets.

Elias instantly dismounted and began shouting commands to servants who hurried to meet them. He directed a female servant, Ana, to help Gabriella to her quarters. There she could refresh herself in private before being presented to the family. As the servant Ana half-carried the girl up the broad steps, Padre noticed the tangled hair straggling from beneath her grimy maid's cap. He wondered how Gabriella, fastidiously clean in her personal habits, would deal with this new trial.

Padre Mero supervised as Miguel unloaded the lone pack mule. As for the stolen baggage, Gabriella had lost two of her new frocks and a few gewgaws. Otherwise the outlaws had grandly enriched themselves with two books of theology — already resold in the plaza for a real or two, Padre was sure — but best of all, several of the convent's famous cheeses and sausages intended as gifts for the Figuroa and Costanza households. The bandits would enjoy them immensely.

Padre Mero mounted the grand staircase of the palace and was shown through a series of anterooms. In the *sala*, an elaborate chamber of coffered ceilings, mirrors, tapestries and gilt furniture, he found Don Avila Flores de Figuroa Beretta with his wife and daughter.

Don Avila, nearing sixty, was a slightly-built, finely-featured man with the effortless courtesy of the grandee. He was richly dressed in satin breeches and a brocade waistcoat. Over them he wore a velvet coat from whose colossal cuffs spilled a torrent of lace. On one hand he wore a spectacular emerald ring. His courtly presence was marred by mismatched stockings and an elaborately-curled peruke too big for his head. He smelled of brandy, and though his speech was flawless, he displayed the uncertain gait and splotchy skin of a gentleman long dedicated to the bottle.

"Welcome, Padre!" exclaimed Don Avila, sidling forward and clasping both of the priest's hands in an enthusiastic greeting. "How good it is to see you again, my fine fellow!"

"And you also, Don Avila," Padre Mero replied warmly.

"So at long last you've fetched Señorita Salgado from the convent, have you? You must tell us about your journey. There were no mishaps, I trust?"

"Alas, we were attacked by a band of outlaws and lost one of our pack mules," Padre replied. "At a *cantina* just beyond the outskirts of the city. I must commend you, Don Avila, on the courage and skill of your guards. But for them, all four of us might this moment be lying dead beside the road."

Don Avila took a moment to absorb the information Padre Mero had given him. His face registered grave concern. "So near the city! The insolence of these brigands increases daily! Tell me, was anyone hurt? The Señorita, was she harmed in any way?"

Padre smiled. "Oh, no. On the contrary. She proved herself as enthusiastic a fighter as Elias or Miguel. But she is tired from the experience, coming as it did at the end of a long, grueling day of travel."

"The viceroy shall hear of this atrocity. I shall personally notify the proper authorities at the National Palace. Expect a constable to call on you tomorrow for details."

A tall, aristocratic woman standing behind Don Avila pointedly cleared her throat. Perhaps fifty years old, the lady was a once-great beauty gone sour. Flowing black silk disguised the shapeless body. Jewels hung from ears, wrists, neck, waist and fingers, clicking with her movements like muted castanets. A tumble of curling gray hair escaped from a torn snood of gold filagree. She stood leaning on a cane, defying the priest with the brooding malevolence of a hungry eagle.

Don Avila bowed. "Padre, I have the honor to present my wife, Doña Dolores."

Padre Mero bowed nervously over the noble lady's hand. Don Avila's wife, cousin of the queen, was deaf and in constant pain from a shipboard injury sustained on the family's journey to the New World many years before. Her ill temper was legendary.

"What took you so long?" the queen's cousin shouted testily at the priest. "We've been waiting all afternoon!"

Her husband explained loudly in her ear, "It's a full day's ride from the Convent of Santa Clara, my dear. And their party was attacked by bandits. I'm sure with Elias in charge they came as quickly as they could."

Then he nodded toward a nearby settee. "And Padre, I believe you have never met my daughter Bonita."

The priest turned to greet a slender girl who rose and curtsied lightly. Everything about this young woman — her shapely form, her beautiful shoulders and arms, the limpid hazel eyes and classic features, the gleaming jet black of her hair, were unbelievable in their loveliness. *No wonder Don Avila guards her so carefully*, thought the priest, his collar suddenly grown too tight.

"But where is María Gabriella?" Bonita asked. "Didn't she come with you?"

"Oh, yes," replied Padre. "You see, she — "

At that moment, the double doors of the *sala* opened. Gabriella appeared, wan but smiling, supported by the serving woman. Padre had expected the worst, but instead he found his spirits lifting with pride and affection. The schoolgirl's tangled braids were burnished and coiled neatly at the back of her head. The dusty skirts had been brushed; a crisp white fichu covered the drooping shoulders. With great dignity, poised and gracious, Señorita María Gabriella Salgado, daughter of a housemaid, dipped carefully. She moved forward a few steps, smiled like an angel and extended her hand to her employer.

Instantly charmed, Don Avila presented his wife and daughter and moved to dismiss the servant, but Gabriella checked him.

"Please," she said. "Don Avila, Doña Dolores, Señorita Bonita, Padre. First, I must apologize. As you see, I am still in my school regalia, which is not suitable attire for Buena Suerte. I have had a wearying day, and it is only with the help of Ana here that I can walk properly. I'm afraid I need rest very badly." Again she inclined her head dutifully to Don Avila. "I would like to offer my respects to you, Señor, and to your family. And then with your most kind permission, I ask you to please excuse me."

Impressed, Don Avila ventured a bow of such sincerity that he lost his balance and nearly toppled. "But of course, my dear. A thousand thanks for appearing here in spite of your long journey and your harrowing experience." Doña Dolores' cane clattered to the floor and the gray curls trembled in agitation. "What did she say?" she bawled. "Why is she holding onto Ana like that? Has Ana stolen something again? Someone hand me my cane!"

As Bonita retrieved the cane, Gabriella smiled engagingly at Doña Dolores. Speaking slowly, deferentially, and above all clearly, she explained, "Ana has been very helpful to me, Doña Dolores. She is helping me to walk because my legs are so weak. I — "

"Bad legs, is that it?" shouted Doña Dolores, jangling her bracelets angrily. "I know all about bad legs! As for this good-for-nothing slut, if she disobeys you, let me know. She will feel my cane on her back!"

With help from Ana, for whom such outbursts seemed to be routine, Gabriella smilingly made her exit. At the door, Bonita pressed her hand. "Don't mind Mama," she murmured. "I'll come to your room in the morning. I'm awfully glad you're here at last."

"Thank you," and the big double doors closed behind them.

"A redhead!" shouted Doña Dolores. "Why didn't someone tell me the girl had red hair! Irish, that's what she is! And Irish women can't be trusted, especially the pretty ones!"

Don Avila regarded his wife with surprise. "Irish? But my dear, as you yourself know so well —"

"And she's sick!" cried the old woman. "Pale as milk! What good is a sick schoolgirl?"

"She isn't sick, Mama, she's just tired," shouted Bonita.

"What's wrong with her legs?" her mother continued. "What's the good of hiring someone to take care of Bonita if she can't even walk?"

"Mama," cried Bonita, "she rode a mule all day long to get here. They were attacked by bandits. She is exhausted. She will be all right when she gets some rest."

Bonita's words finally penetrated her mother's thickened eardrums. "Well, anyway her clothes are terrible. Bonita, do something about that girl's clothes. We can't have her about the house in that silly convent costume."

"Yes, Mama," said Bonita.

Padre Mero, after a mellifluous leave-taking that included three cups of chocolate, six almond cakes and a juicy pear (while making certain that the same fare was being offered to Gabriella as she lay soaking in her hot bath), at last departed in unusually high spirits. For he had noticed something that escaped the attention of the others. Between the time the serving woman, Ana, helped Gabriella up the staircase and later when the same Ana appeared in the drawing room, her drooping bodice had been properly laced, her tangled hair had been combed and her dirty face and neck had been washed.

Padre Mero hummed a little tune to himself as he mounted his mule in the courtyard below. Cheerfully he bade farewell to the night porter and sallied forth into the broad avenue, while behind him the porter closed and made fast the huge doors for the night.

Breathing deeply of the fragrant evening air, Padre Mero's satisfaction erupted in a rivulet of chuckles. *After today, there will be more than one strong-willed woman at Buena Suerte*, he reflected, and rode home with a happy heart.

Early the next morning Gabriella awoke in a narrow bed canopied with velvet. An armoire stood against one wall, and against another a gilt dressing table. Tapestries covered the walls and at the windows, curtains of silk gauze stirred gently in the early morning air.

The night before, she had been overwhelmed by the richness of everything she saw here at Buena Suerte, but now, with the light of day, she was less impressed. The mirrors in their magnificent frames were milky and spotted, the gilt tarnished, the tapestries faded with dust and rank with mildew.

She rose on one elbow and winced. Slowly she slid from the tall bed and searched among the leather cases and bundles which Miguel had stacked neatly in one corner. At last she found the vial she sought, swirled a drop of the yellow syrup in a cup of water and swallowed it.

An hour later, she was groomed and dressed for the day in a frock of sprigged dimity. She was unpacking when a knock sounded at the door connecting her bedchamber with that of her *patrona*. She opened it to find Bonita in a wrinkled peignoir, scrubbing her sleepy eyes.

"Gabriella, you're up and dressed!" she cried. "No one but Papa ever gets up before noon!" She entered, caught Gabriella's hands in her own, held them wide and surveyed her. "Ai, this is better! Mama will approve!"

"I am glad, Señorita," murmured Gabriella with a brief curtsy.

"And now tell me about the attack yesterday. It was exciting, wasn't it?"

"Exciting?" repeated Gabriella, trying to keep her voice from trembling at the memory. "It was terrible! Miguel shot two of the bandits and Elias shot one man full in the face."

"In the *face*?!" Bonita stared. "I want to hear all about it," she cried with glowing eyes. "Every detail!"

She turned away and without warning, uttered a piercing shriek. The cast iron bathtub, still filled with milky bathwater, stood before the fireplace. To one side was a little table with the remains of the meal Gabriella had eaten the night before. Beside the plate perched two large rats feasting on the leftovers.

Bonita rushed at the creatures, furiously clapping her hands. "Go away, you nasty things! Away! Go! Go!" And the rats zigzagged to safety behind the dusty wall hangings.

Her skirts twitching with irritation, Bonita marched down a short hallway to the gallery where she shouted into the courtyard below, "Ana! Come at once! You're needed!"

Returning and slamming the bedroom door behind her, she fumed, "Lazy thing! But then, *all* our servants are lazy, even Elias sometimes! Ana is my maid but yesterday we decided she should get you settled in your room. Slut! She knows better than to leave leftover food standing about like that! It always attracts rats and bugs!"

"Where are your cats?" asked Gabriella. "At the convent, we always had several hungry cats prowling about. So the rats left. Roaches left, too. And snakes. Very useful animals, cats."

Clearly, Bonita had never heard of such a thing. She was interested. "Maybe I'll talk to Mama."

"Have her ask Elias to find some fierce ones. He grew up on a farm. He'll know where to find good ones. And — ah — while you're talking to your mother about the cats, why not ask her about getting rid of the garbage in the courtyard? That's what attracts the rats."

"That's what Federico keeps saying, but then he never does anything about it. Federico Verro, Papa's steward. He runs the household. His rooms are at the back part of the palace. Come. I'll show you."

Bonita led Gabriella to the gallery. She pointed. Below on the ground floor was a wide portal that gave access to the service areas. "The stables are back there, in the rear part of the palace, with servants' quarters on the second and third floors. There's plenty of open space where the blacksmith shoes the horses and mends the farm equipment. Behind the building are the orchards and gardens. But the trees don't bear fruit and anyway the bugs eat everything. I told you our servants are hopeless."

Along the gallery behind them, a *zopilote* waddled aimlessly, its gray head and cruel beak thrusting forward with each step. The creature stood as tall as Gabriella's waist. It paused to examine her with interest and she edged away.

Bonita laughed. "It won't hurt you. You're too big to eat. Let's go back to your room. It smells bad out here."

"Bonita, doesn't anyone ever take the garbage away? The *zopilotes* — the buzzards, well, they're noisy, filthy birds, worse than the rats. Fighting over the garbage in the courtyard! Roosting along the galleries at night! Don't your parents object?"

"Oh, yes, Mama objects," said Bonita. "Always. She never stops finding fault with the way Federico runs Buena Suerte."

"What does your father say?"

"Oh, you know how men are. Papa tells Mama to leave Federico alone so he can manage the palace properly. Federico says women are terrible managers and anyway, well-bred ladies of the aristocracy don't do things like that."

Gabriella remained silent, wondering what Bonita would think of Madre Valderia.

Bonita continued, " — And Federico's word is law. He likes the *zopilotes*. He says they're a gift from God to keep us clean."

A pause. Gabriella asked, "Will I be taking orders from Federico Verro?"

"I suppose so," said Bonita. "In a way, I guess all of us take orders from Federico, even Papa." She sat on a gilt chair, lifted her knees and clasped her arms around them. "He's Papa's agent, an Italian. Manages everything - palace, plantations, buildings that Papa owns here in the city, mines, merchant ships — us!" She laughed. "Papa says Federico's the most brilliant accountant in Mexico."

"He knows about me, then?"

"Oh, yes! He had to approve, you see. He travels a lot, doing whatever it is he does. Elias acts as palace chamberlain when Federico's away."

"Then why doesn't Elias have the servants sweep the rooms and wash the windows? Why hasn't he had the servants clean the courtyard?"

Bonita shrugged. "It's nasty work, I guess."

Gabriella suspected there must be more to it than that. She wondered if she dared seek out Elias for a private talk.

Her attention strayed to a white ribbon at Bonita's throat. On it crawled a tiny bug. At her hairline were two more tiny bugs. The daughter of Doña Dolores Herédia de Figuroa, cousin of the queen, had head lice!

Gabriella's features hardened. "Bonita, I was told by Padre Mero that Don Avila wants me here for two purposes. He wants me to act as your companion, but mainly he wants me to guard your health. Is that your understanding too?"

Puzzled, Bonita replied, "Yes."

Smiling, Gabriella said briskly, "Very well! For the next few days, Ana and I are going to clean your bedchamber and your sitting room and my bedchamber. We are going to take down the tapestries and brush cobwebs down from the walls. We are going to wash the windows and clean the curtains and the bedclothes. For the sake of your health, you need clean surroundings. You also need exercise. This morning when Ana comes, she can help you dress for the day while I finish unpacking. And then we'll go out on the boulevard for a walk in the fresh air."

Bonita was stunned. *Walk? On the street?* She was about to protest but at that moment Ana tapped at the door and immediately entered, panting. Her face and hands were clean, her hair tidy and her bodice neatly laced. Noting her appearance, Gabriella smiled with satisfaction and greeted her warmly.

CHAPTER 4   Buena Suerte
                                                                       May 1774

During the next twenty-four hours, Gabriella learned things she would never have learned at the convent. Bonita explained that among the well-born of Mexico, ladies were expected to dress ostentatiously. They must wear as many jewels as possible, preferably diamonds and pearls. Colored stones were vulgar, though acceptable for men.

Young women following the latest European fashion must lace their bodices tightly, squeezing bosoms up and waists in at least an inch less than their normal measurements. They must wear tiny gloves and tiny shoes, disguising as best they could how poorly they fit. ("Mama knows a woman who hasn't walked in years," confided Bonita.)

Smart young women must be graceful and slender as willow whips with a tendency to swoon, especially if eligible gentlemen were nearby to catch them.

For all her beauty, Bonita deemed her cheeks disgustingly fat. She demonstrated to Gabriella how holding one's teeth apart while speaking caused the cheeks to sink, giving an appealingly slender line to the face in three-quarter profile. Gabriella nodded and filed away this detail, though to her ear the resulting speech sounded as if the speaker had lost several teeth.

Daylight revealed Buena Suerte's surroundings in worse condition than Gabriella had imagined the night before. She wondered that the entire household hadn't died of plague. She felt hesitant about seeking out Elias for fear he might misconstrue her mission. Consuelo had said that men would find her attractive, but not how Gabriella should respond when they did. She admired Elias, respected him. But love him? No.

But the situation was too serious for timidity. Braving the stench, the flies, and worst of all the quarreling, flapping *zopilotes,* she toured the galleries searching for him. Every glance revealed what a noble structure the palace had once been. But the marble-paved corridors sagged dangerously; intricately designed hardware on the doors and staircases was eroded and broken.

She found Elias sorting harness in the tack room. He straightened, pleased to see her, and she abruptly came to the point. "Elias, what I see so far, here at Buena Suerte, is a magnificent palace maintained no better than a cave where wild animals live. Why is that?"

Thrown off by her bluntness, he answered evasively, "Good servants are hard to find, Señorita. They — " A pause.

"Yes?"

"They usually do not stay very long, so it does no good to train them." Elias put down the harness he was untangling and glanced outside the door for eavesdroppers. "The servants do well enough. They try."

"Elias, one of my friends at the convent is from a wealthy family here in the city. I have been a guest in her home. The servants are clean and polite. The windows are washed regularly, floors are shined. The courtyards are swept daily and garbage is hauled away. And it makes me wonder, Elias. Why isn't the palace maintained properly? Why don't the servants clean it up?"

"Well, house servants in the city are not paid very well. They are better off begging. Our Savior's disciples begged for bread, so no one sees anything dishonorable in begging. Most would rather sleep late in the morning and beg on the street for what they need."

"But Don Avila can afford to pay well to keep good servants!"

"It is Federico who decides what to pay them, not Don Avila. Actually, servants like to come here." He scuffed the dirt floor with the toe of his boot. "At Buena Seurte there is more to steal. They come, steal a little food, a few nails, a sheet, a basket. Then they want more time to spend with their families, so they leave."

Gabriella frowned. "What does Federico do when he catches the servants stealing?"

"Nothing."

"*Nothing?*"

Again Elias glanced outside the door. "Maybe he tells them to be more careful. Because Federico steals too, you see. He will expect you to steal. And whenever you steal, you will pay him a little something. Everybody does."

Gabriella's eyes widened. "You, too?"

"No, because I am his assistant. I do not have to pay him."

"But I meant, do you steal?"

Elias met her eyes defiantly. "I have many brothers and sisters at home. And my father's land is poor and nothing he plants will grow. Yes, I help my family when I can."

Gabriella was disappointed to learn that Elias was a thief, but surprised that he was willing to confide so much in her. Surprised and emboldened. "I hope you will tell me the truth about something else. You know that I am an orphan, raised at the convent."

"Yes."

"I never knew my parents — " She faltered.

He waited. At last, helping her out, he said, "You have no family at all?"

She averted her eyes.

Elias explained, "There are servants here with no brothers or sisters, no parents, Señorita. There is no shame, only pity. They seldom mention it but yes, I know who they are. You see, I always attend Don Avila when he goes out playing cards in the evenings. Sometimes it is late when we return. He drinks much wine, Don Avila. At times like that, he tells me secrets maybe he should not repeat. He knows I will guard them. If you want nothing said about your family, nothing will be said. Not by me."

And she saw in the kindly depths of his black eyes that his promise would be kept. "Thank you," Gabriella murmured.

Recalling her reason for coming, she said, "The steward, Federico — but I should call him Señor Verro, shouldn't I?"

"Yes," said Elias firmly. "Even if he asks you to call him Federico, you should call him Señor Verro." He returned to his task of untangling and sorting out the pile of harness. "Don Avila has two maguey plantations near Vera Cruz. Federico is there now. He will be back in a few weeks after the winter's fiber has been made into rope and shipped. You will meet him then."

Gabriella was silent for a moment. "And Señor Verro, he takes orders from — from whom? Don Avila?"

"He takes orders from nobody. He does whatever he wants. Federico, he is usually the reason the women servants don't stay long. He expects special favors from them, and they get tired of it." He sighed. "It is all pretty bad."

"Why doesn't Don Avila do something? I can't believe he'd let Federico bother the women!"

"Don Avila, well —" Elias tossed the harness aside. "Don Avila is an unhappy man, you see. For many years, he hoped to return to Spain. There he lived in a big stone castle. His people bred Arabian horses and the finest sheep south of the Pyrenees. But the Figuroas made him come to Nuevo España to watch over their properties here."

"Why did he come if he didn't want to?"

"He was the youngest. It was his duty. They got him a post in the viceroy's court. That was twenty years ago, before I was born, but old Pepita will tell you."

"Yes," murmured Gabriella. Twenty years was before she was born too, but she wanted to learn about these things. "What does Don Avila do at court, anyway?"

"He is in charge of the king's taxes."

"The king's taxes from the whole colony?" asked Gabriella, stunned. Now that Carlos III of Spain had acquired the vast territory of Louisiana from the French, the colony of Nueva España was larger than all of Europe.

"Yes, I think so. I do not understand such things, but they say clerks do the work and all he does is sign papers."

Gabriella reflected. "I guess that isn't as interesting as breeding Arabian horses, is it? And he's been signing these papers for twenty years?"

"Yes. For a long time, Don Avila thought every year he would return to Spain. He used to tell me about the horses running free over the plains and his children laughing with their cousins in the big hall of the castle. Just talking about it made tears come to his eyes. For a long time he cared about Buena Suerte and the way the servants were treated. Doña Dolores was not so sick then, and her hearing was better. There were receptions and banquets. But he does not care anymore. He drinks to forget —"

"But he's an old man. He deserves to be happy. The family could send a nephew, someone younger —"

Elias looked doubtful. "A nephew could get rid of Federico and install another agent who might be worse. Here in the city we see many noblemen from Madrid and they are all the same. They feel it is the duty of the servants to get along with the steward, not the other way around. When it comes to money for the house, Don Avila believes it is beneath his dignity to argue about pesos and centavos with his steward. That is what Federico is for, he says, to worry about such things."

"But Doña Dolores —." She paused.

"Well, yes. Doña Dolores is different. But she cannot hear, you see. She is always after Federico to take better care of things but he teases her. He pretends he cannot understand what she is saying and goes right on doing as he pleases."

"But you think if only Doña Dolores could hear, Federico would do what she asks?"

Elias smiled wryly. "Señorita, if that old lady had her health and her proper hearing like everyone else, *El Diablo* himself would march to her tune!"

Gabriella knew, then, what she must do, no matter how much she dreaded it. With the awareness came a surge of forgotten pain in her back and legs. She rose and abruptly bade Elias goodby, ignoring the longing in his eyes.

At bedtime that evening, Gabriella sprinkled Bonita's scalp with larkspur petals and bound her hair close to her head. Next morning, she showed Ana how to brush out the dead lice and comb away the nits left clinging to the hair roots.

It was slow work, and Ana's patience soon wore thin. "Such a fuss!" she grumbled. "What's a tiny bug or two?"

"They bite, Ana," said Gabriella.

"Yes, and itch too, sometimes; it's God's punishment for our sins."

" — God's punishment for the sin of sloth," Gabriella said sharply. "As soon as Bonita's treatment is finished, it will be your turn!"

"*Santa Madre!*" murmured Ana.

It was a fine morning with early summer in the air. The doors to the hall leading to the courtyard gallery stood open. Gabriella had seated herself with her sewing so as to watch for Doña Dolores' personal maid Pepita when she passed on her way to Señora's rooms with morning chocolate.

Pepita, bent but cheerful, was an elderly *paisana* who had served the Figuroa family for many years. At last she shuffled past with a covered tray and shortly afterwards retraced her steps with an armload of sea-green silk — Doña Dolores' newest gown to be brushed and aired for the *paseo*.

Gabriella feigned composure though her stomach lurched with dread. "I'll be back soon," she told Bonita. She put aside her sewing, checked her pocket and strode down the gallery toward Doña Dolores's rooms. As she neared, anxiety slowed her step. Arriving at the door, she tapped softly then entered. She crossed the morning room to the bedchamber beyond, where Bonita's mother lay wrapped in a robe of French lace, rubbing her aching leg with her free hand. Beside her bed on a taboret was the tray with chocolate pot and cup of thinnest porcelain.

A moment passed before the old woman acknowledged her visitor. Gabriella quailed before the fierce eyes. At last their owner snarled, "What do you want? Where's Bonita?"

Gabriella's thoughts raced aimlessly and her kneecaps jerked as if on strings. She cleared her throat and said, "I left Bonita in her bedchamber with Ana, Señora."

Doña Dolores coiled like a serpent. "Speak up!" she shouted. "Weak voice, weak mind! Say what you have to say, then go away and leave me alone!"

Damned old bully! thought Gabriella, suddenly angry. She clamped her jaw, approached the bed, and drew the vial from her pocket. Slowly and distinctly she said, "Doña Dolores, I was trained at the convent to help sick people. I have some medicine here that will control the pain in your leg." She showed Doña Dolores the vial of amber liquid she held. "If you wish, I can mix a dose for you."

Doña Dolores eyed the vial, uttered a shout of exasperation and thundered,

"Then stop talking and do it, you stupid toad!"

With a shaking hand, Gabriella mixed the draft with water from a carafe beside the bed and handed it to Doña Dolores. Instead of drinking it down, the old woman peered suspiciously into the glass. Plaintively, she brayed, "People are always telling me lies. Are you telling me another lie? Will this stuff really make me feel better?"

"Yes, Señora."

Doña Dolores wrinkled her nose. "Looks like turkey piss!" she announced.

Gabriella's fragile composure snapped and she gasped. With an effort, she replied solemnly, "It is a dependable medicine that I am offering you, Señora. I took a dose of it myself this morning."

Doña Dolores stared. "Your leg hurts too?" she shouted.

"Both legs, Señora. And my back. Yes, they hurt. From the fight with the bandits. But mostly from riding the mule. The night I arrived, I was in great pain, but today you see that I can walk very well."

Once again Doña Dolores peered at the liquid in the glass and swirled it idly. "Nobody told me your name!" she bellowed. "Nobody ever tells me anything. What's your name?"

"María Gabriella Salgado, Señora."

"María Gabriella."

"Yes, Señora."

"Well, María Gabriella," yelled the old woman, skeptically raising the glass in her visitor's direction, "*Salud!*" She tossed off the medicine and grimaced hideously.

Gabriella knew first hand of the medicine's bitter taste and stood waiting with Señora's cup of chocolate.

After a pause, enunciating carefully as before, she said, "We need to talk about Bonita's health, Señora. I am sure that you, as her mother, will be interested in what I have to say."

Suspicion surged anew in the savage eyes. "Then say it," she brayed. "But don't waste time asking for money because I won't give you any!"

Gabriella placed a small chair beside the bed. As Doña Dolores' pain gradually eased, her ill temper receded and her interest kindled. Thirty minutes later, when Pepita returned to dress her mistress for the day, a tentative truce and numerous projects had been arranged between Doña Dolores and the newest member of her household.

CHAPTER 5

Vera Cruz
June 1774

Ernán Haros mounted the steps to the vine-shaded piazza of Vera Cruz's leading hotel. He selected a comfortable chair and lowered his heavy frame into it. He had come to meet his longtime colleague, Federico Verro, an agent like himself.

Haros was a businessman of expansive temperament, as broad of mind as he was broad of form. He celebrated the joys of the flesh, but not to debauchery. Power, also, he enjoyed more than most men, but in his management of the far-flung Costanza properties, he believed "they govern best who make the least noise." He congratulated himself, in fact, that in executing his most recent assignment for the Costanza family, he made scarcely any noise at all. The family's chaplain — well-loved but in Ernán's opinion not overly bright — was a cheerful aging puppy by the name of Raoul Mero. The family desired Padre Mero's advancement to the rank of monsignor. Ernán quietly located a buyer for one of the archbishop's deserted monasteries in the mountains and *presto!* — the preferment materialized within days.

As Haros waited for Federico Verro, he wondered what new plan the Italian would come up with this time. Verro had requested the meeting, and as always, Haros was glad to oblige, though wary. Verro was a thin-drawn man, quick and peevish. He was pale for an Italian, with skin that never tanned, a narrow blade of a nose, unforgiving eyes shadowed by black eyebrows that slashed across his face without a break.

Federico Verro had done well for himself, reflected Haros. He had been born and raised in the alleys of Genoa, and at the age of ten, stowed away on a Spanish trader to the Indies. Discovered, the boy was too small for work on deck but the captain put him to tallying the ship's cargo of random merchandise. The child proved an anomaly of the time — an honest seaman — and the career of Federico Verro was launched.

According to Verro's story, he left the ship at San Salvador with his employer's blessing and letter of recommendation. The merchant had been gratified to find his inventory perfectly accounted for and was a week at sea before he missed from his safe two bars of gold bullion that were never found. Haros wondered how many bars of gold bullion were missing from the estate of Verro's present *patron,* the senile aristocrat Don Avila de Figuroa. He suspected the worst.

The sunlight filtering through the vines on the piazza grew more intense. Haros hoped Verro would not keep him waiting. He could guess what the meeting would be about. The two maguey plantations belonging to Don Avila were located astride a far larger Costanza plantation amounting to some six thousand acres of well-drained land with two thriving rope manufactories on the premises. For five years, Verro had buzzed with various plans, hoping to purchase parts of the larger plantation, combine the entire acreage, sell all or part of the two smaller plantations — always some new scheme to increase profits. Whose profits were to be increased, Haros was never quite able to elicit from the wily Italian.

Recently Verro's proposals had grown more feverish. Europe smoldered with rumors of war. The French and British were once again at one another's throats. Within the last few months, Britain's tiny settlements along the Atlantic coast from Massachusetts to Georgia had become restive and were threatening to rebel. Mighty Spain, with vast colonies covering half the earth, would have smiled atsuch effrontery, but the thin-skinned British spoke of sending troops to restore order.

Meanwhile maguey was the raw material of rope, and rope was the stuff of war. With three-masted shipping of six nations breasting the seas from Greenland to Tierra del Fuego, the price of rope for rigging had doubled and then doubled again.

"Federico, my friend!"

Haros heaved to his feet and greeted the Italian warmly, planting jovial kisses on each cheek. "By the Madonna," he cried, "you never looked better! God has been kind to you, to give you such good health and good looks."

Verro smiled thinly. Haros had momentarily forgotten how the Italian despised the unctuous colloquy so typical of Mexico's upper classes even as he longed to master it himself. There was great value in being able to conduct oneself like a person of position and influence. Ah, yes, Haros reflected. Great value.

Solicitously, he asked, "It isn't too hot for coffee, is it? No. Let's have coffee and cakes in the dining salon where we can talk undisturbed, eh?"

Refreshments before them, Verro tasted nothing. He lit a cigar and Haros noticed, but ignored, an emerald ring Verro was wearing. The stone was unusually large.

"I should be in the city," said the Italian, "not here wasting breath shouting at lazy Indians!"

"This is not the best time to leave, my friend. You are only halfway through harvesting for the ship's cordage you have already sold."

Green fire flashed from Verro's ring as he drummed his long fingers on the table. "And the yield is as good as ever, maybe better. The saints be thanked for that, at least!"

"I should think so! Over fifty tons of rope my factories have processed for you so far."

Verro snapped his fingers impatiently. "And where are the ships? My fifty tons of rope, down there on the dock it sits, along with yours, gathering mildew and dust."

"Patience, my friend. Clipper ships from Marseille and Liverpool are due next week and they bring with them the gold to pay. We are doing well this year. Why are you so unhappy?"

"I should be in the city," Verro repeated.

"Elias has always managed Buena Suerte to your satisfaction. Is something wrong? The tenants in your warehouses, perhaps?"

Verro ignored the questions. Instead he hunched over the table toward Haros and lowered his voice. "If you should put a price on the Costanza holding out there, all six thousand acres, what would that price be?"

Haros shrugged and turned a palm upward. "With a crop on it?"

"Of course."

"Including the factories?"

"Including everything. Factories, quarters for the workmen, wells, pumps, roads, everything.

Haros considered. "Say 75,000 gold ounces. Why?"

"I want to buy it."

Haros managed to turn a guffaw into an explosive cough. "Don Avila has been winning at cards, has he?" Haros had heard the opposite was true.

"Forget Don Avila. I am asking for myself, Federico Verro. I want to buy it." The seconds lengthened as Haros met the Italian's level gaze. It was not unusual for managers of great estates to make a little something for themselves on the side. And Haros, aware of Federico Verro's nature, never doubted that he had done well while in the employ of the Figuroa family. But had he done *that* well?

Ernán's glance slid quickly over the emerald ring, now set ablaze by sunlight from the nearby window. A glint of amusement touched his eyes. It was no emerald at all, but glass. A fake! Twenty years of appraising Costanza jewels had given Ernán Haros an expert's eye. A true emerald showed luminous color to its heart; this bauble of Verro's had been buffed to a surface brilliance but the cloudiness beneath — . *It isn't even good glass*! thought Ernán, suppressing a smile.

Slowly Haros lowered his coffee cup. "You want to buy a six-thousand-acre plantation?" he inquired softly. "How do you propose to pay for it, my friend?"

"That's my affair. Will the Costanza family sell it to me, Federico Verro, for 75,000 gold ounces?"

Haros considered. Of course, the Italian could be acting for an unknown party, though anyone willing to trust Federico Verro with such a sum was to be wondered at. Considering further, Haros' own *patron*, old Eduardo Costanza, was frail and might not last out the year. His widow-to-be had long wished to be rid of the property. And though 75,000 was a figure he had plucked out of the air, it was an excellent price.

"Possibly," murmured Haros. "Possibly. But not now," he hastened to add. "This is not the proper time. Possibly at the end of two years."

"It is agreed, then?"

Haros cleared his throat. "Of course, you have in mind to offer a guarantee of some kind."

Verro frowned. "A thousand? Would a thousand gold ounces hold it?"

"You can't be serious."

"Very well, two."

A thoughtful shake of the head. "Don Eduardo, I'm afraid, would not—"

"Three."

A pause. Haros gabled his fingers over his coffee. "Federico, let me be sure I understand you. You want to enter into this agreement today. You have this three thousand ounces — remember, that's twenty-four thousand escudos, gold coins, we are talking about. *Three thousand ounces*! You have this amount available now, do you? Today?"

"My note presented at the bank across the street will give you the entire sum. If you don't want a bank credit, you will need a man to carry it. But the money is yours. — And will be deducted from the price of the property when the purchase is consummated, of course," he added hurriedly.

A shrug. Another pause.

The Italian lowered his voice. "And an extra five hundred ounces for yourself,

Ernán. The papers the notary draws up will not mention the extra five hundred. That is — "

But Haros was shaking his head. "Very well," he said. "This three thousand ounces to hold the property for two years."

He leaned back. "What if Don Eduardo says no. Flatly, no. Not in two years. Never. What then?"

"Return my money."

Haros stroked his double chins. "What about security? In case you are unable to make good your purchase, I mean."

Verro's voice rose. "Security? But you would have my three thousand ounces! That is my guarantee. If I do not purchase the property and pay you the balance in two years, I lose my three thousand."

"Not good enough, my friend."

"Not — ! You are unreasonable, Ernán!"

Haros spread his hands. "With the price of rope doubling two and three times every year, who knows what a price might be offered for the Costanza plantation? An investor from London? From Venice? So we'll suppose that today I commit myself to sell to you for 75,000 gold ounces, but next year the land might be worth half again as much. I must turn down this better offer because of my commitment to you. And then at the end of two years, you come to me and say, 'Sorry, Ernán, I cannot buy your plantation as I promised I would.' Then where do I stand? What do I tell my *patron?*"

In exasperation, Verro leaped from his chair. Snapping his fingers like castanets, he strode to the nearby window, his shallow chest heaving. He stood for a few moments, twirling the ring on his finger. At length he returned and slid into his chair. "How much?"

"'How much?'"

"If I do not consummate the purchase at the end of two years, what 'security' are you asking?"

"Both of the Figuroa plantations," Haros said coolly.

Buena Suerte
Late June, 1774

After much indecision, Bonita purchased a muff as a saint's day gift for her friend Irena. The item was a delicate confection of lace and ribbon, intended for midsummer show and certainly not for warming the wearer's hands in cold weather.

"I need a letter to go with the gift!" Bonita announced to Gabriella. "It must be clever and beautifully written." She busied herself at Gabriella's desk, setting out the needed writing materials. "Come! You'll know exactly what to say."

"It wouldn't be proper for me to write a note like that!" laughed Gabriella. "She's your friend, not mine!"

"What difference does that make?" said Bonita. "I can't write and Irena can't read. You'll write it for me and one of her brothers will read it for her."

Gabriella's smile faded. "No one ever taught you to read?"

"Of course not," replied Bonita. "Before Mama left Spain, she could write a little but now she's forgotten how. At the convent school as a novice, Javiera learned, but by now she's memorized all the hymns and rituals and doesn't need to read anymore."

In the colonies as well as in Spain, nuns were expected to read and explain the scriptures to their pupils or to the novices. And occasionally, lower-class widows in business could read and write as well as do sums. Beyond that, a female who could read and write was something of a freak, like a woman with a beard. The rare lady who enjoyed poems and novels kept her hobby discreetly hidden.

"I'll write your note for you," Gabriella agreed. "But you should learn to write your own."

"Why?"

"Out of pride."

"I don't clean my own shoes out of pride," Bonita pointed out. "That's what Ana's for. Why should I write my own letters? That's what you're for."

Gabriella couldn't argue with the logic. "Very well. Tell me exactly what you want to say and I'll write it for you."

"Oh, I don't know," said Bonita thoughtfully. Gabriella obediently began to scribble on the notepaper. "Maybe just say it's a pretty muff and it made me think of her on her saint's day. Something like that."

She waited for Gabriella's pen to stop scratching. "What did you write down? Read it to me."

Gabriella read: "'Oh, I don't know. Maybe just say it's a pretty muff and it made me think of her on her saint's day. Something like that.'"

Bonita flushed.

"I wrote exactly what you said," Gabriella reminded her.

"Yes, but that's not a proper letter and you know it!" Bonita snapped. "What insolence! I shall report this to Papa."

Gabriella sighed, tore up the paper, tossed it aside and took a fresh sheet. "Very well. We'll try again."

Bonita bit her lip, thinking. "My — my dear Irena."

Gabriella wrote.

Bonita sat nearby on a slipper chair, rocking back and forth in concentration.

Gabriella tried to encourage her. "Try to think of what you'd say if you were talking to her."

"Yes, well —." Bonita eyes shifted rapidly. "Write this: 'When I saw this muff, I thought of you.'"

Gabriella wrote, then looked up expectantly. Bonita's head began to swivel gently from side to side. Her right hand had developed a marked tremor which she was attempting to steady against her waist. The tremor grew to a decided jerking. Alarmed, Gabriella dropped her pen.

Bonita slid from the chair, shaken by repeated muscular spasms that now consumed her from head to foot.

"Ana!" screamed Gabriella. "Miguel! Ana! Come quickly!"

Bonita's arms and legs thrashed with terrifying intensity, crashing against the legs of the chair. Her breath came in hissing gasps, her lips were drawn back in a horrifying rictus, and the irises of her eyes disappeared, leaving only the whites of her eyes showing.

Above all, do no harm, Gabriella remembered from Sister Magdalena. She shoved the chair out of the way and unlaced Bonita's bodice for easier breathing. Suddenly, with diabolical force, Bonita flung an arm across her own throat, leaving a bloody scratch from the ornately carved ring she wore. As gently as possible, Gabriella removed all rings, bracelets and a brooch that might inflict similar wounds and heaped them on the seat of the chair.

What especially disconcerted Gabriella was the intensity of Bonita's convulsion. Her extremities were unyielding as iron. Such an attack while riding horseback or descending stairs could result in fatal wounds. For the first time, she understood the gravity of her assignment at Buena Suerte.

It was neither Ana nor Miguel, but Pepita, who responded to her cry for help. Gabriella was kneeling beside Bonita, bathing her jerking forehead with a cool, damp cloth.

"Ah, poor Gabriella," crooned Pepita sympathetically. "Señorita's first attack, and you alone with none to help you. So sad."

"When this has happened before, what did Ana do for her?" asked Gabriella.

Pepita shrugged. "Nothing. It's God's work. When God gets through with her, He will leave her alone. Long ago, I knew a man who had fits. On the farm where I grew up, it was. He foamed at the mouth and make a scandalous mess. My mother, she threw buckets of cold water on him to wake him up. Made no difference. He groaned and mucked about like an animal."

"Does Bonita have these attacks often?" asked Gabriella, worried.

Pepita shrugged. "Once a month. Once a week. Once in six months. Never any warning, just her eyes gone funny, searching back and forth." Pepita lowered herself onto the slipper chair.

"I wish I knew how to care for her," fretted Gabriella.

"Well, that's it, you see," said Pepita. "When Bonita was a little girl, Master would call the priest. Waste of time. He only mumbled a prayer and ran away. Doctors too. They call it the falling sickness."

Gabriella stared. "Alexander the Great had the falling sickness; and the Roman Emperor Julius Caesar. Some say our own blessed Saint Paul was sometimes pale and wan because of it."

The convulsion lasted perhaps a minute; Bonita's rigors became less formidable and her breathing less shallow.

"None outside the family knows of her attacks," said Pepita, shaking outstretched fingers before her lips. "Oh, no. None outside the family must ever know."

"Yes, I understand."

Bonita was rousing. "I'm so tired," she whispered pitiably.

Gabriella supported her with an arm under her shoulders. She reached to retrieve Bonita's jewelry. Pepita had risen, but the chair seat was bare.

Elias' warning told Gabriella at once what had happened. She fixed Pepita with a stony glare. "Give me Bonita's jewels," she demanded, holding out her hand.

Pepita's eyes widened with indignation.

"Bonita's rings and bracelets and the brooch," Gabriella repeated. "They were there on the chair before you sat on it. Give them to me. Now."

The old woman's face blotched with anger. "You call me a thief, do you?! You, a convent bastard, here no more than a month! You stole them yourself and put the blame on me! Wait till I tell Master about this!"

Pepita moved toward the hallway, but Gabriella had already spied the weighted pocket in the old woman's apron. Ignoring her enraged screams and desperate scratchings, Gabriella quickly overpowered her and emptied the pocket of its stolen treasure.

"Now leave us!" Gabriella commanded.

Pepita complied, but the malevolence in her parting gaze sent a shiver down Gabriella's back.

CHAPTER 6

Buena Suerte
June 1774

Gabriella visited Doña Dolores regularly to make certain her medicine was administered properly. One morning as she approached from far down the gallery, she heard Pepita's cracked voice. "No, no, Madrecita! Your hair is all wrong like that! Take your hands away and let me fix it!"

"Leave me alone, you bitch!" screamed Doña Dolores.

Gabriella had drawn even with the open bedchamber door. Pepita stumbled into her arms, followed by a flying perfume bottle which sailed across the room and crashed against the sculptured marble of the fireplace.

Pepita's face was contorted with rage. "She's crazy, that one!" the old servant hissed as she retreated. "They should shut her up like a viper to sting herself to death!"

Gabriella entered the bedchamber and quietly closed the door. Doña Dolores sat moaning at her dressing table, rubbing her thigh as she rocked back and forth. Gabriella mixed the draft of medicine as usual and watched in the mirror as Doña Dolores greedily gulped it down.

Then, carefully enunciating each word, Gabriella addressed the reflection in the mirror. "You shouldn't allow the servants to shout at you as if you were a wild beast. Make them speak slowly and distinctly." Softly she stroked the tumbled gray hair. "In a few minutes the pain will go away. Then I will send Pepita back to help you dress." She smiled gently, then left to attend to her other duties.

During the days that followed, Señora's tantrums diminished. With her cane, she began stumping about the apartments of the palace, usually with two or three servants. When she spoke to them, giving instructions, and when they replied, explaining and suggesting, the exchange took place in a normal tone of voice.

Gabriella sighed with relief. The servants ogled one another, wondering what the change signified.

It signified change. Out went the faded carpets and window drapery and in came the finest replacements money could buy. Railings and balustrades were repaired and painted. Leaks were mended, floors waxed and windows reglazed.

In the courtyard, the refuse disappeared. First two, then seven, then fifteen cats were introduced to chase both rats and *zopilotes*, though at least one great bird made a meal of at least one snoozing feline, to Bonita's delight. She watched and spoke of nothing else the rest of the day.

The household marveled. "What's happened to Mama?" Bonita asked Gabriella one afternoon.

"Her leg doesn't hurt any more."

Comprehension spread over Bonita's features. " — And Mama's setting everything to rights before Federico comes back from Vera Cruz!" she crowed. "She's won out against him at last." She laughed gaily. "Poor Elias, caught in the middle!"

And indeed, Elias was caught. A dozen times a day, Doña Dolores summoned him to her rooms for new instructions. By the end of May, he was exhausted and sent a pleading message to the steward in Vera Cruz: "When are you coming home?"

As spring gave way to summer, Gabriella's responsibilities multiplied also. Three laundresses were hired and she was ordered to train them. A seamstress appeared to refurbish the family wardrobes and Gabriella was ordered to oversee her work. She and the seamstress designed gowns for Doña Dolores and Bonita for a scheduled ball at the National Palace. They settled on wisteria blue brocade for Señora, and for Bonita, cinnamon satin to match her eyes.

Meanwhile, Señora and Don Avila were impressed by Gabriella's skill with herbs and remedies and promoted her to official household *enfermera*. She found herself treating the kitchen staff for burns and the gardeners for blisters.

She continued to measure out regular doses of pain killer for Doña Dolores and when she had trouble dropping off to sleep at night, measured out a drop for herself. Within a short time her supply of medicines was running low. Padre helped her locate a reliable *curandera* in a tiny shop just off the plaza.

Padre Mero often came to Buena Suerte to visit Gabriella and was gratified to see the improvements Doña Dolores had made. "It's working out just as I hoped," he told Gabriella. "You've been a good influence here, inspired everyone."

"Well-ll — "

"You have doubts?"

"What's Federico Verro going to say? He's been managing Buena Suerte his way for years. And now — ."

"Well, 'his way' left something to be desired, you'll admit. Perhaps it wasn't his fault. Perhaps he was too busy with his other responsibilities to supervise the servants. At any rate, the palace looks far more inviting now than it did before you came."

"He'll be angry," Gabriella insisted.

Padre laughed at her. "What is there to be angry about? He'll thank you for helping to bring about the change." He patted her hand. "You worry too much!"

He heard her confession and afterwards strolled the galleries with her, his shovel hat under his arm.

"Sometimes city ways make no sense to me," Gabriella admitted. "Doña Dolores wants very much to call on the wife of Armando de Neve. The family arrived from Madrid two weeks ago. Señora keeps insisting that we can't call on them until she receives their card. She's indignant because the card hasn't been delivered."

"It may seem petty but Señora is correct," said Padre. "When it arrives — which it will — the card will say something like 'Armando de Neve and his Lady, Doña So-and-So inform you of their arrival in the city and put themselves at your disposal'. It's a formal notification that the furniture is in place, the curtains are up and the newcomers are ready to receive callers, that's all. Armando de Neve's brother is the man Carlos favors to become the first governor of Alta California. Don Armando and his wife have two lovely daughters but more important, they have an eligible son, Martín. Martín is unmarried, twenty-nine and a favorite at court. And he will inherit a handsome fortune someday."

"Ah-h-h-h!"

"Yes, indeed. 'Ah-h-h-h.' Remember, you are still new at this. There is a limit to how much you can modify the Figuroa family to conform to your ideas. You must be prepared to modify yourself a bit in return."

"I think I'm modified already," Gabriella replied pertly. "And more than a bit."

"Your hair's different," Padre admitted.

"Do you like it?" Gabriella patted the intricate French knot with side curls. "Ana suggested it and showed me how to do it myself."

"So? Ana approves of your copper-colored hair after all? What changed her mind?"

"The other servants, I think. They're superstitious. Old crippled Miguel and the others want to touch me for luck."

Padre noticed a staircase nearby leading up from the gallery. "Oh? Now this looks interesting! Where do these stairs lead? To the *azotea?*"

"Yes! And the view is gorgeous! Come! I'll show you!" and she darted up the steps leading to the roof.

At the top, she realized she had no protection from the glaring sunlight. "Let me borrow your shovel hat, Padre, so I won't freckle. Bonita will tease me if I'm all spots."

He handed it over. "Don't tell the archbishop."

"Never!"

"And use it while you can. Its days are numbered, poor old hat."

"Meaning what?"

"I understand that next month I am to become a monsignor. Monsignors wear dignified hats, not hats that roll up at the sides like a piece of music."

Gabriella whooped with delight. "They're promoting you! How marvelous!

And high time, too; you're much better than an ordinary padre." Then her face clouded. "This doesn't mean you'll be leaving the city for some other assignment, does it?"

"I should be very surprised if it meant that. It will mean more responsibility though, I'm sure."

"Oh, Padre, I'm so happy for you. Will there be an installation ceremony?"

"Yes."

"Am I invited?"

"You and the whole Figuroa family, if they'll come. Javiera too."

As Padre took his leave, Gabriella asked, "Do you still make regular trips to the convent?"

"To check up on my cousin? Yes. I'm going next week. Have you a letter you'd like to send?"

She ran to fetch it. Blushing, she showed him her very own wax seal made with her very own new signet ring bought with her very own money that she had earned.

"Pride, pride," reproached Padre fondly as he started down the main staircase.

"And *you're* proud!" she laughed. "Of *me*! Admit it!" At which Padre's dimple winked and his double chins shook with chuckles.

Gabriella located a small chapel not far from Buena Suerte where she could attend early mass each day. Always alone. It surprised her to learn that, except for Javiera, the Figuroa family was devout only sporadically.

One afternoon Miguel was driving Gabriella and Bonita home after a shopping expedition when he suddenly reined in the horses, dropped to the pavement and knelt. Men, women and children all around them were kneeling with bowed heads.

"Get out of the carriage!" ordered Bonita.

Gabriella did as she was told, and only then heard the tinkling of a bell. Approaching down the narrow street was a lavishly robed priest bearing a *ciborium* with the Blessed Sacrament. Before and behind him walked acolytes holding over the priest a white canopy embroidered in gold and crimson. In front was another acolyte carrying in one hand a large lighted candle and in the other a little Sanctus bell which he rang with great solemnity. "They're taking the Host to someone who's dying," whispered Bonita.

They remained as they were until the bell could no longer be heard. Then they and all the people in the street rose and went about their business as though nothing had happened.

In the carriage once again, Gabriella asked, "What about Javiera? No one ever mentions her."

Bonnie stiffened. "We don't talk about her much. She's nearly completed her novitiate at Nuestra Señora del Carmen. She'll take her final vows in December."

"I envy her."

Bonita stared. "You don't mean that!"

"Oh, but I do!"

"You'd be happy to — to *die*? Never again to see any of your family, never eat a meal with a friend, never ride in a carriage, never see a mountain or a field?"

It was Gabriella's turn to stare. "Our sisters at Santa Clara work in the fields. They see their friends and relatives all the time."

"But Javiera isn't joining the Poor Clares. She's joining the Carmelites. They lock themselves away, and as far as the rest of the world is concerned, they're dead." Bonita's voice was rising and Gabriella became uneasy. "That's what my sister has made up her mind to do: She wants to die!"

"I'm sorry if I made you unhappy, Bonita. I shouldn't have brought it up."

After a pause, Bonita said, "Papa and Mama worry about Javiera. She isn't very strong and she'll ruin her health. Many of the sisters do. The order is small, tiny actually. So many of the nuns die young."

Gabriella wondered what she had blundered into. She knew the Carmelites were an order devoted to seclusion and self-denial; everyone knew that. But the Poor Clares denied themselves, too. There were even those who claimed Santa Clara's regimen of poverty was more austere than the Carmelites'.

But dying young? Gabriella thought of sixty-year-old Sister Adela bent double with arthritis, who got her wish and died on Christmas Eve. And on the coldest day of January, ancient old Sister Tómasina, toothless and doddery, who was still hemming sheets an hour before her death at 84. But she kept her questions to herself.

Not until they were nearly home did Gabriella say, "Bonita, the next time Javiera comes for a visit, will it be all right if I talk to her? About her order, I mean."

"Of course," Bonita said with indifference. "Talk to her all you please."

Bonita went straight to her rooms, leaving Gabriella with Miguel to sort out their many purchases.

"Waste of time, talking to Javiera," muttered Miguel as he gathered up the parcels. "Javiera won't have nothing to say."

"Nothing to say about what?" asked Gabriella, only slightly annoyed at his interference.

"The real reason she left Buena Suerte," murmured Miguel. "Had nought to do with praying and such. Had to do with a man."

Gabriella snapped, "It's improper for us to be gossiping about such things."

"Yes, Señorita," said Miguel, straightening with an armload of bundles.

Ana appeared, took most of them, and mounted the staircase, leaving Gabriella once again alone with Miguel. In spite of herself, she murmured, "There are many men in the world. It must have been a very unusual one for Javiera to — "

Miguel lowered his voice. "You've never seen Señora Javiera. She's plain, not a beauty like her sister Señora Bonita. And Elias, he was naught but a groom in those days. But he was the man for her, he was! She followed him like a puppy. Mostly he shooed her away, but to her, he was day and night, moon and stars all rolled into one. Took Master a long time to see what was happening under his nose. When he did, he sent Elias to work as a *vaquero* on a hacienda he owns near Guadalajara. Then he arranged a proper marriage for Javiera. That's when she started her talk of a convent. None but the Carmelites for her, neither."

Miguel went ahead with the last of the bundles and Gabriella thoughtfully followed alone.

Her evening visits to administer Doña Dolores' bedtime medicine had become a companionable time for both of them. Señora loved to talk about her plans for the palace and Gabriella, though uneasy over the changes, loved to listen.

One evening Señora cried, "It's the triumph of my life! The palace will be ready by Christmas when Javiera takes her vows! Geese for roasting this year, I think. Rita the cook will approve. A genius with roast goose, that woman. Candles, too. I'll decorate with a forest of candles this Christmas!"

"You must be looking forward to having Javiera at home again," said Gabriella.

The pleasure drained from Doña Dolores' face. "Yes, but the sight of her breaks my heart."

"Señora! Why do you say that about your own daughter?"

"Because it's true." A pause. "The women at your convent worship God by taking care of the sick and the poor. But the women of Nuestra Señora del Carmen see sin as the cause of all that's wrong with the world. They do penance for the world's sin. They spend their days praying and most of the night, too. They never see anyone from the outside world but the priest who comes to say mass."

After a pause, Gabriella asked, "Is it true they aren't allowed to see their families?"

"It's true."

A stunned silence. "You mean *never*?"

"Never." Doña Dolores took a deep breath. "Javiera's father understands her life will be hard but not how hard. Bonita too. Its best they don't know, so please — ." A muscle moved in her jaw. "The Carmelites whip themselves and wear the iron crown of thorns. Next to their skin they wear the leather belt with the iron points turned inwards and sleep on the short wooden bed with bars across it. Around their necks they wear an iron cross with points to pierce the skin and thus ever remind them of the agony of the Saviour on the cross." She paused. "There's more but I don't remember it all."

Gabriella was deeply disturbed. She could not comprehend a group of women who deliberately manufactured their own self-torture, all day, every day — and counted it holy! To her, the convent had always represented the peak of achievement for a woman. She was seeing that for some, it was the valley of the shadow of death.

Doña Dolores was nodding off to sleep, which was a blessing. Gabriella helped the stiff-kneed old woman to her bed, arranged the bedclothes around her and gently bade her goodnight.

Returning to her own bedchamber, she was haunted by what she had heard. Self-inflicted torture was a dark aspect of Mother Church. There were the thirty-five days of public penance in September called the *desagravios* when the men and women worship separately. At Santa Clara, Madre ignored it if possible. Yet every year, three or four sisters asked permission to observe *desagravios*. For thirty-five consecutive days, they went to the chapel in the morning where they knelt on the stone floor with their arms outstretched in imitation of Christ on the cross. For heavy women, the exercise was excruciating and they were unable to walk for hours afterward.

Consuelo had whispered that *desagravios* for the men was far more severe. They came to worship in the evenings. There was a sermon and then the lights were extinguished. The men bared their backs and whipped themselves with the priest reading Scripture from time to time to encourage them. This went on for half-an-hour, sometimes with the sound of blood splashing on the floor. When Consuelo was very young, an uncle of hers wounded himself terribly and after several days died from an infection. "Women are not supposed to know what happens," she had said. "But the wives treat the wounds, so how can they not know?"

In spite of Don Avila's love of wine and Señora's occasional peevishness, Gabriella enjoyed the time she spent with the family. Together they celebrated the religious fiestas and watched the parades, saw the floats go by bearing high the Holy Virgin bedecked in her treasure of gold and jewels, carried on the shoulders of sweating, groaning men. Guarding the floats were hooded guards carrying candles four feet long and so thick both hands were needed to support them. Wax like white tears dripped from their flaming crests, and the hopeful crowds pressed close. A spattering from one of the sacred candles was a highly prized omen of good luck, and sometimes fistfights broke out, quelled by attendants wielding ceremonial halberds.

Each Sunday the family attended mass at the church of San Hipolito and most evenings they went to the Alameda for the *paseo*. Gabriella was especially delighted when she was invited to come along; at the convent, there was nothing half so grand or exciting to look forward to. Though ordinarily the *paseo* carriage was staffed by four footmen — two before and two behind, — when Gabriella went, it was always Elias and Miguel who handed them into the carriage then took the reins for the drive to the plaza.

There, in the slanting sun of late afternoon, they joined hundreds of other carriages, horsemen on prancing steeds, and an army of strolling onlookers circling slowly round the tree-shaded park. Bonita and Doña Dolores, dressed in their lace shawls and diamonds as big as cats' eyes, fanned themselves as they nodded and bowed to their many acquaintances.

The object of the *paseo*, especially for those of marriageable age, was to see and be seen. After one or two circuits of the plaza, Miguel would park the carriage so the ladies could watch the men show off with their horses, making them pirouette and curvette. Bonita was always the most beautiful señorita there and the young *caballeros* posed and strutted to catch her attention, ignoring the traffic problems they caused.

A rule of this courtship game demanded that the horsemen ignore the audience for which they performed. Even if ladies applauded and cheered, which they sometimes did, honor demanded that the riders appear to be executing feats of spectacular horsemanship for their own pleasure.

Elias and Miguel smiled behind their hands at the charade. The first evening, after Gabriella had witnessed an especially elaborate drill conducted by four young horsemen, Miguel had murmured to her, "Don't think this circus goes on all night, Señorita. As soon as the carriages leave, the *caballeros* head for the nearest *cantina*."

When Don Avila was able, he escorted his womenfolk at the *paseo* astride his favorite Arabian gelding. But Gabriella liked best the times when he rode in the carriage and talked about the history of the city, about Spain, or about faraway California.

"At court we keep hearing rumors that Carlos plans to send colonists to settle Alta California," he announced one afternoon, his eyes shining. "It is an unbelievable place, like the Garden of Eden. All twelve months of the year the climate is like April in Spain. Gentle rains and sunshine. Snow on the mountains, as we have here, but in the valleys, never. Think what crops could be grown — what livestock could be pastured and bred in such a climate!"

"If it's such a fine place, why don't more people go there?" asked Bonita.

"And leave Mexico?" He laughed. "My dear girl, Mexico is the most sophisticated metropolis outside of Europe. And by far the largest. A hundred thousand people live here!"

"Do you mean that Mexico is larger than Boston or Philadelphia?" asked Gabriella. "Don't ships from Boston trade at Vera Cruz?"

Don Avila smiled. "A boatload of dried fish occasionally. But then, the English colonies are made up of starving heathen and runaway criminals, living in mud and squalor. Boston and Philadelphia together number less than fifty thousand souls. Mexico was larger than that for a hundred years under the Aztecs, who were heathen, yes, but far more civilized! Mexico was a center of trade under the Aztecs, just as it is today. We have shipping from China, Hawaii and the Philippines as well as from Europe and the southern continent. Fortunes can be made here. Why should anyone want to move to California?"

"Maybe not everyone wants to make a fortune, Don Avila," suggested Gabriella, thinking of the poor farmers at the convent. "Maybe there are *paisanos* who would like to go."

"Oh, I'm sure they would, some of them. But supplies and equipment are needed for such a trip, so they can't afford it. Or perhaps they're afraid. There's an ancient story that California is a land of Amazons where women warriors march about in golden armor killing off all the male babies."

Bonita gasped at such an interesting prospect. "There are no Amazons, my dear," soothed her father. "Probably there are no Amazons anywhere in the world, but it makes a good story. Anyway, the Franciscans have established missions along the coast of Alta California and they have seen no Amazons and no golden armor. They tell only of a few natives. Poor starving creatures quite willing to steal if they have the opportunity, but friendly enough. The padres feed them and teach them how to herd the livestock."

Don Avila's words fired Gabriella's imagination. The nuns at the convent had spoken of California as a desolate island lying off the western seaport of San Blas. Nothing grew on the island but lizards and cactus, they said. But obviously their information must be outdated if missionaries report rich grazing land, perfect climate and docile Indians.

Santa Clara's crumbling walls and musty traditions had always spelled security for Gabriella but suddenly they took on a morbid air. Maybe there were better places and better ways to serve God than at Santa Clara de Asís. If the king sent colonists to California, wouldn't they need a teacher, a school for the children? Or wouldn't the colonists need a clinic run by a healthy young *enfermera?* Possibilities swarmed up in Gabriella's mind like flights of swallows.

California! There was music in the very sound of it!

CHAPTER 7

Mexico
July 1774

Señora's long-for card from Don Armando de Neve and his lady arrived at last. An appropriate date for a visit was arranged and Bonita, demure in lavender silk, was plucked, primped and pummeled into a vision of the latest fashion.

"*Santissima María*, what will we do if she gets sick?" Doña Dolores asked Ana. "Of course, Gabriella must come along."

"They'll talk about her red hair and forget all about me!" pouted Bonita.

In the adjoining bedchamber, Ana rummaged through Gabriella's scanty wardrobe. "Wear the plainest you've got." She held up a cotton frock of drab gray-green. "This will do," she announced. "Take off the frippery there. No bows. No ribbons. Remember to walk three paces behind. Carry the ladies' shawls and Señora's cane. Wear a dust cap under your rebozo."

Gabriella stared. "I'll look like a scullery maid waiting for orders from the cook!"

Ana nodded meaningfully.

The disguise was effective. As the three left Buena Suerte, no one recognized Bonita's redheaded companion. — Only Elias, who stared slack-jawed at the transformation. Gabriella had determined to resist any attraction she felt for Elias. When he turned away without his usual smile, she flushed with chagrin. Willing herself not to think highly of Elias was all very well; it stung bitterly to realize how much she *wanted* him to think highly of her.

Don Armando de Neve had settled his large family in a palace less grand than Buena Suerte, but more spacious. The Figuroa ladies were received and offered abundant refreshments, as was customary. What was not customary was the activity. The Neve family was an energetic clan, playing jokes on one another, singing songs at the harpsichord, organizing complicated games understood by no one but themselves. Aunts, sisters and cousins popped into the room from various hallways and balconies. They curtsied, giggled, disappeared and reappeared again. Bonita was the center of attention with her straight back, tiny waist and sunken cheeks. Doña Dolores simpered triumphantly.

Gabriella hoped in vain for a glimpse of the fabulous Martín. Among the aristocracy of Mexico, ladies paid social calls on the ladies of a family, never the gentlemen. Still, Gabriella — and doubtless Bonita as well — hoped for a glance through an open door or window. But the minutes dragged by and the only sign of Martín de Neve was his portrait at the far end of the *sala,* pointed out to Bonita within minutes after her arrival. The portrait was not overly large, hung with several other likenesses of people Gabriella took to be family members, and painted when he must have been twelve or thirteen. The portrait showed a proud, pink-cheeked, gaudily-dressed version of the other family members, all of whom looked alike as a row of beans to Gabriella.

After the inspection of the portrait, Gabriella perched on a chair in the corner, homely as a wart. For the duration of the hour-long visit, her eyes seldom left Bonita. She watched for shifting eyes or twitching hands signaling that a sudden leave-taking might be necessary. What happened was as bad or worse. Bonita developed a case of hiccups.

Gabriella drifted unobtrusively to the wine pantry and almost instantly returned with a small wineglass containing a half-ounce of golden fluid. "Vinegar," she whispered in Bonita's ear. "Drink it."

Bonita drank, then coughed explosively into the lace handkerchief Gabriella provided. Eyes watering, she breathed deeply several times, smiled, and resumed — free of hiccups — her description of the cunning summer muff she had sent to her friend Irena. Don Armando de Neve's ladies were charmed but were even more intrigued by Bonita's clever, quick-thinking servant. In spite of Ana's success in making Gabriella as invisible as possible, the de Neve ladies determined to hire the mousy creature if she ever became available.

Normally, Gabriella went everywhere as Bonita's companion — visiting, shopping, sightseeing. Distant acquaintances thought they were sisters. Because of Bonita's beauty and their contrasting coloring, they were observed more often, and far more minutely, than they realized.

Together, they went to the Church of San Hipolito several days later to witness the ceremony when Padre Mero was invested with the rank of monsignor. They were unaware that an aristocratic woman of comfortable proportions sat unobserved behind a grill high above the choir. She was dressed all in black. A shawl of finest Venetian lace covered her graying hair. From her neck fell a rope of matched pearls of unusual size. Diamonds and emeralds embellished her square, competent fingers.

"The ceremony will begin shortly, Señora," murmured the priest who had escorted her to her cubicle. "Is there anything you require? Tea, perhaps?"

More than tea, the lady wanted privacy. This particular afternoon was excessively warm and she wished to fan herself more energetically than propriety allowed a well-born lady. Also her feet hurt from slippers bought a size too small, and she longed to slip out of them.

"I require nothing. Thank you." She bestowed an enchanting smile on the young man but at the same time wished he would go away.

This great lady so carefully hidden from sight was Doña María Teresa Gracés de Costanza, wife of Mexico's wealthiest merchant prince, Don Eduardo Hernández Costanza Ortega, rumored to be dying. The place of a proper wife is at the bedside of her sick husband, not at public ceremonials. Nevertheless Doña Teresa had come to witness, unobserved, the investiture of her chaplain, who had recently been honored by the archbishop with the rank of monsignor.

The cubicle door closed at last, and Doña Teresa's plump toes wiggled in an ecstasy of freedom. Her wrist, as strong as that of any *paisana*, fanned a gale about her face and shoulders. Pearls got in her way, and she dumped them into her decolletage to nestle between her ample breasts. Scanning the church below, she hitched her chair closer to the grill.

Suddenly the vigorous strokes were interrupted. Doña Teresa's searching gaze had found what she sought. The girl with the copper-colored hair was entering the nave with another young woman near her own age, a stunning beauty with dark coloring. The dark one, yes, that would be Bonita, the Figuroa daughter still at home. Doña Teresa looked for a resemblance between the two young women but could find none.

After further painstaking perusal, she admitted that no, the redhead was not a beauty. Something better, perhaps. Her face revealed character and intelligence. It was heartshaped, with a kindly, generous mouth and an Oriental's almond eyes. *She looks like her mother!* Doña Teresa suddenly realized. *—Her mother's slender frame and graceful movements. See how charmingly she genuflects, how delicately she handles her missal. Beside her, the dark one moves like a cow!*

The ceremony commenced with an echoing paean from the organ within the church and a crash of bells from the tower outside. For perhaps a quarter of an hour, Doña Teresa feasted her eyes on the girl seated below, studying her every move, her every glance. Satisfied with what she had come to see, she made herself presentable — slung the fan on her wrist by its black ribbon, decanted the pearls, checked the folds of her lace shawl, stuffed unwilling feet into the slippers, and emerged from the cubicle.

The surprised young padre, awaiting her pleasure in the corridor outside the door, leaped to his feet. "I find the heat has given me a headache," she announced. "Please summon my carriage."

As the cleric escorted Doña Teresa down the stairs and into her carriage, he noted with surprise a smile of satisfaction playing about her lips. He wondered how she could appear so cheerful while suffering from a headache. He bade her farewell and re-entered the church, telling himself he would never understand women.

By late July, the consignments of rope waiting on the docks at Vera Cruz had been transferred to the holds of several foreign ships, gold in payment had been transferred to the bank of Vera Cruz for safekeeping, and Federico Verro was eager to return home. He ran six horses into the ground on his ten-day journey from Vera Cruz. At farms and post stations along the way, he secured fresh mounts and left behind trembling, broken beasts with heaving flanks and drooping heads. It was as though no quirt were cruel enough and no blow violent enough to drive the galloping animals as fast as he wished to travel.

The first faint blush of dawn tinged the eastern sky as he arrived at Buena Suerte. His furious shouting and pounding at the gates brought the night porter, quaking with fear. Well-founded fear, for as Verro spurred his lathered horse through the gate, a well-aimed cut of the quirt caught the porter across the cheek, drawing blood.

"Lazy turd!" he greeted the porter. "Send Elias to me immediately!" And he galloped across the inner courtyard and through the access way to his quarters at the far end of the palace.

Dismounting at the staircase where twin torches burned, he unfastened his leather traveling bags from the weary horse and leapt up the steps two at a time. Near the top, his pace slackened and he glanced about. Something was different. The clatter of his horse should have set the *zopilotes* flapping from their roosts along the galleries. But except for the coughing and snuffling of his winded horse below, all was quiet.

The ammonia stench of courtyard refuse was gone! His feet, long accustomed to the broken tiles on the steps, rested on solid surfaces. And instead of crumbling rust under his hand, the railing was firm and freshly-painted.

Under his breath, Verro cursed richly and obscenely. Buena Suerte was supposed to be a tottering shell. He had planned it that way, planned it for years. What busybody had been interfering?

"Elias!" he bellowed. From far down the gallery, he saw the glimmer of an approaching lantern and recognized the sound of Elias' firm stride. He sorted through a ring of keys from his pocket, unlocked his apartment door, entered and dropped his luggage. As he threw off his mud-spattered traveling coat, Elias entered.

"What's this about the old woman" Verro snapped. "What happened?"

Elias set down the lantern. Its light revealed a small but sumptuously-furnished *sala* hung with damask. "What happened?" Elias shrugged. "She got well, Federico."

"She's had the same injury for twenty years. What do you mean, she got well?"

"The Señorita came from the convent."

"The bastard. The companion for Bonita."

"Yes. At the convent she learned about herbs, remedies, things like that. She gave Doña Dolores some medicine. And she got well."

"She no longer walks with a cane? Is that what you mean?"

"She limps, still," replied Elias. "She still has the cane. But the pain is gone."

"Sounds like the orphan may be palming herself off as a witch of some kind. She chanted nonsense and burned incense and now the old woman believes she's no longer sick."

Elias looked doubtful. "I know nothing of witches. And there has been no incense that I know of. Ana says the orphan wants to be a nun someday, like Javiera."

"A nun like Javiera, eh? Not likely, I think. The fee can run as much as three hundred gold ounces." Verro waved the problem away. "Doña Delores is a feeble-minded old hag. She can be talked into believing anything. I should know; I've done it many a time. I'll do it again. When she wakes up at noon, I'll go straighten her out."

"It might not be as easy as you think," said Elias. "Later when the sun comes up, look around and see for yourself. The whole place has been cleaned up, even the orchards. You will be proud of it. Everybody has worked hard. — "

" — You hardest of all, according to that silly message you sent!"

Elias' eyes hardened. "The orphan, she works hard too. You will see. And Doña Dolores no longer yells at us. She makes us talk to her. Slow, so she can understand. Then she tells us what to do."

"And you, you simpleton, you do it!"

"It is either that or have Don Avila ask me why I didn't do it. You were not here to ask. Anyway, that old lady is smart. She would make a good general in the army. I thought you would want me to follow orders."

Furiously, Verro hissed, "The orders I gave you were to run the place as it's been run in the past! By *me*! Instead you've been outsmarted by a gypsy whore and a senile old crone." In exasperation, he pounded the desk with his fist. "Oh, it's a pretty mess you've left me to straighten out, you bumbling fool! I don't dare ask about my commissions; I have the feeling there won't be any forthcoming. That's right, isn't it? The servants no longer pilfer as they once did? Tell me, quickly!"

"They are afraid of Doña Dolores." Elias shifted his weight uneasily. "Well, there were some pins. Miguel went through the seamstress' things but there wasn't much worth lifting."

"Seamstress?'"

"Doña Dolores hired a seamstress. And three laundresses."

A fresh gleam of rage appeared in the steward's eyes. "Without my approval?"

"Yes."

Federico Verro began to snap the fingers of one hand very slowly — ominously. "The sooner we get to the root of this, the better. Send me the girl — Daniella? Marcella? What's her name?"

"Gabriella. Gabriella Salgado. When?"

"When?'"

"When should I tell her to come see you? I doubt if she will be up for another hour or two."

The Italian shouted, "Servants at Buena Suerte come to see me at *my* convenience, you stupid fart! I will see the girl *now!*"

Elias cleared his throat. "She isn't exactly a servant —"

"You baboon!" sneered Federico, losing patience. "I have no right to expect much from a country bumpkin like you, but I keep hoping you can understand simple language. I discover again and again that you have no more discernment than the day you left your father's farm. Perhaps you'd like to return. At this moment, believe me, it's a great temptation to send you."

Elias turned to go.

"You have not been dismissed," Federico reminded him angrily. "Tell the girl to bring with her the medicine that she gives Doña Dolores for her leg injury."

Federico Verro turned to his desk with a nod, dismissing Elias.

Gabriella awoke to the sound of loud knocking on the door of her bedchamber. "Yes? Who is it?"

She struggled out of bed. "Coming!" Drawing a robe over her shoulders, she flung open the door. "Elias? What is it? What time is it?"

"Federico rode in a few minutes ago, Señorita. He wants to see you."

"But — "

"Now, Señorita. He wants to see you now."

It took Gabriella a moment to grasp what Elias was saying. When she did, her heart began to pound. "I'll get dressed," she said.

"Hurry!"

Across a chair lay a modest dress of brown silk trimmed with black braid. Gabriella had worn it to the paseo the evening before. It would do. With no time to think, she threw on her clothes, quickly pinned her auburn braids in a heavy knot at the back of her head and rushed out to meet Elias.

"Isn't this rather sudden?" she asked. "I was — "

"The medicine," said Elias. "He wants you to bring the medicine you have been giving Doña Dolores."

Gabriella stared. After a moment's hesitation, she darted back into her bedchamber. Emerging with the vial, she murmured to Elias, "He's angry, isn't he?"

"Yes."

"Doña Dolores was not supposed to get better and make changes without his permission. That's the problem, isn't it?"

"Yes."

Gabriella's thoughts were busy as she walked quickly with Elias the length of the building to the steward's quarters. A short distance from the door, Elias paused. "Federico Verro has a bad temper," he warned her softly. "Take care. I will wait for you here."

Gabriella knocked and the Italian bade her enter. The very sight of the blade-thin steward with his malevolent stare left her mouth dry and her stomach churning. His malice filled the room, alive and dangerous. She gripped her hands together to stop their trembling.

She dropped her knee dutifully and lowered her eyes. "You sent for me, Señor Verro?"

There was a long pause. Gabriella realized the steward must be taking her measure, probably wondering about her hair.

"Close the door," he ordered, and seated himself behind his desk. Gabriella closed the door and remained standing.

"You brought the medicine?"

"Yes."

"'Yes?' That's all? 'Yes?' Didn't they teach you manners at the convent?"

"Yes, Señor Verro."

"Let me see the medicine."

Gabriella placed the vial on the desk before him. He removed the cork, sniffed, tasted with his finger. "Opium. I thought so."

He recorked the bottle, leaned back and propped one foot on the desk, thinking. After a few seconds a hint of a smile touched one corner of his mouth. Then, a decision apparently made, he stood. "You are very pretty," he said, and her eyes followed him with growing concern as he strolled to the door, locked it, removed the key and put it in his pocket. "I did not expect Bonita's convent bastard to have red hair. Quite a surprise. Quite lovely. What is your salary, Daniella?"

Gabriella swallowed the fear in her throat. "If you please, Señor, my name is María Gabriella. I am paid two pesos a month."

She assumed the steward already knew about her salary and was astonished when his eyes bulged with fury. "*Two pesos!?*"

He sputtered a moment, then said, more calmly, "Well, my little chicken, you will be paid two pesos a month no longer. Starting today you will receive three reals a month. No, wait. Who gives you these two pesos every month?"

Gabriella paused, not understanding the question. "Why, the Figuroa family, Señor."

The reply was hardly out of her mouth before Verro struck her with the flat of his hand so hard she staggered against a table behind her. She could scarcely comprehend the steward's next words, though she readily understood his narrowed eyes and threatening fist six inches from her face.

"Slut! None of your clever evasions! You understand me perfectly. When I ask a question, I expect an honest answer. Who pays you your two pesos every month?"

"Don Avila, Señor." Her face stinging, she straightened and backed toward the door.

"Then we will leave the arrangement with Don Avila the way it is. I remind you that the door is locked. You aren't going anywhere."

"I thought perhaps you were finished asking me questions, Señor Verro."

"On the contrary, our interview has scarcely begun. Listen to your instructions carefully. Every month when you receive your two pesos, you will bring the money to me. An orphan girl as young as you can't be expected to know what to do with so much money. So of your two pesos, I shall give you back four reals, which is extremely generous. And I shall hold the remaining twelve reals in a special account for you."

"Yes, Señor."

"Don Avila does not like to be troubled with details of household finance, so this plan will be between the two of us. Is that clear?"

Very clear, she thought. But far from keeping the matter secret, Gabriella resolved to go straight to Don Avila with a report of her treatment at the hands of his steward.

Perhaps Verro read her mind, for her moment of hesitation brought a second blow, far heavier than the first. And a third, heavier than the second. As she went down, her head struck the brass studs in the door. Blood trickled down her neck into the brown silk of her gown.

Grasping the quirt he had dropped near the door, he bent over her and delivered stroke upon stroke across her shoulders with all his strength. "I asked you a question, you meddling whore!" he shouted. "Is that clear? Answer me!" And he kicked her viciously in the stomach.

"Yes, Señor Verro," she murmured, and curled herself into a tight ball of pain.

"Federico Verro alone is in charge at Buena Suerte, not some presumptuous shit-faced bastard from the convent!" he thundered. "Do you understand?"

Again he applied the quirt, aiming at her arms and face.

"Squeal, why don't you?" he jeered, catching his breath. "A little noise! The deaf old she-goat up front won't hear you! Neither will Papa. Neither will Bonita. Why else do you think my quarters are here at the back of the palace? Come! Make some music, little chicken! Squawk away!" And the Italian kicked her with all his might.

Impatient with the quirt, he threw it aside and strode to the basket of fuel beside the fireplace. From it he chose a cudgel as thick as his wrist. Gabriella saw his intention, cried out in protest and tried to rise. at the same time she heard pounding on the door and Elias' voice.

"Federico! Federico! Open the door, Federico! If something is wrong, maybe I can help."

The words broke the spell and the steward's frenzy dissipated. Losing interest in Gabriella, he unlocked the door. "Take her to her room," he ordered Elias.

Elias gently lifted Gabriella to her feet. Verro watched idly, as he might watch a mother dog nosing her litter. "These lessons for the servants are strenuous but necessary," he remarked, nursing a bruised knuckle. "There will be no more trouble from this one."

In the faint light of early morning, the steward watched Elias half-lead, half-carry the convent girl along the gallery toward the apartments at the front of the palace. Once they were out of sight, he strode along the gallery in the opposite direction, knocked softly at one of the doors, and entered when it was opened to him. Five minutes later, he emerged and returned to his own rooms.

Thirty minutes passed. It was full light now, and the servants were beginning to stir. The same door opened once more and Doña Dolores' maid Pepita appeared. Over her head and shoulders she wore a wool rebozo against the early morning chill.

With halting gait, she left by the rear servants' entrance and made her way down the lane to the boulevard. No one saw her leave the palace, or if so, thought nothing of it. As personal maid to the reigning lady, Pepita enjoyed a privileged status, coming and going as she pleased.

It was two miles to the plaza, and the old woman stopped to rest many times. — To rest and to stealthily re-examine the gold coins carefully tied in a rag and tucked into the front of her bodice. It was worthwhile running errands for the steward, yes indeed. The Italian was both cunning and brave, and she had done well for herself following his instructions.

When at last she reached the plaza, she explored several of the narrow streets leading off it before she found what she was looking for. She could neither read nor write, but at last she spelled out a sign over a certain door and knew she had reached her destination. She opened the door and went in.

CHAPTER 8

Buena Suerte
Late July 1774

Monsignor Mero was so indignant, he feared he might suffocate. "I can't believe what you are telling me, Don Avila! Your agent — without provocation of any kind, mind you! — has beaten this girl nearly to death! The doctor reports she is bleeding from every orifice! Your wife is so enraged that when I arrived with the doctor half-an-hour ago, we could hear her screaming imprecations all the way out in the street!"

Don Avila, seated at his library desk, raised weary eyes. "My wife forgot herself. She was overwrought. I apologize for the scene that she created."

The priest's chins quivered with anger. "I myself am creating a scene!" he shouted. "And I offer no apology whatever! Verro says only that Gabriella 'exceeded her authority'. I have known this child all her life as a model of discretion. How, then? *How* did she exceed her authority? You have no answer because that fiend of a steward has given you none. Who is the master here, you or your agent?"

Don Avila held his head in despair.

Monsignor Mero snorted with disgust. "What am I to tell my cousin at the convent? The Abbess Christina Valderia is a strong-willed woman, I promise you. She would have had the brute hauled away in chains by now. Yet all you have to say to me is, 'My steward and I have settled the matter.'"

Softly, Don Avila said, "Federico has been ordered to leave Buena Suerte. He is vacating his rooms at this very moment, and will not return. His duties as chamberlain of the palace will be permanently assumed by Elias Márquez."

"And that's all you have to say? A loving child came to you two months ago and has brought nothing but blessings to your household. A monster *retained by you* nearly murders her, and as punishment you — you — you tickle the brute's ankles with a willow switch! And that's *all?*"

"Monsignor Mero, there are many details about my estates that even I do not understand. To acquire a new agent and dismiss Federico Verro at this time is not possible."

The priest ground his teeth with impotent rage. He had heard rumors of Don Avila's indebtedness. Too late, he remembered that Gabriella herself had feared the steward's anger and self-reproach seared his heart like acid. What dreadful predicament had he gotten his dearest girl into?

A month went by, and a depression such as Gabriella had never known before settled into the hidden crannies of her body as well as her spirit. Any sudden noise, any unexpected shadow set her trembling. Not even Monsignor Mero's frequent visits dispelled her gloom for long. Sadness was not her nature, and she considered returning to the convent. But the thought of facing Madre filled her with shame and she dismissed the idea. She must conquer her demons on her own. Meanwhile at dawn each day, at the little nearby chapel, her tears flowed freely.

One day an embossed invitation, tied with gilt cord and tassel, arrived by messenger. The viceroy's annual ball in honor of the queen's birthday! The Queen's Ball was always the outstanding social event of the year, and Bonita glowed with excitement. " — And Gabriella, you'll go with us!" she cried.

Gabriella shook her head. "Only court officials and their families attend affairs of state at the National Palace," she replied.

Mischief sparkled in Bonita's amber eyes. "Ah, but Mama is not well, you see. Additional members of our household staff are needed to attend her."

"Elias is better at that sort of thing than I am."

"*Santa Madre*, Gabriella!" cried Bonita, "what a bore you're being about this! Yes, it was awful, what happened to you. Federico is a beast and should be whipped and locked up. But it's been weeks since that night. You aren't still sick. You're just feeling sorry for yourself, that's all. Last week was your birthday and you wouldn't even let us give you a party. What are you afraid of?"

The ceaseless badgering finally wore Gabriella down. The night of the affair found her in Bonita's bedchamber, helping the seamstress with last-minute stitches on Bonita's new gown of cinnamon-colored satin.

At the last moment, Gabriella withdrew and quickly dressed herself, grateful that the bruises on her face and shoulders had faded. Only a slight discomfort in her shoulder remained of the encounter with Federico Verro, discomfort and something more insidious. She tried to imagine that someday she would once again toss her head and laugh with Ana and the footmen, or joke with old crippled Miguel, or sit at Don Avila's feet and listen as he spun tales of golden California.

Only Gabriella knew of Elias' interruption, that terrible night, which saved her from a more severe beating than the one she received. And only Elias fully understood her anxiety. She relied on him more than in the past, and welcomed his reassuring hand at her elbow, his touch at her waist.

And now, as she sat at her dressing table pinning her hair in place, she recognized his voice at the hall door leading to the gallery. "Señorita?"

"Yes, Elias! Coming!" Quickly she rose, turned to check herself in the pier glass between the windows — and stared. For the ball, she wore the only formal gown she owned, a modest costume of black lace. Consuelo had worn it while in mourning after her grandmother died. Gabriella had fingered the expensive lace and objected, "It's too fine for me."

"And too depressing for me," countered Consuelo. Together, they restitched it into a low-cut ball gown for Gabriella to take to the city.

There were no mirrors at the convent and until this evening, Gabriella had never seen how she looked in it. The rich black lace set off the ivory texture of her arms and shoulders and the burnished gold of her hair. The lines of the dress accentuated her slim waist and amplified her modest bosom. With astonishment, she realized that she was pretty!

"Señorita?" Elias called again. Gabriella flung open the door and beheld a tall, broadshouldered footman in full livery. The two stared at one another. Elias, remembering himself, suppressed a smile and bowed with exaggerated formality.

"Elias!" cried Gabriella. There was puzzled delight and real joy in her smile. "The new livery came, I see. But — ?"

"Doña Dolores ordered livery for her new chamberlain — for me. But the chamberlain's livery isn't finished yet. Too much gold braid, perhaps. Still, she wants me to escort the family to the National Palace, so I borrowed an outfit from one of the other footmen. I am taking his place tonight."

Her dark brown eyes met his for the first time. "I'm glad. You look very elegant, Elias!"

Elias' complexion took on a rosy tinge under the white peruke. "Thank you, Señorita. If a footman is permitted the liberty, may I say a lady who looks as elegant as you deserves a far more elegant attendant than a mere footman."

"Beautifully said, Señor," murmured Gabriella, trying to deny her pleasure at his words. To her surprise, though she had never before curtsied to Elias, she dipped and lowered her eyes.

With effort, Elias remembered his errand: "Don Avila wishes to see you in the library before we leave for the National Palace."

Elias retired and Gabriella quickly paced the length of the gallery, silk petticoats whipping about her ankles. She suspected Don Avila wanted to talk about Doña Dolores. After Federico Verro left Buena Suerte, it was several days before Gabriella was strong enough to resume her twice-daily administration of Señora's medication. But though the dosage remained the same, Doña Dolores had changed. The stern eyes no longer challenged everything Gabriella said. Plans for improving Buena Suerte no longer interested her. Elias was relieved at the change but Gabriella knew that something was wrong.

She had grown uneasy about herself, as well. In May, she had begun taking occasional drops of laudanum, at first to relieve her soreness from riding the long distance from the convent. Later, she dosed herself when she was over-fatigued, and more recently to deaden the pain from the beating she had received. It troubled her that the more she took, the more she needed to control the pain. Why wasn't the same thing happening to Doña Dolores? It was a puzzle that made no sense. Gabriella resolved to ask the *curandera* the next time she visited her shop.

When she was within a few steps of the library door, it unexpectedly opened. The man who emerged, unmindful of her presence, was Federico Verro. Her stomach knotted with terror.

The Italian held in his hand a document with seals and a signature upon which he blew delicately to dry the ink. Suddenly his eyes met Gabriella's and an oily smile spread across his narrow features. "Good evening, Señorita," he said.

"Good evening, Señor Verro," she whispered. She hastened past the steward into the library and swiftly closed the door behind her. Through it, muffled, came the sound of mocking laughter.

Trembling uncontrollably, Gabriella stood a moment to regain her composure. Fear blurred her vision and blood pounded deafeningly in her ears. It was unlike Don Avila, that most courtly of men, to allow such a confrontation to occur. The steward's business must have been important.

She steadied herself, then curtsied to her *patron*. The slump of his shoulders told her that whatever the steward's errand had been, it could not have signified well for the Figuroa family.

Don Avila stood beside a table refilling his wineglass. In the stale air of the library, Gabriella caught the distinctive rotten-egg odor of the native *pulque*. Nowadays it was no longer rare Spanish wine that Don Avila poured, glass after glass, until quite late every evening, but *pulque*, the cheap native brandy made from the agave plant.

"Yes, Don Avila? Elias said you wanted to see me."

It was an enfeebled man who turned to greet her. "You met Federico as he was leaving. I'm sure the encounter was distasteful for you, and I apologize. When I summoned you, I had no idea he would burst in upon me unannounced."

"Don't let it trouble you, Don Avila."

He shook his head dispiritedly. "It troubles me very much, my dear child, but unfortunately there is nothing I can do about it." He waved her to a chair. "First, I must thank you for the ball gown you helped the seamstress design for my daughter," he said. "I was in Doña Dolores's sitting room yesterday when Bonita came parading to show it off to her mother. It is indeed very beautiful." And he bowed, lurching slightly.

"Thank you, Señor. I am glad the dress pleases you."

"Monsignor Mero said you were a young woman of many talents," Don Avila continued. "I see that he was correct. You are generous to undertake extra work of this kind. However, I fear we will need to dismiss the seamstress hired by Doña Dolores, as an economy. When we do, you must not feel obliged to sew, either for Bonita or for Doña Dolores. Do you understand?"

"Yes, Don Avila."

"But that is not why I called you here. The viceroy tells me that Martín de Neve will attend the ball tonight with his parents."

"I see," Gabriella said, remembering the applecheeked adolescent in the painting.

"Martín's father is a distinguished diplomat who has spent the last few years watching over Spanish interests at the French court. As for young Martín — he is thirty years old, scarcely young — Carlos has kept him too busy to find a wife. No one calls Martín a spy, I notice, but that's what he is. Or has been. The military strength of Sweden, Britain and the Italian kingdoms are of interest to Carlos. Martín, it seems, is expert at ferreting out such information, always discreetly, always successfully."

"What information is there for him to ferret out here?" Gabriella wondered. "Nueva España has no army."

"Don Martín asked Carlos for a holiday. And in view of his excellent service, his request was granted."

"And he is to be at the ball tonight?" The prospect made Gabriella anxious. "Bonita has been in a turmoil all day about the ball. Ana and I gave her a warm bath this afternoon but it didn't help."

"Then perhaps it will be best if she doesn't know in advance about Martín," said Don Avila. "Be sure to stay at her side. You always do, of course. I only wanted you to have this warning ahead of time."

"Yes. I see."

"Two times now, Gabriella, you have been with my daughter when she had attacks," (*three times*, she corrected him silently) "and both times you handled matters quite well. Pray God we have no crisis facing us tonight, but we must be prepared. Elias will accompany us to the palace. I will say he is needed to assist my wife. He will remain nearby all evening."

Behind Gabriella, the library door abruptly opened and she whirled with a stifled cry. But it was only Pepita, hunched and fawning, leading Doña Dolores into the room. The seamstress had outdone herself with Señora's magnificent gown of blue brocade embroidered with pearls. Diamonds flashed at Señora's wrists and throat. Her gray hair was piled high and held in place with a jeweled plume.

"Oh, here they are, Pepita!" cried Doña Dolores. "I'll take my wrap now" and Pepita draped a light fur mantle over her mistress' shoulders. "We're all here, ready to go. Where's Bonita? We'll be late!"

"I'll fetch her, Doña Dolores," said Gabriella.

At the entrance of the National Palace, Don Avila and his party left their carriage and joined a milling army of guests moving slowly up the grand staircase to the state apartments. There each group of guests was announced by the viceroy's chamberlain, a personage in powdered wig and purple velvet livery trimmed with gilt lace.

As he had done with others ahead of them, the chamberlain thumped his five-foot baton on the floor for attention and intoned their names to the ballroom at large: "Don Avila Flores de Figuroa Beretta, Doña Dolores Herédia de Figuroa, Señorita María Bonita Herédia de Figuroa, Señorita María Gabriella Salgado."

Gabriella knew she should feel impressed, but the chamberlain's vainglorious braying sounded slightly ridiculous. Impulsively she flipped open the fan she always carried on Bonita's account. She started to fan herself but paused, aware of turned heads and speculating eyes following them from all over the ballroom. *Why is everyone staring at us?*

On a dais at the far end of the ballroom was a gilt settee and side chairs upholstered in crimson velour. Footmen in livery of pale blue silk flanked the steps. In a few minutes, Bonita whispered, there would be a flourish from the musicians. While they played a stately march, the viceroy, Antonio María Bucareli y Ursua, and his family would enter and make their way along the crimson carpet down the center of the ballroom, nodding and smiling graciously at guests along the way. Not until the viceroy's party took their places on the dais would the carpet be rolled away. The viceroy would signal to the musicians, who would strike up a minuet and the dancing would begin. Soon afterwards the great ballroom would be filled with dancers, and Don Antonio and his family would begin receiving guests who would mount the dais to pay their respects.

Don Avila steered his ladies to one side of the ballroom where tall doors opened onto the terrace. There Elias magically appeared, having found chairs for them all. He offered his arm to Doña Dolores and seated her with great care and respect.

Taking his place behind Gabriella, he whispered, "I have found a place in case we need it, Señorita. There is a room set aside for the musicians. It opens off the terrace behind us. As long as the musicians are here in the ballroom playing, the room is deserted."

Gabriella nodded. Seated on her little gilt chair beside — but ever-so-slightly behind — Bonita and Doña Dolores, she surveyed the gold and crimson elegance of the enormous ballroom. The mirrors, the music and laughter, the brilliant candalabra, the magnificent gowns and jewels filled her with wonder. *And this is only the court of the viceroy!* she thought. *What must the royal court in Spain be like?*

Don Avila leaned toward Bonita and Doña Dolores. "When the viceroy's party enters, be sure to watch for a tall gray-haired man. He is the Visitador-General of New Spain, José de Gálvez, the king's personal official. It was Galvez who sent the Franciscan fathers to San Diego and Monterey five years ago. Since then, they have established twenty-one missions along that part of the coast. Carlos sent him to take sole charge of the California ventures and his revenues in Nueva España, so I have been working closely with him."

At the mention of California, Gabriella wished yet again that she were a man and could take holy orders with the Franciscans. A missionary in California, what a perfect way to spend one's life! Gentle Indians, rolling hills of pasture land, rivers and the wide blue sea for fishing! No pompous, self-indulgent nobles, no malicious agents to steal and corrupt everything they touched.

A sudden hush descended on the ballroom. The trumpeters played a brilliant fanfare. Seated guests rose to their feet so that Gabriella saw before her a solid wall of well-dressed backs. The thump of the chamberlain's baton resounded and his nasal baritone announced the viceroy and members of his party.

Then like a field of grain before the wind, the guests bowed and curtsied, and before Gabriella herself dipped her knee, she caught a quick glimpse of the viceroy Antonio Bucareli. He was an elegant, middle-aged man with a goatee and long hair, carefully curled and powdered. The modestly-dressed older man beside him looked out of place among the jewels and lace of the regent's party. He was heavier than the viceroy — a grizzled outdoorsman burned by sun and wind. Gabriella decided that whatever such a man chose to do about California, his plans would probably succeed.

As Bucareli and his party moved down the long room, guests in their wake straightened and resumed their gossiping. Gabriella stole a glance at Bonita. The rich red-brown satin showed off her creamy shoulders, her glossy black hair and hazel eyes. Gabriella closely watched those tawny eyes for signs that always heralded her mistress' attacks. She caught Don Avila's glance and knew his thoughts were the same as hers.

Don Avila turned to his wife. "Come, my dear. Bonita. Let us present ourselves to the viceroy before the crowd of guests around the dais becomes intolerable."

With Doña Dolores on his arm and Bonita at his elbow, the three moved through the crowd. Gabriella would follow at a distance as she always did on occasions such as this, but first she turned and swiftly murmured to Elias, "Earlier, as we entered the ballroom with Don Avila, many heads turned to stare at us. Why was that?"

"They stare because Don Avila's daughter is very beautiful, Señorita," said Elias. "And of course, so are you, if you will forgive me."

"Elias, I have seen men by the dozen ogle Bonita. What happened here tonight was not like that. Why did they stare?"

Elias did not answer immediately. Then he murmured, "There are many stories told in the city about Don Avila. Not just at the National Palace but even in the plaza, in the taverns, at the cathedral, everywhere."

"About his drinking, you mean? His gambling?"

"Yes, but also about his steward. Federico likes to boast that he now owns more of the Figuroa business interests than the Figuroa family."

Gabriella stared. The Figuroas owned silver mines and a fleet of mer chant ships that traded among the islands of the New World. They owned many maguey plantations and factories where rope by the ton was made for export to Europe. To steal a rich man's potatoes and porcelain cups was one thing, but to steal his merchant ships and silver mines was quite another. Surely Elias must be mistaken. How could such a thing happen?

But she recalled the look on Federico Verro's face as he emerged from the library with the freshly-signed document. And she remembered something else: the convent, and Madre Valderia's careful management of its business affairs. The Reverend Mother could — and often did — account for every bushel of apples from the orchard, every gallon of cream churned to butter. She knew the contents of every chest and cupboard. She knew which children in the nursery had been infected with measles and when. How different was her way from that of this sleepy grandee, seldom completely sober, who seemed never to give a thought to the heritage of his brothers across the sea.

Gabriella's spirits sank with foreboding. She felt a certain affection for Don Avila, from whom she had never known anything but kindness. But for all his kind heart, he was careless and weak, a man destined to lose money — if not to his agent Federico, then to someone else.

"Thank you, Elias." And now Gabriella rose to seek out her *patron*. Avoiding the dancers, she moved toward the dais at the end of the ballroom. While still some distance away, she noticed a heavily-muscled military officer waiting to greet the viceroy. In his peruke and dress uniform of blinding white, the officer stood forth from the crowd like some shining blade of Armageddon. There was nobility in his carriage, in the proud lift of his chin and the benevolence of his gaze.

The ballroom's blazing candles swam before her eyes. She drew nearer and her heart lurched. The sensuous mouth, the delicate nostrils, the languid cast of the eyes — . Yes, of course! Here in the flesh was the marble statue in the foyer at the convent, the statue of the archangel with his trumpet hovering aloft, his great wings outspread. Gabriella's everyday senses reported her presence at the National Palace, yet she was certain — as adamantly certain as she was of the blood pounding through her own veins — that the vision she witnessed was the earthly manifestation of her patron, San Gabriel Arcangel.

Then Don Avila was leaving the dais. He stopped to speak to the officer, and presented first Doña Dolores and then Bonita, who smiled and swept low in her most ravishing curtsy.

Gabriella paled. Only one man would be so cordially welcomed by Bonita and her parents: Don Martín de Neve! Transfixed, Gabriella watched as the officer led Bonita to the center of the floor and found places for them among the dancers.

Don Avila caught her eye, and the quick nod of his head gave her the order she expected: "Follow them."

She conquered her grief and obeyed, weaving among the guests bordering the dance floor. She had completely circled the ballroom before she realized that Don Martín had noticed her and wondered what she was doing. As Gabriella watched, the officer paused and pointed her out to Bonita.

Bonita turned, and Gabriella recognized panic in the beautiful hazel eyes. Covering her anxiety with a flirtatious smile, Bonita left her partner, made straight for Gabriella and slumped limply against her, murmuring, "I can barely see."

"Smile!" Gabriella whispered, almost gaily. "We must both smile. No one must suspect anything is wrong. Come with me." Quickly and firmly she imprisoned Bonita's right hand, which was already beginning to twitch. She flicked open her fan and shielded their faces as though sharing a secret of some sort, and led Bonita swiftly to the deserted terrace where Elias was waiting.

Without a word, he took Bonita's other arm and between the two of them they supported the twitching girl the length of the terrace to the darkened room. "Over here," he ordered Gabriella. "There is a cot where she can lie down."

By the time they found the cot and lowered Bonita onto it, her seizure had begun in earnest. Quickly it became so intense that the cot itself jerked back and forth. Gabriella deftly loosened Bonita's bodice and removed her jewelry.

Elias closed the door, drew the draperies over the lone window, and lit a candle. Violin cases and music stands littered the room. Chairs and tables were piled with the musicians' capes and tricorn hats.

In a few minutes, the violence of the seizure began to abate. Elias slipped out to summon the carriage to an alley entrance he had located. As Bonita slowly regained consciousness, Gabriella replaced her jewelry and began to gently massage her temples. Always there was a headache, and fatigue.

"The carriage will be here soon," Gabriella told Bonita softly. "At home there will be chocolate for you and then bed."

Suddenly Bonita clutched Gabriella's hand. "Martín!" she cried urgently, almost weeping. "Did Martín see?"

A stab of pain left Gabriella speechless for a moment before she could answer. "No, Bonita. No, he didn't. And now I hear Elias coming. We're going home."

Together, Gabriella and Elias half-guided, half-carried Bonita to the carriage. As they silently drove home, Gabriella remembered what the _curandera_ had once told her about the falling sickness. "Sometimes young people outgrow it," she had said. "Your young lady could marry and have children and never have another attack."

And later?

"Her children could live their lives through without a seizure. No one knows what causes this sickness."

Gabriella had relayed the good news to Don Avila that very afternoon. The tearful relief in his dull, bloodshot old eyes nearly broke her heart. But her pain then was the merest pinprick beside the grinding torment she now felt.

CHAPTER 9   Convent of Santa Clara de Asís
                                                            September 1774

"My dear Gabriella,

"I hasten to reply to your letter delivered to me this afternoon by Monsignor Mero. My dear, you must restrain yourself from ever again writing matters of a certain nature down on paper. A letter such as you wrote takes on a life of its own, and information contained therein can be used to hurt you or your friends, perhaps beyond repair.

"As to the specific business matters you mention, I have nothing to say, and I petition you most solemnly to follow my example and remain silent. Your distress is understandable but in this circumstance you must protect your own reputation and welfare. As to your own future, there will always be a place for you here at Santa Clara where you are highly regarded and deeply loved. Hold this thought uppermost in your heart and never for a moment doubt it.

"In the matter of the medicine, you are treading on dangerous ground. As in the matter above, I counsel silence. This is a difficulty you must overcome privately. Above all, do not mention it to Monsignor Mero.

"I fear you have forgotten Sister Magdalena's explicit warning regarding this remedy. It induces euphoria and can quickly ensnare patients, some of whom come to feel a desperate craving for this drug-induced state. I have known of well-born women, given this remedy by their doctors to control pain, later reduced to sleeping around the clock in darkened rooms or wandering about their houses like ghosts, recognizing no one, eating almost nothing, until they die at an early age.

"As to your own physical welfare, you must cease all medication at once. You may suffer dizziness, headaches, nausea, nervousness and discomfort, but there is no alternative. I repeat: *Cease all your own medication at once.*

"For your patient also, you must immediately suspend this remedy for her pain and substitute other herbs and treatments, including massage and heat. Sister Magdalena is preparing a list which I will include with this letter.

"Your patient presents a confusing picture. Sister Magdalena asks if your supplies have been disappearing. If so, you must hide them or, better still, get rid of them entirely. Sister suspects your patient is more dependent on the remedy than she has been willing to admit and might be getting it from some other source.

"Does your patient know where you get your supplies? Sister suggests you might question the *curandera*. Sometimes these old women are full of superstitious ideas, but the better ones are repositories of ancient lore that we might all wish to share. Do not be afraid to consult her if you feel you need advice and assistance. Remember that even the most mischievous *curandera* is powerless to bring about any condition that is against God's will. Your common sense will lead you to disregard spurious rites and incantations; you should use only those remedies that are likely to work.

"You seem to place great confidence in Elias Márquez. It speaks well for his ability that he has been given additional responsibilities, although with the reduced staff it will be difficult for him to discharge them. The *friendship* of this young man can be a comfort to you, but I would urgently counsel you to avoid unseemly intimacy with him. From what you say, he respects you and has so far kept his distance. If you wish to retain that respect, make certain you retain the distance. Although today you still wish to become a nun, someday you will undoubtedly think of marrying, and the reputation you establish now will determine the quality of the husband you attract later on.

"And now I have written most of the night away and must close. Monsignor returns to the city early tomorrow morning (*this* morning, rather) and will deliver my letter to you.

"I pray the Blessed Virgin will look down upon you in your trials and bring you peace.

> "Sincerely,
> "María Valderia de la Tapiz"

The candle beside the inkstand guttered and sent up a dark spiral of smoke. Madre trimmed the wick and replaced the scissors in a drawer. Shoulders sagging with weariness, she read what she had written, made a correction or two and folded the letter. It was the memory of the slim-waisted guard Elias that made her uneasy. Low-born though he was, a keen intelligence quickened his every move. He was undoubtedly handsome with the high cheekbones, deepset eyes and perfect white teeth sometimes seen in farm lads from the mountains. Of all men, he was the kind most likely to win Gabriella's trust.

— But a *paisano*! Madre bit her lip against such a possibility. For her precious Gabriella to throw herself away on a farmer's-son-turned-footman was almost more than she could bear.

Stirring from her depressing thoughts, the abbess took a bar of red sealing wax from a small chest on her desk and held it in the candle's heat to melt. She watched the red drops spatter like blood on the white paper and an unexpected wave of nausea overtook her. Dropping the wax, head in hand, she breathed deeply to recover control of her heaving stomach.

Her fear that amounted to frenzy was that Gabriella would somewhere, sometime, be compelled to endure an experience like her own. When she was twelve years old, she had been attacked by a trusted older cousin, a favorite of her father's. She was sick in bed with a fever and the young man had volunteered to watch over her while the family and servants attended a gala *paseo*. The house was deserted except for a slovenly maid. Bribed, she retired to the kitchen and ignored the screams that followed.

Her attacker was strong. She fought desperately, but emaciated and ill as she was, he easily overpowered her. Pinning her wrists, he mounted her and brutally plunged deep within her again and again. Afterwards, panting, he threatened, "Mention this to your father, you little whore, and I will tell him how you seduced me."

Deadened with pain and shock, his words had no meaning for her. She had "seduced him?" Her dutiful goodnight pecks on his cheek were a seduction? Her hasty leave-takings when his hands caressed her in unseemly ways — that was seduction?

Yet his warning rang true. From the pulpit at church, the padres repeatedly warned male parishioners to beware of feminine snares. Never once had she heard a priest caution female members of his flock to beware of male lust.

For young Luz, the direction of her life was decided that day. — Not because of what the priests said, but because of what they did not say. The cruel traps and assaults of life lay in wait for the weaker sex, not the stronger, and in secret, she resolved to become a nun.

Only her mother guessed what had happened. At the sight of the blood and bruises, a look of dismay clouded her features. Then wordlessly, tears streaming, she gently washed and dressed the injuries. Only then did she leave to go find the maid. Next day there was a new maid. The old one was never seen again.

From that evening, Luz's mother never left the child's bedchamber. She changed dressings, sponged off her fevered arms and legs, and cradled her gently until the fever and the shock subsided. The two never spoke of the attack, nor did they need to. From the silence, Luz knew her mother must have undergone a similar experience, or perhaps known intimately someone else who had. Protesting to her husband would have been futile. But a month later the cousin found himself unexpectedly transferred to Santo Domingo.

The victim had achieved her goal, and now, as an abbess with girls and women in her charge, Madre Valderia left to others the fighting of sin. What she fought instead was feminine vulnerability. First of all, they must be commercially independent if it ever became necessary. She told her convent students, "You must yourself master the household arts in order to properly supervise your servants." Thus no schoolgirl left the convent without skills to make her own way in the world — teaching, sewing, cheese-making, embroidery, nursing.

She saw ignorance about sex as a crippling disadvantage and despised false modesty. In the dormitory, she commanded her schoolgirls, "The purpose of a bath is to get clean", and forbade the prevailing dictum that women must bathe in their chemises. To the convent's valuable collection of art works, she added life-size sculptures from Italy portraying both men and women without drapery. She made certain that her city-bred nuns, novices and schoolgirls became as familiar with the ways of roosters and hens, rams and ewes, bulls and cows as the neighboring *paisanas*.

But, the abbess asked herself, had these policies helped Gabriella? Like others, the child as a student had worked with Sister Magdalena, keeping late hours at lambing time and waiting for the ewe's afterbirth. Never once had she expressed revulsion, only awe at God's mysteries. And with that, Madre felt she must be content.

She brushed aside her anxieties. Taking up her pen once more, she wrote a letter of a different sort:

"My dearest sister in Christ,

"How I wish you were here so that we might enjoy one of our long gossips over grapes and coffee. (The grapes are especially fine and sweet this year.)

"Our girl has gotten herself in a fine pickle. Don Avila has boozed and gambled away most of his fortune, as you suspected he would, with the major part of it falling into the willing hands of that scoundrel Federico Verro. If you hold any Figuroa notes, best collect as soon as possible or else unload them on someone else. He could find himself shipped back to Madrid any day, in which case I will need all my wits about me. He mustn't be allowed to take Gabriella with him.

"But it may not come to that. A new possibility has arisen in the person of Martín de Neve. This is a soldier and court favorite, recently arrived with his parents and sisters from the Spanish court. He is handsome and accomplished and has all the mothers fluttering behind their fans. His uncle is Philip de Neve, who is rumored to be the leading candidate to be appointed governor of California. (Papa was a diplomat in Paris. Perhaps you know of this family already.)

"Martín has met Don Avila's daughter Bonita and according to our girl, the two fell in love at first sight and now moon about like sick rabbits. Don Avila is especially eager to arrange this marriage for his youngest daughter, but how cooperative the parents will be in view of Don Avila's sinking fortunes is a subject for speculation. It's possible they don't know, of course. I promise to keep you advised of developments. Meanwhile I have reminded Gabriella yet again that a welcome awaits her here if and when she returns.

"One of these days the highwaymen will take Mero and sell him off for sausage, clergyman or no. He arrived yesterday with a new diamond and emerald crucifix. With bait like that, how can the poor rascals resist? He hints that our girl personally expelled the Italian from his quarters at Buena Suerte but in a six-page letter, she has no word of any such confrontation. I suspect Raoul is embroidering, as usual.

"Am sending Boaz with a box of meringues, the kind you like.

"Your ever devoted
"Luz"

Buena Suerte
October 1774

The chill night air of autumn prickled in Gabriella's nostrils as she stood at the gallery railing with her rebozo drawn close about her shoulders. At the *paseo* that afternoon, Martín had come riding on his gray gelding as soon as their carriage approached the Alameda. He was more handsome than ever in his thigh boots and dark blue velvet coat. And his adoration of Bonita would have been obvious even to a child. Unable to bear the pain, Gabriella turned away. She knew she must somehow control her feelings. After all, it wasn't as though she had no loyal admirer of her own. She had Elias!

With most of the servants dismissed, the palace lay silent except for the pulsing splash of the fountain in the courtyard below.

A month had gone by since she received Madre's letter. Gabriella had welcomed the advice and followed it. Most of it. In the meantime, Buena Suerte had changed. Doña Dolores had closed off large parts of the palace — the grand *sala*, the portrait gallery, the ballroom and the guest suites; ordered the bric-a-brac stored, the paintings and furniture covered with sheets and the draperies drawn.

Gradually the servants had slipped away. As for Gabriella, much as she cared for Madre Valderia, she cared for the convent less and less. Once away from Santa Clara and its happy memories, she saw the old place for what it was, a moldy ruin. The thought of spending the rest of her life there as a nun filled her with distaste. Serving as a nun in California, though, or even as a lay assistant to the Franciscan missionaries — that was a prospect that set her tingling with pleasure. Mornings filled with laughter, nights filled with dreams of the future. Ah, to feel her hair, skirts, her very soul flying free in the golden wind from the sea!

Yet now, with Don Avila's fortunes in such a state, she faced the possibility that she might be returned to Santa Clara, regardless of her preference. She would miss Buena Suerte not at all, but she would miss Elias, her trusted friend. She longed for a talk with him. A real talk, between just the two of them.

He had never moved from his old rooms over the storage areas at the back of the palace. Gabriella had sought him out there many times — always by day — to ask about supplies or services. Wondering if he might still be awake so late at night, she decided to find out, and started toward the service courtyard. Her slipper heels tapped noisily on the marble paving of the gallery. She stepped out of her shoes, dropped them off at her bedchamber door and continued on her way barefoot. At Elias' door, she knocked softly.

"Who is it?" he called.

She hesitated and knocked again, more softly still.

At length the door opened. Elias stood with a lantern held high in one hand while with the other he fastened the remaining buttons on his shirt. "Señorita!" he laughed. "Come in."

Her heart thudded against her ribs. *I shouldn't be here,* she told herself sternly — but accepted his invitation anyway.

Elias' quarters consisted of a meagerly furnished sitting room with an alcove for cooking. An arched passageway revealed a bedchamber with doors opening on a balcony overlooking the orchard.

He gestured her to the one comfortable chair in the room and — too eagerly — stirred the coals in the grate. "I neglected the fire," he apologized. "I — I wasn't expecting the pleasure of a guest." He seated himself on an upholstered stool. "Well. Have you come because of an emergency, so late at night?"

"There is no emergency," she murmured, modestly arranging the folds of her skirt.

A thoughtful pause. "Then let me see if I can guess why you are here. Perhaps you came because all over the palace you see signs of great economy and it disturbs you. Is that it?"

"Yes. Partly."

The fire in the grate revived and Elias added fuel. His smile faded. "The answer is very simple. Don Avila has gambled away a lot of his money. When a nobleman no longer has money, he must cut down on his expenses."

"Cut down how far, Elias? When will it stop, this 'cutting down'?"

"Who knows? There was much expense during the summer, redecorating the palace, buying new furnishings. Suddenly there was not enough money. Don Avila gambled more than ever, trying to win the extra money he needed. But he only made things worse. A month ago, he told me to stop finding replacements for servants who left. When he tells me to start replacing them again, I will. But I don't think he will tell me that."

"Aren't you worried? Don't you care?"

"Of course, I care!" His voice rose. "We may not be living here much longer, you and I. Will Don Avila keep one of us and let the other go? I don't know. Will he keep both of us or neither? I don't know. I will miss Buena Suerte. I will miss my quarters, my private balcony where I watch the sun shine and the moon glide by." *But most of all, I will miss you.* The words lay forbidden behind his lips. Instead, he gestured toward the balcony doors opening off the bedchamber. "The lemon trees are blooming again. Come. Bring your rebozo. I'll show you." The balcony was embowered with honeysuckle vines, their perfume like incense. A chair and against one wall a military cot, spread neatly with a blanket.

"Do you sleep out here?" she asked in surprise.

"In the summertime, yes. This is one reason I wanted my own quarters. Federico's rooms stink, like a cave lived in too long. I like the open air."

In the starlight, Gabriella could make out the white splash of the flowering trees below. Elias pointed. "This year the lemons have never stop blooming, never stop bearing."

Gabriella smiled. "At the convent, Sister Agatha used to say God made lemons sour to punish them. They ignore His proper growing seasons and make their own growing season to suit themselves."

Elias smiled. "Sister Agatha agrees with God. She likes God's season best. So do I. In the spring, the peach and plum and cherry trees begin to bloom. If we are still at Buena Suerte in the spring, you must come some afternoon and I will show you. We will enjoy the trees, sip chocolate and watch the sun set."

Gabriella turned to go. The perfume of the blossoms was intoxicating, and her bodice was suddenly so tight she could scarcely breathe. Elias stood near her shoulder, facing her, and as he spoke, he flattened his palm against her back. She knew the familiar gesture from many other occasions with the family and servants about, but here in the dark, it bespoke an intimacy she never intended but could not bring herself to disallow.

Her voice trembling, she asked, "And if spring comes and we are no longer at Buena Suerte? Suppose Don Avila moves away and takes us with him, where will he go?"

"A smaller palace, perhaps. Is that what you mean, Gabriella?"

Never before had he called her anything but "Señorita". Without meaning to, she found her head resting against his shoulder. It felt so right, so reassuring to be leaning, melting into his strength, as though she had always belonged there.

With more sob than sigh, she said, "Suppose he can't afford to keep either of us, Elias. They'll send me back to Santa Clara and we may never see one another again. You've been so good to me. You saved my life, that night."

Quietly, he answered, "And before that, my dearest one, you saved mine. Have you forgotten?"

She turned to look up into his handsome face only an inch away.

"We will always owe a great debt to one another, you and I," he murmured. He stroked her face with gentle fingers. "As to what will happen here at Buena Suerte, we can only wait and see. These things are in the hand of God." His gentle arms encircled her and he bent to her lips. The sweetness of his mouth on hers was an experience such as she had never imagined. Tenderly, he kissed her cheeks, her eyelids, her hair. Gladly she yielded to the hard curves of his body. At first slowly and then hungrily, her arms found their way around his shoulders, savoring the feel of his warm flesh beneath the fabric of his shirt.

A sudden storm of hunger shook her. She pressed against him and her straining breath became audible moaning. "Sh-sh-sh," he gently quieted her.

But she was mad with longing. "Oh, Elias, hold me closer!" she whispered. "Elias, I couldn't stand it if we had to part! Hold me closer!"

Suddenly his strong hands gripped her shoulders and held her away from him. "You are a virgin, Gabriella," he said firmly. "You may yet decide to become a nun someday. In the meantime, you must not let your body trick you out of your most important possession."

Then she knew. She recognized it, her childhood dream at the convent so long ago. It had never been God's plan for her to become a nun, never. For the way she felt toward Elias was the way a woman should feel toward an earthly husband, not toward a Celestial One. Elias was right. She must be more careful in the future.

"You know best, Elias. I — I must go now."

Saying goodnight at the door, she tried but failed to face him. She arranged her shawl over her tousled hair and drew the ends tight around her shoulders. Standing near him, she said, "Elias, I liked it very much when you held me close. You were right to stop me when you did. Maybe it would be better if we didn't do it again."

She paused, then catching his hand in both of hers, pressed it to her cheek, turned, and quickly drew the door closed behind her.

The cold of the gallery's marble paving stung her bare feet as she hurried to her room. But she welcomed the pain, welcomed the penance. For the mother's hot blood had at last scalded the daughter, and to the daughter's astonishment, had brought not pain but a glimpse of paradise!

Could this be lust, then? — the sin that Padre had warned against? If sin, why did she feel no guilt? Maybe what she felt for Elias was love. But how to explain Martín? In spite of Martín's devotion to Bonita, her own heart beat faster whenever he was near. Was it possible for a woman to love two men at the same time? Why would God pose such a riddle? But then she reflected that God's riddles were many and human understanding feeble. All that she knew for certain was how she felt: She would have made a sour and surly nun, but given the right husband might yet make a happy, lilting wife surrounded by her babies. Her bare feet skipped and twirled for happiness.

And she wondered what she would say at confession.

CHAPTER 10

Mexico
December 1774

Martín Felipé Mendoza de Neve Ortega alighted from his horse at the Convent of Nuestra Señora del Carmen. The courtyard gates were closed. No groom appeared to take his mount so he hitched it to a nearby tree.

Seeing no sign of life anywhere, Martín nervously paced the rocky path in front of the convent entrance. The late afternoon sun bore down cruelly upon him. He wore dark blue silk breeches and a coat of fawn velvet with touches of lace at throat and wrists. Beneath his plumed tricorn, his dark, soft-spun curls were tightly ribboned at the back in the latest European fashion.

Though his clothing was simple, he worried that he might be overdressed. His vocation was the military. That was the area in which he was at ease and the area he preferred. Yet he was conversant with the correct apparel for balls, fetes, theatre parties, duck hunts, *paseos* and the many rites of the church. Fifteen years of occasional court life in Madrid, Paris and London, together with a mother who made a fetish of such details, had made certain of that.

But six months in Nuevo España had taught him that although *gachupin* ways conferred status, they could make for unnecessary discomfort. In the viceroy's court, the native-born *criollos* accepted the vagaries of a climate where the heat of summer sometimes interrupted the chill of midwinter. The natives preferred cotton to heavy satins and brocades and suffered less from the heat. Not for the first time that afternoon, Martín drew from his sleeve a lace-bordered handkerchief to mop perspiration from his face and cursed the silk shirt sticking to his back.

The occasion made him uneasy. Martín was an unbeliever, a natural skeptic who had sampled just enough of the French philosophers to confirm his doubts. He saw no inconsistency in his equally firm conviction that piety warded off bad luck. He had, in his younger days, observed that a pretended devotion to Mother Church brought him friends whereas a noticable lack of it made enemies, so he kept his views to himself.

But religion *per se* was not the source of his uneasiness. What bothered him was that he had never before attended rites for a young novice upon her entrance to full participation as sister in a convent. He had been told that a day-long fiesta usually preceded the ceremony, with hundreds of invited guests.

After a lavish feast at the family's residence, the candidate in all her finery — ceremonial dress, jewels, flowers — was paraded in an elaborately decorated carriage through the city to the convent where fireworks were set off and a band played.

But Martín's invitation, a personal note from Don Avila, had merely asked him to meet the family at the Convent of Nuestra Señora del Carmen to witness the induction ceremony of the Figuroa daughter Javiera — no fete, no feast, no fireworks. And as he could see for himself, no guests other than himself.

The implications both depressed and elated him. He had heard the gossip about Don Avila's financial reverses but ignored it as irrelevant. He looked forward to a military assignment in Nuevo España which would provide income and possibilities for investment. Even without the military post, he had a modest inheritance from an uncle and would someday come into his father's imposing fortune. Others might need a rich bride; he did not.

But Martín's parents took a different view. They too had heard the whispers and firmly rejected Bonita as a prospective daughter-in-law, beautiful though she was. He had not mentioned Don Avila's invitation to his parents or even to the servants. Fortunately, since it would have roused curiosity, and the Figuroa family's curtailed celebration for Javiera more than substantiated the rumors.

However another aspect of Don Avila's invitation set the blood singing merrily in Martín's veins. Of the many suitors who would have walked ankle-deep through a pit of vipers to win a glance from the flirtatious eyes of Señorita Bonita Dolores y Avila Figuroa, he alone had been singled out to join her family on this important occasion. His palms grew moist at the thought, for this gay, laughing young woman had captured not only his heart but his very soul. "Fall in love with a fortune you can count on and forget this girl," his father had ordered. But in his heart, Martín knew that the clouds would rain turnips before he was likely to forget his beautiful Bonita.

His thoughts made him impatient. He peered frowning down the narrow lane. He first heard, then saw cresting the hill, a fashionable carriage escorted by an older man on horseback. Martín recognized Don Avila's favorite Arabian gelding and the lone Figuroa footman, Miguel, at the reins of the carriage. He winced to see the Figuroa family arriving at the convent in such modest circumstances, friendless and alone.

"Ah, young Martín!" Don Avila exclaimed. He dismounted and tossed his reins to the convent porter, a gawky boy emerging from the entrance. "I hope we haven't kept you waiting."

"Not at all, Señor." Martín swept off his tricorn and bowed low. "Even if you had, such a delay would be more than justified, would it not? After all, this is the most important day your lovely daughter Javiera will ever know."

"Yes-yes," agreed Don Avila absently. "You have never met Javiera, have you? I must present you."

Martín saw that Bonita's maid Gabriella, the shy one with hair the color of fox fur, had already alighted and was assisting Doña Dolores. The old woman's eyes seemed not quite in focus and she smiled uncertainly as Martín bent over her hand with the studied indolence of a grandee. From the coach, Miguel handed down the honoree, Javiera. Covering her dark hair was a white veil, held in place by a crown of fresh flowers. Jewels gleamed at her fingers, wrists and throat. She wore an exquisite ceremonial gown of delicate white lace with many petticoats that set the skirt billowing in all directions.

A pale version of her sister, Martín judged, *but the dress is nice.* Bonita had told him Gabriella made the dress and with hooded eyes, he glanced lazily at the redhead. If he succeeded in making Bonita his bride, he must make certain her personal servant was included in the bargain.

"And this is my dear Javiera," Don Avila presented his daughter with tears in his eyes. "She has never looked lovelier nor been more deeply cherished by her father than on this, her special day."

Martín bowed over Javiera's thin, cold hand. "My family and all we possess are at your service, Señorita. May the gracious Holy Mother grant you everlasting happiness in the life you are about to undertake."

"Many thanks for your kind wishes, Señor," she whispered, and her father led her up the steps and into the convent, followed by Doña Dolores on the arm of the servant Gabriella.

Martín turned to feast his eyes on his beloved, who gazed up at him adoringly. "My dearest love!" he murmured, and kissed her hand.

"Sh-sh," she warned, glancing at her mother's retreating back.

"I thought you'd never come!" Martín whispered.

"It was Javiera's crown that made us late. That and some other things. Papa will tell you later."

"Can't you tell me now?"

"It will be better if Papa — " Her voice faltered. She smiled. "Anyway, we're here at last. With the crown."

Martín glanced after Javiera through the convent entrance. "It turned out well, in spite of the haste. Very lovely. But instead of such a crown on Javiera's head, I'd rather see a bridal crown on your own head at our wedding. I live for the day when you will be my bride."

Bonita's lace-edged chemise revealed a tantalizing blush rising from her high young bosom. "It is not for me to speak with you about such things. Not now."

It sounded serious. The smile left Martín's lips. "Why 'not now'? What's the matter? Tell me."

"I can't. I was wrong to have spoken at all. We should go in now or Papa will come looking for us!" And she hurried toward the entrance ahead of him, her small feet dancing up the stone steps. Following, Martín found it impossible to brood.

The party crossed the flagstoned entryway to the sacristy where candles had been lighted and a frail elderly nun awaited them. Javiera went to her immediately and the two clung together, whispering. At last the nun turned to the other guests.

Don Avila bowed. "Good evening, Sister Mathilda. On behalf of my family, I present myself as your most humble servant."

"You honor our establishment with your distinguished presence, Señor," replied the nun, "and I beg to be of service to you. I speak not for myself, for I am a person of no importance, but for the sisters of my order. Our prayers in this house are ever with you and your family." She then embraced Doña Dolores and Bonita, depositing dry kisses on the air beside their cheeks.

Don Avila presented Martín. "It is a rare honor to be received by your holy sisterhood on such a solemn occasion, Señora. I am at your disposal."

"Ah, but Señor, it is a festive occasion," Sister Mathilda corrected him, smiling. "Javiera's preparation for this day has been long and arduous. We have grown to know and love her during the years she has served her novitiate. It is with great joy that we welcome her into the company of Christ."

But there was no responding joy from the family. Shortly afterwards, Sister Mathilda indicated the ceremony was about to begin. The time of final parting had come. Martín knew already of Don Avila's personal grief over losing his daughter. His own eyes studiously examined the pavement at his feet as Javiera's father and then her mother in turn folded the girl in their arms for the last time.

To Martín's surprise, it was not Don Avila but Bonita who broke down in wrenching sobs. Clinging to her sister, she cried, "Oh, Javiera, you're too young! We never had a chance to know one another, you and I. And now you're leaving forever and we'll never see you again!"

It was the servant Gabriella who went at once to the younger sister's side, whispered to her, clasped Javiera's hand warmly in farewell, and then led Bonita away, still weeping.

Javiera was summoned and left the room by a small door leading to the vestry. Sister Mathilda explained to the family, "The ceremony consists of three parts. At the close of the last, Javiera will be allowed to come look upon you once again, but you must not speak to her or touch her. After the ceremony, refreshments will be waiting for you here in the sacristy.

"Come," she continued. "I will show you to your places. And then I must beg you to excuse me, for I too must take part in the ceremony."

Escorted by Sister Mathilda, the guests made their way down a corridor to a large archway with an iron grating. A black curtain entirely covered the grating and blocked the view into the convent church beyond, now empty of worshipers, where the ceremony would take place. Arranged in the corridor before the grillwork was a rank of prie-dieus for the guests who would witness the proceedings from this privileged spot.

Soft music from the pipe organ drifted from the church, echoing in the empty nave. The music stopped and was followed by a long silence. Suddenly, with a thunderous fanfare from the organ, the black curtain parted and the guests found before them a brilliant tableau of crimson and gold. A thousand tapers burned in sconces and candelabra throughout the church. Scarlet velvet hung in panels flanking the gilded altar; the same fabric covered the walls and antique chairs on which sat the priests and the bishop who would conduct the ceremony. Lying prostrate on either side of the choir and the priests in their rich robes were twenty nuns, each covered from head to foot in her heavy black habit.

A wide purple carpet bordered with garlands of fresh flowers had been spread before the altar. In the center knelt Javiera in her ceremonial dress, her veil, flowers and jewels.

As the pipe organ within the church and bells in the church towers outside pealed in exultation, the nuns rose to their feet. Accompanied by the organ, they sang a hymn, after which the abbess came forward, raised Javiera and brought her to face the bishop. He questioned her at length. Satisfied at last, he directed her to kneel while he pronounced his blessing. The black curtain was slowly closed.

After a wait of several minutes, the curtain parted again. This time, the church was not so brilliantly lit. The bishop and priests were seated as before. Fully veiled, the nuns stood like dark shadows in a wide circle before the altar. Lying prostrate on the purple carpet, completely covered by a black cloth, was a motionless form. Again accompanied by the pipe organ, the nuns, chanting, came forward to kneel in a circle around the prostrate figure.

Wondering about the symbolism, Martín turned to ask Bonita at his side. Observing her stricken face in the dim light, he thought better of it and instead leaned toward the servant girl Gabriella who knelt behind him. "What does it mean?" he whispered.

"Javiera has renounced the world," Gabriella whispered in reply. "The black shroud symbolizes her death."

Without removing the black cloth, the nuns raised the figure at the foot of the altar and led her to kneel before the bishop, who pronounced the benediction. Solemnly, as the organ intoned a dirge-like hymn, the figure embraced each nun in turn.

As the black curtain slowly closed for the second time, Bonita wept quietly and an involuntary sob escaped Don Avila. Martín was not surprised at their reaction. From the corner of his eye, however, he glimpsed Doña Dolores stifling a mighty yawn. He glanced over his shoulder at the servant girl kneeling behind him, but she appeared to be lost in prayer, her face hidden by the folds of her shawl.

When the black curtain was drawn open for the third part of the ceremony, the church was once again brilliantly lighted. Javiera, now in full regalia as a sister of the order, knelt before the altar, surrounded by the other nuns. The bishop took his place in the pulpit and delivered a short sermon reassuring the new initiate of the correctness of her decision to become a bride of Christ. Music followed the sermon. Accompanied by Sister Mathilda, Javiera slowly turned from the altar and approached the grillwork behind which sat her parents and her sister. Looking upon her family for the last time, tears coursed down her cheeks. Martín thought he had never before witnessed such sorrow on a human face. Slowly, the black curtain was closed for the last time.

Martín had always understood that traditionally such rites were occasions of joyful dedication for both the family and the initiate. But after witnessing Javiera's ceremony for himself, he wondered that any family could maintain a festive mood in the face of such leave-taking.

Punch, cakes and fruit were laid out in the sacristy but the food, though appetizing, inspired little interest. Sister Mathilda did not appear. In the end, Gabriella passed around goblets of punch, but unnerved by grief as the family members were, most of the refreshments went untouched.

At length Don Avila rose from his chair, replaced his goblet on the table and turned to Martín. "We must beg your forgiveness for our lapse in hospitality," he said. "Our sorrows are endless, it seems. We were late arriving today because the servants are packing. Bucareli, the viceroy, has transferred me from my post at the National Palace."

They've found a way to get rid of him, thought Martín.

Don Avila touched his lips with his handkerchief and cleared his throat. "My new assignment is at Alamos, a settlement far north of here in the province of Sonora. Perhaps you have heard about the overland expedition that is being planned to colonize Alta California. Ultimate destination of the expedition, I understand, is to be the great river of San Francisco which lies north of the presidio at Monterey. The commander of the expedition has already been appointed, Captain Juan Bautista de Anza."

Martín nodded. "I have the honor to be acquainted with Captain Anza. If you will forgive me, he is now a lieutenant colonel, not a captain. Earlier this year, he was promoted for blazing a trail from Sonora to the missions on the coast."

Martín knew of the expedition being planned and had even considered joining it. But from boyhood he had dreamed of finding a treasure like Bonita for his wife. He had almost given up hope that such a woman existed. Now that he had found her — had even designed her bridal ring and left the drawing with the goldsmith for execution — for him to undertake a trek to California leaving her behind was unthinkable!

"The viceroy feels that a representative from his court must undertake the fiscal obligations for the expedition," Don Avila was saying, "and he has asked me to assume that responsibility. A small staff of clerks will accompany me. I am to oversee payroll and settling of accounts from the branch of the king's treasury at the mines at Alamos."

Martín felt the muscles straining across his cheekbones as they always did when he had to lie. "Antonio Bucareli obviously thinks highly of you, Señor, to entrust you with such a responsibility. When do you plan to leave?"

"In a few days. As soon as our furniture and goods are packed." A rueful smile twisted his face. "We will — "

"'We', Señor? A thousand pardons for interrupting you. By 'we' you mean yourself and your clerks."

"My family will go with me."

"Your — ?" Martín's hooded eyes widened in disbelief. Ten years of military spying for the Spanish crown had taught him self control, otherwise he would have exploded. "Don Avila, Alamos is a mountain outpost often under attack by Apaches. Apache Indians, do you understand? Apaches are nothing like the gentle mountain people we see every day here in Mexico. Apaches are the cruelest savages known!" In spite of himself, concern had raised the pitch of his voice. "Alamos is nearly eight hundred miles away! It will take you three months of hard overland travel to get there. At least three months. And you propose to take your wife and daughter to this place?"

"I have no choice."

Bonita appeared at her father's side. "Papa, we had better go now. Mama —"

Don Avila's eyes followed Bonita's gaze. Across the room, Gabriella approached Doña Dolores and offered her a goblet of punch. The older woman, trembling and gasping, gulped it greedily.

"Yes," Don Avila agreed. "Bonita, please find Miguel and tell him to bring the carriage. Martín, I must escort my family to Buena Suerte. You are welcome to join me if you wish."

Darkness had fallen and a three-quarter moon rode the evening sky when, four hours later, Martín de Neve mounted his horse in the courtyard at Buena

Suerte and Miguel let him out at the main entrance. Martín's head ached, partly from the sooty, ill-trimmed lamp in Don Avila's sitting room and partly from the dizzying news he had heard.

For many years, Don Avila had gambled recklessly. Sometimes his losses were great, but his steward unfailingly raised money to pay his debts, borrowing against the many business investments belonging to the Figuroa family. Little by little, it became more difficult to borrow; it became necessary to sell.

Don Avila no longer owned seven of his ten silver mines. Three of his four maguey plantations were no longer his. He appeared to have lost his entire fleet of seven merchant ships and most of his valuable Arabian horses. When he attempted to sell the family jewels to repay debts against some of these properties, he discovered most of the jewels were glass — imitations so cleverly contrived not even the owners could tell they had been substituted for the original gems. "My servants betrayed me," acknowledged Don Avila sorrowfully.

Most of the ships, the mines, the plantation equipment had been allowed to deteriorate so that their sale brought a poor price. Thanks to a stroke of luck Don Avila did not explain, Buena Suerte, which had never belonged to Don Avila but to his brothers, was in good condition. Put up for auction, it brought a handsome price. It was now the property of his former steward, Federico Verro, and the Figuroa family had been ordered to vacate.

Upon hearing this recital of dispossession, Martín had in turn felt anger and dismay, pity and disgust. He asked at last, "The viceroy, the people at court, did they know all this was happening?"

"How could they not know?" Don Avila said, unsteadily refilling Martín's glass and then his own. "Every family, every servant, every *lepero* in the city knew it. From my own chamberlain, Elias, I learned the true reason Carlos sent the visitador-general to Mexico."

"What reason?"

"I am the reason. For fifteen years, it has been my responsibility to collect the king's taxes in Nuevo España, and I have accounted for every centavo. The amount collected was never enough, of course. In fact, the amount we managed to collect shrank a bit more each year. Many of the silver mines have flooded with groundwater, as I am sure you know. Farmers claim the land is worn out and will no longer grow crops. Merchants claim business is bad and their creditors will not pay what they owe. But under the circumstances it was natural, I suppose, for the king to think I was stealing from him." And for the first time, Don Avila betrayed the full measure of the bitterness he felt. "My monarch, Carlos III. He believed I was stealing from him. My shame is complete."

"But Gálvez didn't come here because of you," protested Martín. "He came here because of the California ventures!"

"That is the reason he came five years ago," agreed Don Avila. "Five years ago, he sent the Franciscans by sea to San Diego and Monterey. This time he and his auditors spent six months going over our tax records."

Don Avila waved his hand wearily, and Martín realized the evening was getting on. Still unanswered — because Martín carefully avoided the question —

was what would happen afterward? Within a year, Anza's expedition would have reached California and the bills would all be paid; what then? Would Bucareli bring Don Avila back to the city or leave him to rot in disgrace at Alamos. Martín was afraid he already knew the answer.

"Don Avila," he said. "If it will not offend you, I would like to talk about your daughter Bonita."

One corner of the old man's mouth turned up wryly. "Offend me? Not unless you plan to say something offensive about her, which I doubt."

Martín realized he was being teased and smiled dutifully.

"I love Bonita with all my heart, Don Avila. I want her to be my wife. I — I believe she cares for me as well."

Don Avila nodded sagely. "I too believe she cares for you."

In a rush, Martín blurted, "My parents know how I feel about Bonita but they have forbidden me to marry her."

Silence. "I feared as much."

"Don Avila, I am twenty-nine years old. For me, there have been sweethearts in the past." Don Avila nodded understandingly. "My parents see my feeling for Bonita as an infatuation like the others. They think it will pass away. But there has never been anyone like Bonita, not for me. I want her at my side for the rest of my days."

"Yes-yes."

"What I propose is that I go to Alamos with you."

A pause. "What?"

"I would rather marry Bonita before you leave. I long to make her my bride now — tomorrow! tonight! — and keep her here with me."

"But then your parents — "

"They would not accept her." Martín cleared his throat. "They would be very — angry. But I believe if we wait, if I show them how much I truly care for Bonita, they will come around in time."

Don Avila examined the contents of his glass. "And once you get to Alamos, what then? Do you plan to spend all day every day chatting with my daughter? I promise you, nothing will more quickly kill a woman's love for a man than having him constantly underfoot."

"Well, I — "

Don Avila straightened. "You seem to know something about Alamos. It is, as you said, little more than a settlement in the wilderness. No theatre. No fetes. No balls at the National Palace. How do you propose to occupy yourself?"

"I propose to serve as a military attache on your staff."

Don Avila blinked. Then he nodded. "Now, there's an interesting idea!"

"Perhaps you have heard the rumor that my uncle, Felipé de Neve, is to be appointed governor of Alta California. So you see, I have more than a casual interest in Colonel Anza's expedition. I will petition the viceroy for a military appointment to accompany you to Alamos. Once there, I will be available to both you and Colonel Anza to help supply and equip the expedition. I believe my petition will be granted."

Silence.

Martín coughed discreetly. "If you'll have me."

"Oh, I'll have you, I'll have you. And the viceroy would pay your expenses, would he?"

"If not, I'll pay my own expenses!"

"Astonishing!"

They summoned Bonita and Doña Dolores and told them the good news. Suddenly everyone was ravenously hungry so they rousted out the cook to prepare a huge supper. Don Avila sent to the cellar for the last bottles of his finest wine. Later, for five whole minutes under the approving gaze of her parents, Bonita allowed Martín to hold her hand — *so like a soft white dove*, thought Martín. And his spirits, dove-like, took wing and flew in dizzy circles around his head.

Much later, Martín's exalted state cleared somewhat and he perceived that, since the plates were empty and so were the bottles, the time had come to say farewell. After a giddy ferment of bowing, he descended to the courtyard. He crossed under his horse's head, twice, hunting for the reins and then under the horse's belly hunting for the saddle girth, which he was sure needed tightening.

By then the harness was badly snarled. Miguel sorted reins from stirrups and after twice retrieving Señor's hat, helped Señor mount his horse. But Señor three times headed his mount toward the open gates only to end up in the fountain. Miguel at last led the bewildered animal gently through the portal, and it seemed relieved, at last, to find a street with which it was familiar.

"Go with God, Señor," Miguel called anxiously after Señor Neve.

Señor Neve belched softly, waved, and ambled off down the boulevard aboard his horse.

CHAPTER 11   Mexico to Culiacán

January 17, 1775
Dearest Reverend Mother,

It is the first night of our journey and very late. Traveling is hard. We make many mistakes but we are learning.

Monsignor Mero gave me your letter the morning we left. He wanted me to stay in Mexico, as you did. When I kept saying no, he said I was a monument to stubbornness. (He is more stubborn than I am by far.) He had already made arrangements without a word to me. I was to go to the archbishop's palace as governess to His Excellency's two nieces. I told him I would have caused a lot of gossip there but he did not agree.

Ana needs me now to help make up Doña Dolores' bed in the carriage.

January 19, 10 am
We came to a grassy place near a brook and Elias said the animals need to graze. Elias says we will stop for the animals to eat and drink

whenever we find a good grazing spot. Anyway we are taking our mid-day rest though it is not mid-day.

We took the Camino Real north out of the city. If Carlos could see his "King's Highway," he would make the viceroy give it a different name. Mostly the stone is broken or washed out. Usually we see only pine trees and cactus and mesquite and chaparral but the mountains are beautiful.

(Are you really interested in all this? Your letter says you want to know "everything.")

Martín de Neve volunteered to go with us to Alamos. He wanted to be near Bonita. He already bought her wedding ring. I saw it. It is very pretty. Before we left, Señor Neve told Don Avila he should charge Federico Verro with fraud but Don Avila took the blame on himself for all that happened. They had a very loud discussion. We could hear it all over the palace. We were afraid Señor would refuse to go with us to Alamos but he fumed and sulked and went anyway, maybe because of the ring.

Padre thinks I place too much trust in Don Avila. I am not as trusting as Padre thinks. Don Avila is a good man but he is weak. Our Lord loved gentle, meek people and said they would inherit the earth. I hope not. I have seen a weak man cause great suffering to others. I wish you were here to explain.

I trust Elias and Señor Neve, not Don Avila. He is kind when drunk but drunk just the same. Without Señor Neve to make decisions, I would go to the archbishop's palace and worry later about the gossip. Señor Neve thinks people going to California are lucky. I think so too. The expedition is important to the empire and to Mother Church. Most of all, it is important to the poor farm families who are going there. They will make a new beginning without landlords to grind them down or rich merchants to cheat them out of their harvests. Colonel Anza is doing a good thing. I want to take part, even if only in a small way.

January 24, 6:30 pm

You wanted to know about closing up Buena Suerte. Don Avila made Elias dismiss most of the servants and the others wandered away. Even Doña Dolores' old Pepita walked out one day without saying goodby. So there was no one to help with the packing.

Señor Neve and Don Avila made an inventory of everything in the palace. I wrote it all down. They even listed the statuary and sacks of meal in the storeroom. Then they decided what to take to Alamos and hired men to pack.

Señor Neve limited Doña Dolores to four gowns and Bonita to six pairs of shoes. There was a big argument but Señor won. He made Don Avila auction off everything else. It was sad to see the silver tureens and Sèvres plates carried away. Bonita wept rivers. But the auction raised enough to pay off more of Don Avila's debts and buy fifty more mules. Don Avila wanted to buy back a few of his Arabian horses but Señor talked him out of it. "Arabians are no good as pack animals," he said. "Too costly, too nervous, too skinny."

(Bonita wants me to call him "Martín" but when I did, he frowned. Elias says Martín knows about my trouble with Federico Verro and would rather Bonita found another companion. He thinks I will "cause trouble." Elias did not explain what kind of trouble I am supposed to cause. Meanwhile I explained to Bonita I must call Señor Neve what *he* wants, not what *she* wants.)

Señor Neve found two *arrieros* to handle the pack animals and the extra mounts. He had to promise to get them back to Mexico as part of the bargain. Then three clerks arrived from the National Palace, sent by the viceroy. They were staff for Don Avila's paymaster's office in Alamos, but Don Avila claimed they were hangers-on the viceroy wanted to get rid of.

Señor Neve talked to them. The one named Pedro could write and do sums so Señor sent him to help Miguel who is in charge of supplies. Elias took the other two, Alex and Manuel, to work with the livestock. We have now been six days on the road and the not-so-good clerks have turned into not-so-good *arrieros*. But Elias is patient.

And now I hear the "*arrieros*" shouting to the mules. We are ready to move on. Goodby for now, dear Reverend Mother.

January 28, 5 pm
The day we left Mexico, we went to early mass and found a robin drinking at the vessel of holy water. Everyone says a robin is good luck, so we left the city in high spirits. Señor Neve ordered our line of march and it has never changed. Señor and Don Avila always head the column. Next comes the family carriage with Miguel at the reins. Doña Dolores, Bonita, Ana and I ride inside the carriage. Behind the carriage are Elias with the four muleteers. They tend the *remuda* of spare mounts and guide the strings of pack animals. All the men are armed with muskets, pistols and sabers but so far no bandits. Last comes Rita the cook, on horseback. She has her own pistol and claims she knows how to shoot it. She leads six mules with coops of live fowl for food along the way. Behind the chickens comes poor Pedro, herding fifteen sheep for the same purpose. (Pedro is a not-so-good shepherd. He lost three sheep the first day.)

The carriage is bumpy but keeps us dry in the rain. Sometimes there are places in the road so bad the carriage might turn over, so we get out and walk. Don Avila will sell the carriage in Mazatlán. North of Mazatlán, the road is a rocky trail and people travel only on horses and mules. We have a litter in the baggage for Doña Dolores who sleeps most of the time. Bonita and I sometimes leave Ana with Doña Dolores in the carriage and ride horseback to get some fresh air and relief from the jolting.

After we left the city, the trail was downhill and easy on the animals. We pass villages with houses built close beside the trail. Women and children work in the fields with the men. They are very poor and stare at us as we ride by.

Our biggest problem is finding places to stop for the night. Señor Neve says travelers are usually men who roll up in blankets on the ground. But there are thirteen of us (five women). That means we need a level place for tents but also water and pasture for the animals.

This is the dry season, and the mountain lands are greenish brown with cactus, greasewood, mesquite and last summer's scrub grass. There is moisture in only a few of the streams, so water is a daily worry. (Elias said he would show me how to get water from a dry stream bed but he hasn't done it yet.) Our cavalcade has been nearly two weeks on the trail and we have eaten two of the sheep. Still, that leaves nearly a hundred hungry beasts needing grass and water.

January 30
Last night a rainstorm brought a flash flood that nearly washed us away. We traveled all day with wet clothes. This afternoon, Elias found a high well-drained spot where we can spend the night in safety.

I am writing in the carriage with Doña Dolores. The others are tending to the animals, putting up tents and cooking the evening meal. We are getting used to living outdoors. Before we left the city, only Señor Neve and Elias understood that a journey like this is hard work. Everyone helps. Even Bonita turns the spit while the ducks roast.

I did not finish telling you about Buena Suerte. I soon understood why Doña Dolores was so quiet. Pepita had been buying FLOWERS (I remember your warning in your letter) and giving her all she wanted every three or four hours. The *curandera* told me to wait till Alamos to start holding back on the dosage. She sold me all she could spare for the trip north but my supply will not last. She told me of a woman in Guadalajara. There is no source north of Culiacán.

Elias has known about Doña Dolores for a long time. After Pepita left, I told Don Avila but I don't think he understands. I haven't told Señor Neve yet. He will blame me, and I deserve it. She would not be the way she is if it were not for me.

Don Avila spends as much time as he can with Doña Dolores. I think he tries to atone for the family's loss. Miguel and Rita spend their evenings planning the next day's meals and arguing with Pedro, who is careless with the sheep. Señor Neve and Bonita whisper and tell jokes and ignore the rest of us. It is disappointing that Señor Neve holds himself above everyone else, though he is a good man to have in charge.

Elias and I are often together. He knows I miss Monsignor Mero and he finds ways to cheer me up. He teases me and tells funny stories. Pedro settles his sheep at night with falsetto baby-talk. When Elias imitates him, I laugh till I choke. His black eyes sparkle and the way he handles a horse is a wonder. Ana is five years older but she flirts with Elias anyway. I used to hope Elias and Ana would fall in love but if they did, I would miss him very much.

I would like to talk to Sister Magdalena about Bonita's attacks of SNEEZING. The *curandera* says she may have outgrown them. She had her last attack the day Pepita left. She could surprise us all and START SNEEZING while fording a stream on horseback. Señor Neve does not know about her attacks. I hope he never finds out.

Rita is getting ready to serve our evening meal. I must waken Doña Dolores. Don Avila is better at coaxing her to eat than I am. She calls me a prissy little fart and worse. I do not indulge her as Pepita did. (Neither do I steal her jewels!)

February 8, 9 p.m.

I am writing in the carriage where the lamplight makes it easier to see. Ana says she can't sleep because Doña Dolores snores. So I am tending Doña Dolores in the carriage while Ana shares the tent with Bonita. Her sleep will be disturbed in Bonita's tent too, but not from snoring.

We have reached Morella. It is a few huts with a tiny plaza and a tiny church. The *paisanas* offer us all the water we need from their wells. The padre is supposed to come say mass on Sunday (tomorrow). If he does, we will stay an extra day.

We pitched our tents on the plaza but Señor Neve and Elias pastured the animals outside the town. Don Avila is paying some farm boys to watch the animals for two nights while our men get some rest. Before we leave on Monday, I will seal these pages and hire one of the farm boys to take the bundle to Padre in the city. He will have it delivered to you.

Señor Neve drew a map to show us Alamos, the town where we are going. When I left the convent, I was not a very adventurous person, but now it is exciting to think about new places and the people who are going there. Colonel Anza plans to take his California expedition to Monterey, on the coast. Alamos is halfway between Monterey and Mexico! From the first time I heard of the California expedition, I wanted to go. When we reach Alamos, we will be halfway there! It is hard to believe it!

Pedro dozed in the saddle and lagged too far behind the column. His mount wandered off the trail and the sheep followed. It took Elias and Miguel all afternoon to round them up.

February 13, noon

Don Avila never wears his wig any more. His natural hair is rust-colored with gray at the sides. He fell off his horse again this morning. It is a miracle how drunk he can get and still sound sober as a Jesuit. Ana no longer plays cards every evening with Alex and Manuel. She says they cheat.

Miguel got in a fight with Pedro because of his carelessness with the sheep. They were quickly parted but Miguel has a black eye. To keep peace, Elias put Manuel in charge of the sheep. Pedro will now tend the horses and mules with Alex.

Señor Neve is sometimes too arrogant and Elias is sometimes too easy, but they are good friends. Señor Neve is embarrassed to be sarcastic when Elias is so good-natured, so even when things go wrong, they are both cheerful and kind. God has blessed us with good men to lead our caravan! They make us ashamed to complain, so we don't.

Next week we will reach the sea. We will have easier country along the coast and can travel farther each day. Then north to Culiacán. If anything interesting happens, I will write again from there. If not, I will wait till we reach Alamos in early April. A silver train leaves for Mexico once a month, taking mail and bringing back supplies. Six months is a long round trip, but better than none.

Please say hello to Consuelo. At the Alameda in December I saw her, home for Christmas. We had a short visit — too short.

Please remember me in your prayers, dearest Reverend Mother, as I remember you in mine. Traveling as we are, without early mass, I say a rosary every morning instead.

> Your loving
> Gabriella

> Culiacán to Alamos
> March 1775

Gabriella's account to Madre Valderia told only partly of her relationship with Elias. Six months had now gone by since their midnight meeting above the blossoming lemon trees at Buena Suerte. Afterward she was more on her guard than ever lest her emotions betray her. She had pretended their meeting had never happened, and Elias had followed her lead.

With the decision for Alamos, Gabriella was at first overjoyed that Martín de Neve, her secret idol, would be leading the family's expedition. The joy faded as she realized the daily pain she would experience as she witnessed his adoration of another. She tensed her shoulders to still their shuddering. The ordeal would be more than she could bear. But her alternatives were the crumbling towers of Santa Clara or the snares of intrigue at the archbishop's palace.

At last she admitted that, Martín or no Martín, she wanted most of all to see Colonel Anza's expedition on its way to California. And with her decision, a change came in her feeling toward Elias. Her trust in him — and in herself —

grew and strengthened. She often felt his steadying touch at her waist and, more rarely when they were alone, she rested her weary head on his shoulder. There was no recurrence of earlier intimacy, only that the earlier intimacy was no longer denied.

Elias supervised the pack train at the rear of the caravan. Gabriella endured long days of boredom in the saddle, awaiting late afternoon when she could fetch his food from Rita's cooking pots and hear his humorous version of the day's happenings.

After Culiacán, no more laudanum was to be had for Doña Dolores. Gabriella substituted valerian and soon ran out of that too. The old woman's returning pain was as virulent as ever, and in her weakened state there followed days of feeble rages and exhausted tantrums. At first the mules bearing her litter shied with alarm, but they soon grew accustomed to their unruly passenger and even stopped without being told when she fell out.

"Maybe brandy would help her," Don Avila suggested after an especially difficult day on the trail. Gabriella was certain Doña Dolores lacked her husband's ability to drink and still comport himself with dignity. But for lack of a better plan, Don Avila began sharing his generous supply of brandy and pulque with his wife. From that time on, she was never entirely sober. She complained of nausea and headaches, but was relatively free of pain.

With the passing weeks, the travelers became accustomed to one another, as members of a big family are inclined to do. When they camped at night, Don Avila and Doña Dolores shared a tent. Bonita slept in a second tent with Ana and Gabriella, and the men shared a third. Miguel and Rita improvised shelters of their own to be near and protect the caravan's supplies.

The travelers saw one another in all conditions: refreshed and exhausted, neat and disheveled, even — occasionally — doused in unexpected thunder showers. The experiences strengthened Gabriella's devotion to Elias. Supervising the men, he was resolute but never unreasonable. He never forgot a promise or failed in his thoughtfulness toward Bonita, Doña Dolores and even toward Rita. Observing that he wore his boots without stockings like a *paisano*, she knitted him a pair.

Like all those in love, Gabriella thought her secret well-kept. She was wrong. "Look who's swooning over Elias!" teased Bonita late one afternoon as she and Gabriella washed their long hair side by side in a brook not far from the tent.

For weeks, Gabriella had laughed with Ana and even with Don Avila about Bonita and Martín, the lovebirds, forever preening and flirting. To find herself the butt of the same joke was mortifying. Quickly Gabriella rinsed her auburn hair, wrapped a towel around her head and went to sun herself on a boulder above the camp. Elias found her there.

"I'm giving you a different mount tomorrow," he said.

"What's wrong with the one I had?" she asked tartly, still irritable from Bonita's teasing.

"Her back is sore. Come, I'll show you. I'm going to work on her now. Recognize this?" Suppressing a smile, he showed her a container of linament.

In spite of herself, she laughed. She had prepared it for Elias months before when one of Don Avila's Arabians was lamed with an infected cut. Closing up the palace was a busy time and Gabriella had snapped at Elias, "I didn't come to Buena Suerte to doctor horses!" Then, ashamed of herself, she had put aside a half-dozen other tasks and prepared the linament anyway.

Elias led the way through a grove of cottonwood trees where the animals had been corralled for the night. Shouldering his way among the horses and mules, he paused at the chestnut mare she had ridden every day since leaving Culiacán. He pointed to the oozing lesions on her back, and began to apply the soothing linament. "When Alex saddled her up this morning, he forgot the blanket."

"The villain!" cried Gabriella. "Because of him, I rode her all day and didn't realize I was hurting her!"

"I'll have to keep a closer eye on his work," said Elias. "He seemed to know what he was doing, but I see he's apt to get careless. We can't afford carelessness. It's a good way to lose our mounts, and we need every one."

Elias finished doctoring the mare, then walked slowly among the animals, stroking them. He inspected a scratch here, probed a hoof there. Gabriella followed, caressing the long noses that turned her way seeking affection. She enjoyed being among the animals, liked their strong smell and their trust.

Elias glanced toward the camp to make certain there was no one nearby to overhear. Without preamble, he said, "Don Avila will never return to the city, Gabriella. Anza's expedition was Bucareli's excuse to get him out of the way."

Gabriella was speechless for a moment. "How do you know that?"

"Martín has been free with his words. Alamos is the end of the road for Don Avila. And the end of the road for us. For you and me."

"What do you mean?"

"Don Avila will have no money to pay us. Are you willing to work for nothing, like a slave? I'm not! Do you have the money to hire men and pack animals to escort you back to Mexico? Don Avila doesn't. I don't."

"Martín does."

"Martín won't commit himself, but I think he plans to marry Bonita, stay in Alamos and invest in a silver mine. He's been asking questions about Miguel and Rita. His household would need a cook and a footman. But — "

The silence lengthened. Gabriella had assumed her service with Don Avila — and perhaps Elias' service as well — would end after a year or two, and she would return to the city, most likely with Bonita and Señor Neve after their marriage. But both she and Elias recognized how fragile those marriage plans could prove to be. What would happen to Señor's ardor after witnessing one of Bonita's seizures with cracking joints, gnashing teeth and staring white eyeballs?

And without Señor Neve, what? Spend the rest of her life in Alamos, sleeping every night dreading Apache raids? Maybe Madre Valderia and Monsignor Mero would send a proper escort for her. Maybe Don Avila would raise the money somehow and send his womenfolk back to Mexico and she could go with them. Maybe. Maybe.

She glanced at Elias. "What about you?" she asked. "Do you mind staying at

Alamos?"

"Yes. I mind very much." He pinched off a twig from a low-hanging limb. "To get the Figuroa family to Alamos, get them settled, no, I do not mind that. Don Avila has been good to me. I owe him that much loyalty. But in Alamos, the only place for me is with the military garrison. And to spend my life on the frontier fighting Apaches, no. That is a life for soldiers, men who like fighting. I want my own place to farm, to raise sheep and cattle."

"Maybe you could farm and raise cattle at Alamos."

"With the Apaches burning down my house and stampeding my herds two or three times a year? No, thank you. Besides, to farm and raise cattle you need fertile land, not mountains covered with rocks. Most of the land around Alamos is good for mining and nothing else."

"Then go to work for the mines."

"Go to work for — ? Gabriella, are you serious? Is that what you think of me? Do you honestly think I would be content burrowing in the earth like a worm?"

It was the first time she had ever heard challenge in Elias' voice. She quickly shook her head and placatingly stroked his arm. "No, Elias. Please don't be angry. I was thinking of overseeing the silver shipments to the city, supervising the smelting, something like that." Then she looked up at him, impatient. "Elias Márquez, you have something on your mind or you would never have brought this up. What is it?"

Thoughtfully, he twirled the cottonwood shoot between his fingers. "In a few days, we will arrive at Alamos. Colonel Anza is on the trail behind us, at Culiacán. He is right now, today, recruiting families for the expedition to Alta California."

"California?" she repeated, wonderingly. "You're thinking of going to California?"

Elias' eyes began to sparkle. "And you. Why shouldn't Anza recruit you, too? You and me?"

"Oh, Elias!" cried Gabriella, overwhelmed with hope and joy. "To go to California!"

"Listen," Elias continued. "Martín has copies of the supply orders. It's unbelievable! The government is supplying *everything* for the colonists — not just to get them to the coast but to set them up farming and raising cattle once they get there! The colonists, they get their clothing — stockings, ribbons, hats, shoes, petticoats, underwear! They even get pots and pans to cook in, blankets, tents. Soldiers *get paid* — "

"I thought you didn't want to be a soldier."

"I don't!" Elias placed his dusty tricorn over his breast and mockingly raised his eyes to heaven. "It is against my principles to kill people," he pontificated, "but to get to California, all expenses paid? For free land, free seed for planting, a small herd to start out — "

"They're taking cattle too?"

" — I will compromise my principles and be a soldier for the king. For four or five months only. Oh, and Bucareli says soldiers are to be issued muskets and ammunition."

"What about carts? Wagons for all those supplies?"

"No carts," said Elias. "The terrain is too rough. Horses and pack animals only."

Suddenly curious, Gabriella remarked, "You know an awful lot about this expedition."

"*Martín* knows an awful lot about it. I've had six weeks to pluck him like a chicken. Everything he knows, I know. For instance, do you know where the colonists will be selling the hides and tallow from the livestock they raise? To merchant ships from Hawaii and the Philippines! Already there is trade with the California coast. There are fortunes to be made there!"

A pause. "Is that the reason you're interested in going, Elias? To make a fortune?"

He sobered at the disappointment in her voice. Gently, he took her hand in his. "I want to go, my dearest Gabriella, because it is a chance to see what I can make of myself. Maybe in California I will be only a small farmer. But if I am, it will be because I decide to be a small farmer, not because someone else condemns me to be a small farmer. Do you see the difference? The opportunity, that is why I want to go. Isn't it the same with you?"

It was a pointless question. He knew the answer already. She merely nodded and smiled at him, her soul in her eyes.

Then she grew wistful. "Elias, every farm family in Sonora will flock to join the expedition. We don't have a chance, do we?"

"Maybe we do," Elias said. "Many of these farmers will be suspicious. What does anyone really know about this California? They will think it must be a pretty bad place for Anza to be offering such a big bribe. Or at least that's the way some of the *paisanos* will see it. And Anza wants only young, healthy people. Children, yes, even babies. But no invalids, no grandparents. That rules out dozens of families, right there. They can't abandon their parents who are old and need them."

A pause. "Don Avila is old and needs us, Elias."

"Not after he's settled in Alamos. He'll have Martín."

Gabriella said shrewdly, "We're experienced travelers, aren't we, coming all the way from Mexico? Colonel Anza would especially want people like us."

"Of course he would." Elias' grin returned. "And not only are we experienced travelers! Here is a lady who knows how to doctor horses!"

"*You!*" cried Gabriella in mock anger. She reached for a twig above her head, stripped off a handful of cottonwood leaves and threw them at him. Elias dodged, chuckling.

Through the twilight, they heard but ignored Rita's little bell announcing dinner.

"I tease about it, but what you said is true," said Elias. "Anza will want families who already know that the trip to California will be hard. Once signed up, there's no backing out. Or sneaking out. Deserters will be caught and whipped."

"'Families'. You keep saying 'families.'"

"Yes," said Elias carefully, avoiding her eyes. "There are a few unmarried soldiers who will go to California with Anza and then come back. An armed escort. But only the families who remain in California as colonists will be supplied and equipped. To stay there, I mean."

"Then we aren't eligible, are we, Elias? We can't — "

Silence. Elias scrutinized the stream a few feet away. "We will be a family if we marry," he said softly.

She stared at him and began to smile. "Marry?!" she teased. "Marry each other? What a hideous fate!" And her laughter came tumbling out.

Suddenly they were in one another's arms, shouting with merriment. Elias swung her round and round, frightening the horses. And Gabriella, to her profound surprise, was ecstatically happy.

CHAPTER 12   Culiacán
                                                                            March 1775

Unknown to Gabriella, the California expedition was to bring about political intrigue more threatening to her welfare than any she might have encountered at the archbishop's palace. Also, the expedition would demand of her far more resourceful improvisation than had ever been required at the decaying Convent of Santa Clara. The individual who might have explained both to her was Juan Bautista de Anza, lieutenant colonel in the king's cavalry and the appointed leader of the expedition.

One afternoon in early spring, in the palm-shaded plaza at Culiacán, Colonel Anza stood waiting beside the derelict bandstand. Beside him flew a banner bearing the royal arms of Carlos III and around him gathered a tense group of barefoot *paisanos*, many in rags. At Anza's side, also in uniform, was Sergeant Juan Pablo Grijalva.

Anza was a tall, spare man in his thirties, with glittering black eyes, a neat goatee and a great prow of a nose. He was a third-generation frontiersman in service to the Spanish crown, widely known for his gallantry, courage and ability to restrain the Indians. Colonel Anza's grandfather had served thirty years in the frontier post of Tubac, located 450 miles north of Culiacán in an area later to be known as southern Arizona. Anza's father had served at the same presidio, but his life was cut short in the Apache wars.

Colonel Anza was the present commander there. He was eager to recruit the colonists he would lead to California and return with them in time to leave Tubac in late September. As he enlisted families in the farming communities of Sonora, his garrison to the north was scouring the neighboring rancheros, missions and settlements, gathering mounts and pack animals needed for the expedition.

"Maybe we'll get another family with nine children today, colonel," remarked Grijalva jovially.

"Let's hope not," replied Anza. "Five or six per family is more than enough."

With such swarms of children, no wonder the farm families are starving, thought the colonel. A comforting exception was the Sandoval family he had enlisted the day before. The mother of nine, suckling her two-month-old daughter, was sharp as pepper and tough as rawhide. If her husband made it alive through Apache country, she might easily honor him with another nine offspring once she reached California.

But the Sandovals were unusual, and so many juveniles made Anza uneasy. His career hinged on the success of this journey, and to ensure it, he had planned the minutest details, tried to foresee the unforeseeable. But who could foresee what children would do? Sicken and die along the way? Misbehave and torment the animals? Wander from camp and get lost? Whine and complain?

At least none will complain as loudly as Font, the bastard! An angry muscle twitched in the colonel's cheek. When the viceroy had notified him that Pedro Font would accompany the expedition as official chaplain, Anza had lost his temper.

"That self-righteous peacock!" he had exploded in Bucareli's office. "I shall have trials enough coaxing two hundred ignorant farm people and a thousand animals through the desert; why must I be weighed down with that ailing priest?"

"You forget yourself, Juan," the viceroy had replied softly.

Anza had, indeed, forgotten himself. No one, not even the king's favorite of the moment, talked that way to the Viceroy of Neuvo España, and he quickly apologized.

"Why do I recommend Pedro Font?" Bucareli continued. "Because he is a mathematician with the equipment and skill to take latitudes, my dear fellow. You have gone to enormous trouble to blaze this overland trail to the sea. It was your father's dream, you say. Surely you would agree it is important to have a record so it can be accurately traced on a map. Is that so unreasonable?"

Anza breathed deeply. "No, Excellency," he said.

Bucareli heard the suppressed fury in the officer's tone, and tossed the papers he was holding onto his desk. The viceroy respected Anza. No officer in the province saw issues more clearly or came straighter to the point in discussing them. What was troubling him?

"I fail to understand," Bucareli said plaintively. "Font is a clergyman like any other. I met him once. He seems agreeable enough. A pedagogue and a bit haughty, perhaps. But beautiful manners. Perfectly harmless. Yet you military men, one and all, loathe him to distraction. Why?"

"He is a pompous jackass," Anza replied evenly.

Suddenly Bucareli had the key. Font, born and educated in Europe, for ten years a professor at the College of Santa Cruz de Queretaro, considered himself a gentleman. "Ah, yes," the viceroy said with a smile. "He is a bit too proud of his education, his Spanish background. That's it, isn't it?"

"Perhaps it is merely that he has so little else to be proud of."

"Juan!" scolded Bucareli mildly. "Font is a man of God, after all!"

"With all due respect, sire, Font is a fool. Francisco Garcés is a man of God."

Bucareli threw back his head and shouted with laughter. "Francisco Garcés is a wild man! He eats locusts and honey in the wilderness like John the Baptist!"

"And he converts more Indians for Mother Church in a fortnight than Pedro Font will win in a lifetime."

Garcés was Anza's trusted neighbor from the mission at San Xavier del Bac north of Tubac. He had proved invaluable on the exploratory expedition to the coast the year before. Garcés knew the Indians, had lived among them — eaten, laughed and danced with them. Anza had hoped to have him again, this time as official diarist and religious administrator for the colonists.

But like it or not, Bucareli had saddled him with the ever-sickly, ever-critical Font, and Anza felt the reins of authority slipping in his grasp. Garcés would escort the colonists only as far as the Colorado River where he would conduct missionary work among the Indians until Anza's return. Or at least, that was the plan.

The excited crowd milling around the pavilion recalled Anza's attention and he mounted the steps. When the murmuring subsided, he spoke.

"Many of you know me already. I am Colonel Juan Bautista de Anza, here to address you by authority of his majesty King Carlos III. My mission is to enlist colonists to take part in an expedition to missions in Alta California, which lie some 1800 miles northwest of Culiacán. "For two hundred years, Spain has claimed the territory of upper California but so far, few Spanish citizens live there. The area is hard to reach by ship. Fog, stretching far out to sea, often hides the coast, and adverse winds and currents carry our galleons hundreds of miles off course. Every year, ships are lost and never heard from again.

"In spite of these difficulties, five years ago, our king sent Franciscan fathers to establish missions along the California coast. Their purpose was to bring the Christian faith to the docile Indians who live there, and in this the padres have been successful.

"His majesty has long wished for a way to reach Alta California by land, and now there is such a way. The trail is not an easy one because of the scarcity of water. Yet with proper care and supplies, colonists and their wives and children can be transported in safety. Last year, his majesty made it possible for me to travel this route with an expedition of armed men. I certify to you that once beyond the region of the Apaches, the Indian inhabitants along the way are friendly.

"I must tell you," he continued, "this is no journey for the sick or elderly. There will be hardships beyond their endurance. But for colonists able to withstand the difficulties, the rewards are great. They will receive free land and everything necessary to set up farming or ranching on locations of their choice.

"The land in California is rich. There is pasture — wild grasses cover rolling hills as far as the eye can see. There are great forests for lumber and rich river bottom land where fruit trees grow wild. As to the climate, on the lands near the coast, there is more rain than you have here, and the weather is cooler.

"Your king is aware that times are hard and that the farmers of Sonora live in poverty. He does not expect those who enlist to provide for themselves for this venture. My commissary officer is under instructions to supply food and clothing for all the men and women, and fabric to make clothing for the children. He will issue pots, pans, tents and eight blankets per family." Gasps and murmurs from the crowd. "Recruits will be provided with horses to ride and pack animals to carry their household goods." The murmurs became a clamor, which was quickly stilled. The listeners wanted to hear more.

"The first two weeks of our journey will be through territory inhabited by the Apaches. In case of attack, we will need men willing and equipped to fight. For that reason, most of the men will be enlisted as soldiers and will be issued military gear, including muskets and ammunition. These soldiers will be placed on the royal payroll and will begin receiving their salaries the day they sign up with their families." Exclamations of amazement. "Do you have any questions?"

A man stepped forward and bowed awkwardly. "Colonel, sire, how long on the trail? What I mean to ask is, what of women with babes on the way?"

"Your woman is expecting, is she?" asked Anza.

"Yes, sire."

The same question had been asked before, and it made Anza uncomfortable. To cut corners on the budget, he had listed himself as medical officer. From his command on the frontier, he was knowledgable enough about fevers and wounds. But he was childless, and anything bearing on midwifery or the ailments of children found him unprepared.

He answered the question as honestly as he could. "At times of childbirth, the expedition will halt for a day or two to allow the new mother to recover. Overlong delays cannot be allowed because our supplies are limited. We must leave Tubac in September and reach the coast by the first of the year."

The man seemed satisfied with the answer. Another stepped forward. "About the pack animals, sire. I have a good mule. Can I take her along?"

"Is she fit?"

"Fit enough, sire. She brought us three miles from the farm this morning."

"She'll be examined. If she is in good condition, yes, bring her. On the trail, she will be provided feed and will be corralled at night along with the other animals."

Another asked, "How many will there be, traveling?"

"We have allowed supplies for forty families," Anza answered. "Ten soldiers from the garrison at Tubac will escort the expedition to the coast and return with me. So will two padres and their servants."

A torrent of questions arose, which Anza interrupted.

"Tomorrow, my commissary officer and I will travel to other towns in this area. Some of you may want to think over the proposal I have made and talk to me on my return. Those who wish to talk to me today, please come to the alcalde's office across the plaza."

Anza nodded his head in dismissal and descended the pavilion steps. The crowd parted before him. The sergeant struck the royal banner and followed his commanding officer as he strode across the plaza toward the alcalde's office.

Half the barefoot, ragtag crowd followed in their wake.

Alamos
March 1775

As Colonel Anza enlisted colonists, the Figuroa caravan, far to the north, drew near the mountain mining town of Alamos. Their future there would be profoundly influenced by the alcalde, Ignazio Antonio y Fimberes Gónzales.

Don Ignazio was proud of his small city: While the entire colony of Nueva España lay paralyzed in economic depression, little Alamos prospered. Silver mines elsewhere had played out or flooded, but Alamos' abundant stream of silver bullion to Mexico seemed destined to flow forever. The king had designated his mines at Alamos the Royal Treasury; it was here that his silver ore was mined and his bullion refined.

Others besides the monarch owned silver mines nearby. Several palaces of wealthy silver lords lined the town's streets; its social life was Mexico in miniature with rigid protocol and even a distinguished *paseo*.

And now, to the mayor's gratification, the viceroy had at last sent to Alamos an official worthy of the community's economic rank. The newcomer's party was encamped for the evening three miles outside of town and Don Ignazio had planned a formal welcome.

His steed trimmed with ribbons and flowers, the flamboyant little mayor rode proudly at the head of a gala party composed of the town's officials. At the rear of the procession rumbled a gaily-painted cart decorated with flowers and overflowing with food and other gifts.

The mayor guided his horse to the Figuroa camp, dismounted and strode toward a worn, elderly gentleman struggling to his feet from a campstool beside the fire. With a flourish of his plumed tricorn, the mayor bowed low. "I am Ignazio Gónzales, Señor, alcalde of the city of Alamos," he said. "Don Avila Flores de Figuroa Beretta, it gives me great honor to bid you welcome on behalf of our citizens. We look forward with joy to having you and your family living among us!"

The courtly old man, obviously weary, bowed in return. Indicating the alcalde's festive procession, he said, "You offer me more respect than I deserve, Señor."

"Ah, but the personal representative of the viceroy and a relative of the queen deserves infinitely greater veneration than our small city is capable of bestowing, Don Avila."

"You are too kind, Señor. But I neglect my duty as host. Please allow me to present the members of my party."

Following the introductions, Don Avila continued. "I regret that you find us in traveling dress and unfit to receive you as propriety dictates."

"Do me the kindness of dismissing such a thought from your mind, Don Avila. Your journey from Mexico has been a long one, a fact which we residents of Alamos are in a special position to appreciate. My companions and I will tarry only long enough to present you with these few tokens of our good will."

Don Ignazio waved his hand and the cart, drawn by a garlanded donkey, was led forward for the inspection of the travelers. Their trail-weary eyes gladly noted the baskets overflowing with oranges, mangoes, grapes and melons; the hams and sausages; the hampers of wine and jugs of ale.

"We shall leave the cart and donkey with you," Don Ignazio informed them. "Much of what it contains is intended for your new residence, which is waiting in readiness. Tomorrow at daybreak, we shall send a carriage with footmen so that your ladies may be transported to the palace in an equipage more in accord with their taste.

"A fiesta has been planned in your honor upon your arrival tomorrow. In the plaza, there will be food and drink for all, with dancing and juggling and contests of athletic prowess. Tomorrow evening our priest, Padre Mendoza, will say a special mass of thanksgiving for your safe arrival."

Don Avila acknowledged this recital with a bow. "Your generosity reduces us to beggary, Señor, as we have no means at our disposal to reciprocate."

"Ah, but to reciprocate would demean our errand, Don Avila," the mayor protested, smiling. "And now, we understand your weariness at the end of your long journey. We will withdraw to allow you to refresh yourselves in privacy and prepare for the morrow." With a parting bow, Don Ignazio and his officials remounted and clattered down the trail toward Alamos.

If Don Avila had won several gold ounces in a card game, he could not have been more invigorated. The alcalde's visit left him standing two inches taller. A flush of exhilaration brought color to his cheek and eagerness to his eye. As always, his instinct was for the courtly gesture. He indicated the cart and announced, "We have not yet properly acknowledged the young lovers among us. Now that the means to celebrate has been so generously bestowed upon us, I herewith order a festive banquet in honor of the weddings to come!"

From the hampers, Miguel brought out crystal goblets together with the wine to fill them. Under Rita's supervision, he set out dishes and platters on the long trestle table. From the largess of fresh flowers, Ana fashioned tiaras for the honored ladies.

Seated at the table, Don Avila prompted round after round of toasts — to the brides-to-be, Bonita and Gabriella; to the husbands-to-be, Martín and Elias; to the alcalde; to Alamos; to the viceroy; to Colonel Anza; to California.

It was a leisurely meal. Gabriella rarely drank wine but on this occasion her brown eyes sparkled and her well-mannered, ladylike chuckles sometimes broke into open-throated laughter. As they lingered over walnuts and chocolate, Elias murmured in her ear. "I have a wedding gift for you." From his pocket, he produced on the table before her a rough stone the size of a baby's fist. It was a rich dark blue, veined and mottled with black — the color of the distant sea on a cloudless day.

"Elias!" she exclaimed, turning it in her hand. "How beautiful!"

"Martín says it's a turquoise," he said. "I found it beside the stream where the horses are picketed."

"No turquoise mines in this part of the world," Señor Neve remarked. "It had to come from far north and east of here."

Don Avila looked on with interest. "A traveler could have lost it," he said.

"This is an ancient trail we've been following. Coronado came this way. Indian traders too, in the time of Montezuma. The Aztecs traded a little of everything. A priest at the cathedral once told me that exotic birds by the thousand were raised at Montezuma's court for their feathers. The feathers were used for ceremonial robes, but also they were traded to the north for furs, clay pots, flint tips for arrows. Turquoise too, probably."

Gabriella held up the stone, admiring it. "Pity the poor trader who lost this."

The travelers lingered over wine. The sun sank behind the mountains. Martín and Bonita excused themselves. Elias and Gabriella exchanged glances. At her tent, she tucked the turquoise stone in her traveling case and together they slipped away.

"Poor Martín!" said Gabriella, laughter bubbling up. "He'll hear the terrifying details about the tarantula Bonita found in her camisole this morning."

Elias frowned. "Before she put it on, I hope!"

"If *after* she put it on, all the saints in Heaven would have heard her screaming!" He took her arm affectionately. After a pause she said, "You were worried, weren't you?"

"Of course! A tarantula doesn't deliver much of a bite, more like a stinging ant. But such a sight, for Bonita, might excite her too much."

"I'm glad you're here to worry about it."

He raised her chin and gently kissed her lips, smiled and held her close. The deepening twilight enfolded them, and the world seemed far away. Did she love Elias? She admitted she did not, but his gentle regard for her made up for so many of the hungers and fears in her life. He was loyal and strong, would always think of his wife and children first — a far greater boon in life than most women enjoyed.

Arms entwined, they walked slowly along the dim path.

"I'll be glad when we're married, Elias," she breathed.

"It won't be long now. Perhaps tomorrow." He stopped again and gazed critically at her faded crown of flowers. One by one, he began removing the wilted blooms. "Three hours ago, these were pretty. Not now."

Feeling his fingertips in her hair, Gabriella closed her eyes, relishing the moment. Thanks to Elias, her life during these last months had taken on a new dimension. To the silence of her loneliness, he had brought laughter and music. She pressed her cheek against his hand. "You are a gift from God, Elias," she murmured. "Thank you for the turquoise, but especially thank you for being so good to me."

"Come," he whispered huskily. "I want you to see Alamos."

"Alamos? It's an hour's ride from here!"

Elias shook his head and pointed to a ledge fifty feet above their heads. "We can see it from there. I explored the path this afternoon to make certain there were no Apaches. If we hurry, we can reach the ledge while there's still light to find our way."

Leading her by the hand, he climbed swiftly through a series of sharp turns, helping her along the steep shelves and boulders. In a few minutes, out of breath, they stood side by side on the high ledge. Far below lay their campsite with the horses picketed nearby. But Elias pointed in a different direction. Through a cleft in the mountains could be seen a toy village spread out across a valley.

Gabriella stared, spellbound. "That's Alamos?"

"Yes."

The town plaza was enclosed by a church and sturdy masonry buildings, their carved facades lit by torches. Leading off the plaza were narrow streets lined with adobe houses. Tiny figures hurried back and forth across the plaza, carrying boxes, erecting platforms, draping garlands among the trees.

"They're getting ready for the fiesta tomorrow," she whispered.

"Or for our wedding," Elias murmured. He shrugged out of his leather coat and hastily slapped the dust and gravel from the broad ledge. "No tarantulas," he announced lightly.

He spread his heavy jacket on the stone floor of the ledge. One arm beneath her shoulders and the other under her knees, he lifted her gently and knelt. Their lips joined as she lay back against the pungent leather. Desperately yearning, their bodies pressed together in an embrace both had denied for far too long.

"My dearest treasure," Elias murmured against her ear. "As husband and wife, I think we are going to be very happy."

"Yes," she agreed breathlessly, but an inner warning cooled the fire rising within her. They were not yet husband and wife.

She rose on one elbow to rearrange her clothing against the chill air of early evening. The campsite below, to her dismay, had disappeared in the gloom. "It's dark, Elias! How will we get back to camp?"

"The moon will rise soon. Last night it was full, remember? We will have plenty of light."

Close against the curve of his shoulder, she said gravely, "Elias, there's something I want to explain to you."

"Yes?"

"I don't know if I can make you understand."

"Try."

She took a deep breath and plunged. "When I was growing up at the convent, I worked very hard. Harder than anyone else."

"Because you were an orphan," Elias said softly, "with no family like the other girls. You felt yourself a person of no importance. And you worked hard and did all the proper things so that everyone would respect you anyway."

"Yes. I had to be responsible. You see, Elias, there was never a time when — when I could think something like the tarantula was funny."

Silence. "Not even when you were a little child?"

"I make it sound too grim. We had good times at the convent. We laughed. Sang. Played games. But — the one who led the games was always me. Nobody said I had to. It was just that once I started, the girls would say, 'Gabriella, what shall we play?' And I tried to think of games they'd like. So that each time someone new would have a chance to win. I tried to choose songs to sing that everyone would like, not too hard. Not too high or too low."

"Didn't anyone ever think about what *you* would like?"

"I'm sure they did. Maybe they did and I just don't remember."

"Weren't the nuns good to you? None of them ever blamed you because you were an orphan?"

"No, never. Everyone was good to me. Always. But — "

Sensing her mounting distress, Elias softly kissed her brow. "But what, Gabrielita?"

"Always I had to make sure the tarantula didn't hurt anyone, so I couldn't laugh. I had to be grown-up about it. There was never a time when I could think the tarantula was funny. Never till you."

The tears came then, tears of release and gratitude. He drew close in his arms the orphan girl who had never been a child. And that night, as the moon rose over the shoulder of the mountain behind them, both knew that as man and wife they would find a greater joy in one another than either had imagined possible.

CHAPTER 13   Alamos

"Gabriella!" Elias' cry, ringing with excitement, echoed through the stone corridors of the palace. "It's come! The message from Anza!"

Eagerly Gabriella ran to meet him. Their hopes, their dreams depended on this letter. Arms about one another's waists, they walked swiftly to their favorite hideaway on the south gallery. Gabriella broke the red seal with trembling fingers and began to read:

"Date: July 5, 1775
"From: Colonel Juan Bautista de Anza, Onavas, Sonora
"To: Elias Márquez, in care of Don Avila Flores de Figuroa, Beretta, Alamos

"Your application to join the expedition to Alta California is hereby approved. Your pay as a cavalryman of His Majesty's troops will commence immediately.

"When I was in Alamos, I spoke to you and to Señor Martín de Neve about an anticipated authorization from Mexico, which has now arrived. Recently at the presidio of Tubac, of which I am commander, Apache raiders made off with 500 expedition horses and mules which my men had been collecting for over a year. The loss of these animals is a serious setback, one we must rectify as quickly as possible.

"Your orders, therefore, are to gather as many assistants as you deem necessary and visit all ranches and settlements within a 50-mile radius of Alamos, buying as many horses and mules of good quality as possible. Bear in mind that these animals will be required to carry heavy loads over desert and mountain trails where sufficient water will not always be available.

"After you have purchased your mounts and are headed back to Alamos, you will be an especially attractive target for Apache warriors. Let me know by the bearer of this message when you will be transferring these animals from Alamos to Horcasitas. I will send military personnel as extra security, as you will be moving not only the livestock, but your wife and personal effects.

"Draw the funds necessary for this excursion from the paymaster, Don Avila de Figuroa. Separately I am sending him a requisition for the funds you will need.

"I wish to thank you for your assistance when I was in Alamos last month. It was generous of Don Avila to extend to my officers and me the hospitality of his palace, but I equally appreciated your aid with the colonists' encampment nearby.

"Please be advised, also, that your wife will be welcome for her convent experience in attending ailing mothers and their children. We have several pregnant wives traveling with us. I expect their infants will be born along the way to California. I welcome you and your wife to the expedition and convey my personal congratulations on your recent marriage.

"Juan Bautista de Anza, Lt. Col.
"Commander, Expedition to California"

Too happy for words, too happy even for tears, they exchanged a long wondering look. *This is our future in California, our opportunity, the life we'll build for ourselves and our children,* thought Gabriella. Almost reverently, Elias folded her in his arms to share the sacred moment together.

"We've been so lucky, my treasure!" breathed Elias. Yes, they had, Gabriella had to agree. Their marriage, the breathless nights they had shared together as man and wife, the storybook wonder of it all was certainly beyond anything Gabriella had ever dared hope for.

After a moment, she drew away. "How are we going to tell Don Avila?"

"Show him the letter and just — tell him," said Elias practically.

In Don Avila's office, they were a bit crestfallen at his response. "Your decision doesn't surprise me, you know," he told them, smiling. "We'll miss you. But Martín is my strong right arm. We'll get along comfortably enough."

When Martín heard of Elias' assignment to buy mounts for the expedition, he insisted on coming along. "You'll accomplish nothing alone," he told Elias bruskly. "The ranchers will only laugh at you, offer you a plate of beans for your lunch and send you on your way. We'll enlist a couple of the garrison soldiers and make a party of it."

Martín's arrogant way of handling matters as though Elias were a person of no consequence always infuriated Gabriella. She wanted to cry out to Martín, "Colonel Anza appointed my husband as head of the party, not you!" But Elias didn't need the burden of a shrewish wife, and she was determined not to saddle him with such a handicap. Instead, she turned affectionate eyes on Elias and said, "I'll start getting your things together."

Elias' party had been gone perhaps three weeks. One warm afternoon toward the end of July, Don Ignazio, the alcalde, found himself confronted in his neat office with two haughty but travel-worn gentlemen claiming to be relatives of Don Avila Flores de Figuroa Beretta. The mayor stared at the document they placed before him. "But — but Don Avila has been here scarcely four months!" he stammered, struggling to his feet. "And you are saying that already he is ordered to leave? Such a long trip —"

The two gentlemen might have been anybody. One claimed to be Don Avila's son from Jamaica and the other a cousin from Madrid. What convinced the mayor was the document. The large square of parchment stated that Don Avila Flores de Figuroa Beretta, together with his wife and daughter, was to leave Alamos immediately and proceed through Mexico to Vera Cruz and from thence by ship to Madrid. The document bore the seal of Carlos III.

The son (Alesandro, was that his name?) replied crisply, "Don Avila is needed at his majesty's court. That's all you need to know."

"But, Señor, in a few months there is to be a wedding," protested Don Ignazio. "It is my understanding that Señorita Bonita and Martín de Neve are to —"

"Plans for my sister's marriage do not concern you, Alcalde," interrupted Don Alesandro testily. "Nevertheless to forestall gossip, perhaps I should say her marriage has been arranged for quite some time. She is to be wed to a marquis from Seville."

Pause. "I see," murmured the alcalde, though uncertain if he did or not. The marquis from Seville must be incredibly rich. Either that or the stain on the de Neve escutcheon must be incredibly vile to interest Bucareli and even Carlos himself! Surely there must be more to the situation than that. Don Alesandro continued, "My cousin and I inform you of Don Avila's transfer to better acquaint you with our requirements and to command your assistance." He produced a piece of paper. "We must replenish our supplies before returning to Mexico tomorrow."

"Tomorrow!" exploded the alcalde. "But, Señor, your father is a frail old man! He will require —"

"Tomorrow," repeated Don Avila's son firmly. "Our train is camped just outside town where there is pasture for the horses and pack animals. This is a list of the supplies we will need. See that they are delivered to our campsite by sundown."

A glance at the paper horrified the little mayor. "The quantity! Señor, the expense of these provisions —"

Whereupon Alesandro de Figuroa Herédia produced a third document. "I have here an order from the viceroy, Antonio Bucareli, in Mexico. It commands Martín Felipé Mendoza de Neve Ortega to assume the post of the king's treasurer and paymaster being vacated by Don Avila. The new paymaster is authorized to disburse funds as necessary to defray the traveling expenses of Don Avila and his family."

The alcalde returned the document and coughed delicately. "Martín de Neve will regret having missed you," he said, straining at the understatement. "He is away, buying mounts for Colonel Anza's California expedition."

"When will he be back?"

"In a few days. A week, perhaps."

The two travelers exchanged glances. "If Martín de Neve is out of the way, so much the better," said Don Alesandro. To the mayor, he indicated the list. "Keep track of what you spend. There will be no difficulty collecting the money when the new paymaster returns."

Don Ignazio examined the list of supplies more carefully. "Suppose what you have written here cannot be had but a substitute is available. Where can you be reached to discuss the matter?"

"At the residence of Don Avila. Incidentally, where is it?"

Remembering the obligations of his office, the alcalde bowed. "Allow me the honor of personally escorting you to the palace."

"Is it nearby?" asked Don Alesandro, moving toward the door.

"But of course," said the mayor, pointing. "There. Just across the plaza. The most distinguished establishment in the city."

"Then an escort will not be necessary, Alcalde," said Don Alesandro. "Thank you for your trouble."

Trouble it would be, too, thought the alcalde as he watched them go. More trouble, even, than the upheavals of the month before when Alamos was overrun by Colonel Anza's California expedition traveling north to Horcasitas. The colonists had kept out of the way, the Madonna be thanked. But there had been incidents with the swaggering soldiers and especially the drunken *arrieros*, who accosted respectable women on the street.

Now the mayor studied the list of supplies, made notes, and hoped for the best. He sent word to his wife that he would not be home for dinner. Next he went to see the sergeant in charge of the town's tiny military garrison. The remainder of the morning and the entire afternoon he spent bullying fellow townsmen and shaming housewives to collect the provisions he wanted. He organized forays into the countryside and dragooned Indian porters to transport supplies to the Figuroa campsite on the outskirts of the town.

By sundown everything on the list had been procured and delivered except three pipes of wine, about which the alcalde refused to worry. He had noticed that the king's paymaster kept an ample supply of wine on hand. The Figuroa relatives need only apply to their host's wine cellar for as many pipes of wine as their mules could carry.

Don Ignazio was a man who liked to keep an eye on things, and especially on the mysterious affairs of Don Avila and his household. In the four months the Figuroa family had been in residence at Alamos, they had been something of a disappointment. Regular shipments of royal coin arrived at the paymaster's headquarters as expected. Emissaries from Colonel Anza came and went as expected. Two or three times a week, the ladies of the family, dressed in their finest gowns and most spectacular jewels, ventured out in the carriage for an afternoon's diversion at the *paseo*. But the town's socially prominent families who had hoped to entertain, and be entertained by, the new aristocracy had so far met with frustration.

They would have been even more so had they known the more intimate facts of Don Avila's menage. It was not the glittering household attended by footmen and grooms as the local people imagined. From Mexico, Don Avila brought with him a token staff of servants and, with the exception of a scullery girl supplied by the alcalde, hired no more. In the great banqueting hall, no sideboard displayed the family's awesome collection of toureens, salvers of precious metal or jeweled goblets of Venetian glass. Furthermore, the head of the Figuroa household was not Don Avila, a fragile and forgetful shell of a man, but Martín de Neve, the agreeable young military officer who was soon to become Don Avila's son-in-law. Or, at least, so everyone thought.

From this little scullery maid, the mayor also learned the real reason why Don Avila's lady, on the eve of her formal entry into Alamos, nodded off to sleep in the middle of the mayor's welcoming presentation. She was drunk. She was drunk during most of the journey from Mexico and she had been drunk ever since.

Another curious secret dropped into the ready ear of the alcalde was that during the height of the Alamos fiesta honoring Don Avila, his beautiful daughter Bonita was mysteriously hustled to her bedchamber at the palace where she remained, alone with her companion, for two days. Don Avila explained to officials that the girl was exhausted. But the little maid pointed to her temple and made cryptic circles.

As for the pretty redheaded bride, said the scullery girl, she had lately been suffering from morning sickness. *Morning sickness!* worried Don Ignazio, who with his wife had witnessed the marriage and found Gabriella and Elias a charming couple. *Perhaps they will change their minds about California.*

As dusk fell on the afternoon of Don Alesandro's arrival, the alcalde walked across the plaza to the palace. The courtyard gates stood open. Inside, the Figuroa footman Miguel was harnessing a team of husky mules to an ore wagon overflowing with baggage. Several porters, strangers to Don Ignazio, were loading a second wagon, bringing from the upper rooms a succession of carpet-wrapped bundles, wooden boxes, chests and trunks. Don Ignazio wondered if some of them had ever been unpacked.

To Don Alesandro, the alcalde explained about the wine and presented his list with a copy of the itemized bill which would later be presented to the new paymaster. "Please convey my respects to Don Avila," the mayor said. "I shall not interrupt him, as I realize he has much on his mind at present. Would you please notify him that the people of Alamos deeply regret that circumstances have cut short the time he might have spent among us. To him and his family, we wish Godspeed."

"I shall tell him," Don Alesandro replied. "On my father's behalf, I thank you. He has told me of the cordial welcome extended by you and the people of Alamos. It meant a great deal to him."

For once, words failed the mayor. In the deepening twilight, he nodded a farewell to Don Alesandro, and with downcast eyes departed.

So many unanswered questions left him sleepless that night, and the first crepuscular shades of dawn found him in his deserted office, staring at the palace across the plaza. Every window of the big building glowed with light. A bedchamber door on the second floor opened and onto the balcony stepped a slim woman dressed for traveling. That would be the daughter Bonita, perhaps seeking a moment alone under the glittering stars to whisper farewell to her absent lover. Don Ignazio was a romantic at heart and the sadness of it all stung his eyes and knotted his throat.

Someone called. The young woman returned to the room and closed the door. After a short wait, the courtyard doors were swung wide and a carriage emerged — delivering the women to the campsite, obviously. Don Ignazio could make out, inside the carriage, the silhouettes of three women: mother, daughter and — who? Not the redhead. Don Alesandro would never take a wife without the knowledge and consent of her husband, and the redhead's husband was away buying horses with Señor Neve. Not the cook, of course, since the travelers had their own cook. It must be the maidservant Ana.

The carriage skirted the plaza and made off down the narrow street that led to the campsite. Following in its wake were a half-dozen armed horsemen, some leading additional mounts. The courtyard gate was drawn shut behind them and the rustle of hoofs on the hardpacked earthen roadway faded to silence. At the palace, the windows darkened one by one. *Poor Señor Neve*, thought Don Ignazio, and went home to breakfast.

Later in the morning, the mayor sent a messenger to Señora Márquez. He offered his respects and asked if he could be of assistance in setting the palace to rights after Don Avila's whirlwind departure. She favored him with a written reply:

"Don Ignazio,

"Thank you for your kind offer. When my husband returns, I am sure he will confer with you about the furnishings of the palace. In Don Alesandro's haste to be off, he left some of the Figuroa belongings behind, and also mistakenly took a few items that should have remained here.

"Señor Neve and my husband are away from Alamos on business for Colonel Anza. They should be back in a few days.

"Respectfully,
"María Gabriella Salgado de Márquez."

The few days turned out to be less than forty-eight hours. The next morning, near noon, Don Ignazio glanced up from his desk to see, across the plaza, a half-dozen armed horsemen turning in at the gates of the palace. Recognizing Martín de Neve's dapple gray in the lead, the mayor sprang to his feet. Señor Neve drew behind him a chestnut gelding, riderless but bearing a long blanket-wrapped burden slung across the saddle.

"*Santa Madre!*" breathed the alcalde. Rushing out the door of his office, he flung instructions to his clerk. "Locate the padre. Tell him he's wanted at the palace. Immediately!"

Don Ignazio raced across the plaza and arrived in the courtyard to see Señora Márquez, frozen with shock, standing in the midst of the silent horsemen.

"It was an ambush," Señor Neve was explaining to her. "Our first thought was to save the horses we'd bought for Anza. Finally we chased the Apaches away. Only then did anybody wonder where Elias was. We found him with an arrow in his throat. He must have died instantly. He was already growing cold."

CHAPTER 14   August 1775
                                                        The California Coast

No one — neither Martín at Alamos nor Bucareli at the National Palace in Mexico, and certainly not Colonel Anza encamped at Horcasitas — had the faintest inkling that the expedition's intended destination, the San Francisco River emptying into the Pacific Ocean, did not exist. Yet as last rites were being said over the grave of Elias Márquez in Alamos, that stunning fact was being discovered on the coast of California.

The sun shone brightly on the sparkling sea as the little packet ship *San Carlos* rounded a promontory covered with barren hills. The captain on deck was unprepared for what unfolded before his eyes. Instead of parallel riverbanks confining a single flow of water, distant rocky shores stretched away in every direction.

"I don't believe it!" he murmured. "The viceroy said we would find a river here. That's where he's sending Anza with the expedition, to establish a presidio on the shores of the San Francisco River!"

"Then obviously we're in the wrong place," said the long-limbed, redheaded Franciscan friar at his side.

"You saw the chart!" exclaimed the captain. "It's the right location, no doubt of it. But *Santa María,* how could anyone mistake this — this gulf for a river?"

As the little craft cleared the headland, the captain was stunned at the mighty expanse of water spread out before them. "There's no harbor in the world this big!" he cried. "It's large enough to hold every ship asail on the seven seas!"

The friar was less sanguine. "We can't see the north shore. This headland could be an island, you know."

"Even so — !" The captain's experienced eyes took in everything — water currents, velocity of the waves breaking against the far rocky cliffs, arroyos in the mountains suggesting clearwater streams. "It's a bay, all right, Gómez. *The* bay! In 1570, 1580, around then, a Spanish explorer reported finding an anchorage like this."

"Drake said he found a harbor and named it the Bay of Saint Francis," ventured the friar. "But that was earlier, around 1550. Anyway, the bay Drake described was nothing like this."

"Drake!" spat the captain. "Who'd believe any claims of that English scum!" Spyglass to his eye, he scanned the shoreline. His excitement grew. "Think of the political advantage of controlling a place like this — the commercial possibilities, military defense, shipbuilding! The nation that commands this bay commands the entire west coast of the continent!"

The captain polished the spyglass lens with his handkerchief and handed it to Fray Gómez. "This is the harbor the visitador-general talked about. The story goes that Gálvez said to Junípero Serra, 'If Saint Francis wants a mission, let him show us his harbor and he shall have one.'"

The cleric smiled, glanced above at the heavens and crossed himself. "Then Saint Francis has honored us!"

"Indeed!" said the captain. "Gálvez can now rejoice. What puzzles me is why no one found it before."

"Who'd be likely to find it?" asked Fray Gómez. "Ships avoid the California coast. Treacherous winds, treacherous currents. You should know; you've braved them often enough!"

"Yes, and gotten blown off course and starved in the calms and wrecked by the currents and lost half my crew to scurvy because there was no safe place to come ashore for fresh meat. Not even at Monterey. In a gale, there's not enough shelter at Monterey to harbor a raft! Still, our Manila vessels have been up and down this coast a hundred times. Well out to sea, of course. But desperate for just such a refuge as this. Yet not one of them ever found it."

The friar looked over his shoulder and pointed behind them. "There's one reason. Look at the narrow opening."

Following his gaze, the captain agreed. "Hmm. And I see another reason. That fog bank out there. The long gray smudge along the horizon, see it? If it behaves like most fog banks, it will drift in to shore at sundown. Who knows? Maybe the opening stays hidden in fog most of the time."

"Now *that's* an uncomfortable idea," said the friar with mounting concern. " — Hidden from the land side as well as the ocean side, naturally. Let's leave while we can!"

"It's only hidden, Gómez," reassured the captain. "It doesn't disappear. Bucareli will want a report. While we're here, we'll chart this place from one end to the other."

The friar cleared his throat. "I am expected at the mission at Monterey, you know," he reminded the captain. "I'm needed there. My assignment —"

"All in good time, Brother Gómez. All in good time."

The friar rolled his eyes in frustration. The ongoing rivalry between religious and secular authorities was an old one; the secular won most of the skirmishes but Gómez, remembering that the religious nearly always won the wars, held his peace.

After a moment of reflection, he mused, "Sailors all over the world will laugh about it, you know. I can hear the taunts already. 'You Spaniards discovered the Bay of San Francisco, not that it did you any good. With all your other real estate to watch over, you mislaid it and two hundred years went by before you found it again. What a pity.'"

Eye glued to his spyglass, the seaman replied grimly, "It won't be mislaid this time, Fray Gómez, never fear. No, it will never be mislaid again."

Alamos
August 1775

Meanwhile at the palace in Alamos, with the loss of Don Avila, official business had slowed to a halt. It had now been ten days since the family had departed in the dusk of early morning. That inauspicious day was followed by one much worse: The convent orphan Gabriella had lost her husband to the savage Apaches, and Señor Neve, though he had ridden twenty miles in pursuit of his lost bride, had returned to Alamos two days later without her.

Within an hour of his second arrival, Señor had changed mounts, demanded provisions for a five-day journey on horseback, and left yet again. The clerks in the paymaster's office upstairs dozed and gossiped the days away. The young widow Gabriella, numbed with grief, kept to her room. She had shrunk and hidden within herself, searching for someone new to be now that her former self no longer existed.

Only in the cavernous kitchens below the palace, dungeon-like with their hoists, chains, spits, presses and ovens, was there any sign of life. The echoing rooms were sufficient to prepare meals for a battalion or two. Rita the cook, however — who the week before counted a mere fourteen stomachs to fill and was now further reduced to cooking for six — had partitioned off a small work area beneath the morning windows for her knives, pots, spoons and spices.

Rita the cook was a hunched, highstrung but capable farm woman of middle years, the wife of Miguel the footman. She had been the oldest of her parents' offspring but the last to marry. There had always been their crippled neighbor, Miguel Esala, but who would have Miguel? — Or so thought Rita and her father. Miguel had come with his family from the city. Trained from birth as a professional beggar, he had spent the first ten years of his life with one leg tied up to counterfeit an amputation. His pathetic aspect brought to his parents enough money to buy the small farm they owned but left the boy with a limp from which he never recovered.

Rita's younger brothers and sisters found spouses and began producing grandchildren. They humiliated their unmarried sister with mock sympathy and wry suggestions — bitter toxins which she hoarded against a day of vengeance.

For over a year, Rita and Miguel eyed one another at Sunday mass from pews on opposite sides of the village church before their fathers reached an agreement. Man and wife at last, they made their way to the city and established themselves as servants at Don Avila de Figuroa's palace known as Buena Suerte, from whose mighty walls Rita mightily snubbed her hated siblings.

Rita aimed higher. Bullying her rivals and perfecting her skills, she became head cook at Buena Suerte. Long before the orphan Gabriella Salgado joined the household, Rita told her husband Miguel, "Don Avila's fortune is disappearing down a rat hole. The relatives in Spain won't stand by and let it happen. Someone will come. You'll see."

She felt quite certain that loyal family retainers such as Rita and Miguel would be pensioned off, at the very least. Or taken along to Spain to continue in service to the aristocratic Figuroa family and its royal connections. And what would Rita's grubby brothers and sisters have to say *then*?!

But the family was exiled to a mountain wilderness and still no relatives had come from Spain. When at last they did, as Rita the cook had always known they would, they laughed at Miguel's request to be taken to Mexico with the family. Jeered at him! Rita's disappointment was as bitterest gall.

"There's others with worse disappointments than us," Miguel reminded her. "That orphan upstairs, now. Think of it. So poor in spirit she comforts herself with a rock!" Waiting to deliver Gabriella's breakfast tray, Miguel watched while Rita heated corn cakes on a *comal*, buttered them and arranged them on a plate.

"Yesterday you said she was sewing," said Rita.

"For the silly rock!" replied Miguel. "She's sewing a silk pouch for it. 'Broidered all over with little flowers and such!"

"Well. Keeps her fingers busy."

"Such a pity!" he sighed.

"She's young and healthy," Rita muttered. "Give her time. She'll be all right."

"She's not even sick in the mornings no more. You don't suppose the little one inside's dead like its father, do you?"

"A blessing if it is, I'd say," replied Rita. From the fire, she brought a small kettle of steaming chocolate and began whisking the contents. "A child's naught but a curse."

"Holy Mother, woman, you've a heart of stone!" Miguel cried over the racket. "Elias and the orphan girl, they had a real love match! She might want something of her husband to hold onto, hadn't you thought of that?"

"It's devilish hard for a woman alone to care for a babe, hadn't *you* thought of *that*?" Rita transferred the foaming chocolate to a pot and set it with the corn cakes on a tray. "She's got her memories. Lucky he died when he did. Love in a marriage don't last. Look at Don Avila. Flames for a year, ashes for thirty."

"O-ho!" chirped Miguel. "I notice it's not all ashes with you, old woman. I notice you flaming up every now and again."

"I'd flame up quicker and better was we on our way to Mexico with the family," Rita grumbled accusingly.

"*Santa Madre*, how you nag!" cried Miguel. "I did my best. You heard me ask Don Alesandro."

"Yes, I heard," said Rita, and the tears she brushed away were closer to despair than any she had ever shed. "Ana must've asked better than you since she's gone and we're stuck here."

She brought a fresh napkin from the linen chest and placed it, folded, on the breakfast tray. Hands on hips, she shook her head and with unsteady voice said, "She won't touch nought but the chocolate." Rita could face with courage the worst of life's ordeals, but her world crumbled to dust when food was returned to her kitchen untasted.

Understanding, Miguel stroked her arm. "Maybe today, my love. The child can't starve herself forever, now, can she?" He picked up the tray to deliver it.

Rita squared her shoulders. "At least the clerks'll eat. Lazy villains. While you're gone, I'll set them up in the servants' dining room."

A footstep drew their attention. "Señora!" exclaimed Miguel.

Gabriella wore a pale morning robe of pink gauze. Her face was drawn and pale, her step that of an invalid.

"I came for breakfast. Can I have breakfast now?"

Rita jerked her head at Miguel. "Take her upstairs. The sitting room off the courtyard. I cleaned it yesterday."

But Gabriella shook her head. "It's too lonely up there." She indicated an empty table. "Here. Could I eat here, Rita? Please?"

Miguel placed a stool and brought her tray. Gabriella whispered grace, nibbled experimentally and then began to consume her meal in earnest.

Restored, Rita straightened with a smile. "The clerks?" she reminded Miguel.

Gabriella seemed in no mood for conversation, so husband and wife murmured together as they worked. They served breakfast to the clerks and Rita set about the morning's chores.

"Señor Neve will be glad to see you feeling better, Señora," Rita remarked experimentally as she skimmed cream for churning.

"Where is he?"

"He rode north to Horcasitas to talk to Colonel Anza," said Rita. "Something to do with money, most likely. Señor Neve is the new treasurer and paymaster, you know. He's appointed to take Don Avila's place."

At length, Gabriella said, "I don't remember much about the day we buried Elias."

"Understandable. Your own husband and all. It was a nice funeral. The church was full, with people standing outside. Afterwards we went up on the mountain behind the palace for the burial. In the orchard there. Remember that part?"

"Not very well."

Miguel asked gently, "Would you like to see the grave, Señora?"

Rita glared at her husband. "Maybe she'd like another corn cake, or more bacon."

"I'm finished," said Gabriella, laying aside her napkin and rising. "Your breakfast tasted very good, Rita."

Miguel led the way through a network of passages to the rear entrance of the palace and up a flight of stone stairs.

The steep mountainside had been banked into terraces and planted with pear, peach and cherry trees. Miguel climbed to the top of the orchard and paused beside a mound of freshly-turned earth.

Gabriella expected to feel — what? — loss, grief, shock? But the sight was meaningless. A mound of earth. "I can't believe my husband is buried there," she told Miguel. "I can't believe he's gone."

"Maybe he isn't, Señora," murmured Miguel. "What I mean by that, he was a fine man, was Señor Elias. People will remember him for a long time. Life is sweet, and no one wants to die. But if die we must, it is good to go on living in people's hearts."

Gabriella nodded, only half understanding what he said, and glanced about. "Where are the flowers?"

"The day we buried him, the grave was covered with flowers, Señora. You remarked about them. Many brought bouquets and wreathes of sweet grasses. But they withered. Yesterday Rita took the dead flowers away. She didn't want you to see the grave uncared-for like that."

"There should be flowers."

"This afternoon, I can — " began Miguel.

Gabriella shook her head. "I'll do it. I need something to do."

"Señor Neve ordered a headstone," Miguel was saying. "He asked the padre what words should be on it. The stonecutter had to know, you see. What they decided was 'In loving memory.' Rita said she thought you might like that. Is it all right?"

Gabriella nodded. "Yes. That's very good, I think."

From the flagstoned courtyard below came the rattle of horses' hooves.

Martín de Neve on horseback, leading a pack animal, had entered the gate and was circling the fountain.

"There," said Miguel. "I'll be needed to take the horses. Best I hurry down."

Miguel's sudden movement attracted Martín's glance. From the courtyard he called, "Gabriella! Wait there! I want to talk to you!" Minutes later he strode up the path.

Gabriella recalled the night at the National Palace and her first exhilarating impression of Martín de Neve. Her enchantment had faded rather quickly. People of Martín's own rank found him charming, but to servants he was cold and demanding. He regarded Gabriella as a talented but not very trustworthy member of the household staff. From Ana, she learned he had even questioned Elias' decision to marry her. She had looked forward to her departure, with Elias, for California, leaving Martín and Bonita behind.

But now everything was changed. With Don Avila virtually a prisoner on the way to Mexico, who was her employer? Martín de Neve? She resolved to change that, too, as soon as possible! In the meantime, better watch herself.

While still some distance away, he called, "You're up and around, I see!" It sounded like a challenge.

He removed his dusty tricorn, drew his shirtsleeve across his perspiring face and surveyed her critically. "I talked to you before I left, but I don't think you understood anything I said."

"No, I'm sorry. Everything happened so fast." Indeed it had, thought Gabriella. Don Avila, on meeting his son after so many years, had fallen into a storm of penitent weeping; Doña Dolores had drunk herself into a coma; and Bonita had responded with the most destructive convulsion Gabriella had ever witnessed. With Ana, Rita and Miguel, she had packed as best she could in the confusion of the moment. Then, before recovering from the shock of losing the family, she was overwhelmed by the loss of her husband.

No, Gabriella recalled few of the details. "If you please, Señor Neve, maybe you would tell me again what you talked about before you left."

"Lieutenant Neve," he corrected her absently. "I'm going to California with Anza."

She heard the words but his meaning eluded her. She stared blankly.

He dropped his coat and hat on the grass and sat beside them. "You've never asked for particulars about Elias' death. Don't you care how he died?"

"Yes, I do. Very much."

"I was leading the column," he said. "I thought Elias was farther toward the rear with the men but they say no. Anyway the Apaches were unexpected — no warning at all. There were five, six of them. We'd planned many times, even practiced bunching the animals together and surrounding them, keeping them moving. We were armed, our pistols loaded.

"The attack lasted maybe five minutes. The Apaches were losing horses and men. So they — just — disappeared. When we were sure they'd gone, we couldn't find Elias. At first we thought maybe they'd taken him prisoner, but one of the men noticed his horse far back along the trail. He went to check and found him with the arrow — ."

He glanced at the raw new grave, picked up and thoughtfully crumbled a clod of earth. "I'm going to miss Elias. He was my friend."

"Mine, too." Tears brimmed in Gabriella's eyes.

Martín gazed at her curiously. "Funny you'd say that," he murmured. "Bonita and I thought you and Elias behaved more like father and daughter. I guess an orphan finds her parents where she can."

He knocked the dust from his hat and replaced it on his head. "Elias and I, we had it all planned, you know. Beautiful plans, all smashed. Bonita and I were coming to California later. Maybe Elias told you that."

For Gabriella, memories began to stir. "He mentioned it," she said. *And discounted the possibility. He thought Bonita's marriage would never take place.*

The lieutenant spoke idly, absorbed in his thoughts. "My uncle's been planning with the king for years about this venture. Carlos worries about the Russian settlers moving down from Alaska. They're coming, you know, for the fish, the timber, the fur. — Sealskins. To fend them off, Carlos wants thousands of families in California. This first project with Anza, it's a demonstration. To show others the land route is feasible. You and Elias were to go with Anza. Later, in a year or two, after Bonita and I were married, we planned to follow."

What would have happened once Martín learned of Bonita's frailty? Gabriella wondered. When she collapsed at the fiesta, Don Avila had kept him away, pleading his daughter's "nervous exhaustion."

"I'm sorry about Bonita," said Gabriella. "She loved you very much."

"We should have run away, Bonita and I. We could have talked a padre somewhere into marrying us. We could have disappeared — vanished — and started over in Peru. Or better still, one of the British colonies. Virginia maybe, or Massachusetts."

"Don Avila would have found you," said Gabriella. "He wouldn't have let Bonita slip away like that."

Lieutenant Neve clenched his fist. "And that's exactly what *I* did, *I* let her slip away!" His voice grew harsh. "She is to marry Emilio de Obregon, a pockmarked old nobleman with the soul of a sewer rat. He's so wealthy he secretly loans money to Carlos III and two or three other monarchs besides! He owns sixteen palaces scattered over Europe, so many he forgets where they are. There are some he's never seen." He swallowed a sob and ducked his head. Through clenched jaws he said, "Bonita will be his third wife. The first two died."

The lieutenant stood and went to Elias' grave. He gave the soft earth a nudge with his booted toe. He looked tired and worn. Gabriella said, "You've had a long ride, Señor. Probably Rita has hot food waiting — "

"Later," he interrupted. "First there are things I need to tell you and I don't want the others overhearing." He paced and talked. "I found Anza at Horcasitas. Colonists were camped in the plaza, about thirty families. I reported to Anza about Elias and the mounts we were able to buy, maybe a hundred head. I'll be taking them along to Horcasitas with muleteers hired here in Alamos.

"I managed to convince Anza that after the colonists move north, there's no more need for a treasurer and paymaster at Alamos. Supplies and equipment will all be paid for by then. Coin for meeting payroll will go with Anza. He could use me better with the expedition than paying me to sit and do nothing here at Alamos. So Anza is sending a request to Bucareli to let me close the paymaster's office and go with him as regular military personnel with the rank of lieutenant."

"But after your plans with Bonita —. Without her, do you really want to go?"

Angrily he cried, "Holy Mary, why wouldn't I want to go? It's better than staying cooped up here where every room, every flower reminds me of the filthy pimps who took my Bonita to sell to the highest bidder!" His voice threatened to break and he turned his back on Gabriella.

After a long pause, she asked, "What about the clerks?"

"Anza authorized their expenses back to Mexico. They can go with one of the silver trains."

A pause. "What about me?"

"Anza says Miguel and Rita can come along to California if they like."

"Lieutenant?"

"What about you? Yes." He turned to face her, not bothering to hide his disapproval. "What Anza really needs, with that many people, is a medical staff — a doctor and a *yerbera* who knows medicines and dosages and perhaps a *partera*, a midwife. At the very least, he needs an experienced nurse who can do a little of everything. It looks as though there will be over two hundred people, counting the mounted escort, muleteers, everyone. And over half are children!" He cast his eyes heavenward. "*Santa Madre de Dio!*" he muttered, shaken with dread of the military difficulties involved. "No one on Anza's staff knows how to take care of sick children. Every time the commander talks about it, that big nose of his turns white. And he certainly doesn't know how to take care of pregnant women. Some will give birth before the expedition reaches California. If any of those babies survive, it will be a miracle."

He interrupted himself. "Isn't there something a pregnant woman can do if she doesn't want the baby?"

Shocked, Gabriella stared. "Murder her child? Is that what you mean? Yes, but it's a mortal sin. Her penance would —. How could a woman live with herself, if she murdered her own child?"

"According to Anza, there are a few of the *paisanas* who wanted to go on the expedition but felt they couldn't because of a baby coming. They're the ones who asked, not me. But you say yes, there is something that can be done."

Reluctantly, she answered, "There's a potion made with savin. Any *yerbera* can mix it. Once at the convent, a farm girl was pregnant because of a rape. Madre Valderia asked the archbishop for a dispensation. But there's agonizing pain and hemorrhaging. Recovery is slow. A month or maybe two."

"A woman couldn't take this remedy one day and get back on a horse and ride the next?"

"It could kill her."

The lieutenant shrugged, dismissing the subject. "From the beginning, when Elias first talked to Anza, the commander wanted you as the expedition *enfermera*. In fact, the thing he talked about almost entirely, when I was with him a few days ago, was you. He knew about Elias, of course. I told him how young you are and how little experience you've had. He nearly exploded. He wanted to know about the people you treated before you left the convent. I didn't know. But I said there's no doctor at Alamos and you'd treated some children here. 'Did they get well?' That's what Anza kept asking, 'Did they get well?' He's uneasy about taking a lone woman along at all, let alone giving her that much responsibility. But even without Elias, he needs you.

"Because of your age, he must put you under the protection of someone and the logical person is Padre Font, chaplain of the expedition. The chaplain's tent is large — for holding mass, hearing confessions, things like that. Padre Font and his servants will eat and sleep in this tent. You'd be the only woman and it might get lonely for you. One of the other servants is supposed to be a cook so hopefully you wouldn't be called on to prepare meals. But you shouldn't count on it. "The biggest problem is Padre Font. From what Anza says, he's disagreeable. Gives himself mighty airs. He's very critical, very superior."

Like you, Gabriella almost said. Instead she said, "Priests *are* superior."

"Superior to God?"

"Well, no, not — "

"Anyway, Anza wants you on the expedition. But if you come, you'd be under the thumb of this chaplain who is hard to get along with."

"Maybe I'd get along with him better than Anza."

"Possibly."

A pause. "Lieutenant Neve, I haven't really thought much about what I would do. Now I see that — . Suppose I went on the expedition, without Elias. What about after I got to California? I mean, a widow alone, could I expect — ?"

"To get married, yes."

"That's not what I meant."

"I know it's not what you meant. You haven't been a widow very long. A woman alone, well, face it: The law doesn't allow a woman to own property — other than that bequeathed by her husband. And of course Elias didn't have any property to bequeath, did he? A woman can't even inherit from her own father unless there's a husband or brother to take responsibility for her." He waved the subject away. "But this won't be a problem once you get to California. There are plenty of lonely soldiers in the garrisons over there. The padres will find a suitable husband for you."

"I was thinking of opening a clinic or a school."

"That would be up to your husband."

Gabriella bit her lip. "Actually, Colonel Anza may not want to take me to California. I'm — I'm pregnant. I'm carrying Elias' child. It will be born in January."

"I suspected it," muttered the lieutenant. "Something Miguel said."

Another silence.

"Lieutenant Neve," said Gabriella, "Even before Elias and I were married, I wanted to go to California! Even more, now with the baby, I'd still like to go. There's no future for the baby and me in Mexico. I have no family there. But on the frontier, things like that won't matter so much. In California, the baby and I would both have a chance."

"Then go."

"But Anza won't allow it if he knows I'm pregnant. You know he won't."

"Don't tell him."

A gasp. "Deceive him?"

"What deceit? You aren't incapacitated. He wants someone to care for the sick women and children. Will being pregnant keep you from attending to the sick along the way?"

"No."

"Then you'd be living up to your part of the bargain. So forget you're carrying a child. You don't look it."

"But before we get to California, he'll know."

"And what can he do about it then, hundreds of miles from nowhere? Send you back?"

Gabriella kneaded her hands, then shook her head. "I couldn't do it without his knowledge. What would Reverend Mother say? It's too dishonest."

The lieutenant cried, "It was that damned convent rectitude of yours that got you into this mess in the first place! You could have stayed comfortably in Mexico but you thought Don Avila needed you! Listen to me, my girl! Your precious Madre is a thousand miles away. You are an orphan with no family. You are a widow, alone in the world with an infant on the way.

"Your survival is at stake here, the survival of you and your child. So I have some advice for you: You'd best forget your dainty little convent code of honor that demands that you do this and demands that you do that. Where you're going —

wherever it turns out to be — that way of thinking will do you a great deal of harm and no good whatever!" He snatched up his coat from where it lay on the ground.

Gabriella squared her shoulders. "I am not alone in the world, Lieutenant Neve. I have a home at the convent of Santa Clara any time I want."

"Fine! Then go there!" And he strode off down the hill.

CHAPTER 15   Convent of Santa Clare de Asís
                                            August 1775

"You're talking nonsense, Raoul!" Madre Valderia's wideset black eyes blazed with anger. "Why isn't Gabriella on her way back to Mexico with Don Avila?"

"My dear Luz," Monsignor Mero tried to sooth her, "the day Don Alesandro took his parents from Alamos, Gabriella was a married woman. She wrote you herself about her marriage to Elias."

"Answer my question," ordered the abbess through clenched teeth. "Why is she still in Alamos?"

"*Because that's where she wants to be!*" shouted the exasperated priest, instantly checking over his shoulder to make certain the office door was closed. He tried to control his quivering jowls. "Luz, please. This is as difficult for me as it is for you. The messenger arrived late last night. I came as soon as I could."

"That has nothing to do with anything!"

"Luz, Elias is *dead!*"

The silent air was tense with disbelief. The abbess squinted. "You're lying."

It took several minutes for Monsignor Mero to sort out his information to Reverend Mother's satisfaction. How could Elias possibly be dead? The Apaches. Was Elias protecting Don Avila's son from the Apaches? No, Elias and the Apaches had nothing to do with Don Avila's son. The message was sent from Culiacán. Why Culiacán? The Figuroa caravan had traveled that far beforeBonita could persuade her brother to send a message. Why persuade? Was she a prisoner? Yes. The family was kidnapped.

The abbess threw up her hands. "You've gone mad!" she pronounced.

"You don't believe me? Here," urged Monsignor Mero. "I brought the message with me. Read it."

"My father is no longer himself," Bonita had written. "Alesandro trusts him with no one, not even Gabriella. My brother agreed to bring Ana from Alamos only when he realized I could not care for both my parents. I thought you would want to send for Gabriella since she is now alone."

A few more minutes were required for the abbess to completely absorb the situation. At last she slammed the message down on the desk. "A pretty fix!" She reflected a moment longer. "Of course, she must be sent for. The sooner, the better."

"Perhaps we can organize a party in the city," Monsignor ventured. "There should be a trustworthy priest available to undertake a mission of that kind. In fact, I think I know of two or three possibilities. I will see what I can do."

"What about you? I should think you'd be the logical one to lead a rescue party."

Monsignor squirmed. "Doña Teresa expects me to officiate at the christening of her tenth grandchild. She says the archbishop has been invited to attend. The christening is to take place in three weeks."

"Then the christening will have to be postponed."

"The father of the baby is scheduled to sail for Spain. The date cannot be postponed."

"Very well, christen the child tomorrow and let's get on with more important affairs!"

"Doña Teresa says two of the baby's aunts and the other grandparents must be summoned from Vera Cruz. They cannot get here sooner than three weeks."

Reverend Mother folded her arms over her heavy breasts. "Then surely," she said grimly, "with a city full of priests, Teresa can find someone else to christen her tenth grandchild."

Guilt shadowing his face, Monsignor said, "I am told the baby's mother insists she wants me and no one else to baptize her child."

A silence. In years past, all five of the Costanza daughters, one after the other, had been students at Santa Clara. The mother of the five daughters, Doña María Teresa Gracés de Costanza, was a generous patroness of the convent and well known to the abbess. But not well enough, apparently. Why was she placing these obstacles in the way? What was she up to?

Frowning, Madre Valderia heaved to her feet. "But Teresa agrees that after her grandchild is christened in three weeks, you will be free to head this caravan for Alamos?"

"Yes."

"At her expense?"

"Oh, yes. Or mine. It doesn't matter."

"Can a messenger be sent now, notifying Gabriella you're coming?"

"Oh, indeed! Yes! An excellent idea, Luz! Excellent! I'll dispatch a messenger the minute I return to the city."

Alamos
August, 1775

Without a word to anyone, Lieutenant Neve abruptly packed his personal belongings, closed out the paymaster records, sealed them and sent them to Mexico with the clerks. Then he hired muleteers, supplied his train for the journey north and set out with the hundred horses and mules to rendezvous with the expedition, already encamped at Horcasitas.

Gabriella's bravado to Lieutenant Neve concerning her home at the convent began to fade as soon as the proud words left her lips. What echoed in her mind was his remark about the survival of her child. Could she, pregnant, weather the trek north through the wilderness, braving hostile Indians? Or was it wiser, for the sake of the baby, to return to the safety of Mexico?

With California actually within reach, her desire was stronger than ever. Nevertheless after a prayer for guidance at her husband's grave and a thoughtful stroll down the mountainside to the palace, she knew the safest place for Elias' baby was in the capable hands of Sister Magdalena at the convent. She would return to Mexico.

Minutes later she found Miguel in the kitchen turning the spit at the hearth while Rita removed pastries from the oven. Rita called without ceremony, "Señora! We decided to go, Miguel and me."

"Señor Martín says the colonel will take us," crowed Miguel, clearly delighted.

Knowing of the couple's contempt for farmers and farming, Gabriella asked skeptically, "You're going to California to sow seed and raise crops?"

"I've not forgotten how," Miguel declared. "We'll have the best farm in California!"

"Listen to him!" scoffed Rita. "He can milk his cows and gather his eggs. Me, I'll cook for the fathers at the mission. A good cook never goes hungry!"

Busy with plans of their own, they gave Gabriella no chance to speak of hers. She would have welcomed their advice. The morning was young so she sought out the alcalde in his office. Did Don Ignazio know of any ladies who would be traveling to Mexico within the next month? No....She had a little money; could guards be hired who would take her to Mexico? No. The money needed was far more than she could supply, and anyway, he would never give his permission for such a project. Her reputation would be forever compromised traveling such a distance unchaperoned with a group of men....Then the only alternative was to send word for her people in Mexico to come fetch her. This would take four to six months. Did the alcalde know of a household where she could make herself useful as a companion or governess until spring?

The alcalde immediately thought of his wife and two teen-age daughters. But not only had this lovely redhead been married, she was pregnant; his wife most certainly would not approve such a governess for their daughters.

Don Ignazio promised to see what he could do. Scarcely encouraged, Gabriella returned to the palace and took stock of her belongings: her valuable turquoise stone that Elias had given her; six months' wages in coin, held for her in the vault adjacent to the paymaster's office; her personal wardrobe, mostly servicable; a few bits of jewelry, none valuable; a supply of splints, bandages, scissors, scalpels, tweezers, vials, cruets and other medical equipment; a dwindling supply of oils, powders, tinctures, dried herbs and remedies. Even if Elias were still alive, she reflected, she was not prepared to go to California as Anza's *enfermera* for an expedition of thirty families. And a pregnant woman sharing a tent with a priest was too shocking to consider.

"Before Elias died, you wanted to go to California," said Rita that night as they sat talking in the kitchen.

"With Elias to help me, there was little to worry about," said Gabriella. "We'd have had our own shelter. When I was too tired, he could bandage cuts and measure out cough medicine. But without him — and the baby on the way, —

living in the same tent with a *priest!*! — It wouldn't work out, that's all. It would never work out."

"Why do you have to live in the same tent with the priest? You could share our tent with us. If Anza insists on only immediate families living together, maybe he'd let us claim you for a sister."

"I'd get so tired, Rita," said Gabriella. "The last days before the baby comes are exhausting. I don't know if — "

"Couldn't you tell Rita what to do?" asked Miguel. "Couldn't she help when you are too tired?"

"No matter what the colonel decides, the *paisanos* need you for doctoring," insisted Rita. "I'll help with the sick babies. My broth will cure them. My broth will bring a horseshoe to life."

"As for the rest," Miguel continued, "Anza will already have medical supplies. Not enough, maybe. Maybe not the right kind. Let's ask the alcalde. If there's expense, he'll collect from Anza."

"And in return for my help with the sick, Gabriella will help me cook!" cried Rita, her enthusiasm growing. "We'll eat better at our campfire than the colonel himself!"

And so in the cheerful firelit kitchen in the palace at Alamos, Gabriella found herself planning to do what she wanted to do all along. They must be off as soon as possible, for the expedition was due to leave Horcasitas in early September.

By noon next day, the alcalde had been consulted and was gathering medical supplies. He had given their plans his qualified blessing. The footman Miguel Esala and his wife would do well in California. But the pretty young widow — pregnant! — undertaking such a journey with no male relative to protect her left him frowning with apprehension.

That afternoon, the alcalde went to the palace to deliver several bundles of supplies but could rouse no one. He wandered hallooing through thirty rooms before exploring the lower levels where he found Señora Márquez, Señor and Señora Esala enjoying dinner together in the kitchen. Invited to share their meal, he swallowed his pride of station and sat among them gladly, for the cook's reputation was well-known in Alamos.

"I brought a gift for you," he said to Gabriella, handing her a neatly wrapped parcel. Removing the paper, she found two tent-like maternity frocks, beautifully trimmed with embroidery and braid. "My wife sent them with her regards," explained the alcalde. "She says you will need them later on."

"She's the kindest lady in Christendom!" cried Gabriella. "Please tell Señora how much I appreciate her gift! She is very generous and thoughtful."

"She instructed me to inquire about your shoes. She says your journey will be long and hard, and ladies will require heavy boots the same as the men. She says also there will be no shoemakers in California as there are here in Alamos. She says if she can be of assistance in providing you with the extra footgear you will require, she will be glad to help."

Gabriella and Rita exchanged relieved glances. "We are deeply grateful to her for reminding us, Señor," said Gabriella. "Again, we are indebted to your wife."

Don Ignazio asked Miguel, "You are armed against the Apaches?"

"Señor Neve lent me a sword," replied Miguel uncertainly.

The mayor closed his eyes and opened them again. "Well, against the Apaches, I suppose a sword is better protection than a packet of pins, but what you need are firearms and plenty of ammunition. If you are not well armed, the savages will rip out your guts while you watch, toast them over a hot fire and make you eat them. The women will get off more easily. They will merely be taken as slaves."

The travelers froze with dismay, as Don Ignazio intended they should. The discussion ended with the alcalde assigning two armed guards from his garrison to escort the party to Horcasitas.

Two days later, with footwear, arms and ammunition, the guards helped Miguel lash the travelers' baggage and supplies on the dozen pack mules. The palace keys were turned over to the alcalde, Miguel mounted his chestnut gelding and they were off.

All were glad to leave Alamos, the scene of so much sorrow. Rita and Miguel accepted Gabriella for what she was, a convent girl who had married too young and still needed the caring eye of sympathetic adults from time to time.

The trail that the little party took north seldom left the mountains. Every ten to fifteen miles, the landscape was marked by great trampled areas, littered and desolate, where Anza's colonists had camped the month before. Foul-smelling trenches, insufficiently refilled with earth, remained from the expedition's *excusadas*. Forage was grazed to the roots, as had been the pastures at Alamos after the colonists departed.

Miguel and the guards avoided the expedition campsites and sought, instead, overnight situations of their own. The streams were dry this time of year and natural tanques of rainwater among the mountain rocks had been drunk dry by Colonel Anza's livestock. Rita and Gabriella helped dig shallow *pozos* — wells two to three feet deep, in the dry stream beds. Gradually they filled with pure sweet water for the horses and mules.

Late in the afternoon of the fourth day, the travelers saw on a rise ahead the palms and spires of Horcasitas, ancient capital of Sonora. Gabriella dreaded her meeting with Colonel Anza. Instinct warned her to tell the commander of the baby she was expecting, even though Miguel and Rita, like Lieutenant Neve, saw no need. She longed for the interview to be over and everything settled.

The whole town of Horcasitas seemed to swarm with busy people. The colonists' encampment occupied the tree-shaded plaza and spilled over into neighboring streets. At one end of the plaza, situated on an elevation, was the baroque church, pillared and pitted with scars where the centuries-old plaster had fallen away. Nearby was the camp's headquarters tent with its banner bearing the royal coat of arms.

Most of the male colonists had been issued soldiers' uniforms, and as they worked and conferred with one another on the streets surrounding the plaza, wore random articles of military apparel. The children wore garments sewed by their mothers from cloth issued by the commissary officer, one bolt of cloth per mother. Toddlers and older boys and girls, laughing and swooping bird-like to chase their friends, sometimes came together in flocks of one color, brothers and sisters of the same family unit.

Each family had improvised its own shelter from blankets, cactus ribs, lumber or palm thatch. As Miguel's party approached, most of the encampment had finished dinner. Women joked back and forth as they scoured pots and put away leftover food. The men gathered to gossip or play cards.

The gathering was more than twice the size of the group they had seen at Alamos. Rita, bewildered, asked, "Who are all these people?"

"This is the expedition," replied Miguel. "They're going to California."

"*All* of these people are going to California?"

"And Señor Neve says sixty more are waiting at Tubac."

"Where's Tubac?" asked Rita.

"Up north somewhere." Miguel was examining a uniformed sergeant approaching to meet them. Over regulation pants and boots he wore a *cueras,* the frontier soldier's famous knee-length jacket made of seven thicknesses of cured deerhide. Miguel noted the pockets and red flannel lining, and hoped desperately that the commissary officer would issue him one. A *cueras* was known to be warm and waterproof; it could serve as a blanket or a tent as well as armor against Apache arrows. In emergencies, the leather could be used to improvise shoes, water bottles and harness. If the emergency was dire enough, it was said, the whole thing could be boiled and eaten!

"You must be Lieutenant Neve's party from Alamos," said the sergeant. He was a short, stocky man, weathered and abrupt, who introduced himself as Juan Pablo Grijalva. He showed Miguel where to picket his party's mounts and then led them to the large headquarters tent.

"Lieutenant Neve is with the *arrieros* outside of town," the sergeant explained. "There's a big valley where the livestock are being held. Lieutenant has his own tent out there. You can see him tomorrow. He comes in every morning to report to Colonel Anza."

Gabriella had expected someone older than the tall cavalry commander who rose from his desk to greet them. Jet-black hair fell to Colonel Anza's shoulders, and a forest of black beard covered the lower half of his face. Barely visible were his lips, now wearing a warm smile that softened the harshness of his beak-like nose and smoldering black eyes.

"Señora Márquez?"

"Yes, Señor."

"It is good to see you've arrived safely. Your services are needed. I regret to say the mothers bring their children to us with colic and toothache and there is little we can do to help them."

He sent a messenger for the chaplain, explaining that "Padre arrived only yesterday from the mission at Ures, where he has been waiting."

Gabriella presented Miguel and Rita. "Lieutenant Neve brought us your message that a place would be saved for Señor Miguel Esala and his wife" she explained. "Señora Esala was chief cook for many years at Don Avila de Figuroa's palace in Mexico."

Rita curtsied respectfully.

"Indeed?" said Colonel Anza, immediately interested. "We are losing our headquarters cook. He agreed to come only as far north as Horcasitas. If Señora Esala and her husband would be willing to take his place — ?"

Rita, beaming, exchanged a delighted glance with Miguel. Prompted, he bowed low and replied, "Quite willing, Señor."

" — Then this is a lucky day for us," continued the commander. "Sergeant, we have a new cook. Find room for Señor Esala's party somewhere nearby. If you need to move one of the other families, offer them a side of bacon with my compliments."

From a desk at the other side of the tent, a corporal beckoned. "Señor Esala, there are some papers here for you to sign. Then I will issue your gear and supplies."

At Anza's invitation, Gabriella seated herself beside his desk. "Please accept my sympathy on the death of your husband, Señora. The Apaches are a treacherous foe. They prize horses above all else; on a raid, they will make short work of anyone who stands in their way."

The sergeant approached the colonel's desk. "Here is Padre Font, Colonel."

A mottled, wasted Franciscan friar entered the tent, walking with the aid of a staff. Wisps of white hair stood out like wings behind his ears and the musty stench of failing health surrounded him like an aura. He was a man of great dignity with a jutting brow and narrow delicate hands.

"I'm glad you could come, Padre," Colonel Anza greeted him.

Ignoring Anza, Padre Font remarked, "So this is the young woman from the convent." There was a musical, caressing quality to his voice. Noticing Gabriella's unusual coloring, he asked, "Your parents are European, are they?"

"No, Padre. My mother was *criollo*. I was born and grew up at the convent of Santa Clara de Asís, just outside Mexico."

The welcoming smile faded from Padre Font's lips. He fastidiously raised his eyebrows and looked away. "I understand." His tone left no doubt as to what it was that he understood, and Gabriella's cheeks burned with humiliation.

He questioned her delicately. "The convent of Santa Clara, you say? I have heard many discussions of the religious establishments in the valley, but I never heard of the convent of Santa Clara de Asís. Perhaps it is only a coincidence."

"Probably so, Padre," murmured Gabriella.

"And you are Señora Márquez, a widow?"

"Yes, Padre."

"And you claim to cure sick people?"

Claim?

Gabriella replied evenly, "I have never claimed anything for myself, Padre. At the convent, I was put to study with Sister Magdalena, our *enfermera*. She taught me many things. With God's help — and hers — I was sometimes able to promote healing among the *paisanos* and their families who came to the convent for help."

"You are very young to be healing the sick. I should think a more pressing occupation for a young woman in your situation would be finding a new husband."

Colonel Anza broke in harshly. "Señora Márquez' husband was killed by the Apaches scarcely a month ago. He was under my orders, requisitioning mounts for the expedition. She is capable of judging for herself when she is ready to search for a new husband."

The priest held up a reproachful hand. "My dear Colonel, I know what I am doing here. You who deal at all times with soldiers could not be expected to know in what ways the devil tempts those of the weaker sex. There is a matter here that must be settled." He turned again to Gabriella. "Could it be, my dear, that your healing sometimes involves magic potions and incantations?"

This is an evil man, Gabriella realized, a*nd it makes not a particle of difference that he is a man of God.*

"I'm afraid I know nothing of such things, Padre, unless by incantations you mean prayer," she said. "At the convent, I was taught by the sisters always to pray for those who suffer."

She made a quick decision. "However, yes, Padre, there is a matter here that must be settled. I'm sorry that I have not yet had an opportunity to inform the colonel that I am carrying my husband's child. My baby will be born in early January. Under those circumstances, Colonel Anza, though I hope very much to be allowed to come along on the expedition with my friends Miguel Esala and his wife, I do not believe it is appropriate for me to serve the expedition as you planned. Thus I'm sure you will agree, Padre Font, that it will be impossible for me to join your personal staff."

Silence. The sounds of children playing outside the tent, and even the faraway clang of a dropped kettle seemed unnaturally loud. Colonel Anza stood staring at Padre Font with a look of raw hatred.

The Franciscan was unaware of it, for he, in turn, was gazing intently at Gabriella, one corner of his thin lips raised as though undecided whether to be pleased.

At length he said softly, "Thank you, Señora Márquez, for delivering us both from an embarrassing situation." Nodding absently to himself, he turned and, with the aid of his staff, slowly hobbled from the tent.

CHAPTER 16

Horcasitas, Sonora
September, 1775

Gabriella and her friends had been at Horcasitas a week when early one morning the expedition's livestock stampeded. A general alarm was sounded. Even the townsmen saddled their horses and went to help round up over a thousand horses, mules and cattle.

Suddenly the camp seemed deserted. At the church on its eminence above the plaza, Padre Font opened the doors for early mass.

"There won't be many to pray this morning," Rita muttered.

Gabriella had a special reason to pray. She had not been feeling well and was worried about the baby she carried. Still, she felt no urge to disagree with Rita. Even on the best of days, Padre Font attracted few worshipers. He whispered the service as though sharing secrets with his thumbs. The one time she had gone for confession, he had badgered her about mysterious "offenses" of which she knew nothing. She had mentioned his behavior to no one, nor had she gone again to confession.

Returning to the shelter with Rita after seeing the men off, Gabriella spied a lone woman toiling up the slope to the church. "There goes poor Josefa," she murmured.

"'Poor?'" mocked Rita. "Seven children and the eighth due any minute. 'Poor' by her own choice, the stupid sow!" Everyone in camp knew about the Bellis family and the plight of the mother.

"I wonder who's taking care of her children," said Gabriella.

"Before long it could be you if you aren't careful," warned Rita. "*Santa Madre*, you have worries of your own. Why can't you leave the poor woman alone?"

"That's just it, Rita, she *is* so alone. All the *paisanas* in camp avoid her."

"For good reason!" Rita said. "If they give her half a chance, she'll drag them down with her. People like Josefa Bellis are to be feared, don't you know that?"

"*Feared*?! What a heartless thing to say!"

Rita turned and faced Gabriella, hands on hips. "Let me tell you something, my pretty one. Let's suppose you keep on as you have with this Josefa Bellis. You help her before her baby comes. You act as midwife when the child is born, you wash and cook for her family till she gets her strength back, you wheedle and coax to keep her worthless husband from drinking himself to death. D'you know what will happen next? Before the year is out, she'll be pregnant again. And who will she come to for help with baby number nine? You!"

"But she's so sick!" Gabriella insisted. "She shouldn't be with this expedition at all. Her feet and ankles are so swollen she can hardly walk, and nothing I give her seems to help."

"Of course not! She's worn herself out bearing children, but that's none of your affair. If her man won't leave her alone, and she can't *make* him leave her alone, then it's her lookout, not yours."

By nightfall that same day, at least half of the livestock had been located and driven back to the valley. By noon the following day, all but a few dozen head were accounted for. Serving the officers' mid-day meal, Miguel overheard their conversation about the stampede. Rita asked, "Where was the colonel during all the excitement yesterday?"

"Busy," teased Miguel.

Rita glared. "You know where he was but you're too busy to tell us, is that it?"

"No offense, my love! No offense!" He looked outside the shelter for anyone who might overhear, then lowered his voice. "The poor man was with his new wife."

Gabriella stared in amazement and Rita nearly dropped the big olla she was cleaning.

"He hasn't been married long," Miguel whispered. "Everyone says the colonel got himself a rich wife. Pretty, too, but she's willful. Likes to get her own way, they say. He found a place for her to stay, not far from town at a hacienda belonging to a friend of his. He slips away to see her every chance he gets."

Jealousy for their happiness stung Gabriella, and she was instantly ashamed.

Miguel continued, "The Franciscan's been busy with his forked tongue. He's spreading the tale that Anza was dallying with his woman when he should have been attending to business. It wouldn't have made any difference where the commander was, the animals would've stampeded anyway, but not according to the padre. The viceroy will hear of it in good time, you can be sure."

Gabriella said, "Lieutenant Neve was supposed to be on duty with the herds. Where was he when the stampede began?"

"In the middle of it, that's where," said Miguel. "Working with the greenhorn muleteers. Them's the ones that caused the stampede. Lieutenant said Anza got 'em cheap."

"The cattle didn't like it that Anza got 'em cheap?" Rita asked, bristling.

"Cattle didn't care, my love. Cattle get along fine when the animals is all used to each other. But there's been three hundred new head of livestock brought in since the colonists got to Horcasitas. Well, Lieutenant had three experienced *vaqueros* and about six *arrieros* who knew to keep the batches separated. Trouble was the nine new fellows who didn't. Anza's plan was for the lieutenant's men to train the greenhorns in time to leave next week. Eye on the money, y'see. It was a good plan but what happened, the critters started milling around and the new men didn't know what to do. Next thing, Lieutenant had a stampede on his hands."

Hacienda Vallejo, on the outskirts of Horcasitas
September, 1775

Don Juan Bautista de Anza lay in bed gazing sourly at the two identical tents formed by the sheet over his long feet near the footboard. They reminded him of the message received an hour before from his contractor in Culiacán: "Have searched Guadalajara and Culiacán but at the price you name, no tents are available."

Tents for the soldiers had already arrived but now it was too late to search elsewhere for smaller tents for the families. Wanting to attract the best people, he had spent lavishly for the colonists' clothing and household equipment. Too lavishly, for now he had placed his colonists at risk for illness from overexposure to the weather. And his military career depended on getting the colonists to California unharmed. Wearily he closed his eyes. These last few days, so many things had gone wrong.

— But not everything. Resting on his bare shoulder was the beautiful head of his bride, Ana Regina Serrano, the love of his life. Their time together was spinning out. "Bucareli wanted me to leave two weeks ago," he murmured.

"Ah, no, my dearest!" Doña Ana crooned. "Don't think of such things! Not now!" And she arched against her husband's naked length, enjoying the sensuous pleasure of his bare skin against hers.

"Vixen!" He kissed her milk-white forehead and held her close in his arms. "It's our future I'm concerned about, you know."

"Let the future take care of itself. What's another day or two?"

He punched up the pillow beneath his head. "Strangely enough, another day or two — better still another week or two — would give us more time to train the herdsmen. The stampede proved how little control they have over the livestock. It's frightening!"

"All they need to do is tie a string of mules together and lead them," said Doña Ana. "I could do that."

"We have considerably more than one string of mules, my dearest. I have never taken you to see that valley outside town. A thousand animals is a lot of livestock. And I promise you, each animal has its own idea of where it wants to go and when."

"When the extra guards come from Tubac, can't they help with the herds?"

"The extra guards are to look out for the Apache, not for the livestock."

"Oh."

"The first two weeks of the journey are the most dangerous. We'll be going through hostile country, with spies behind every rock. Our men are expected to drive the animals in an orderly march, feed and water them, help load them each morning and unload them every night. Many of those animals have never before carried any cargo, mind you! Never been trained for trail duty at all."

"Oh, dear."

"The worst of it is the new men. They need more training."

"Isn't the new lieutenant working out?"

"He's doing his best but he can't perform miracles. To leave Horcasitas now would mean disaster. Before the end of the first day's march, we'd have horses and mules scattered for a hundred miles. —With all our supplies and equipment strapped to their backs. That would make Font happy, wouldn't it? He'd have all the rope he needed to hang me."

"Why not simply announce that the expedition won't leave for another two weeks?"

"I've already announced that we can't leave until the guards from Tubac arrive. With the Apache menace what it is, it's insane to risk leaving without the extra protection; at least everyone understands that. But if I announce yet another holdup, then in Font's official diary, he'll write that 'Anza's poor planning has caused all these needless delays.' Which is the truth, I guess, except that no expedition of this kind and on this scale has ever been mounted before. I'm having to improvise as I go along, and unavoidably some arrangements aren't going to work out."

Doña Ana entwined affectionate fingers in her husband's beard of silken black curls. "Why must Font's diary be the only one? Write your own diary. Tell your side of it."

Anza gazed at his bride with new respect. "Well, of course! Why not?" His laugh rang with relief. "What wonderful luck that you're on my side and not Font's. Thank you, my dear, for the idea!"

"I should think that way you could parry most of his thrusts if not all of them."

"No, not all of them. His favorite charge is that 'Anza is a slave to his animal appetites and keeps delaying the departure to be with his wife.'"

Ana nuzzled her husband's ear where she knew he was most vulnerable. "And could such a charge be true, Colonel?"

Laughing, they scuffled and then embraced ardently. "Partly, yes," he admitted. "It's partly true." He disentangled himself from the bedclothes and searched on the floor for his boots.

Doña Ana propped herself on one elbow and pouted. "Font! What a trial he is, the old scarecrow! Catalina's a good friend of his. Maybe Catalina and I together can think up a way to trick him."

"Easy there!" warned Anza. "Your friend Catalina is sly as a snake. I've trouble enough with Font. It won't help at all if you two fabricate still more!"

"How could you possibly be in *more* trouble with Font?" wondered Doña Ana.

"How indeed? Almost anything I do or say brings another fusillade of complaints. There's no pleasing the man." The colonel buttoned his coat and stood before the mirror to tie his military sash. "At least the old scoundrel finally named a patron saint for the expedition, after fuming about it for two months."

"Ah. He found someone worthy enough to suit him?"

"Not some *one*. Nothing as ordinary as a mere mortal. He chose an archangel — Saint Michael."

"What an interesting coincidence! Saint Michael is my little brother's patron saint. His feast day is, let's see, the 29th of this month. That's almost two weeks away."

Anza swept up his hat. "I'm late, kitten. Wish me luck." He swiftly kissed his wife goodby and dashed out the door.

Doña Ana gazed after him lovingly, and slowly smiled.

Horcasitas
September, 1775

Two days later the weather was beautiful and clear with the smell of sage in the mountain air. Gabriella and two of the older expedition children had spent the morning hunting herbs in the surrounding hills and canyons. Sergeant Grijalva sent an armed escort with them and to Gabriella's happy surprise, the guard knew nearly as much of herbal remedies as she did. He located a red raspberry thicket and found patches of golandrina. He showed her outcrops of wild hyssop and above all garlic, a preventative against scurvy which she had been hoarding for the journey.

She returned in time to help with dinner at the headquarters tent. As she readied the table and Miguel fetched chairs, Sergeant Grijalva and Anza continued their conversation at the tent entrance. "It's definite," announced Anza. "We won't leave until the 29th. I've notified everyone. Mainly Font's idea. It's the feast day of Saint Michael."

"The patron saint."

"Yes. Since we're running late anyway, Font thinks it would be appropriate to wait another few days and commemorate his feast day."

"Every day we delay, Colonel, we're eating up food intended to last until we reach Monterey!" Gabriella heard anxiety in Grijalva's remark.

"You've forgotten," said Anza. "The party of hunters I appointed the day after we arrived here? They've brought in game for the cooking pots and extended our rations. That solution won't last much longer, however. They tell me there isn't a jackrabbit left within a radius of three miles! Last night one of our hunters shot a heifer that stampeded but was never found!"

Gabriella, arranging the table, wondered if Colonel Anza realized he was about to be served beef cutlets from that very heifer. She smiled and looked up to see Padre Font hastening angrily down the hill from the church, raising puffs of dust with his footsteps. His brown habit swirled about him, his white hair stood straight up above his ears and he brandished his wooden staff like a weapon.

"What's this?" cried the priest. He waved a piece of paper above his head. "You say here we will wait to leave until the 29th because I requested it! What kind of treachery is this? I requested no such thing! Why are you blaming me for your delays!"

Anza stared at Padre Font. "Didn't you tell Doña Catalina you thought it would be appropriate to celebrate mass on the feast day of Saint Michael before we left?"

Font took a moment to collect his wits. "What? Yes, but that was only a casual conversation with a good friend! Words, words! Doña Catalina and I talked of many things when she came to call on me yesterday. I had no intention of changing your plans for departure!"

"She also reported that you were feverish and needed extra time to rest," continued Anza.

"But my infirmities are not — "

"You did tell her you were ill, did you not?" insisted Anza.

"I spoke in confidence. It was a private conversation with a lady. I had no idea she would repeat what I said. My illness is a matter of no importance!"

"Certainly it is a matter of importance to me, Padre," said Anza with a slight bow. "If you are ill, we will delay until you are restored. A messenger was sent to Bucareli yesterday afternoon advising him of our new date of departure."

Padre Font's eyes widened with indignation, then narrowed with fury. "And giving me as the reason!" he shouted. "The presumption! The impertinence of you — you self-appointed frontier potentates is not to be believed!" Finding the written message still in his hand, he crumpled it and threw it violently to the ground. "This is a deliberate trick! You and that Jezebel of yours put Doña Catalina up to this!"

"I counsel you to take care how you speak of my wife," said Colonel Anza, his face forbidding as stone.

"I'll speak of her as she deserves!" hissed Font, glaring up into Anza's face. "You can't stand to leave your pretty wife's bed, can you, *Captain* Anza? Oh, yes, I know for the expedition you have been given the rank of *Lieutenant Colonel* Anza, but in actuality you are nothing but *Captain* Anza and will never be anything more than *Captain* Anza as long as you live. You are incompetent beyond belief, negligent of your duties and ill bred as any savage. A gentleman would keep his word. You promised me servants. What do you offer me? This twit of a girl here who stole off in the bushes and got herself pregnant — "

"That's enough!" Anza shouted.

" — Oh, yes, I've seen the wedding ring she wears. I know she claims to be a widow. *She claims.* Just as *she claims* she can cure people of their diseases. I've seen no proof of either. The only proof of anything I've seen is that you have added four unauthorized servants to your own staff, enabling you to indulge your gluttony for rich food as you keep delaying the departure of the expedition to indulge your lust for your beautiful wife. Well, I must tell you, *Captain* Anza, the viceroy will have a second message from Horcasitas, from Fray Pedro Font, apostolic preacher of the Colegio de la Santa Cruz de Queretaro. And the second message will give the whole truth of the matter!"

The Franciscan turned and furiously stumped back up the hill.

Sergeant Grijalva broke the silence. "He has his own private messenger service, does he?" he asked in surprise.

"You know he doesn't," replied Anza. "Font also knows he doesn't. The only way a message of his can be delivered to the viceroy is by my courier, the one who left yesterday. In his enthusiasm, perhaps he forgot." A pause. "You were present the day I invited Font to share the officers' mess here in the headquarters tent?"

"Yes," answered Grijalva.

"He declined, did he not?"

"Ho-ho! Indeed, he did!"

Anza turned. "Señora, I understood that Miguel has been delivering meals to Padre Font at his quarters. Doesn't Font eat the same food we do?"

"Yes, Colonel," Gabriella answered. "Miguel takes food to Padre while it's hot. He stays to serve it and pour out his wine."

"Is the food satisfactory?"

"Well — . No, it isn't. He says Rita's cooking gives him indigestion. Miguel thinks he would rather have porridge, soups, things like that."

"How much of an added burden would it be for Rita to prepare special meals for Padre Font?"

"I don't know, Señor. I can ask."

"And Miguel has more duties than he can handle already. We need a servant for Padre Font. How about the oldest Sandoval boy? The tall one. Hasn't he been acting as acolyte at Mass?"

"Tómas," said Grijalva.

"If he agrees, put him on the payroll as one of Padre Font's servants. Ten days after we leave here, we're scheduled to pick up Padre Garcés at Tumacacori. And we have two additional servants for the padres waiting to join us at Tubac. Tómas can decide then if he wants to stay on with Font. If so, fine. If not, we need an errand boy at headquarters."

"Colonel Anza?" Gabriella quietly interrupted.

"Yes?"

"If there should ever be any doubt of my marriage, the church records at Alamos show my husband and I were married before witnesses on April 15. My husband asked to have a certificate prepared verifying the wedding. I have it with my things if you should ever need to see it."

Anza's stern features softened. "I'm sorry you were present to witness Padre Font's outburst. He was overwrought. You mustn't let him worry you. As for your certificate, I don't need to see it. Your word is good enough for me."

CHAPTER 17

Horcasitas, Sonora
September 1775

Gabriella coughed delicately to attract the commander's attention. "Colonel Anza, may I talk to you about Josefa Bellis?"

The commander was busy at his desk. "Bellis," he repeated, trying to remember. "Is her husband Vasco Bellis?"

"Yes. Vasco Felipé Bellis."

"The lazy one. Always needs help loading his pack mules. Never knows where his children are. Yes, I remember Vasco. But you say it's his wife you're worried about?"

"Her baby will be due in two or three weeks. She needs all her strength to give birth but there's no time for her to rest. There are seven children already and her husband isn't very good with them. It's a bad situation. I don't know what to do about it."

"Well, I do," replied the colonel crisply. He stood. "Leave them behind if necessary. I've had to talk to Vasco before and from what you say, it's time to talk to him again. Thank you for calling the matter to my attention." Gabriella turned to leave. "Before you go, Señora Márquez! Within the next few days, six more families will be arriving. Please check them for contagious diseases. I am fairly sure of the colonists who came with me from Culiacán, but we need to look at these new people. We have enough troubles riding with us to California without adding plague or typhus."

Six more families? Already the extra supplies Gabriella brought from Alamos were half gone, and still more colonists were scheduled to join the expedition at Tubac. "Colonel Anza, I don't have enough medical supplies for so many people."

"Then get what you need here in Horcasitas," he said. "You can find many things — herbs, cloth for bandages, olive oil. Requisition whatever you need."

Without warning, Gabriella was seized by an agonizing pain in her lower abdomen. She gasped in anguish and the commander frowned. "What is it?"

"Nothing, Señor. Thank you for your concern. It is nothing."

Abruptly she turned and groped for the entrance. Outside she stood breathing deeply, the heel of her hand pressing against the piercing pain in her belly. She and Elias had rejoiced at the prospect of becoming parents so soon. To avoid false hopes, she had warned him: Young mothers sometimes failed to carry their babies full term. The younger the mother, the greater the risk.

She had experienced backaches on the trip north from Alamos and had begun taking raspberry tea every night and morning as a precaution. When the backaches disappeared, she thought the medicine had done its work. The morning of the stampede, she'd waked to find her nightdress faintly streaked with blood. Afterwards, she had avoided heavy work and taken naps every afternoon. Again there had been no recurrence, and again she was optimistic.

But there was no denying the agonizing pain she felt now. She had seen too many young mothers miscarry not to realize that the hemorrhaging had begun. What she dreaded most of all was happening. She was losing Elias' baby.

Mexico
Palace of the Costanza Family
September 1775

A maid appeared at the door of the sitting room of Doña Teresa de Costanza. "Señor Haros is downstairs, Señora."

"Ask if he wants coffee," Doña Teresa instructed the maid.

Ernán wanted coffee, served his favorite way, Viennese style with whipped cream. "Delightful!" he breathed.

"Delightful as the news you have for me, I hope," said Señora. "What of Verro? I want to hear it all."

Half-an-hour later, she was disappointed. "The wretch has admitted nothing, of course."

"Verro? Nothing." The steward touched his lips with a napkin from the tray. "He insists he is innocent and that the charges against him are spurious. Insists convincingly, I am loathe to add. The man could lie his way through a stone wall with no difficulty at all."

"And the case comes before the *audiencia* next week, you say."

"Yes."

Haros drew from a leather case at his feet a document to which seals had been attached. "Don Avila's deed transferring ownership of Buena Suerte," he explained. "Verro turned it over as evidence. It was left with the bailiff for safekeeping and the bailiff was kind enough to let me borrow it for the afternoon. The wording is a little unusual. I thought you might want to look over it."

"Where is Verro now, by the way?"

"Safe. Until the investigation's over, he's being held under guard at the National Palace."

"I want the villain shot," Doña Teresa said briskly.

Haros swallowed. He already knew what Doña Teresa wanted. She had told him many times. Rascality was one thing — she herself had committed her share of rascality over the years — but Verro's offense, violent abuse of a favorite, consigned him to the nethermost realm of her vengeance.

Doña Teresa unrolled the parchment. The dangling seals swung busily as she surveyed the text. Her gaze lingered over the signatures.

"Excuse me a moment," she murmured to Haros, and took the deed to the adjoining chamber where she tossed it on the bed. Making a selection from the rosary of keys hanging at her waist, she unlocked a large teakwood chest and lifted the lid. Rummaging through jeweled scarves, fine lace, richly embroidered tunics, slippers and jackets, she retrieved a brocade-covered box no longer than one of the shoes she had laid aside. Another key, a tiny one, opened it. Inside were various papers and documents. She searched again, at last flipping open a letter stiff with age. Rising to her feet, she took it to the bed and examined first the deed and then the letter for several minutes.

Satisfied, she replaced the chest's contents, carefully secured the lock, and returned with the deed to Haros in the morning room.

"Don Avila's signature is forged," she announced. "Listen carefully while I tell you what must be done."

Horcasitas
September 1775

Though Gabriella did not share their enthusiasm, the colonists were giddy with anticipation. Tomorrow was departure — September 29, the feast day of St. Michael, patron saint of the expedition. Her packing completed, she sat listlessly on a shady bench at the edge of the plaza. The afternoon sun sifted through the palms and cottonwoods, sprinkling fragments of sunlight on the hardpacked earth below.

After her final farewell at Elias' grave at Alamos, she had the sensation of descending, alone, into a foggy abyss from which she would never emerge. In the beginning, there were tears. Now, only despair remained — despair of the empty nights without his loving touch, without their shared laughter and delicious secrets, without the joy of waking each morning to find his beloved face pressed close on the pillow beside her. How patient Elias had been! He had married a girl afraid of her own body and the tricks it might play on her. He had left behind a widow of many hungers, tormented and alone.

She secretly wondered if she might have been better off at the convent, where she could anesthesize herself with work and drop, exhausted, to immediate sleep every night. She remembered that September 29 was also the feast day of her own patron saint, San Gabriel. At the convent, there had always been a little fiesta in her honor on September 29, and presents made especially for her.

She wondered if San Gabriel was watching over her, protecting her? It was hard to believe. The loss of Elias' baby had added new grief to an already heavy burden. Rita, that least motherly of women, had held and comforted her through the storms of weeping and had tolerated her depression ever since.

"Please, Rita, let's keep the miscarriage to ourselves for awhile," Gabriella had pleaded. "Just you and Miguel and me. I don't think I can bear talking about it to strangers."

"Of course," Rita agreed. "You're quiet and much too pale. People will wonder what's wrong. If anyone asks, we'll say it's the strain of leaving."

With the eve of departure come at last, fiesta was in the air. The townspeople had blazoned the plaza with banners and streamers. It was early afternoon, and a fandango was already in progress.

Lieutenant Neve, uninvited, joined Gabriella on her bench. His presence disturbed her, as it always had. She nodded a greeting, smiled noncommitally and thought of ways to escape.

He broke the silence. "Gabriella, customs that we all thought were proper and necessary in Mexico and Alamos seem out of place here. Don't you agree?"

"Yes."

"I think it would be better if you called me 'Martín' instead of 'Lieutenant Neve'" he said. "You aren't really a servant, you know. You never were."

You and Federico Verro are the only ones who ever called me a servant, she thought despondently, but shrugged. "Whatever you wish."

A pause. "Apparently I offended you, that day at Alamos behind the palace. But what I said was true, you know. I think you are wrong to go on sulking about it."

The accusation jolted Gabriella from her dispirited mood. She glared at him irritably. "Sulking, am I?"

"Yes, you are," he said firmly. "You seem to resent what I said to you that day. I'm not apologizing, make no mistake about that. You're Elias' widow and I owe it to him to think of your welfare. This pouting of yours because I spoke frankly doesn't go over well, you know. The officers notice it. It's very unbecoming."

Her ragged nerves rebelled. "Lieutenant Neve, perhaps I should speak frankly — "

"Martín."

"Lieutenant Neve," she grated through clenched teeth, "you are twice my age, and I'm sure you know more of the world than I do. Both at Buena Suerte and at Alamos, you seldom favored me with any remark that wasn't some kind of lecture about this or that. As long as we were part of Don Avila's household, your behavior was appropriate. It was never welcome. Usually it was just a bore. Now such behavior on your part is no longer appropriate. No one appointed you to be my guardian. You are *not going to be* my guardian! Your arrogance is just as unpleasant to me as what you call my 'sulking' has been to you."

The lieutenant was speechless. Not even his own father had ever spoken to him so harshly. "*Arrogance*'!?" he cried. "I give you the benefit of my advice and you call it 'arrogance'? My dear girl, I care very much what happens to you!"

"I am not your 'dear girl'," she snapped, ashamed of the hurtful things she was saying but, now that the dam had broken, unable to soften her words. "And please stop pretending you care what happens to me. You don't. You just like to preach. It's your nature."

The lieutenant could scarcely believe his ears. — Such insolence from an orphan girl with no more social standing than a lizard sunning itself on a rock! Unnerved, he challenged feebly, "It's my nature, is it? And I suppose you're going to tell me that Elias never preached to you!"

"Never once!" She rose to leave. "When I asked my husband for information, he gave it to me. It's not the same thing as preaching, but I doubt if you would understand the difference."

He rose to face her. "Gabriella, there's something *you* don't understand. This petulance of yours — "

She fought back tears of fury. "How could you possibly know anything about my 'petulance'? Why can't you leave me alone? Stay away from me. Padre Font says women are sinks of iniquity. That should be enough to warn you off, right there."

It was Martín's turn to be angry. "Why should I care what that old fool has to say? I'm not interested in being warned off. I'm interested in seeing that you and Elias' baby get to California. Safely!"

His words broke her down. She buried her face in her hands. "Elias' baby will never see California."

Not sure he heard aright, he moved to her side. "What's that?" He tried to read her anguished features. "Gabriella? What was that you said?"

Suddenly aware they were being stared at, she whispered, "There was a miscarriage. There won't be any baby."

"Won't — ?" At last comprehending, the lieutenant was overcome with guilt. He closed his eyes and bowed his head. "Oh, Sweet Jesus!"

Gabriella blotted her nose, caught the curious eye of a passerby and smiled, pretending nothing was wrong.

"When?" he asked.

"A few days ago."

After a moment, he stirred and looked about. "Let's walk," he murmured, and gently took her elbow. "Do you feel well enough to travel tomorrow?"

She nodded.

They had strolled a short distance along the path when he said, fervently, "Gabriella, I'm knocked in a heap. Holy God in heaven, this is a terrible blow!"

With heavy sarcasm, she asked, "Do you expect me to comfort you in your sorrow, Lieutenant Neve? That would be hard for me to do since I am the bereaved in this case, not you."

Another silence. They reached a fork in the path. Gabriella said, "I must go help Rita now. She's putting together a fine dinner for you officers to celebrate the departure tomorrow."

She walked purposefully past the bandstand but he followed her like a determined shadow. A crowd whistled and cheered as dancers whirled, stamped and clapped to music from a wailing violin and a battered cornet.

"Let them enjoy today," said Martín, "they won't enjoy tomorrow. The colonel said he hoped loading would be completed before sundown. The expedition will ford the shallow stream north of the city and camp on the other side — maybe three miles. If we don't complete loading before sundown, he will regard the day as rehearsal and we'll leave the next morning."

"Why will it take so long?" asked Gabriella, curious.

"Inexperienced *arrieros* showing inexperienced *paisanos* how to load pack mules that never carried a load in their lives."

"That should be interesting to watch," mused Gabriella, glad that she and Rita had Miguel to depend on. The long journey from Mexico had taught her that strapping cargo, even on a seasoned pack animal, could be exacting work. The padding had to be right and the load had to be balanced. If not, the animal could be lamed for days or possibly forever!

"We don't have enough stock," Martín was saying thoughtfully. "A rule of thumb for military transport is ten animals per man but we need extra transport for each family's supplies and household baggage. Thirty animals per man would be about right. Forty would be better. Even allowing ten, we're still short some eight hundred horses and mules."

Gabriella tried not to show her boredom. She felt drained of energy and longed to be with Rita who understood and left her alone with her silences.

"And because of the Apache raid at Tubac," Martín went on, "we have less than seven hundred head! Not very good ones, either. A poor horse can't carry as much and can't carry it as far as a good one."

Gabriella said absently, "Colonel Anza's had one stroke of bad luck after another, hasn't he?"

Martín's eyes were solemn. "You've had some bad luck yourself, Señora."

In spite of herself, his words stirred her. Thoughtfully, she replied, "So have you."

Had the lieutenant been at church next morning, instead of readying the livestock in the valley, he might have been surprised to learn the commander's thoughts during the High Mass held for the colonists. Colonel Anza knelt at his prie-dieu near the altar with a consecrated look carefully arranged on his face. His thoughts were less of consecration than of thanksgiving for the group that had come to him, like a gift, from Alamos. In Señora Esala and her husband, the colonel had gained a wizard of a cook and a personal servant of singular discretion and competence. Bucareli's haughty grandee Martín de Neve, of whom Anza had at first been suspicious, was hardening up nicely. The man's jowls and paunch no longer jiggled when he put his mount into a trot and he was losing some of his overpowering egotism.

With Señora Márquez as *enfermera*, Colonel Anza had also been fortunate. Being widowed and left pregnant at such a young age could have broken the spirit of many girls her age. But Señora was a resourceful young woman who had set aside her grief when her duties demanded attention. To the expedition mothers, she gave cheerful advice about their infants. With the children she could be gentle, stern or clownish, as required. She was everyone's bossy sister, with a saucy smile and warmhearted ways. In the weeks at Horcasitas, the colonists had come to trust her skill, and as news of her second loss inevitably became known, to marvel at her courage.

The service was drawing to a close. In the distance, the commander heard the unique thunder of an approaching army of horses. The *arrieros* were bringing the pack animals to the plaza for loading. Inside the church, the priest pronounced his final blessing. Worshipers greeted the last words with catcalls and whistles.

Anza had ordered packs to be ready for loading the moment Mass was over. Families who had journeyed from Culiacán quickly selected out their horses and pack animals from the herds as they were brought up from the pasture. Steady-handed, they went about readying the animals with little trouble.

For others, there were difficulties. Some of the loads were painstakingly lashed on the backs of the mules only to slip off immediately. Some of the animals, never having carried baggage before, bucked and reared; others took to their heels, galloping back to the pasture strewing pots, pans and bedding along the way.

The townspeople, who had come to see the colonists off, laid bets among themselves as to when the expedition would depart. Out of sympathy and genuine friendship, they tried not to laugh. At last the more experienced men stepped in to help with the loading and gradually others, shamed, followed their example.

The sun climbed in the sky. Mealtime came and went. Women of the town brought food for the sweating colonists and their helpers. The tavern owner took pity on the overworked muleteers. Wanting to help, he passed word among them to come for a brief rest and a free tankard of cool beer. Lieutenant Neve angrily rebuffed the offer as soon as he heard of it but the damage had already been done.

While the mounted *arrieros* — the sober ones — led more and still more pack animals and saddle horses from the pasture into the crowded plaza, and as more animals were readied for the journey, a rough line of march began to form in the avenue that surrounded the plaza. Space toward the head of the line was reserved for the colonists with their mounts and a younger child or two. Scattered among them were their wives and older children with their saddled horses and mules. After the colonists came the pack animals, their loads given a final check by Lieutenant Neve and Sergeant Grijalva. As the teeming hours passed, the line grew longer and longer, circling the big plaza once, then twice, then three times.

At four o'clock, Colonel Anza appeared in dress uniform, the plumes of his wide-brimmed hat tumbling in the breeze. Frenzied cheering broke out. With Sergeant Grijalva riding at his side, the commander guided his charger down the line, inspecting every animal, every rider, every child sharing a mount, every loaded mule.

As Colonel Anza was finishing his inspection, Gabriella asked Rita, "Where's Padre Font?"

For answer, Rita jerked her head in the direction of the church on its elevation at one end of the plaza. At the entrance stood Tómas Sandoval towering over his little mare and at his side, a sturdy mule. Reins in hand, Tómas waited.

In the plaza, the buzz of conversation slowly died. All was silence except for the occasional stamp of an impatient horse or cry of a hungry infant, quickly stilled. Colonel Anza completed his review, wheeled his mount and trotted to his place at the head of the column. Behind him, the bugler mounted his horse.

"What's the delay?" asked Miguel querulously.

Rita gazed sourly at the church. "Our official chaplain wants to make his grand entrance."

"Rita!" Gabriella cried reproachfully. "That's not fair! Padre Font is praying for us, for the expedition. It's his duty!"

"Pah!" scoffed Rita. "The old buzzard's had all afternoon to do his duty. It pleases him to keep us here sweating in the sun."

Suddenly, with no announcement, unseen hands drew open the massive church portals and the official chaplain of the California expedition emerged. With great dignity, he stood a moment surveying the silent throng in the plaza. The gentle wind stirred his brown habit and ruffled the white tufts above his ears. He sketched his blessing on the air, and from one end of the plaza to the other, eager hands crossed the breasts of the pious. Even the not-so-pious, such as Martín de Neve, crossed themselves for luck.

Having discharged his obligation, Padre Font mounted his mule and slowly proceeded to his place beside Colonel Anza at the head of the line of march.

The commander turned for one final supervisory glance, then shouted, "Mount!"

Colonists yelped, the townspeople cheered, harness jingled, startled animals whinnied, excited children squealed, and leather groaned. The bugler unfurled the great banner bearing the royal arms of Spain and sounded the military call to march. The brassy tones of the trumpet carried over the shouting throng and echoed among the surrounding mountain peaks. At last the huge gathering in the plaza began to move. Colonists and wellwishers alike shouted and whooped themselves into a state of intoxication. The California expedition was on its way at last!

CHAPTER 18

En Route to Tubac
October 1775

After the first full day of travel, Padre Font wrote in his official diary that one group of pack animals "remained behind on the road with packs scattered and the mules lost, and with so many setbacks that it was not able to reach camp during the whole day."

On subsequent days he reported additional losses. One of the lost mules carried on its back the wafers, holy oil and cruets needed for religious services. And the church bell. Padre Font borrowed from Anza a heavy tankard, suspended it on a cord and struck it with a mallet to summon worshippers to Mass.

Borrowing and improvising became the rule for everyone. Most submitted with good grace, but not the expedition's chaplain. "The mules are overloaded," he complained to Tómas. The caravan had halted for the day and Tómas had brought up the padre's pack animals to unload. "One can't blame the poor beasts for running away. They are too frail for work of this kind. If the commander had excercised a little foresight, none of these troubles would have occurred."

"Yes Señor."

"Be careful there with my psaltery! You nearly ripped the keys off yesterday."

"Yes Señor."

The priest reached for the triangular zither-like instrument and plucked a chord or two, testing to see if it was still in tune. It was not. He seated himself on a camp stool and tried the strings, listening and strumming.

Finally satisfied with the corrected pitch, he put the instrument aside with a sigh. "I brought it all the way from Spain," he mourned. "If a mule runs away with it, I'll never have another."

"No, Señor."

"I was wrong to let myself be talked into bringing it but the commander insisted. He said the music would amuse the Indians. I can't imagine why ignorant savages should be amused by music from a civilized instrument like a psaltery, can you, Tómas?"

"No, Señor."

"It's just another example of poor judgement on the part of our frontier potentate. But then, his whims must be obeyed, I suppose."

"Yes, Señor."

The priest looked on with increasing impatience as Tómas, himself tall and lean as one of the poles, struggled to erect the chaplain's large tent. At last he shouted, "Every evening it's the same! You shuffle and wobble endlessly putting that thing up! Go get one of the soldiers to help you!"

"Yes, Señor." With relief, Tómas dropped the poles and ran.

"—And if the commander stops you, tell him you are acting under *my orders!*" Padre shouted after him.

"Yes, Señor."

"The blackguard promised me *three* servants, not *one!*" the priest grumbled to himself. But then, he reflected, enduring such affronts was the lot of the religious and he piously crossed himself. Anyway, within the next few days, the frontier potentate would find his power somewhat diminished. The priest smiled in anticipation.

The Apache threat was seldom far from anyone's mind. The commander kept his garrison soldiers busy monitoring the train for limping mounts, faulty harness or family members separated from one another. Outriders scouted ahead. The third day out, one of them sighted a distant file of riders. He hastened to alert the commander but an hour later the alien horsemen had disappeared.

The land was sparsely settled. Beyond the dry, shallow streambeds and tumbled arroyos through which they journeyed, mountain ranges lay in every direction. Guarding their flanks were scatterings of *sinaloa*, straight slender cacti pointing like stern fingers to the sky. Above and on all sides vaulted the dome of the blue October sky, incredibly vast, frighteningly empty.

—Empty, except for the mark of the expedition itself. The travelers grew accustomed to the sight of distant dust tornadoes whirling hundreds of feet into the air. "Dust devils," the soldiers called them, common to the desert. But the most imposing dust devil was as nothing compared to the mammoth tower of dust raised by the expedition itself. One rancher claimed he could see it coming sixteen miles away.

Encamped at the end of each day's march, the expedition looked like a large village of makeshift huts and lean-tos perhaps a half-mile across. The headquarters staff, arriving first, pitched its large tent at what became the hub of the community. Nearby was the tent of the expedition chaplain, which doubled as a chapel, and the large barracks tent for the leatherjackets, who would return with Anza after accompanying the families to California.

"Avenues" were staked out as the terrain permitted. Families unpacked their mules and set up their shelters at the ever-broadening outer edges, from which *arrieros* led away long strings of weary, unburdened animals to the pasture areas.

Each day's march began between eight o'clock in the morning and noon. While the *arrieros* and soldiers were loading packs and saddling mounts, Padre Font said Mass for those available to participate. After the day's travel — five miles or twenty depending on many circumstances — the new camp site was reached between one and five o'clock in the afternoon.

Gabriella early decided such long hours on horseback were too restrictive for the expectant mothers. For exercise, she had them dismount and walk beside their horses for a half-hour each day. An exception was Señora Bellis, who was too weak for so much exertion.

The expedition ascended the Magdalena River valley to the chain of missions established a hundred years before by the Jesuit missionary Eusebio Francisco Kino. "The farther north we go, the greater the danger from the Apache," Anza warned his officers. "Alert the colonists. They should report anything they see that might be suspicious."

"Should we tell them again, Colonel?" asked Sergeant Grijalva. "We've already had two Apache alarms, both from youngsters and both false."

"Surely the missions are armed," said Lieutenant Neve. "Can't we count on security there in case of attack?"

"Very little," replied Anza. "The Indians have no qualms about attacking the missions. On the contrary, there's good plunder to be had there."

" — For which the Holy Mother be thanked," murmured Sergeant Grijalva. "Maybe we can replace some of the supplies we lost with the runaway mules."

On the thirteenth day out of Horcasitas, Anza halted in the early afternoon. Ahead lay the tiny settlement of El Guambut, and beyond it a narrow, dangerous pass hemmed in by steep cliffs. Many a bloody ambush had occurred there in the past. "It's no place to straggle through," Anza warned Lieutenant Neve. "By stopping early, the cattle will have a chance to catch up with us by nightfall. Early tomorrow we will move through the pass slowly and as close together as possible."

They had stopped for the night at a location with insufficient wood for cooking fires. Many families doubled up to prepare their evening meal. Others did without a fire, and threw together cold meals of jerked meat and beans.

Autumn chilled the desert air and Gabriella, sraightening from her unpacking, noticed thunderheads building on the horizon. Worried about Josefa Bellis, she gathered an apron full of corn cakes, apples and cheese and went to search. Before she had gone far, a husky ten-year-old girl with happy eyes and black curls fell in step beside her. "I know you," she chirped. "You're the doctor lady."

Gabriella laughed. "I'm no doctor! I'm only a nurse and my name is Gabriella. What's your name?"

"Ynez. Can you read and write?"

"Yes. Can you?"

"No, but my two older brothers can. Tómas can read almost as well as Papa. So can Ricardo."

"Tómas is Padre Font's assistant, but who is Papa?"

"Gilbert Sandoval. If you can read and write, will you teach me?"

Gabriella flushed with pleasure. "I'd like to very much, but I don't know when I'd do it. I work for Colonel Anza, you know, and he keeps me busy."

"Doing what?"

Gabriella glanced at the food in her apron. "Well, doing things like this. Do you know the Bellis family?"

Instantly the child was on guard. "Yes."

"Well, Señora Bellis is expecting a baby right away. She is not very well and I'm afraid her family doesn't have enough to eat. So I'm taking some food to her. Would you like to come with me?"

Shaking her head, the child took a few steps backward. "No. I have to go now." She turned and disappeared running among the shelters.

Gabriella frowned, puzzled. She shrugged and continued her search. A few minutes later she found the pregnant woman huddled with her children beside their baggage. The oldest son, age eleven, was halfheartedly trying to unpack.

"Where's your father?" Gabriella asked the child.

"He said he felt sick from worrying about the Apaches," the boy replied. "He went to hunt for some medicine."

Gabriella knew what kind of "medicine" Vasco Bellis was hunting for — a nip from the forbidden flask of a friendly colonist. Or, better still, a doze under a shady cottonwood. She marveled at a man who could neglect his wife when she needed him so desperately. Colonel Anza would be angry.

She told the boy, "Stop what you're doing and go look for your father. Don't give up until you find him, because this is very important. Tell your father that Colonel Anza wants him to unpack his baggage and help his family. If your father is too sick to help his family, Colonel Anza has some medicine for him. Do you understand?"

"Yes, Señora."

The child's mother appeared more dead than alive. Her skin had a grayish pallor and her dull eyes responded to little that took place before them. Gabriella parceled out among the family the food she had brought, setting aside a portion for the older boy when he returned.

"Your husband will be back soon, Señora," Gabriella told the wretched woman huddled beside the family's belongings. "I have my own work to do just now. Later I will come back to help you. Do you understand?"

The woman seemed too dazed to comprehend.

"Stay close to your mother," Gabriella ordered the children sternly. "Help her all you can. It is your mother who is sick, not your father."

She returned to headquarters and reported to Colonel Anza what she had found. "Señora Bellis's baby could come any time," she told him.

"You have your own duties here," replied the commander, and sent a leatherjacket to attend to the Bellis family.

Gabriella taped a child's sprained ankle, treated and taped a soldier's infected blister, and made willow bark tea for a feverish baby.

Late that afternoon, Anza called the travelers together. "The next few days are especially dangerous," he explained. "The Apache know methods of torture cruel beyond imagining. The threat is real. For your own protection and the protection of the expedition, stay together; obey the soldiers; maintain a quiet, orderly line of march."

The setting sun drenched the landscape in crimson light. Mothers glanced uneasily at their husbands and children tinged blood red by the dying sunlight. An ill omen? Many thought so, crossed themselves and quietly wept. Even Gabriella searched out Elias' talisman in its silken pouch and laced it tight in her bodice for luck.

Voices were more hushed than usual that night; uneasy eyes returned again and again to search the deepest shadows. Families softly sang the *Salve* or the *Alabado* together, but even as rosaries were fingered and prayers whispered, weapons were never far from any hand. The leatherjackets stood watch all night.

Next morning without pausing for Mass or even to cook breakfast, the colonists rolled up their bedding, packed their tents and saddled their horses. By eight o'clock, the long line of march was passing through the gorge beyond El Guambut. Nor did the caravan pause until the column reached the little settlement of El Sibuta, ten miles beyond, where they once again made camp. The commander found a messenger waiting for him with dispatches from Tubac.

Lieutenant Neve rode in from the pasture for his usual conference with the commander and paused at Miguel's shelter. Gabriella sat beside the fire picking out pine nuts for a cake. "Another long march tomorrow?" she asked, determined not to be cross.

Martín nodded. "At Tubac, we'll rest for a few days."

"And still no Apaches," she remarked. "Maybe they don't even know we're here."

"Oh, they know, all right," replied the lieutenant. "They've had lookouts spying on us every step of the way."

"How can you tell? No one ever sees them."

"They choose not to be seen. The colonel says an Apache can hide behind his own shadow."

Tómas was kneeling by the fire toasting a muffin for Padre Font's evening meal. He found as many reasons as possible to be near Gabriella, whose esteem he secretly labored to earn. To earn it now, he scoffed at the joke. "That's stupid!

How can anyone hide behind his own shadow?"

Miguel solemnly explained. "Easy. First you draw a line around your shadow on the ground, then you dig it up, crawl in the hole and pull in your shadow after you. Not even a badger can find you."

But to Martín, as to the other officers, the Apaches were no joking matter. "They could have attacked," he remarked, puzzled. "Many times. What's holding them back?"

"They're afraid," said Rita, turning chops on the grill. "Too many people. We outnumber them."

The lieutenant shook his head. "Anza says by now they know how many women and children there are. They know most of the men are not professional soldiers and probably never loaded a musket before in their lives. They know the *arrieros* are inexperienced. We're a massacre begging to happen. What are they waiting for?"

"You'd think they'd at least steal the cattle," agreed Miguel. "They could stampede the cattle with no trouble at all."

"And would," allowed the lieutenant, "except Apaches hate the taste of beef. They'll gorge themselves on mule meat, but won't butcher a steer unless they're starving."

Tómas broke the short silence. "Rita is right," he said. "The Apaches don't attack because of so many people riding together. It looks suspicious."

"Suspicious?" asked Martín. "Why?"

Tómas arranged his thoughts before he spoke. "Our farm in the mountains was near an Indian village. When they traveled together, there are thirty, forty people. But our expedition has many hundred. To the Apache, it must look like a whole nation moving from one place to another."

"To get away from something?" suggested Martín. "Disease, maybe?"

"The pox, that's it!" said Miguel. "Indians are scared of the pox. They'll pack up and move a hundred miles to get away from it. Whole families have died from the pox, whole tribes."

"Or ghosts," said Tómas. "They would think the ghosts must be very bad to make so many people run away. And run so far. All the way from Culiacán. Maybe the Apache, he wonders if maybe we brought the ghosts with us."

Again silence fell.

"*Or —* " said Miguel, mischief in his eye. "Maybe they found the runaway mule with the padre's holy oil and communion wafers. Maybe they gobbled it all down and it made 'em sick."

The suggestion brought peals of laughter. Both theories made their way from shelter to shelter before dark.

After dinner, Colonel Anza came to Miguel's shelter, as he often did, to compliment the cook for her excellent meal. Leaving, he turned to Gabriella. "Señora Márquez, would you accompany me to the headquarters tent? I need to confer with you."

Gabriella followed in the fading light, expecting a discussion of the Bellis family. The headquarters tent was deserted but the bright lamp hung as usual over the commander's desk.

"The messenger from Tubac brought a communique from the viceroy," he told her after they were seated. "It covered many topics but one is especially disturbing." He unfolded a document. "I'd like to read to you the pertinent section. 'It has come to my attention that the *enfermera* I authorized you to add to your staff is of doubtful reliability. Gabriella Salgado was born of an unmarried mother and raised as an orphan at the convent of Santa Clara de Asís, a highly-regarded institution. Nevertheless, questions have been raised as to the innocence of her motives. On investigation here in the city, I find that after she attached herself to the Figuroa family, her ministrations led to the opium addiction of Doña Dolores, the mother, and to convulsive fits on the part of the younger daughter."

Gabriella felt as though she had been suddenly and brutally slapped. Scarcely able to catch her breath, she gasped, "Colonel Anza, that's not so! That is such a terrible, terrible lie! Who said I 'attached myself' to the Figuroa family? I never wanted to leave the convent! Madre made me go! And Bonita — "

"Wait," commanded Anza. "Let me finish. Bucareli goes on to say, 'Indeed, Don Avila's fortunes took a turn for the worse from the day she entered his household. Both parents and the daughter have since returned to Spain broken in health and fortune.'"

Again Gabriella cried out in protest but Anza held up a restraining hand. "'Interrogation of former servants,'" he read, "'particularly a loyal old woman named Pepita, who served Doña Dolores for many years, confirm that several in the household suspected this girl of practicing witchraft. They cite the cats she introduced at the family mansion and her close association with a *curandera* in the city, who is widely known for her expertise with spells, potions and magic incantations.'"

"*Pepita!*" gasped Gabriella, incredulous. "That letter is quoting Pepita! Pepita was helping Federico Verro steal the Figuroa's jewels! Instead of asking someone like Pepita about me, why don't you ask Miguel and Rita? They were former servants at Buena Suerte, too! And good ones, not thieves like Pepita! They knew me from the day I arrived there. Ask *them* if I'm a witch!"

"That will be enough, Señora Márquez," said Anza coldly. "I am not the one who conducted the investigation. The viceroy conducted his own investigation. I am only reading to you what he has to say."

Gabriella fought to control her panic. "I apologize, Señor, but what you are reading there are wicked, false accusations."

"There isn't much more, but you must hear it," said Anza, and he read on. "'I doubt if you would have added Señora Márquez to your staff if you had not been certain of her ability and the purity of her religious beliefs. Still, it is perilous to continue with her in such a sensitive position considering the possible damage she can do to the expedition. I must therefore command you to relieve her of all duties effective immediately.'"

Gabriella stared at the commander.

Harshly, Anza continued, "So, effective immediately, you will no longer treat expedition patients. I have already spoken to Sergeant Grijalva, who will take over your duties. At Tubac, he will leave the expedition for a few days to fetch his family from the presidio at Terrenate and I will appoint a corporal to substitute for him. Later, with the train once again underway, he will be administering first aid each evening here in the headquarters tent. So I must command you to leave all supplies and equipment where they are. He will see to their transport. You are not to involve yourself with the expedition's medical concerns in any way. Do you understand?"

Gabriella was stunned. "*You* believe those lies, don't you?! You believe what the viceroy says is true!"

The commander would not meet her eyes. "Señora Márquez, it is not my place to judge in this matter, one way or the other. The viceroy gives me my orders, and I must obey them."

A sudden storm of trembling overcame Gabriella and she slowly rose to her feet. She glanced over her shoulder at the table, two primitive stools and cupboard full of supplies near the headquarters entrance that had been her work station. Indicating them with a trembling hand and trying to regulate her voice, she said, "Most of what you see over there is mine. Things like the scalpels, lancets and the extra pairs of scissors, tongue depressors — all those I bought with my own money in Mexico. My flint knives, mortar and pestle, and glass vials were given to me by Sister Magdalena. Those things will be irreplacable in California. Some of the herbs — the oil of camphor, the senna, myrrh, wolfsbane and many others are rare and hard to find, even in a city the size of Mexico. I brought most of my rare herbs with me from the convent. I bought a few in Mexico and some in Guadalajara. So you see, I want to be sure I understand. Is the viceroy ordering you to confiscate my dispensary? And am I expected to turn it over to you without a protest?"

It was uncharacteristic of Colonel Anza that he had failed to think through this part of the transfer. He was silent for a moment. "An equitable arrangement will need to be worked out," he admitted. "For example, I doubt if Sergeant Grijalva will know how to prepare many of your medicines, or to prescribe them. Isn't there a notebook, a manual of some kind with a list of your remedies and what they are to be used for? He will need written instructions to know how to proceed."

Gabriella replied evenly, "Yes, Señor. There is my notebook, there on the shelf. I would offer it to Sergeant Grijalva but most of it is written in Latin. He told me once he does not read Latin."

"Couldn't you write something down for him, some basic instructions?"

Gabriella felt her right knee crazily lock and unlock in a bewildering spasm. *Holy Mother of God, don't let me fall down*, she prayed. *Please don't let me grovel on the floor before this cruel man who has so monstrously betrayed me!*

"Colonel Anza," she began, cleared her throat and began again. "From the time I was ten years old until I left the convent at age fifteen, Sister Magdalena was teaching me how to care for the sick and injured. It would take a long time to write down instructions that would help Sergeant Grijalva. Anyway, most of what I wrote for him would be useless unless I could show him with live patients.

That I cannot do, for you say I am not to be involved with the patients in any way." She straightened. "Perhaps some of these details can be worked out later, Colonel Anza. But for now, I ask you to please excuse me so I can return to my shelter."

The commander dismissed her with a wave of his hand, glad that a difficult interview was over. She felt her way blindly through the tent's entrance and disappeared into the night.

Juan de Anza thought yet again of Josefa Bellis and slowly resumed his seat behind his desk. He had just dismissed the only midwife within two hundred miles, thanks — he had no doubt — to the treachery of the expedition chaplain.

The deepset black eyes narrowed to furious slits. So be it. He would keep impeccable records, fully documented. Bucareli must be advised in full of the consequences of his reckless order.

CHAPTER 19   En Route to the Convent of Santa Clara de Asís
                                                October 1775

Ernán Haros watched as the girl riding ahead of him guided her horse down the steep rubbled bank of the arroyo. The summer rains had washed a deep gash across the road leading to the convent of Santa Clara de Asís. The party of seven included an escort of five armed guards from the Costanza household. One by one, the party picked their way down to the dry streambed and up the other side.

Watching the girl's slim form dip and bend with the movements of her mount, Haros wondered how many disappointed young suitors she had left behind. Consuelo Felicia de Vao was too pretty to become a nun, he decided. Her skin was the color and texture of a tawny rose and her deep-lashed eyes were like black pools with hidden glints of passion. Yet her serenity of manner indicated a strength that a man could trust without a flicker of hesitation.

Such women were rare. Pious as he was — up to a point — Haros had sometimes wondered if Jesu as a youth had encountered such a woman, would the history of the world have been different? He knew better than to dwell on such a riddle — it was heresy, after all. Still, he wondered.

Ahead of him, Consuelo negotiated the farther bank and turned to wait for him. Haros remembered many years before, the gay family outings when Doña Teresa's daughters were transported to and from the convent school. The roads were better then. Her youngest brother — Consuelo's father — was a toddler in dresses at the time. But now the niece Consuelo, her decision made, was returning alone to the convent to become a novice. The armed escort, even the horse she rode had been furnished by her aunt, not by her angry father. An outstanding debt had been canceled to surmount his disapproval.

When Haros drew even with Consuelo, she asked, "How will you get the bull across?"

"On the return trip tomorrow? I have no idea. After I deliver you to the abbess, young lady, my assignment is completed. I plan to leave at first light in the morning. Alone. I'll be halfway to the city before the problem arises."

Amused, Consuelo asked, "Do you mean to say Tía Teresa sent five guards to protect the bull? I thought the guards were to protect you and me!"

"You, yes. Me, no. The Costanza family learned long ago not to waste military personnel on their steward. When Don Eduardo was still alive, he insisted on furnishing me with a guard, but it was I who usually ended up guarding the guard instead of the other way around. I asked to be relieved of such responsibilities."

"You don't care about the poor bull?"

"'The *poor* bull?' In view of the price Doña Teresa is paying your abbess, I care for him a great deal! As to getting the creature across the arroyo, I imagine the guards will find an easier crossing. The leader is a seasoned *vaquero*. If all else fails, he might pull it across by the horns, for all I know. Whatever method they adopt, true love will triumph. Your aunt's lonely heifers will have their sweetheart, come what may."

Consuelo laughed. "The family always depends on Tía Teresa to arrange the marriages."

"And why not?" replied Haros. "She's very good at arrangements of all kinds. She is a better business man than most business men. Better even than me!"

"Now you're teasing me."

"No. The cattle, now. The dear lady once broke a tooth on a gristly bit of beef the cook had purchased at the market, It was the usual sort of meat brought to the city by the *paisanos*. After that incident, she began to think in terms of juicy roasts and cutlets for the city's leading families. With hides and tallow for export, of course. From the beginning, her cattle operation was a success and she established a second ranch near Guadalajara. She has mentioned a ranch in California, largely fantasy, I trust, at least for the present. Her interest now is in improving her herd."

For Consuelo, a mysterious family puzzle suddenly became clear. In a remote hallway at her family's city mansion was a portrait of Uncle Eduardo, his wife and covey of daughters. When she was a young child, she remembered seeing, in that portrait, an auburn-haired youth standing at Uncle Eduardo's shoulder. On re-examining the painting years later, she noted with surprise that the youth had disappeared — painted out of existence and replaced by a blossoming fruit tree.

Don Eduardo and his son had always been enemies, or nearly so, and his disappearance had come as no surprise to their dozens of relatives. When Consuelo was a schoolgirl at the convent, she suspected that Gabriella was her cousin; but the Costanza branch of the family was not to be provoked lightly, so she kept her thoughts to herself. And now Gabriella was with Anza on her way to California. To Tía Teresa's steward, a ranch in California might be "largely fantasy," but Consuelo felt certain that someday, somehow, it would materialize.

The strong wind at their backs pushed tatters of cloud ahead of them across the pale October sky. Along the dry streambeds, the cottonwoods were losing their autumn foliage, leaving bone-white boughs to crack together in the gusts. Far ahead among the barren hills, the travelers could make out the bell tower and bright green irrigated pastures of the convent.

Haros cleared his throat. "The abbess was quite ill. Exhaustion, was it? Has she recovered?"

"Not completely. But I had a letter from Sister Magdalena. She's spending an hour in her office each day."

"She'll be glad to see you," said Haros, who knew of Consuelo's heavy load of convent responsibilities.

"Gabriella used to say none of us understood all the work that kept the convent running. And she was right; we didn't. Such little things, usually. In the dormitory, our cots are made of wood, very lightweight. We used to get up in the morning in a hurry and go to bed at night in the dark, and the cots were shoved this way and that. We didn't realize it at the time, but it was Gabriella who straightened the dormitory cots each day. What she did was nothing, really. Yet a week after she left, the room looked like trolls lived there. It was like that all over the convent. With Gabriella gone, it —. Well, it wasn't the same. Still isn't."

" — And you think your decision is the proper one, do you?"

"In spite of Father's objections?" she smiled ruefully. "It will take him awhile to get used to the idea. But yes, I'm sure I'm doing the right thing. Before I left school in July, I talked to Reverend Mother about it. She was still in bed, talked in a whisper. She told me to think carefully about it. But I could tell she was glad I wanted to come back to stay."

"She needs you now more than ever, of course."

"Yes. Madre's whole life has been dedicated to the convent. She wants to feel that someday there will be nuns here that she trusts. She trusted Gabriella but with Gabriella married — widowed —, even if she comes back to Mexico, she can never take her vows."

"Sad," mused Haros. "So now, who will succeed Madre Valderia as abbess? You, perhaps?"

The shadowed black eyes were noncommittal. "It isn't a question for me to decide, is it? I want a life that is useful in the service of Christ. Beyond that, He will decide."

For the second time that morning, Ernán Haros felt a twinge of envy for the carpenter of Nazareth.

The Journey to Tubac
October 1775

At least, I have boots, thought Gabriella gratefully as she made her way across the pre-dawn encampment and beyond toward the vast livestock pasturage. An hour before, Rita and Miguel, already astir, were preparing the officers' breakfast when the commander summoned Gabriella to his tent. Padre Font stood, stone-faced, at the colonel's elbow.

Anza cleared his throat, averted his eyes, and spoke. "Señora Márquez, in view of the changed situation, it has been decided that you will no longer travel in the main line of march as you did before. I have relayed orders that the *arrieras* in charge of the *remuda* are to expect you as their permanent responsibility — "

"The *cattle!*" spat the priest in disgust. "She should march and sleep with the *cattle* — with leavings from the men's meals for her food! A witch scarcely deserves more than that!"

The colonel ignored the interruption. "At the end of the march each day, you may return to your usual overnight accommodation with Señor and Señora Esala. They are sorely overtaxed as it is, and you may assist them by tending fires, sweeping out the headquarters tent, and mending the officers' clothing as they may require. Under no circumstances are you to touch any food or cooking utensils — other than food eaten by yourself, of course. Before dawn each day, you must have eaten your breakfast, left the encampment and returned to the *remuda*."

"Phah!" sneered the priest. "Your weakness in this matter is typical of your incompetence in everything else! A proven witch should be banished *totally* and left to starve among the lizards! Yet she is to be allowed to contaminate the innocent here in camp."

"Begging your pardon, Chaplain, she is not a proven witch," responded Anza with determination. "She has undergone no trial of any kind, and her behavior with us has certainly shown no evidence of witchcraft. That Bucareli has charged her at all is due to the testimony of doubtful witnesses. My order stands. She will march with the *remuda*."

Gabriella expected disciplinary action of some kind, but not this. She recovered from her shock enough to ask, "Will I be allowed my regular mount?"

"You will not be mounted, Señora. You will travel afoot. You are dismissed."

Her jaw dropped in astonishment. Colonel Anza avoided her gaze, but Padre Font eyed her levelly, with the beginnings of a triumphant smile playing at the corner of his mouth.

Hearing what her sentence was to be, Miguel shook with rage and swore he would poison the chaplain's porridge before the day was out. Rita was more practical. "Colonel put her there so Lieutenant could see she comes to no harm." To Gabriella, she warned, "Lieutenant can't help you much, or he'll get you both in trouble. But he'll make sure the men treat you with respect and that you get water when you need it."

She dug out the two pairs of heavy boots that she and Gabriella had bought in Alamos. "If you wear out your pair, you'll have mine. Your feet will blister. I'll have ointment from the dispensary waiting tonight."

Weeping, Gabriella threw grateful arms around her old friend.

Rita plucked Gabriella's rosary from the tiny stand beside her pallet and handed it to her. "Count yourself lucky, that's what I say," she murmured. "It could have been worse. Now hurry. Before dawn, he said."

At the pasture, Gabriella settled herself under a mesquite tree to wait. Saying her rosary had calmed her, and her mind began to work again. She thought of the fate she had escaped with the bawling, nervous cattle, whose hooves and horns were so quick to slash at the unfamiliar. Afoot and lost in the dust, she would have died before the day was out. She crossed herself and offered up a prayer of thanksgiving for Colonel Anza.

The light was growing, and the *arrieros* began the hour-long chore of driving the pack animals to camp for loading. It would take another hour to form up the line of march — a long time for someone as active as Gabriella to sit idly watching other people work. Dirty work it was, too. Nowhere was the dust thicker, nowhere was the sludge underfoot more revolting. Still, Gabriella liked horses. — Far more than she liked the smelly, rough-spoken *arrieros*. She reflected that, traveling afoot, she herself would soon be smellier than they, high above the filth on their mounts. Still, if given a choice, she preferred honest dirt that could be scrubbed away to the deadly acid of Padre Font's malicious intrigue, the scars of which his victims would bear to their graves.

And except for the muck, walking wasn't so bad. Hadn't commander's Yuma interpreter walked every step from Culiacán, refusing a horse? "A human can outwalk a horse in any weather and do it with less food and less water," he claimed. She hoped the interpreter was right. Concerning such matters, the natives usually were.

She found herself watching for Martín, even though she knew he would be farther ahead with the pack animals, where he always rode. The expedition was traveling north that day, with a breeze from the west. Gabriella walked at the margin of the trail, thanking the Holy Virgin for her stout boots and keeping the wind at her left shoulder. To her right, the nodding heads of the listless trudging animals were scarcely discernible through the dust. Only the nearer ones were clearly visible. It troubled Gabriella to see many among them in poor condition — dull-eyed, gaunt, with ears drooping and coats rubbed raw. They badly needed currying, doctoring, and above all, rest. Anza, the cavalry officer, had scheduled a layover of several days at Tubac — their day's destination — perhaps for that very purpose. The animals were never long out of his mind.

Maybe if the expedition's official witch was not allowed to doctor its human members, perhaps the commander would let her doctor its horses. The thought brought a smile to her lips and a glow to her heart as she remembered Elias and their happy times together. Elias would be much more likely to laugh with her at her present predicament than to be angry about it.

At first, the *arrieros* seemed anxious about the young widow who was accompanying them. But when she behaved like the spunky sixteen-year-old girl that Lieutenant Neve insisted she was, their spirits rose. A holiday lay ahead, after all. At Tumacacori Mission, the expedition chaplain would be dropped off with his servant, Tómas, — supposedly to spend the holiday period discussing theology with the other padres stationed there. A few miles beyond Tumacacori lay the secure fortress of Colonel Anza's presidio at Tubac.

Around the bend from — and out of sight of — Tumacacori, there drew up beside Gabriella a gelding upon whose back rode a grizzled muleteer, his cheeks wrinkled into an enormous grin. "Lieutenant Neve's orders, Señora," he called down, and handed her the reins of a trim, long-limbed little mare, saddled for a lady. "He thought your feet might be gettin' sore."

The man turned and galloped toward the head of the line, leaving her to mount as best she could without help. Ungallant, maybe, but as they both knew, if reported in the right place, such good will could bring a thunderstorm of punishments for them all. The horse alone was risk enough.

She led the mare well away from the other animals and there discovered, tied to the cantle, a bottle of fresh water. She drank gratefully. The saddle was of a quality better than the one she regularly used, but the stirrup was too high for mounting. She unbuckled the stirrup strap and adjusted it as low as it would go, mounted, and from the back of the puzzled mare, readjusted the leather for a more comfortable ride. That done, she flipped the worst of the dust from her rebozo, draped it becomingly over her head and shoulders, treated herself to a second drink of water, replaced the bottle, and rode like a queen the rest of the way to Tubac.

The garrison was located on high sloping ground above the Santa Cruz River. Like most such garrisons, it consisted of several structures fronting on an open plaza with access from the surrounding countryside by stout gates. Along the north side of the plaza was a headquarters building with a square lookout tower, maintenance shops and a spacious stable area. To the east was a chapel and rimming the south side, a barracks for the soldiers, sheltered across the front by an arcade.

The expedition's travel-worn families were relieved to reach the garrison with its protecting walls, safe from Apache arrows. The women busied themselves with laundry. Bedding, shirts, trousers, and camisoles waved like pennants from a hundred improvised clotheslines.

Gabriella hung out her wet clothing with more composure than she felt. Scorned by the other women, she had done her laundry last, using the dirty water left behind by the others. Still, she was lucky. In Europe, a woman accused of witchcraft would be ordered before the Inquisition and if found guilty, burned at the stake. Madre had detested the Inquisition. "Soured bishops snooping after lost souls," she jeered. They were the shame of Europe, she said, with their torture of feebleminded old women or derelicts guilty of nothing worse than poverty. "Convenient victims," she called them.

Gabriella was coming to realize that without a husband or male relative for protection, she also was doomed to the role of convenient victim — not only of Federico Verro and Padre Font but of untold others yet to come. The injustice brought angry blood to her cheeks. But justice was a luxury reserved for men of rank; others must eke out what justice they could arrange on their own terms. For herself, she resolved in future to trust her own judgment, even — perhaps especially — when it conflicted with the judgment of her superiors. If she must dissemble and even betray those in authority to get her way, then so be it. The results could be no worse.

Vengefully, she finished arranging her damp clothing along the clothesline she had improvised. So what about the present? She would take everyone's leavings or do without, that seemed certain. What else? She would avoid Martín, for her own sake as well as his. For as long as she lived, her favorite memory would be Martín de Neve as she first saw him at the National Palace. She had felt exalted, transfigured. Her disillusionment had been slow in coming and ended in bitterness. His gift of the horse was out of character for the Martín she had come to know. It was as though an unexpected benefactor had thrown a warm, protecting cloak about her shoulders. Beneath her heart something twisted painfully. Was it gratitude that she felt? Perhaps, but she stiffened. She must watch herself.

She turned from the clothesline to meet the bashful gaze of Amanda Jiménez, a twelve-year-old expedition girl that Colonel Anza had hired to do housekeeping and laundry in Padre Font's tent. Gabriella and Amanda had been easy comrades from their first acquaintance at Horcasitas. A smile touched Gabriella's lips, but Amanda panicked and hurried away.

Stupid little twit! Tendons in Gabriella's grimy neck stood out and sour rage burned in her dirt-smeared face. *THEY ARE NOT GOING TO DO THIS TO ME!!*, she resolved, eyes blazing with fury. Miguel, mallet in hand, looked up from hammering a tent stake nearby. Reading her mood was easy enough. "It's a shameful thing, all right," he grumbled, "and all due to our high and mighty padre. That's the treachery you can expect from a Franciscan! The king was wrong to throw out the Jesuits. I said it five years ago and I say it now!"

"Don't be silly, Miguel," she snapped. "You can't condemn the whole Franciscan order because of Padre Font. And anyway, we only suspect he wrote a letter to the viceroy. No one can prove it."

"The notion about witchcraft didn't come to Bucareli in a dream, y'know! It had to come by courier. By a courier from the expedition, riding night and day both ways."

However the viceroy received his news, the garrison stewed with gossip, and Gabriella knew it. Gossip and fear. Over the length and breadth of Christendom, every household from the noblest palace to the meanest hut had its collection of witch stories. It was true that Gabriella Márquez was young, attractive, friendly and pious whereas witches were usually old, ugly, ill-tempered and profane. Still, the viceroy himself had spoken, so the charge must be true.

Nor were Gabriella and Miguel alone in believing the chaplain to be the instigator. Everyone in the encampment believed it. And Padre Font, formerly looked upon as an ineffectual prig, gained respect as a careful guardian of the expedition's welfare, conscientiously doing his duty. In his absence at Tumacacori, his reputation improved remarkably.

Colonel Anza agreed to a rental fee for the use of Señora's dispensary, payable in California. The terms were generous, and Miguel agreed with Gabriella that a promise of payment later was better than nothing.

After dark that first evening, Gabriella stepped outside the tent to shake out some bedding preparatory to rearranging her sleeping pallet for the night.

"Psst!"

To her surprise, she discovered Ynez Sandoval hiding in the shadows. "Ynez!" she murmured. "What are you doing here?"

The child moved closer and whispered, "I came to tell you Papacito thinks everyone is silly to say you are a witch. Some people are just ignorant. That's what he says. Mama says so too."

Tears of gratitude formed behind Gabriella's eyes. "Tell your parents I am glad they have confidence in me."

"I saw you yesterday walking by the soldiers' barracks. Does it make you feel bad when people turn their backs on you?"

Gabriella nodded and sighed. "It makes me feel all hollow, like a person without any insides. It's not a nice feeling at all."

Ynez thought for a moment. "Mama says now that you aren't a nurse, maybe you'll have time to teach me to read."

Gabriella hesitated. Being seen with Ynez could compromise them both. Was the witch seducing the child? Being seen entering and leaving the Sandoval shelter wouldn't do, either.

The silent moments lengthened. Ynez sighed. "Ricardo said you wouldn't do it. He said you'd be mad at everybody."

"Ricardo?"

"He's my twelve-year-old brother."

"I thought your brother was Tómas."

"Tómas is sixteen. I have five brothers. Oh, and Tómas is in love with you. But I guess you knew it."

Gabriella gulped. She decided to ignore the news about Tómas. "Five brothers is a lot of brothers."

Ynez heaved another sigh. "It sure is!"

"Ynez," said Gabriella matter-of-factly, "I want to teach you to read and write. Ask your Papacito to think of a good place for us to meet so the expedition people won't gossip."

"He already thought of that," said Ynez. "He said we should meet where they keep the livestock. The men who take care of the animals won't know or care who we are."

Martín will know, Gabriella thought immediately, but could name no better spot. Reluctantly she admitted, "It's true not many expedition people would be coming there."

"If they did, we could always hide behind a horse."

Gabriella nodded thoughtfully.

Ynez said, "If it's all right to teach me, maybe you would teach Juan too."

Gabriella smiled. "Another brother? I'd like that very much."

"And Ricardo?"

"I thought you said Ricardo could read as well as your father."

"My father can't read so good."

They agreed to meet the following day. Ynez slipped away into the darkness.

CHAPTER 20   Tubac to Canoa Ranch
                                                  October 1775

Sergeant Grijalva took charge of the dispensary as ordered, but in name only. His departure to collect his family from the garrison at Terrenate, some twenty miles away, left the commander with sole responsibility for the problem of Josefa Bellis.

For Colonel Anza, as with most men of his time, childbirth was an intimate matter that women took care of among themselves. He liked it that way, but obviously Señora Bellis had no friends interested in her welfare, and expedition wives were too busy with their own families to be assigned to care for the family of another. He gritted his teeth at assigning a soldier to do "women's work" for the Bellis family. Yet he saw no way to avoid it with the family's rightful father either drunk or sick or both and the rightful mother scarcely strong enough to stand, let alone attend to herself and her children.

The busy days at Tubac raced by. The expeditioners cleaned and repaired saddles and harness, repacked their belongings, and cooked food against the long journey ahead. With no Padre Font to scold her into submission, Gabriella determined to ignore the witch charge and behave around camp as though nothing had happened. With time to spare anyway, she arranged a smile on her face and took brisk walks around the presidio, exchanging cheerful banter with anyone who would favor her with a reply. The women heard her lighthearted conversation and turned to stare — resentfully at first, then with bewilderment.

Lieutenant Neve, from the moment he heard of the viceroy's order, recognized the witchcraft charge for the mischief it was. Power struggles were an old story to him. He had learned long ago to weather them by standing clear, saying nothing and avoiding any contact with the adversaries, Yes, it was a difficult time for Gabriella, but she had endured worse and the furor would pass more quickly without his interference.

He scarcely knew what to think the first day she appeared in the meadow with three of the expedition children. He watched as they found a shady spot under a cottonwood tree, opened their books and began to read. He strode toward them, then paused. He longed to talk to Gabriella, longed to see her almond eyes laughing up at him as they had the day she teased him about the Apaches. But small tongues could wag as dangerously as big ones. He thought better of it and returned to his command tent.

Rita provided the officers' meals as usual and watched with a hopeful eye as more new families arrived in Tubac to join the expedition. "Others besides Josefa Bellis will need help birthing their babies," she remarked to Miguel. "There's four more little ones on the way that I know of, maybe more. Sergeant can't do birthings. Colonel won't let Gabriella do it."

But there was more to Rita's worry than that. Without Gabriella to help, the headquarters work was too much for Rita and Miguel. Neither was as vigorous as in their earlier years, and half the distance to California — the most difficult half — still lay ahead.

Anza was aware of their need. The second day at Tubac, he brought Amanda Jiménez to the Esala shelter. "When the padres arrive from Tumacacori," he told Miguel, "Amanda can cook, launder and clean for them. In the meantime, if it is agreeable with you, she can make herself useful here."

The girl was cheerful, pious and neat in her habits, but she was not one to take responsibility, not like Gabriella, and Rita longed for an older woman she could depend upon.

Next day, she crossed herself with relief when Sergeant Grijalva arrived from Terrenate with his family. His wife Rosa was a quiet, full-bodied woman of few words. Her four well-behaved children were independent and resourceful. She became a frequent visitor and then a trusted addition to the headquarters staff.

Tómas returned to Tubac under a cloud of self-pity. Accompanying Padre Font was Padre Francisco Garcés of the TumacacoriMission. By the viceroy's order, Garcés was to join the expedition as far as the Colorado River. There he would remain and pursue missionary work among the Yuma Indian settlements. In the meantime, Tómas Sandoval, the padres' only servant, was attending to the needs of both men.

Upon his arrival, Tómas was heartened to learn that, with Miguel's assistance, Amanda Jiménez had already pitched and swept out the padres' tent. Also she expected to take over many other responsibilities that had formerly been his. Also she was pretty. Tómas brightened considerably.

The Sunday before departure, Padre Font officiated at a High Mass for the continued success of the expedition. Again he admonished his families to set a good example for the heathen Indians — not the Apaches this time, but friendly village tribes through whose territory they would soon be traveling. Josefa Bellis was too exhausted to attend the service. She still had not given birth to her infant.

On October 23, the following day, cargo was packed on mules and saddles were flung over the backs of the horses with less confusion and wasted effort than at the staging area at Horcasitas. Shortly before noon, the California Expedition under the command of Colonel Anza set out once more. It traveled some twelve miles north along the river to a ranchero called La Canoa where the expedition made camp.

Late that afternoon, Josefa Bellis went into labor.

The autumn dusk had fallen and families clustered about their campfires. Miguel and Rita had gone to check Rita's mare, which had developed a limp during the day's travel.

Gabriella was alone when Sergeant Grijalva slipped like a shadow into Miguel's shelter. "It's Señora Bellis," he whispered. "Her baby's coming, Gabriella. Rosa's busy taking care of a baby that nearly choked with whooping cough. Nobody knows what to do!"

"How far along is she?" whispered Gabriella.

"How far along? How would I know that? She just lies there. Every four or five minutes her belly bunches up and turns hard as a knuckle."

Gabriella nodded. "Contractions. Is she working with them?"

"What d'you mean?"

"She's had seven babies, Sergeant. She knows what to do. She should be bearing down every time one of the contractions comes. Her face should turn red. Tendons in her neck should stand out." But the sergeant looked bewildered.

Gabriella blushed, wishing Rosa had come instead. Looking away, she asked the sergeant, "You've watched your little boy have a bowel movement. He strains. Well, giving birth to a baby is like that, only much harder."

The sergeant's black eyebrows skipped halfway up his bald forehead. "Really?"

Gabriella poked the fire. "Josefa. Is she straining?"

"No. Like I told you, she just lies there. Colonel Anza keeps checking her pulse. A good thing, too. She looks dead to me."

Gabriella was puzzled. "But that's so painful, when a woman ignores her labor pains like that! Hasn't she cried out?"

"No."

"Hasn't she said anything?"

"If she has, I haven't heard her. On the march today, Tom rode along with her and her kids every step of the way. Colonel's orders. When we made camp, he helped the family unpack. He and the kids were getting a meal together when he noticed Señora looked funny and that fool husband of hers started to cry. He wept! Real tears! You know, Gabriella, that guy — "

"Josefa," Gabriella reminded him. "Tell me about Josefa."

"Well, the colonel sent a litter for her. The men had to lift her in and then lift her out again at headquarters. That's where we've got her now."

"I hope they're keeping her warm."

"Oh, sure. There's a couple blankets on her. Good warm bed. But God's britches, Gabriella, she hasn't opened her eyes or said a word! Not once. Rosa finally got the kid with whooping cough settled for the night. She's there too."

"Good. Has she had anything to eat?"

"Señora Bellis? Well, no. I guess not since before we left Tubac this morning. You think maybe that's all that's wrong with her? She's just hungry?"

Gabriella stepped outside the shelter where she opened a food chest and removed a covered jar. "Rita made broth for Padre Font and there was a bit left over. It's still warm." She quickly poured the jar's contents into a clean bowl. "Give her this. Get your wife to feed it to her. Here, take a spoon along. Then come back and I'll tell you what to do. Hurry!"

Shortly afterwards, Miguel and Rita returned. The three whispered beside the fire, then Miguel and Rita arranged their bedding for the night and withdrew.

For two hours, Gabriella waited. Once, to assuage her loneliness, she stole into the darkened shelter for Elias' turquoise stone in its silken pouch. Clasping it tightly, she returned to the fire where she gazed at its lustrous blue surface, caressing and stroking it against her cheek.

Without warning, a slender figure silently materialized out of the darkness and she started with surprise. "Tómas?"

"You're awake," the boy observed. "I came to see for myself." A mischievous grin spread over his face. "I've never seen a witch before."

"In the daylight with the horses, I'm more convincing," she teased solemnly. "Dust from head to foot, I look like a huge spider." She screwed her mouth in a mock sneer and her hands into ferocious claws.

Tómas was not impressed. He made himself comfortable beside the fire. "Padre's wrong," he said. "You're no witch. I could have told him."

"Could you, now?"

"I can tell by looking. You can't suck your heels."

"Idiot!" Gabriella stifled her laughter, not wanting to attract the attention of the neighbors. "Whoever heard of witches sucking their heels?"

"Padrecito says all witches suck their heels. That's how they move so fast. Wet heels. But you're too stiff, so you can't be a witch. You can't even suck your elbows."

"Please notify Padre Font," requested Gabriella. "Maybe you'll convince him. Where is he, anyway? In bed asleep?"

"The colonel sent for him. They're at the headquarters tent with Señora Bellis."

Gabriella's smile faded. There was only one reason the colonel would summon Padre to headquarters at a time like this. After a moment's silence she asked, "Is it the end for her, then?"

Tómas nodded solemnly. "I went along to carry Padre's things." He brightened. "There are two of us now, working for the padres. Things are easier with the girl Amanda. She is all right." He shrugged. "She is pretty enough, I guess."

"Who?"

"The girl." He realized that Gabriella was lost in thoughts of her own. "Soon I must go back to headquarters and wait. Padre Font says Señora will not take long to die."

Gabriella bit her lip. Where was Sergeant Grijalva? Why hadn't he returned?

Orange points of firelight reflected in Tómas's black eyes as he examined her. "You lost your baby?"

"Yes, Tómas."

"Were you sad?"

"Yes."

After awhile, Tómas said, "I understand your being sad about your baby. But why are you sad about Señora Bellis? That family, they are scum. Even a *lepero* would look down on Vasco Bellis and his wife. Why do you care?"

"I don't know, Tómas. I suppose because everyone else judges Señora the same way you do. At the convent, sometimes we had a *paisana* like her, very sick. But her husband was always with her and you could see the love they had together. The children were there, the woman's mother, her sisters. And no matter how poor the family was, they sacrificed to give a moment of pleasure. Maybe they would bring the sick woman a bit of lace or embroidery, or a picture of the Madonna. Sometimes just a blossom. But poor Señora Bellis has never known blessings like that. She carries a terrible load of hardship, all by herself."

Tómas' young features shifted. "Maybe you think too much about the loads other people carry. Maybe you should sometimes think about your own load."

She glanced at Tómas and noticed his solemn, grown-up look. She reached out and squeezed his hand. "It will be a lucky girl who gets you for a husband, Tómas."

She shifted and drew her rebozo closer about her shoulders. She wished the sergeant would at least come tell her what was happening.

Tómas rose to leave. There was an awkward pause. "Ynez says you are going to teach her and my brothers to read. Will you teach me? I can't always come when they do."

The request pleased Gabriella. "Of course, Tómas! We can work out a separate time for you."

Tómas vanished into the shadows, Gabriella spread a pallet before the fire and at last dozed off. The stars were fading when the sergeant returned. His bowed head confirmed what she had already guessed. Padre Font had been wrong: the woman had taken many long hours to die. Gabriella closed her eyes against her sorrow, crossed herself and whispered a prayer.

The sergeant squatted beside the fire. His face was reddened and swollen from shock and fatigue. Gabriella whispered, "What about the baby?"

"He's fine." Sergeant Grijalva stared despairingly into the coals. "I guess he's fine. It's a little boy. Rosa cleaned him up."

"The baby will need to nurse."

The sergeant nodded. "The Sandovals took him."

Gabriella stared. "The Sandovals already have nine children of their own!"

"Yes, I know. Rina Sandoval is nursing that baby of hers but says she has enough milk for two. At least, that's what she told Rosa. Rosa said the baby started nursing right away."

The sergeant's speech was slurred and a muscle in his cheek twitched from exhaustion. "What went wrong?" Gabriella asked.

"Rosa said something else was supposed to come out of her after the baby."

"The placenta," Gabriella said. "The afterbirth."

"But it didn't come."

"Sometimes you have to press on the mother's abdomen. Press hard. You have to make it come."

Grijalva gestured weakly. "I guess Rosa didn't know what to do. None of us did."

"I could have told you what to do! Why didn't you come back? I thought you were coming back after you gave her the broth."

"Padre Font made me stay."

"What?"

"When I got back with the broth, Font was there. The colonel had sent for him. He didn't want the woman to die without the last rites."

"But the broth — "

"Font wouldn't let Rosa feed her the broth. He said it might be cursed somehow."

Gabriella was stunned. "'Cursed?'"

"He recognized the bowl. He knew I'd gotten the broth from you." Grijalva covered his face with trembling fingers. "He made me stay there and watch it all. Holy Saints, Gabriella, I've got four kids of my own but I never knew it was like that when a woman had a baby!"

He fought to control a sob rising in his throat, then continued. "At the last, she had convulsions, one after another. She nearly bit her tongue off and there was blood everywhere. She nearly drowned from the blood in her mouth. I thought she was going to break her arms or legs, she was thrashing around so. Font kept saying she was possessed of the devil and it was God's will that she had to die."

The sergeant had spoken softly to avoid waking nearby sleepers but now his voice hardened. "And you know what? The bastard enjoyed every minute of it! Anza was half out of his mind, wanting to try this and try that to save her, but Font wouldn't hear of it. 'Let God's will be done,' he kept saying. Hell, he didn't care a damn about God's will. With the woman dead, that would put the colonel in a bad light with the viceroy, that's what Font cared about! *He* wanted her dead!" He looked away. "At the very end she was staring like a crazy person. She was looking straight at me. I saw the light fade out of her eyes. I saw her die."

Suddenly the sergeant leaped to his feet, found a stick and furiously jabbed the dying coals to flame. "Damn!" he shouted.

But weariness quickly dampened his anger. "Hell, what do I care? It's their quarrel, not mine. Anza and Font between them, they'll fight it out, I guess. But I'll tell you this, Gabriella, I'd rather take my chances with fifty Apache warriors than one mother about to give birth! *Santa Madre,* I'll never understand you women. Before tonight, I never knew what it was like. But you knew. You've watched dozens of women give birth. And still you came on this expedition pregnant, with no husband, expecting to have a baby of your own in a few months. You're crazy, Gabriella, you know that?"

He turned to go, then whirled and shook a formidable fist in her direction. "I'll tell you something else, Gabriella Márquez! I make a sacred vow here and now, with you and Almighty God as my witnesses: My sweet wife Rosa will never bear another child." His voice broke and he struggled to finish what he wanted to say. *"Never!"* And he turned and stalked away through the fading night.

Later that same morning, the physical remains of Josefa Bellis were placed in the care of Padre Garcés. With a small military escort, the priest traveled north ahead of the expedition to San Xavier Mission where a proper funeral was held upon the later arrival of Colonel Anza and the settlers.

The newborn infant was welcomed by the older Sandoval children, who watched over him with the same care given their own younger brothers and sisters. Among the other expedition families, there was concern over the remaining seven Bellis children; ill-clothed and sickly though they were, several willing foster parents immediately came forward and the children were taken in.

The father was another matter. Vasco Felipé Bellis pleaded his own failing health to disclaim responsibility for the tragedy. Now, he maintained, he was without children, wife, or a soldier to care for him and wondered what was to become of him. By the time the expedition broke camp, Bellis had approached every family begging for assistance. Next he sought out unwed teenage daughters with offers of marriage but they either laughed or fled in alarm.

Word reached Colonel Anza that the new widower, despairing, was returning alone to seek shelter at Tubac. The commander thereupon reminded Private Bellis of his military status as a cavalryman. The penalty for a deserting soldier was the firing squad.

Vasco Bellis hurriedly gathered his belongings. Weeping pitiably, he harried his beasts through the dusty livestock until he caught up with the main line of march. For the next few days, he grieved quietly for his departed wife.

No one ever came forward to help with his chores so he cooked and carried on his own account. The exercise improved his health.

CHAPTER 21   San Xavier Mission and Beyond
                                                    Late October-Early November 1775

Beyond the San Xavier Mission and the little settlement of Tucson, Gabriella said her rosary each morning before dawn, then returned to her assigned place with the *remuda*. The expedition was moving north into territory that was both dryer and cooler. The alkali dust had been a nuisance. Now it became a formidable enemy. Walking beside the surging horses, Gabriella could scarcely make out their forms well enough to stay clear of them. Nor could she see large boulders and drop-offs in her path before stumbling into them.

An hour away from the mission, she became aware of a shadow looming at her elbow, a mounted *arriero*. "Grab my stirrup and hold on!" a male voice shouted. Groping, she found the harness and gratefully accepted the man's guidance. She buried her nose and mouth in her rebozo and shut her eyes tight against the grit that stung like acid.

Another hour passed. Her hand gripping the horseman's stirrup had lost all feeling. She frequently stumbled and once took a bruising fall into a great thicket of prickly pear. She was slow recovering, and at length heard the *arriero* cantering off toward the rear of the line of march.

She thought herself deserted, rested awhile, and renewed her efforts to free herself from the clinging, crumbling thorns. At last she stood, rubbed her scratched and bleeding legs, adjusted her rebozo to keep out as much of the dust as possible, and continued, limping, beside the turbulent roar of the horses. She had covered no more than a dozen yards when an unidentified *arriero* nudged forward with a mount for her.

Encamped late that afternoon, Gabriella found two expedition mothers waiting for her, one with a red-faced, coughing baby and the other with a weeping toddler. The women, themselves bedraggled, were shocked at Gabriella's appearance. Glancing at her reflection in Rita's mirror, Gabriella understood why. Head to foot, she was colorless as a wraith, her hair as stiff as wood shavings.

Tears of pity came to Rita's eyes at the sight of her. "You need a wash," she said, "but the only water we have is for drinking and cooking, and precious little for that. Miguel is with Sergeant and the men, digging *pojos* in the riverbed. Later, we can clean ourselves, but Colonel will water the horses first so it will be late tonight."

And the women? "Sergeant Grijalva said you would help us," said one. "He said you know about the dispensary and would know what to get for the babies."

Rita and Gabriella exchanged bitter glances.

"Well," sighed Gabriella, "I can't go to headquarters tent looking like this," and she began flipping the caked dust from her clothing. Rita stopped her. "There's no one to see you at headquarters. The officers are all at the river with the men digging *pojos*. If the chaplain sees you helping these women, let him see you just as you are. Tell him you are following Sergeant Grijalva's orders."

Later, as the women were leaving the deserted headquarters tent with their children, a leatherjacket limped by, furtively thrust his head through the tent entrance and asked her to look at a contusion on his knee. The injury had been improperly cleaned and clumsily bandaged. There was extensive infection. Lacking water, Gabriella wiped away the foul matter with wine and expertly rebandaged it.

Putting away the dispensary items, she sensed someone behind her and turned. Two naked Pima Indian men stood well inside the tent, staring. They frightened her, but apparently the gray corpse-like Spanish woman frightened the intruders even more. Their eyes wild with terror, the men wheeled and ran.

Gabriella remembered what Tómas had said of the natives' fear of ghosts. Well, she supposed to them she looked more dead than alive. *Convenient*, she thought, with a sigh of relief, and wondered why she hadn't crossed herself and thanked the Blessed Virgin.

Before Gabriella awoke next morning, word had already spread that the expedition "witch" had lost none of her skill as a nurse. Word also spread quickly that Padre Font was so enfeebled by the dust that he kept to his bed whenever possible; Padre Garcés was now hearing confessions and saying Mass each morning.

That day — and on subsequent days — Gabriella found the long-legged mare saddled and waiting at the shelter for her before dawn each morning, and an ailing *arriero* or two waiting for her attention when she reached the livestock area. Before long, Lieutenant Neve invited her to ride farther to the front of the line of march with the pack animals, where the dust was not so bad. A few days later, Sergeant Grijalva suggested that she "would be more help to Rita and Miguel" if she rode in her old place with them where the dust was not bad at all. Padre Font disapproved but was disarmed by his frailty.

The colonists were relieved to be free of the Apache threat but the "friendly" Pimas were a threat of a different kind. The larger settlements offered good water and occasionally the welcoming natives built brush arbors and brought fuel for the colonists' cooking fires. The commander reciprocated with gifts of glass beads and tobacco, which the natives gladly accepted. But the natives also snooped at will among the shelters and took whatever they happened to fancy.

The farther the expedition journeyed, the colder grew the nights. Eight blankets per family had seemed ample in the sunny plaza of Culiacán, but several hundred miles to the north, they did little to warm the shivering travelers after the sun went down. Tómas was grateful for the cast-off habit Padre Font gave him. It was old — frayed at wrists and hem — but warm. The chaplain, in his weakened condition, found it harder to take readings from the sun for establishing the latitudes through which they traveled. He was teaching Tómas to make the necessary journal notations, and spoke of formally appointing him his notary.

Tómas coveted the assignment. As the chaplain's notary, perhaps he would no longer be expected to wash the chaplain's feet and empty his slops.

In view of the cold, the natives astonished everyone with their nakedness, Tómas most of all. He tried not to look at the female Pimas with their bare breasts and short rackety skirts of willow bark that barely covered their buttocks. One of them had gone so far as to leer and stroke his shoulder in a suggestive way.

The expedition had first seen these friendly natives at the mission at San Xavier, but the San Xavier Indians went to Mass each morning and wore real clothes. These new Indian tribes were what Padre Font called "the godless heathen". Four days north of San Xavier, Colonel Anza read out a list of penalties for colonists who attacked the "godless heathen" or stole from them or violated their women.

The Pimas were a dark-skinned people with short legs, thick torsos and long hair cut short in front. Padre Font said they were ugly. Tómas guessed they were, though the Pima woman who had smiled at him looked tempting. She was young, clean and not too fat. Tómas asked himself if she was worth fifty lashes on his bare back if he got caught. He decided it was safer stealing kisses from skinny little Amanda Jiménez. Or trying to. He had succeeded only once.

Farther north, the expedition encountered Pima natives — a different tribe — the men wearing cotton breechclouts and the women loose-fitting deerskin tunics. Both men and women warmed themselves with cotton blankets thrown about their shoulders. They were successful farmers. The harvest season was over except for winter-grown crops, nevertheless these northern Pimas proudly showed off their fields and explained their irrigation systems. They demonstrated the wheels on which they spun their cotton thread and the looms on which they wove their blankets. A lively trade developed between the natives with their soft blankets and the shivering colonists.

Food was offered to the expedition leaders. The chaplain turned away with a shudder but Rita gladly accepted melons, vegetables and freshly-ground cornmeal for the officers' mess. Padre Garcés was a true man of the wilderness with his yellow peg teeth and worn Franciscan robe, more rags than raiment. Garcés had long dined and danced among the natives and particularly relished the squash, cantaloupes and stewed desert game which Padre Font found revolting. There was ample food for the colonists as well, but the *paisanos*, as squeamish in their own way as was the chaplain in his, preferred their beef and beans.

Each successive encampment brought them to a new population of Papago, Pima or Yuma natives. Gabriella, with most of the dust washed from her auburn hair, grew impatient with their curiosity. "They snatch handfuls of my hair and won't let go," she complained at the shelter. "What pests they are!"

Rosa looked up from the meat she was slicing. "They want to see if it's real. They're trying to pull it off."

"Worse than that," Miguel said solemnly. "Remember the Pima men at headquarters who thought you were a ghost and ran? They've passed the word along the trail ahead of us. They claim you tricked them to challenge their manhood."

Gabriella fumed. "The stupid scoundrels tricked themselves! All I did was stand there, filthy as a scarecrow! Anyway, aren't they supposed to fear witches?"

Miguel shook his head. "They know you're not a witch," he said. "They see you giving people medicine on the sly. And the people don't die, they get well. What the braves don't like is a mere woman showing them up as cowards. Especially savages like these. They treat their chickens better than they treat their women. They think you scared them on purpose, and laughed when they ran."

Rita was suspicious. "How do you know all this?" she demanded.

"The interpreter," said Miguel. "He told me to warn Señora Márquez. The Pimas know to look for the woman with red hair."

"With no husband to protect her, they can mistreat her any way they want and get by with it!" exclaimed Rosa.

"Tie up your hair like a nun," advised Rita. " — And never be caught alone. Take two or three children with you wherever you go."

"They know which shelter you live in," warned Miguel. "That turquoise, the stone Elias gave you. Guard it close, even when you sleep at night. Yesterday I caught a couple of the rascals here in the shelter going through Rita's chest. They'd broke the lock! What do you think of that?! And made a neat stack of things they planned to take! So if you treasure your blue stone, leave it in its pouch pinned inside your camisole."

For the most part, Gabriella complied. Finding children to attend Mass with her each morning was nearly impossible but she wrapped and draped herself against the prying Indians and went anyway.

She sought out Padre Garcés for confession. The first time, as she stood to leave the closet, he murmured to her, "You must be the red-haired one, the *bruja*."

"Padre, I am not a witch," Gabriella replied evenly. "I have been falsely accused."

"I was told you could cure people. Have you had training as a *curandera*?"

"I knew a *curandera* in Mexico. It wouldn't be true to say she trained me. But I have watched her work with her patients so I know something of her cures."

Garcés was puzzled. "You 'watched her'? Is that what led Colonel Anza to appoint you official nurse for his expedition?"

Gabriella smiled. "No," and she told him of her background with Sister Magdalena. "But that doesn't make me a witch, does it?"

"No," Padre Garcés replied easily. "I had my doubts anyway. You don't look the part."

Gabriella saw that others were coming for confession. "Several of the families have asked me for medical advice, Padre," she said. "They know it's against Colonel Anza's orders. They also know Padre Font would disapprove, so they are quiet about it. Please advise me. I don't know what is proper for me to do."

"I shouldn't think a word or two of medical counsel would be amiss. Discreetly given, as you suggest. Other than that, you are teaching — how many? — eight boys and girls to read and write?"

Her face softened with pleasure. "I have three Sandovals, four Garcías, and an Alvarez."

"Very laudable! And I understand you hold your classes always near the corrals, with your friend Lieutenant Neve nearby for protection against the unpredictable natives? A wise precaution for an attractive young widow. My colleague Padre Font thinks so, too."

She stiffened. "'Padre Font thinks so'?"

Garcés smiled and said archly, "Your expedition chaplain is actually a very prim priest. Unattached individuals, he says, are prone to sin. They make him nervous. He feels more comfortable with all the world's creatures neatly paired off, as on Noah's ark."

Other parishioners required his attention. Quickly, he added, "But you asked about medical assistance for the expedition families. I should say if, with your other duties, you can also find time to assist Sergeant Grijalva with medical advice, you would be making yourself useful and we would all be better off."

Except that I no longer have my salary, thought Gabriella coldly.

With a jovial nod, Padre Garcés dismissed her. She went to the chapel, knelt, and fingered her rosary. But her thoughts were muddled and the prayers would not come. So Padre Font had paired off Martín the *gachupín* with a woman he had formerly accused of witchcraft. He had known all along his charge to the viceroy was false, and cared not at all that he had brought about the death of Josefa Bellis, an innocent woman, and the spiteful punishment of herself, another innocent woman. The crisis had never been anything but what Sergeant Grijalva said it was, a scheme to blacken Colonel Anza's name at the National Palace.

"You must see what the world is like beyond the walls of the convent," Reverend Mother had explained to her that frightening afternoon in her office. "You will find wickedness, even depravity." Indeed Gabriella had found both, not only in the world beyond but within Mother Church itself. She had been terrified to leave the security of the convent, but the security was an illusion.

Well. She would watch for the right time to talk to Colonel Anza about resuming her former salary.

Gabriella continued to teach the children each afternoon near the enclosures put up for the horses and pack animals after the day's march. Often Martín was miles away supervising the *vaqueros* with the cattle, a day behind the main part of the expedition. On rare occasions when he appeared, he was busy with duties of his own.

One afternoon Gabriella had seated herself in the shade of a boulder and was busy teasing Tony Alvarez, who on that day's march had taken a tumble from his pony. The Sandovals approached. Ricardo carried a large basket under his arm.

"A picnic?" wondered Gabriella.

"We brought José," called Ynez. "He'll be quiet, Señora. Mama just finished feeding him. He'll sleep and won't bother us."

"Aurelia's starting to cut teeth," Ricardo explained. "She cries all the time and has to be held. Mama fed José first to get him out of the way so she could take care of Aurelia."

"Please, can he stay?" begged Ynez.

"Of course, he can stay!" said Gabriella. "May we look at him?"

Ricardo held out the warmly-lined basket, and for the first time, Gabriella saw the infant that was born that terrible night at Canoa. Drowsing among his wrappings was a sturdy infant with dark blue eyes in a round pink face. A trickle of milk leaked from one corner of his rosebud mouth. His finespun hair was a dark chestnut color with red glints reflecting in the late afternoon sun.

Gabriella held her breath as she touched the tiny perfect hands, the delicate unblemished skin.

"He has red hair, like you," Ynez pointed out.

"It's not red," scoffed Ricardo. "It's only brown."

"Would you like to hold him?" Ynez asked Gabriella.

Deeply moved, Gabriella picked up the infant son of Josefa Bellis. How perfectly the tiny bundle fit in the crook of her arm! She brushed her cheek against the infant's hair, soft as spiderwebs, then looked up, embarrassed, to find the children staring at her. She ignored the tears in her eyes, smiled brightly and said, "He's a fine baby. Your family has taken good care of him. What did you say his name was?"

Ricardo explained, "We decided to call him José because his mother's name was Josefa."

"Why are you crying?" Ynez asked.

It was a fair question, for a tear had coursed down her cheek. "You see, Ynez, my own baby was born before its time. So it's — it's almost a miraculous thing, to me, to be able to cuddle a tiny newborn."

"We could bring him every day when we come for lessons," volunteered Ricardo. "It would give Mama more time with Aurelia."

Gabriella welcomed the proposal. She would like to have seen more of Martín, but according to rumor, the natives were keeping him busy. They pressed on him their offers to help herd the livestock but were actually more interested in stealing a horse or a mule if not carefully watched.

Others of the expedition besides Martín found the Pimas hard to bear. "There are too many of them and they take too many liberties!" cried Padre Font. "They swarm over us like insects."

"You don't need to put up with it, you know," said Padre Garcés. "If you don't like it, stay in the tent."

"What good does that do?" cried the chaplain. "They come right inside, picking up this, picking up that, feeling and twisting, taking things apart, *licking* things — ugh! One of the filthy creatures nearly ruined my psaltery! Twanged at the strings and then tried to rip them off the instrument!"

"Come now, Pedro," protested Garcés. "These people are innocent children, after all. Any music more sophisticated than a deerskin drum is a fascinating mystery. Play for them. Show them yourself what your psaltery is supposed to do, and they won't be tempted to find out for themselves. Didn't you tell me Anza wanted you to bring it along to play for the natives?"

"He did," sulked Padre Font. "Or at least, that's what he said. But has our mighty frontier commander asked me to play? Not once! Here I have brought the thing all this distance. And for what purpose?"

"Play!" urged Padre Garcés. "Play something now. For me."

Clearly tempted, the chaplain plucked several experimental chords. Then he sighed, put the psaltery firmly out of sight in a chest and locked it. "I would only be criticized."

The old missionary smiled and turned away. He had no intention of giving up.

The commander ordered encampment near a lake that was later called Laguna del Hospital. It was said to offer good water and ample pasturage. In the weeks ahead, the expedition would cover difficult terrain, and Colonel Anza had scheduled a lengthy rest beside this lake to strengthen the livestock and hearten the colonists. Also, there was a holiday to celebrate.

"Tomorrow is the king's birthday and the feast day of San Carlos," Garcés reminded Padre Font as Tómas set up the chapel. "It is a celebration that deserves our best efforts. Let me say Mass this evening while you assist with your psaltery."

More persuasion was needed, for cold wind and rain on the march that day had stiffened Padre Font's arthritic fingers. But he consented at last and at twilight the delicate chords of the psaltery alternated with Padre Garcés' prayers. The Indians stood, as always, at the rear of the tent behind the worshipers. The unfamiliar sights and sounds of the liturgy rendered them spellbound. "Did you see them?" murmured Font afterwards. "How wonderful it would be if all our services could be so effective!"

His satisfaction was short-lived. That evening, the commander ignored the chaplain's objections and distributed a pint of brandy to each soldier in honor of the holiday. Many of the women drank, danced and sang as lustily as their husbands. Gabriella the widow and still-suspect witch braved a sip of brandy from Rita's mug and went to bed early.

It was a noisy night with little sleep. At dawn, yawning and scrubbing her eyes, she left the shelter on her way to Mass. Usually there were several worshipers making their way to Padre Garcés' early service, but glancing about in the morning dusk, she found herself alone.

Halfway to the chaplain's tent, she was relieved to hear galloping hoofbeats approaching. Someone else was coming to Mass after all, perhaps one of the *vaqueros*. She expected the horseman to halt at the padres' tent but to her dismay, he neither slowed nor veered. Neither saw the other clearly in the dim light and only at the last moment did the cavalryman rein in his mount to avoid running her down.

"Damn you, woman!" he shouted testily, struggling to control his rearing, neighing horse. "Take care where you're going!"

Gabriella drew aside. "Martín?"

"You could have been killed!" cried the lieutenant. "What's a lone woman like you doing wandering around at this hour, anyway!"

"It's Gabriella, Martín! I'm on my way to Mass!"

The horse circled and tossed its head. "Gabriella?"

"I'm sorry I got in your way. I thought you were a *vaquero* coming into campf or the early service. I thought you would stop."

The horse calmed somewhat and Martín dismounted. "You're going to Mass?" he repeated, not quite believing her. Except for hasty reports to the commander, he had lost touch with the encampment these last few days. "They let you go to Mass?"

Gabriella's temper rose. "Padre Font's charge was false, Lieutenant," she said icily. "He is not well. Padre Garcés has taken over his duties as chaplain. I come and go as I please."

He was glad of her news but baffled by it. He swore. "Look, Gabriella, down there by the lakeshore, we've got livestock getting sicker by the hour. The forage is brackish and the water worse. The expedition is in trouble, believe me! When I jumped on this horse to report to the commander, I wasn't thinking of you or your silly feud with Padre Font. I was damned worried about getting us all to California!"

Gabriella caught her breath. "'My silly feud — ?'"

"I can't waste time talking to you now! I've got to report to Anza." And without so much as a parting nod, he pulled his skitterish mount behind him up the path to the headquarters tent.

Gabriella stood looking after him, trembling with angry humiliation. To be scorned as though she were a stupid, misbehaving child — ! Armed with a quirt, she would at that moment gladly have struck Martín de Neve across the eyes as she had attacked the bandit on the road to Mexico! Before continuing on to the chaplain's tent, she waited for her angry tears to subside, but instead of subsiding, they coursed in miniature rivers down her cheeks. Her bosom began to heave with suppressed sobs.

She gave herself an angry shake. What was wrong with her, crying over that boob, Martín? And suddenly, like a fetid miasma, her true fear beset her. The lieutenant might take pity on Elias' unfortunate widow, send her a horse to ride and take thought for her welfare. But it could well be that Bonita de Figuroa, of aristocratic birth and breathtaking beauty, still reigned in his heart and nothing would ever change it.

Brushing away her tears, she decided that perhaps Mass was not such a good idea after all, and returned with lagging footsteps to the shelter.

Because of the brackish water and forage, Martín and his men spent the entire day moving the livestock to fresh pasture.

Anza's scouts located two springs of fresh water for the colonists. — But not before several of them became ill and one of the pregnant women went into hard labor before her time. When darkness fell that evening, Sergeant Grijalva quietly appeared to notify Gabriella.

"She's miscarried, hasn't she?" Gabriella asked.

Grijalva nodded. "Rosa's still with her."

Gabriella thought of her own lost baby. "The woman is lucky," she murmured. "She has her husband. She can try again."

Before departing, the sergeant hesitated. "Funny thing. A few days ago, one of the leatherjackets said he was too tired to eat. Well, for a soldier, now, too tired to eat, that's pretty tired. I gave him a tot of brandy and got a little color back in his face. Next day there were two more men. I thought they were after booze. I bawled them out and sent them back to work. An hour later, one fainted dead away!"

"'A few days ago?' Then it wasn't bad water from the lake?"

Grijalva shook his head. "Yesterday, a couple of women said they were aching and tired all the time. And now this new one today, Señora Jiménez. Colonel doesn't know what to make of it. He's worried. He said talk to you about it."

Gabriella had never found the right time to talk to the commander about her reinstatement; maybe the opportunity was closer than she thought. Jiménez? That would be Amanda's mother. Whatever ailed Señora must not be contagious, otherwise Amanda would also be ill, and she wasn't. "Have you examined any of these people?" she asked Grijalva. "It could be scurvy."

"Only sailors get scurvy."

"Anyone can get scurvy."

"Women too?

"Women more easily than men," said Gabriella, "and children most easily of all. Would Señora Jiménez let me examine her, do you think?"

"Maybe. I know Colonel would want you to, though he can't say so. Come on, I'll take you."

Gabriella threw her wool rebozo about her shoulders and left the shelter with the sergeant.

"What causes scurvy, anyway?"

"No one knows," answered Gabriella. "It has something to do with fresh food. When a ship is away from land too long, the sailors get so weak they can't leave their bunks. Their gums bleed and their teeth fall out. Some of our colonists haven't had fresh food since early summer in Culiacán."

"Our food supplies are holding up all right," said Grijalva defensively. "At least, we don't have anyone going hungry."

"It's *what* people eat that's important, not how much. And it's serious. Ask Colonel Anza. With an outbreak of scurvy, everyone could die before we get to California."

Sergeant Grijalva looked skeptical.

They approached a dimly-lit lean-to. The sergeant exchanged a few words with a soldier at the entrance, the woman's husband. Inside on a pallet lay a shivering female figure, her knees drawn up beneath her chin. "Señora Jiménez, I've brought Señora Márquez to examine you."

The sick woman drew back in terror as she recognized the expedition's redheaded "witch." She crossed herself, then snatched a crucifix from the tiny makeshift shrine nearby. Holding it toward Gabriella as if to ward off evil, she cried hoarsely, "Get away from me, *bruja!* Leave me alone!"

Gabriella stifled an indignant exaclamation. She had been patient with Amanda, the Jiménez daughter, when the girl trembled at Gabriella's touch. But hysteria from this worn old *paisana* was too much!

You silly she-goat! she thought. *It's a dramatic scene you want, is it? Then so be it."*

She spoke sternly to Señora Jiménez. "Señora, I came to see for myself if someone has put a spell on you. If you won't let me examine you, I will do exactly as you say and leave you alone, for I won't be able to help you."

The sergeant stared at Gabriella.

In Señora Jiménez' hand, the crucifix wavered. "You are a *curandera?*"

"Of course not," snapped Gabriella. "To become a white witch requires a lifetime of study. Someone as young as I am could not possibly be a *curandera*. But I know when a victim is under a wicked spell and I can tell you how to strengthen yourself against it. I need to examine your mouth."

Señora Jiménez snatched the covers over the lower half of her face. "Padre Font says you are in league with the devil."

"Padre Font is quite right in one respect," Gabriella improvised glibly. "The devil is at work in this camp, but Padre Font doesn't know where to look. One of the Pima men is the witch, not me. But no one knows which one it is, not even the interpreter. Padre Font believes prayer is the only way to overcome evil spells. You and I know there are other ways."

Cautiously, the woman lowered the quilt. "Why do you need to examine my mouth?"

"That is the only way I can tell. The Pima witch was able to put a spell on some of the colonists' food. People ate it and it made their mouths tender and sore. Some of them got sick. They had dizziness and a heaviness in the stomach. Their gums bled. If they keep on eating this poisoned food, their teeth will fall out. They will be too weak to ride a horse and Colonel Anza will leave them behind for the Pima witch to eat. Are you going to let me examine your mouth?"

For a long moment the woman hesitated. Then, with anxious eyes, she nodded.

A sputtering candle lit the shelter. Gabriella took it from its nearby stand, handed it to Sergeant Grijalva and motioned him to hold it close. She knelt beside the pallet and took the woman's chin firmly in her hand.

"Open wide," she commanded.

She carefully completed her examination, then felt for swollen glands in the woman's neck. She didn't like what her sensitive fingers told her.

She rose. "I can see that your gums will soon be starting to bleed if you are not careful what you eat," she said sternly. "You must not eat any more of your own food as long as the spell is upon it. In about two weeks, the spell will dissipate. Until then, eat the squash and melons and fresh-picked beans that the Indians offer you. They know about this witch and know how to protect their crops from his wicked spells. Do not eat anything the Indians have cooked. Eat their food only if it is fresh. If they offer you cornmeal, have your daughter Amanda make bread from it and eat that too."

"What about the rest of my family?"

"Amanda is safe where she is. As for the others, do you want them to get sick like you and be left behind?"

The woman sobbed. "No. My littlest girl is already weak, like me. I will see that all my family eats the Indian food."

"Good. That shows you are a wise mother. You will keep your family well." She turned to Sergeant Grijalva. "We will go now."

Safely out of earshot, the sergeant said indignantly, "Will you please tell me what that was all about? God's britches, she'll repeat what you said all over the camp!"

"That was the point, of course!" Gabriella said curtly. "I hope she does!"

"And people will believe it."

"Of course they will. Stupid bleating sheep, they'll believe anything. With luck, maybe they'll change their eating habits so they won't die of scurvy."

"And they'll tell Font what you said."

"He's as superstitious as they are, so maybe he'll believe it too. As it is, he's slowly killing himself with his watery broths and gruels."

"Scurvy, you said?" Grijalva squealed. "She's got scurvy?"

"I think so."

"God's holy britches! What do we do now?"

"Pray."

Wordlessly they returned to the headquarters tent. When they were nearly there, Gabriella broke the silence. "Sergeant, about Padre Font. Amanda said his malaria flared up again. In the dispensary, you have plenty of *sauz*. If you give some to Amanda, she knows how to brew the tea."

"I already offered him some," replied Grijalva, avoiding her eyes. "Font won't touch anything from the dispensary."

Gabriella stared. "Because of me?"

The sergeant nodded.

"But after we leave Padre Garcés behind at the settlements, he'll be our only priest! And he's killing himself!"

Grijalva shrugged.

Gabriella crossed herself. *Santa Madre de Dios!* The expedition chaplain had proved himself her enemy, yes, but suppose he sickened and died before the expedition reached California. Only a priest could say Mass and absolve sin, christen babies and perform the last rites for the dying. The threat of such a loss set her heart knocking against her ribs.

The sergeant was asking, "If more people come to the dispensary claiming to be tired, what do I do?"

"Keep plenty of fresh fruit on hand — watermelons and cantaloupes. When people come complaining of fatigue, give them a melon. Tell them to take it home and eat it or their teeth will fall out."

Grijalva winced. "Melons are food for pigs! That's what the colonists think. They'd almost rather have their teeth fall out."

"Very well, let them fall out!" she snapped.

Grijalva himself disdained most fresh food, as she knew from tending the headquarters mess. And clearly, he was not convinced that scurvy represented a threat. Most men were like that. Hearing of others' misfortune, they invariably blamed the victim's weakness and discounted the weight of the burden.

And what would happen when Señora Jiménez' story reached Padre Font, as it certainly would? To fudge on her sentence in the line of march was one thing; Font would disapprove but do nothing and Garcés would look the other way. But to exorcise evil spells, that was a priest's work. To take upon herself such a task was to compromise the Holy Faith itself. And no matter how frail Font might be, or how permissive Garcés might be, they would put a stop to it. Font would be very likely to tell his flock — from the pulpit if he could, or from his bedside if he must — that it was the witch Gabriella Márquez herself whose curse had brought sickness to the colonists!

And she realized — with anxiety turning her knees to jelly — that in all probability his flock would believe him.

CHAPTER 22   The Colorado River Crossing
                                             November 30, 1775

Reaching the Colorado River was a relief to officers and colonists alike. Fording would be dangerous but once across and several miles on the other side, the expedition would leave the meddlesome natives behind.

On the day scheduled for the river crossing, Martín was worried about the livestock, now being held on scrub pasture a half-mile away. By quick action in moving them from Laguna del Hospital, he and his men had held losses to six steers and two mules. But the animals were still weak, and they faced the crossing in icy water, often over their heads. The healthier among them had grown protective winter coats, shaggy and thick. But others were in such poor condition he knew they were doomed.

The lieutenant was again taking his meals with the other officers at headquarters as theft of the livestock was no longer a concern. After the continued threat from the "friendly" braves, Martín had requisitioned extra firearms and ammunition for his *vaqueros*. Game was needed to extend the colonists' rations anyway, and his cowboys were expert marksmen. When the young Pimas saw how readily the vaqueros brought down rabbits and quail with their muskets, their interest in "helping" to herd the expedition's animals quickly dissipated.

The day specified for the crossing was colder than usual because of the frigid wind. Water in the canteens rattled with slivers of ice, and even inside the headquarters tent, warmed by a stove, the officers' breath showed white vapor when they spoke.

Martín heard Gabriella's low-pitched voice at the entrance delivering a message to Colonel Anza. What a joke that he had once thought himself a charmer of the opposite sex! He had done his best to please Gabriella — or at least avoid displeasing her — but every effort had gone wrong. Bonita's stunning beauty had taken his breath away — the very thought of her moved him, even now. But she was a gorgeous prattling doll, her thoughts and moods as predictable as the dawn.

Gabriella was different. For resourcefulness, she would put the wiliest Apache to shame. From the pulpit, Padre Font accused her as the source of Señora Jiménez' illness. But the colonists, on their way home after Mass, found Señora Jiménez playing lively games with her children and praising this same "witch" who had brought about her miraculous cure! People were laughing behind their hands, a result that Gabriella, the minx, no doubt intended. Poor Font must be apoplectic with rage!

"Saddle your mount and come with me, Lieutenant."

Martín started from his reverie to find Colonel Anza speaking to him. He rose, saluted, and left to obey.

The colonel was annoyed and Martín knew why. For weeks the officers had looked forward to the junction of the Gila and Colorado Rivers. There the expedition was to meet Salvador Palma, an energetic, ambitious chieftain with wide influence among the tribes along the great Colorado River. The year before, Anza had come with Garcés on a trailblazing journey through this territory, scouting a safe route for the colonists. Palma had welcomed the Spaniards and warmly endorsed the colonists' passage through his lands. His men would do everything possible to make the river crossing a safe one for the expedition, and he even begged for a missionary to come live among his people.

And now that Anza had brought Padre Garcés as promised, Palma had suddenly changed his mind. His braves would not be available to help the colonists ford the river after all. The current was too swift and the water too cold.

Anza was considering various plans to set Palma's judgment aside. By the time Martín returned to headquarters leading his mount, Palma was on hand with an interpreter. Anza announced, "Tell him no matter what he says, the expedition must cross the river. Tell him I have already given orders to have rafts built to carry the colonists and our freight over the water."

Palma erupted in shouts and gestures. The interpreter turned to Anza. "The chief says it will take all day to get one raft across. The water is very cold, he says. It comes from the mountains where there has already been much snow. He says such a plan with the rafts is too dangerous for your people and too dangerous for his men who would assist you."

Anza's great nose lifted in irritation. To Martín, he muttered under his breath, "The scoundrel intends to keep us here as long as possible, using the river as an excuse. Having us here as his guests gives him great prestige among the other tribes."

"Maybe it would be better to remain here for awhile, Colonel," Martín suggested. "Give our animals a rest. We lost another steer and three more saddle animals last night."

The commander's face clouded. "In addition to the ones we lost the night before?"

"Yes."

The commander observed gloomily, "The cold weather has come earlier than I expected. We have sick colonists too, perhaps a dozen. Grijalva and his wife got little sleep last night or the night before. Even with help from the natives, I wonder if the sick can stay on their horses long enough to make it across."

"If you give the order, Sir, they'll try."

The lines in Anza's face deepened. "We must risk it. Once safe on the other side, we can rest as long as necessary. But the longer we remain where we are, the more obstacles Palma will invent." He summoned the interpreter. "Ask Palma to assign us a guide. My officer and I wish to explore the riverbank."

With great reluctance, Palma summoned a young Yuma brave with face and torso decorated with the tribe's typical red, black and white markings. The interpreter reported to Anza, "Palma says he and his men have already searched the riverbank for five miles in both directions. The only way across is the way he came with his men, by swimming."

"We shall see," said the commander, mounting his horse. "Tell the guide to fetch his pony and follow us."

Nudging his mount into a fast walk, Anza turned in the direction of the river with Martín at his side. Beyond a rise, they found the watercourse — a raging torrent some 240 yards wide, with treacherous eddies and crosscurrents. "In we go!" ordered Anza.

They spent the entire morning on horseback, weaving back and forth across the surging river and its many channels. Trying first one crossing and then another, they worked their way slowly upriver. Not until early afternoon did they test a ford where the river divided into three channels, relatively shallow, measuring in all some 350 yards from one bank to the other. "This is it," announced Anza. "This will do."

They scouted a site on the far shore for a temporary encampment and another for a holding area for the animals. "We will take two days for the crossing," the commander decided. "We'll bring the sick across first. Colonists and baggage the first day, cattle the second. We'll camp an extra day here on the riverbank to let the families dry out and re-pack their goods properly. All cargo animals will carry reduced burdens for the crossing. We mustn't risk losing equipment or food supplies."

One last time, they fought the charging currents to the east bank of the river and Anza led the way back to camp. To their dismay, they found their trail blocked by a heavy growth of mesquite so dense as to be nearly impassable. Dismounting, the men hacked and slashed their way through the maze and arrived at camp at sundown.

Anza ignored Palma's arguments and issued orders for a march next morning at daybreak. He sent a detail with lanterns to cut a road through to the crossing, a task which occupied most of the night.

Sergeant Grijalva was needed, and Gabriella found her official ostracism unofficially set aside — Señora Jiménez' recovery had effectively set it aside anyway. Grijalva told her, "The patients are with their families now. You'll need to get them collected first thing in the morning. There's a woman in labor but her pains start and then stop. I didn't know what to do about her. Oh, and you'll need to pack the dispensary." And off he rode.

At sunset, the wind died but the night was cold. For Gabriella, it had already been a hard day. She had helped Rita, who in the emergency was cooking for the *arrieros* as well as the officers. Then she had met with her eight pupils for an hour and sent them home. As darkness fell, she threw her own things together and had just finished securing the dispensary equipment when she was summoned to the woman in labor.

Lighting her way with one of Miguel's lanterns, she found the shelter. The young husband bowed awkwardly in greeting. Inside, the stricken wife lay drawn up in pain. "Oh, Señora, please help me," she whispered. "I've started bleeding and it won't stop."

Quickly Gabriella arranged for the couple's two children to spend the night with another family camped nearby and sent the young husband for more fuel for the fire.

She secured the entrance, scrubbed her hands at the basin, then carefully and gently examined her patient. Afterwards, she scrubbed her hands again and mixed a draft for the young mother to drink.

"This will make you feel better," she told her patient. "Now listen carefully. You are a healthy woman with strong muscles. You have already had two healthy babies and you'll have many more. But there is no way to save this one."

Tears slipped down the woman's cheek. "My husband will say I have caused the baby's death."

"I will talk to him," Gabriella assured her. "Expedition life is hard on all of us, but hardest of all on mothers with babies on the way. For you, the bleeding will continue for awhile and then your little baby will come but it will be dead. I will send your husband to summon Padre Garcés to bless the infant."

The woman sobbed. "There is something wrong with me or this baby would be healthy too."

Gabriella gave the woman's shoulder a sharp shake. "There is nothing wrong with you!" she said firmly. "Sometimes things go wrong with babies before they're born. They may be blind or malformed. And it is the fault of no one. It just happens. Remember, God is merciful; He doesn't want those poor malformed babies to live sad, unhappy lives, unable to look out for themselves. So He takes them back to heaven sooner than the rest of us. God knows what He's doing about these things. We must trust Him."

When the young husband returned with the wood, she sent him to fetch Padre Garcés. Not long afterwards, the woman gave birth to her dead infant.

Outside the entrance to the shelter, an unfamiliar voice called, "Señora Márquez? Are you there, Señora Márquez? Colonel Anza wishes to see you."

She suppressed a groan. What now? It would soon be dawn and she needed rest. She straightened and answered, "Tell him I'm coming right away." Her patient was asleep. She found clean linen and closely wrapped the tiny corpse. Padre Garcés would have to worry about the burial.

At the headquarters tent, the commander looked up from the journal in which he was writing. He waved her to a chair before his desk, stern eyes following her. "I'll come to the point, Señora. An hour ago, at the crossing, I asked Sergeant Grijalva who was taking care of our sick people. He tried to evade the question but finally admitted that you were with the farmer's wife who went into early labor."

"She lost her baby about an hour ago. But she is comfortable now and had dropped off to sleep when I left. Padre Garcés is there by now."

"Garcés!?" Anza leaned back in his camp chair. "There seems to be a conspiracy here to reinstate you as *enfermera* without my knowledge or consent. However, we haven't time now to thrash it out. We have ten invalids on our hands, two of them seriously ill. A possible cause of all this illness is the water at Laguna del Hospital three days ago. In all, we have lost seven saddle horses, fifteen pack animals and four steers. We'll undoubtedly lose more."

"Señora Jiménez was not sick because she drank brackish water."

The commander glowered. "Is she the one you warned about the evil spell?"

Gabriella blushed scarlet. "Yes, Señor. I think she was showing early symptoms of scurvy. I told her to eat melons and the fresh cornmeal that the Indians gave her. She did, and she is now recovering."

The colonel stared. "Scurvy? Why scurvy?"

"Ordinarily Señora Jiménez would be at home in Culiacán, eating bananas and oranges fresh-picked from the trees at her back door. But since summer, she and her family have eaten beef and dried beans and corn cakes. I know the colonists don't like the natives' squashes and cantaloupes but they need to eat them anyway. Señora Jiménez said her little girl is sick, too."

Anza chewed his moustache thoughtfully. "You rule out cholera? The ague?"

She replied wearily, "Yes. With all of the sick people, it is the same. Every one of them comes from a family that has been longest without fresh food."

"Why don't the officers have scurvy? They've been without fresh food longer than the families."

"Rita has been cooking for them and she knows what to cook. If she forgets, I remind her. Colonel Anza, could we talk about this later? I am very tired."

"Yes, yes." Anza stood and cleared his throat. "I wish to officially ask you to continue to work with the patients until further notice."

She turned to go. "Padre Font won't like it."

"If he complains, I shall give him the option of caring for the sick himself."

"He can't. He has malaria."

"I know."

"And won't take any medicine for it. Also he is suffering from malnutrition."

Anza snapped, "Will you take care of our invalids or not?"

"Yes, Colonel Anza."

"I have ordered Miguel to accompany you at the crossing tomorrow. The patients will go first on the tallest horses. You must go with them and care for them once they reach the other side."

"May I ask Rosa Grijalva to help me?"

"Yes."

Her shoulders sagged with fatigue. She had already turned toward the entrance when an unexpected spark of rebellion straightened her spine. "Am I to be paid a salary?"

Anza jerked as if stung. He considered. "Why not? Yes. You have made a reasonable request. Your former salary will be reinstated. Good night, Señora Márquez. Sleep well."

That night was very cold. Eight more animals died.

The early morning frost numbed the colonists' hands and dark clouds warned of rain, but Anza ordered the crossing to proceed as planned. Palma had promised to organize his men for the work but he failed to appear. Some five hundred native warriors gathered, apparently intending to watch while the travelers undertook to cross the river by themselves. When Colonel Anza indicated through the interpreters what was expected of them, they shied like timid sheep.

The Yuma people were tall and well-formed, more handsome in appearance than the stocky Pimas. Since they were so vigorous, their reluctance was surprising. Martín found it hard to blame them as most went naked as eggs from the waist down, summer and winter. Anza, however, who knew of their year-round custom of bathing in the river daily, was less sympathetic. He threatened to have them seized, bound and whipped on the spot unless they kept their bargain.

"Señor," protested the interpreter, "if I tell them what you said, they will run away."

Anza's face reddened. "Then tell them — "

Behind him Padre Garcés approached. "Perhaps I can help," he said to Anza. "I suggest you let me talk to them. I will ask how they can expect to be rewarded with tobacco and glass beads if they do nothing to earn the reward. Also I will remind them that the viceroy in Mexico will not be eager to keep sending missionaries and gifts to tribes known to break their promises."

"Very good, Padre," said Anza gratefully. "Thank you. Please proceed."

Colonel Anza was not surprised when Padre Garcés' plan succeeded. Garcés' plans always succeeded.

At the ford, Martín placed a half-dozen of his men at intervals downstream to catch anyone, children especially, who might be swept from the saddle in the strong current. It was equally important that they intercept any of the precious cargo that might be worried loose by the swift water.

Soon Gabriella appeared, her tantalizing hair warmly capped under a wool rebozo, riding slowly down the trail on a towering mule. At the water's edge she dismounted and had a private word with each patient, some of whom Miguel had lashed to their saddles to prevent their falling.

She had just scrambled back onto her mount when Ricardo Sandoval on his pony trotted toward her. In his arms he bore a closely bundled infant. "Señora!" he shouted. "Señora Márquez! Wait!"

Approaching her at the head of the line, he called, "Mama asked if you could take José across with you. Papa gave up two of our tall horses for the invalids.

Now we have barely enough horses and mules to carry us and our baggage too."

"Of course, I'll take him!" Gabriella cried, beaming with glad surprise. She took the wiggling infant from Ricardo, planted a firm kiss on the tiny forehead, cradled the bundle comfortably in one arm and reached for the reins with the other. "Tell your mother he'll be happy in his new home!" and kicking her mule's massive sides, moved off toward the water's edge.

What a pointless thing to say! she thought, glad that Ricardo had already turned away. What new home? None of them had a home — not the baby, not the Sandovals, and Gabriella Márquez the orphan witch least of all. She held the infant close. Before Elías died, her dream of having her own baby in California had been a cherished one. Maybe, if everything worked out, her dream might yet come true.

Martín, who knew how to avoid the many treacherous drop-offs underfoot, led them into the churning river, thanking God for the strength of women like Gabriella and Rosa Grijalva who calmed and reassured the timid. As they entered the swirling waves, each rider was accompanied by a Yuma brave to walk alongside and provide additional support through the water. Support was needed, for within minutes the restless waves were cresting against the shoulders of the horses. Miguel came last, to assist any who fell behind or needed extra assistance.

Once the invalids were safe on the other side, Martín loitered briefly to be certain that Gabriella was safe. Then he left Miguel in charge and returned, with the Yumas swimming easily beside his gray gelding. He was soaked to the waist and numb from the cold, but if the natives could stand it, so could he.

"Lieutenant Neve! Lieutenant Neve!" cried Tómas Sandoval as Martín approached the shore. "Padre Font wants his mule. He says he will not cross the river on the horse you picked out for him."

"The idiot! I saved one of the tallest horses especially for him so he wouldn't get wet. Tell him!"

"I already told him. The big horse prances and blows. Padre Font says Colonel Anza wants him thrown off in the water and drowned. He refuses to cross unless he has his mule."

Martín bellowed angrily, "Tell that pompous fool — !" Immediately he checked himself. Instead he approached Tómas and said reasonably, "Ask Garcés to talk to him. Padre Font will have to ride the horse assigned to him." Martín returned to his work, calling over his shoulder, "Remind him that the one who chose that horse for him was Lieutenant Neve. The frontier potentate had nothing to do with it."

Tómas hid his smile behind his hand. He turned his pony and, threadbare monk's robe flying, cantered back up the trail.

Next across were the women, several with infants in their arms. Most also carried a young child mounted in front or behind. Nearly all rode barefoot, ignoring the cold. When they were accepted as members of the expedition, they were issued the only shoes most of them had ever owned, and there would be no replacements in California. Such treasures were carefully bound around waists or hung around necks, safely above the water.

Several horses carried three children riding one behind the other. Difficult as the natives were about many things, they vigilantly guarded the children in their care and saw them safely to the other side.

They guarded Padre Font with even greater caution. Font required three assistants, a brave to lead his horse and one on either side to hold him in the saddle. Behind him came Tómas carrying on his shoulders, out of the way of the water, a leather case containing the psaltery and the altar accoutrements. Another pack animal on a lead behind him carried holy oil and the vestments.

The smaller mounts were left for the men, some of whom were also responsible for a child or two. The wind had grown colder and stronger, and instead of riding, most led their mounts to spare them. Not Vasco Bellis, however. Josefa's surviving husband carried, riding behind him, one of his daughters, several rolled blankets, and two large baskets containing food and clothing.

The ford was a carefully plotted trail through the water following the shallowest route; riders were warned that each in turn must carefully follow the rider ahead or risk being washed away by the current. Knowing this quite well, the natives who accompanied the sick, the women and the children, all guided them carefully along the route which their own feet searched out with no trouble.

At last, the men started across, and were well into the stream. The first warning of trouble was a shout from one of the Indians, followed by a chorus of masculine cries, then screams from the women ahead. A heavily-laden saddle horse had been ridden far beyond the line of march, disobeying strict orders, and suddenly lost its footing on the riverbottom. The overladen beast, eyes rolling with terror, bucked and charged, shaking loose its riders and baggage. Swimming free, head held high, it raced downstream with the swirling, roaring current, its mane entangled with foam and twigs.

"Bellis!" shouted one of the men from the line of march. His voice could scarcely be heard over the rushing water and others joined with him in shouting to the *arrieros* downstream. "It's Bellis and his daughter!" "They can't swim!"

Two of Martín's men had already lunged for and caught the terrified horse. Together, they firmly led it back to the Yuma brave responsible for it in the line of march. The baggage floated swiftly with the current and the *arrieros* retrieved one of the baskets farther downstream. Once caught, it was difficult to hold onto. Soldiers from the opposite shore, seeing the difficulty, quickly mounted, chased the final basket and caught it as it floated a quarter-mile downstream.

The two riders were nowhere to be seen. The loss of Vasco Bellis would have brought few tears from the colonists and none from the officers; the man was a whiner and shirker. His oldest daughter Ramona was a slatternly but capable girl of sixteen. Though little admired, she was at least pitied.

Bellis' flat-brimmed hat was clearly visible on the crest of the waves, carried swiftly downstream by the raging water. Bellis was not under it. Undertows had apparently dragged down father and daughter.

"There!" screamed a woman in the line of march, pointing. "There's Ramona! See her?!" A swirl of Ramona's blue printed skirt appeared briefly at the top of the water. Three of the *arrieros,* swimming and wading, made their way toward the flash of color as speedily as the churning waves would allow. They fetched her up, more drowned than alive, and slung her, belly down, over the nervously waiting horse.

The line of march proceeded once more, with many eyes scanning the water for any sign of the missing colonist. On the western shore, Colonel Anza mounted his horse and followed the waterline south for a mile but returned no wiser than when he left. More than most of the colonists, Anza knew Bellis for a useless, self-pitying blackguard, but his goal was to arrive in California with no human losses at all. Morosely, he rode back to camp, cursing Vasco Bellis under his breath. On the opposite shore, the last of the men had started across, and the Yuma braves began leading the long file of cargo animals into the charging water. At the riverbank, Martín noticed Padre Garcés standing to one side. Threading his way through the crush, he found the Franciscan in leisurely conversation with the interpreter.

"Padre!" cried Martín, "You should have gone across an hour ago! Why are you still here?"

"There's no reason to hurry, is there?"

"Yes," exclaimed Martín, "there is! Those people on the other side are wet and miserable. Don't you think you should be there with them?"

"Well, yes, I suppose you're right, Lieutenant. I should."

"Where's your horse? Your own horse, Padre! I told one of the men to make certain you had your own horse."

Garcés avoided Martín's gaze. "As a matter of fact, I — well, I loaned him to a man who needed him worse than I did."

Dismounting, Martín noticed that Garcés' florid coloring had faded to an oily gray. "Can you swim, Padre?"

Biting his lip, Garcés shook his head.

Martín sighed. He wound the reins of his mount around the stub of a mesquite limb and beckoned to the interpreter. Together, they plunged through the milling pack animals and at length Martín found what he was looking for, the headquarters store of arms. From the back of a big mule, he untied a long box, opened it, drew out a lance and tested it for strength. To the interpreter, he explained, "We'll send Garcés across on a stretcher. It should take six of these lances, three lashed together on each side. We'll need blankets and four men, two at his head and two at his feet."

The smiling interpreter left to search among the braves for the strongest, most reliable men. He returned with three. A fourth had gone for blankets. Among the headquarters stores they found rawhide thongs. By the time the warrior arrived with the blankets, they had finished lashing the lances together.

With Gabriella safe on the other side and Padre Garcés launched, Martín was now most concerned about his *arrieros* who had been on duty in the freezing river for three hours. The last of the cargo would soon be across. He ordered fires kindled, dry clothing laid out and a hot meal prepared against the moment when his men emerged from the swirling water.

As Martín moved about, making arrangements, he became conscious of angry voices beside one of the cooking fires. Vasco Bellis, washed to safety far down the eastern shore, had made his way back to the crossing. Unnoticed, he had already helped himself to dry clothing laid out for the *arrieros* and was preparing similarly to enjoy their hot meal.

But Bellis found the men's insults unbearable. Martín told him he could cross next day astride one of the steers or swim, whichever he chose. Deeply offended, Bellis withdrew and ate his stolen meal alone. Lieutenant Neve sent word across the river that the lost traveler had been found.

Not long afterward, Colonel Anza ordered Martín to hurry with the last crossings for the day. At the new camp site, the command tents were up. Most of the families had erected their shelters, with cooking fires lit and damp clothing set out to dry.

Much later, Padre Font would write in his official diary for that day that Padre Garcés was the last to cross, murmuring prayers all the way and "lying stretched out face up as though he were dead."

CHAPTER 23

West of the Crossing
December 1775

The wind continued unabated during the night. Next morning, the travelers awoke to an opaque, pale-brown world. Those venturing out could distinguish vague forms a few feet before them, nothing more.

Desert dust storms were commonplace to the troops from Tubac but came as an astonishment to the colonists. Miguel and Rita, along with the others, had to be instructed to tightly cover food, clothing and equipment to keep out the sand, and to realign their shelter with its back to the grit-laden wind.

From the headquarters tent, after seeing the sickest of her patients, Gabriella had just groped her way back to Miguel's shelter which she recognized by the sound of a baby crying inside. She lifted the cowhide covering at the shelter's entrance, slipped inside and took the hungry baby from Rita's weary arms. "Ramona hasn't come yet?" she asked, frowning.

"She's shiftless as her father, that girl," grumbled Rita.

Gabriella drew a stool near the tiny fire, sat and wrapped the infant close in her arms and rocked it, crooning. When it grew quiet, she said, "It's not fair to blame Ramona, Rita. She won't stay with her father, says he's 'after her' all the time. So she sleeps wherever she can, to avoid him. Others are like us, they use her like a donkey, ask her to do all kinds of things. If she wants food and shelter, then she's afraid to refuse."

Rita snapped, "The baby is her brother, after all!"

How I wish he were mine! thought Gabriella, smiling into the infant's eyes.

"Lusty little tyke," said Miguel. "Best of the lot, by the look of him. And poor Señora Bellis never set eyes on him, poor woman."

Rita was busy cleaning desert game that one of the natives had brought for the commander. "Ramona's not so bad looking," she said. "She's big and strong from taking care of her no-good father. In California, what with building and farming, strength will be a blessing. She'll catch herself a husband."

Outside, the wind hissed through the branches of the palo verde trees. "How did the patients fare through the night?" Miguel asked Gabriella.

"The few I've seen are improved a bit," she replied.

"Señora Jiménez was here," he said. "She wants you to come look at that little one of hers. Flora."

"Again?" asked Gabriella, worried. "I examined her. She hasn't any temperature. No inflammation. No swollen glands. No runny nose. Doesn't seem to hurt anywhere. She just lies on her pallet and stares."

"Maybe her mother's driving her crazy," proposed Miguel.

"She's driving me crazy!" retorted Gabriella, not amused. "She says it's the *mal ojo*. Flora's a pretty little girl. Señora says it was the other mothers' envy that brought on the spell. She wants me to exorcise the evil spirits."

Rita nodded. "You brought it on yourself, speaking out of turn."

Miguel said, "If you watched the curandera in Mexico, can't you make Flora well again if you want to? Why not try?"

"I know about the ritual," admitted Gabriella. "I wish I didn't. Things are complicated enough without people thinking I'm a *curandera* when I'm not."

Finished with her work, Rita placed the meat in a covered pot for stewing on the headquarters stove and reached for her rebozo. Gabriella noticed the deepcircles under Rita's eyes and was disturbed. Having the baby in the shelter was hard on Rita, interrupting her sleep at night. But in the Sandoval shelter, tiny Aurelia was teething and restless. Gabriella had gladly volunteered to care for José between feedings.

"There are some who still think you're a witch, you know!" reminded Rita, adjusting her rebozo. "A black witch, a *bruja*. A *curandera* is several steps up the ladder from a *bruja*. Go do some hocus-pocus over the girl," she urged. "If it works, you're that much ahead. If it doesn't, Señora will find a dozen reasons why it didn't, none of them your fault."

" — And then there'd be no end to it, Rita. Not here, not after we get to California. I've already told Señora. No."

"This — ritual, is it hard to do?" asked Miguel, shrugging into his coat preparatory to escorting his wife to the headquarters tent.

"Not really," said Gabriella. "It takes concentration more than anything else. I know what to watch for, what to avoid."

Miguel leaned over the baby, whose unsteady gaze returned his own. "Sweet child!" he murmured.

Suddenly the covering at the entrance flew open and Ramona Bellis appeared, an untidy giant of a girl with hair like wire and half-crazed eyes the color of granite.

"I'm sorry, Señora!" she cried to Gabriella. "Pa's shelter blew away last night and I had to help fix it! Señora Sandoval will be wondering where I've got to!" She took her baby brother and snatched up a blanket to protect him against the dusty, bitter cold wind outside.

"Sergeant has extra building material," Miguel reminded Ramona as he held back the entrance covering for his wife. " — A little lumber, some cowhides, a few blankets. The officers keep it on hand in case anyone needs it for repairs."

Miguel and Rita departed and Ramona, with the baby, was about to follow them.

Gabriella touched her arm. "Wait." The two were alone in the shelter. "Ramona, what Miguel just said gives me an idea. Why can't you and I ask Sergeant Grijalva for some of his material to make a shelter of our own? For you and José and me. I'd have a place to teach the children."

Ramona's coarse features glowed briefly with excitement which quickly drained away. "That wouldn't work out, Señora," she said bleakly. "With no man around, Pa'd show up first thing, ready to move in. Anyone could come after us. The Indians could steal anything we had, even take the baby!"

"But wait, Ramona." Gabriella's mind worked busily. "Maybe — I don't know if he would agree, of course, but maybe Lieutenant Neve would agree to act as our protector."

"You'd marry him?" Ramona cried, overjoyed. "Then everything would be fine, Señora. He likes you, the lieutenant. I can tell. I've wondered why you don't talk to him more, or even smile at him."

The hungry baby's complaints accelerated from whimpers to shrieks. "Later!" said Gabriella. "We'll talk about it later, just the two of us."

"Yes!" cried Ramona, her pale eyes shining. "Yes, Señora!"

The big girl headed for the Sandoval's shelter. Gabriella knew she must talk to Padre Garcés, but on the way to the chaplain's tent, her step slowed. She was uncertain of her feelings about Martín. In Mexico, the sight of his sensual lips as he talked, smiled, or whispered into Bonita's ear had melted the marrow in her very bones. At Buena Suerte, she had often quietly left a room when he entered it because of a weakness that flowed over her at the sight of his rebellious curls and hooded gaze.

But as the weeks passed, she had seen those sensuous lips slobbering and drooling from too much wine. She had seen them sneer at a clumsy footman, and snarl at a maidservant slow to answer his command. There was cruelty in Martín's character, a quality remarkably absent in Elias. She forced herself to admit the truth: She could easily come to despise Martín, for though brave enough to his face, she was afraid of him — afraid of that cruelty which might easily, one day, be turned against her.

On the other hand, she told herself, if she was afraid of Martín, so was everyone else in the expedition, with the exception of Colonel Anza. — The possible exception of Colonel Anza. She had seen the commander jerk to attention at a simple question from Lieutenant Neve. Yes, she thought her plan was a good one.

After seeking Padre Garcés' advice, she went to check on the remainder of her patients. All had heard of Señora Jiménez' recovery and had begun to eat squash, fresh corn cakes and melons. None enjoyed the natives' food but all were better, one remarkably so.

Two prospective mothers had miscarried many days before and had received no care of any kind. Gabriella found the women weak, flabby and pale, with brass-colored spots on their foreheads and cheeks. Their bellies were still loose and soft; milk leaked from their breasts, staining their clothing. Gabriella braced them both with tea of canutillo and manzanilla to enrich their blood, and showed them how to bind themselves with heavy cotton fajas for support.

In another shelter, she inspected the infected cut on a youngster's foot, cleansed it with olive oil and applied a fresh poultice of egg white and garlic paste.

Outside, the wind was dying down. Replacing the brownish mist overhead were sluggish gray-bottomed clouds threatening snow. She returned to head-quarters for supplies and caught her breath when she found Lieutenant Neve reporting to Colonel Anza. She hadn't yet thought through what she wanted to say to him about her plan.

— Nor did she have time now. The lieutenant's report was frightening. Four more mules and six steers had died of exhaustion and exposure during the night.

"We can't delay any longer!" the commander said grimly. "We're losing more animals every day!"

"We'll lose more yet, Colonel," warned the lieutenant gravely. "The horses and mules I brought from Alamos were second-rate to begin with. Heavy exertion leaves them so fatigued they can't keep up with the column. These cold nights will finish them off."

Anza turned to Gabriella. "What about the sick? Could they leave tomorrow?"

"Yes, Colonel, I think so," she said.

"Then that's it. We're to leave Garcés with Palma. The men are nearly through constructing a hut for him. I'll have the camp notified immediately. We'll march in the morning."

Lieutenant Neve brightened when Gabriella favored him with a smile, and they left the headquarters tent together. A reddish haze lingered in the air, all that remained of the retreating dust storm.

Gabriella groped for words. "The — ah — the journey will be more difficult now, won't it? Farther on, I mean. With less water."

"Anza says the first few days won't be bad," said Martín. "We follow an easy route along the river. Beyond that, we'll have nearly sixty miles with almost no water at all."

"Miguel said the expedition would split up into sections," said Gabriella.

"A *tordeada*," said Martín. "Colonel says there are sources of water along that sixty miles, there just isn't much of it. It won't do to have several hundred thirsty animals trying to drink at the same places at the same time. So the expedition will divide into three parts, leaving on successive days. Anza will probably take you and your patients in the first group with him. His men will dig deep pozos, dozens of them, and water their animals. By the next day, the same wells will fill up enough to water the next group, and so on."

Gabriella hesitated, then plunged. "Martín, I have a question to ask you. The thing is, I think the Sandovals will let me keep Señora Bellis' baby if I ask them."

The lieutenant was wary. "To raise, you mean? To adopt? You're remembering the scum that fathered it."

"And the saint who mothered it, Martín," pleaded Gabriella. "José's mother was kind and good. I already talked to Padre Garcés about church sanction of an arrangement like that. — A widow adopting a motherless baby, I mean. With a family friend acting as godfather. Padre said it was irregular but he would bless the arrangement if we came to the chaplain's tent before we leave."

Lieutenant Neve was baffled. "What are you talking about? I don't understand."

"I — I'm asking you to be my adopted baby's godfather. Will you?"

The request stunned Martín. After Elias was killed, he had briefly fantasized about marrying Gabriella. Nothing unusual about that; half the expedition men would admit they had done the same. But this was an adopted child, with a scoundrel of a father hanging about, notorious for making a pest of himself with the expedition's women. If Gabriella adopted the baby, she would need a husband more than ever for protection.

So what was this "godfather" game she was playing? Was she deliberately shutting him out of any future role as a husband? Martín disliked being shut out. "Ask someone else," he suggested coldly. "Miguel might be willing."

"If I had wanted Miguel, Martín, I would have asked him," Gabriella said sharply. "I want you!"

He sighed, wondering what had happened to the sweet- tempered girl he had known at Buena Suerte. "Gabriella, you've changed," he said.

She gazed up at him, almond eyes shining like black mirrors. "I changed because you advised me to, Martín," she said softly. "Before we left Alamos."

Remembering, he coughed, swore under his breath. "You want me to be godfather to this child," he repeated. "Personally, I think it's a stupid idea. Do you have a reason?"

"Of course, I have a reason. Having the baby in the same shelter with Rita and Miguel, as we do now, is an ordeal for them. They work hard all day and they need their rest at night. Ramona and I want our own shelter — for us and for my little school. But two women and a baby need a man's protection."

"There's always marriage, you know."

Gabriella gazed at him levelly. "Ramona's too young. And there's no one I know well enough to want to marry."

Damn her insolence! thought Martín. In a few months the wench would take a husband, all right. In California, that gaudy hair and tinkling, merry laugh would snare some unlucky leatherjacket. Martín pitied the poor bastard.

"Then if all you want is a godfather for protection, any soldier will do."

"The garrison soldiers will be returning to California. All the other men are married and have responsibilities of their own."

"Is that the only reason you asked me, then? Because you think I'll stay in California? Gabriella, I haven't decided yet," he lied. "I may go back to Mexico with Anza."

"You won't, though."

Martín's eyebrows lifted. No woman ever talked to him like that, not even his own mother. But Gabriella always did. — Not as a saucy woman of the street, challenging him, but as an equal. "You seem very sure of yourself," he said.

"Of course, I'm sure. You think court etiquette is silly."

She wasn't saying what she meant, of course. Martín knew what she meant. Mexico's tightly-knit social world was actually a suffocating prison constructed of rules like iron bars. Each individual was sentenced for life to his own cell, never to escape. Gabriella wanted no part of that life, had joined the expedition to escape it. She wanted freedom, a future of her own making. Before he left Mexico, Martín had wanted the same thing. Gabriella believed he still did.

At last he said, "Court life may be silly, but there are advantages. I am not a suitable godfather for José. You've asked the wrong person."

"I respect you. You are a deeply admired official of the expedition. I did not ask the wrong person."

"You don't mean what you say."

"I would never say something like that if I did not mean it."

What was she up to? Martín wondered. More important, what would he be getting himself into if he agreed? He might be called on to chase off a few natives or perhaps give that rascal Vasco Bellis a knock on the head — which would be a pleasure. Such minor inconveniences were offset by a huge advantage — a closer friendship with a bewitching woman. He would have access to Gabriella, her shelter, her trust (didn't she say she respected him?) at all times. And no competition. As godfather to the adopted baby of the expedition's *enfermera,* not even Colonel Anza would cast a speculative eye in her direction.

Martín bowed stiffly over her hand. Gabriella Márquez was a dilemma played on a mystery to the tune of a paradox. But he would go along. "Then, Señora, it will be my greatest pleasure to accede to your wishes. You are too generous in your judgment. I shall always endeavor to live up to your high opinion of me, which I do not deserve."

A chuckle surged against Gabriella's lips. She sobered, curtsied with a grand *gachupín* flourish, sucked in her cheeks and replied mincingly, "My family and all I possess are at your service, Señor. And now it seems I must proceed to the palace of Don Miguel Esala and his lady. Though I am nothing in the eyes of the world and unworthy of your distinguished company, I would nevertheless be deeply honored if you would escort me to their establishment."

Martín tried to conquer his amusement but failed. She dropped her court pose, and with a peal of laughter took his arm, squeezed it, and set off with him along the path.

Santa Madre, forgive me for such wicked deceit, thought Gabriella.

If the bitch plays me false, then as God reigns in Heaven, she'll walk the rest of the way to California, thought Martín.

The expedition's route was marked by scattered Yuma villages, and there were often gifts from the natives of food and fuel. Like the other women with infants, who needed their hands free to control their mounts, Gabriella and

Ramona improvised a sling for José, then took turns carrying him. The horse's steady motion was soothing and he slept through most of each day's journey.

As the expedition traveled west of Palma's village, painted braves followed on their ponies. They raced up and down the line of march, shouting and raising clouds of dust. They were a special annoyance to Padre Font, so fevered and weak he said Mass feebly or not at all. The colonists missed Padre Garcés.

Late one morning, Tómas on his little mule drifted back along the line of march for a few sociable moments with the *enfermera*. "This dust isn't helping Padre Font's malaria," she said to Tómas. "Can't you keep the braves away from him?"

"As long as he's near Colonel Anza, they stay clear," replied Tómas.

"And Amanda?"

"She travels with her family, not with us. She does her work each afternoon and then goes to her father's shelter. She takes care of her little sister who is sick." Tómas cast an aggrieved glance at Gabriella.

"Tómas, why do you blame me? You like Amanda and you want Amanda to like you. I too would like for Amanda to like you. But I've examined Flora Jiménez many times. She's as healthy as you are."

"Then why does she look like she's dead?"

Gabriella shrugged. "Maybe she's tired of traveling. A lot of us are, you know."

"Amanda and her mother say it's my fault. They think I've made you hate the Jiménez family. You joke and laugh with your pupils and the other colonists but with them you turn away."

"Señora nags all the time," Gabriella said impatiently.

"Amanda says you know how to cure her little sister of the *mal ojo* but you won't. It is only out of spite, she says."

"That's ridiculous."

"But Señora — !"

"I mean it, Tómas. The answer is no."

The expedition reached its evening's destination and the long line of march began winding down in the usual way. Ramona took her little brother to Rina Sandoval to nurse, then erected their shelter. At the dispensary Gabriella lanced a boil, inspected two dozen mouths for bleeding gums and prescribed two dozen cantaloupes just in case.

At her new shelter, Gabriella found the infant José fed and sound asleep. Ramona was depressed. "Señora Sandoval hates to nurse him," she remarked.

"How do you know?" asked Gabriella. "Did she say she hated to nurse him?"

"She never says so but I can tell. Gets a woman roused up, nursing a boy baby."

"Roused up'?"

"Makes her want a man." She gently caressed her tiny brother in his basket. "Never happens when a mother nurses her girl babies, just boy babies."

Gabriella stared. "Ramona, are you telling me the truth?"

"Why lie about something like that?" asked Ramona with a trace of irritation.

"Ma, she always dreaded a new boy baby. Every time she fed it, Pa'd be hanging around, knowing she'd want him afterwards no matter how much work she had waiting. I should know; I was the one had to do the work!"

Rummaging through her memories from the convent clinic — a hint here, a clue there — Gabriella suspected that Ramona was telling the truth. Poor Rina Sandoval. Sexual desire might be welcome and manageable at home, but it could be an ordeal on the expedition with living arrangements open for the whole family to see.

Ramona was in a mood for confidences. "José, he'll have a better chance than Ma's other babies," she went on. "When we lived in Culiacán, Pa liked to get to Ma and suck all her milk. Wasn't none left for the babies. I had a little sister that died and a little brother, both starved to death. Ma finally told the priest and the priest told Pa he had to stop."

"What?!" cried Gabriella, flinching.

Ramona said with disdain, "I guess there's a lot you never learned in that convent." She tucked the baby's blanket more snugly about him. "That's what kept Ma so poorly after we left home. Her milk already started for the new baby and Pa sucked her dry. Wasn't no one to stop him."

Gabriella was horrified. "She should have gone to Padre Font! He'd have done something!"

"Psh!" exclaimed Ramona angrily. "That old man helped kill her! Pa got to him first. Told him Ma was a complainer not to be listened to."

— So Josefa Bellis was not listened to. And she died. Gabriella felt so ill she dared not speak. Seeking reassurance, she fumbled in her traveling chest for the small leather case in which she kept her valuables. She removed Elias' blue stone and gripped it tightly until her nausea passed. Elias and his gentleness, his thoughtfulness of her were a comfort. Awaking in the deep of night, as she so often did, to his soft kisses on her neck and shoulders, his strong protecting arms, even the silken way he entered her, were proof of a love that few women ever knew in a lifetime.

Eyes closed, lips parted in the ecstasy of her memories, she felt Ramona's curious glance upon her. She opened her fingers to reveal the deep, rich blue of the mottled stone. "It's a turquoise," she explained softly. "My husband gave it to me before we were married. He was nothing like your father, Ramona."

"Not many men as rotten as Pa," the big girl murmured.

For which Almighty God be thanked! thought Gabriella.

Ramona readied herself for bed, smoothed the blankets of her pallet. "You ought to get you another husband," she advised Gabriella. "Lieutenant Neve for godfather is better than nothing. But two of us alone with the baby, anybody could come after us."

Gabriella stirred impatiently. "Ramona, please stop talking like that! Miguel and Rita are scarcely twenty feet away. All we need to do is call for help."

"You don't know Pa. He's a slick talker. He'll go talk to that old priest, like he done with Ma. He'll claim you taken over two of his kids, me and José. So by God's law, he'll claim you must needs take him too."

Ramona's words penetrated Gabriella's euphoria like a thousand stinging wasps. Their muted buzzing continued on and on. Through white, stiff lips, she said, "That won't happen."

"All the same," said Ramona, "you ought to catch that lieutenant fellow and make him marry you."

CHAPTER 24

The National Palace
Mexico
December 1775

Hundreds of miles behind the expedition, in the city of Mexico, an event was about to take place that would affect Gabriella and her descendants for decades to come. It involved Antonio María Bucareli y Ursua, Viceroy of Nueva España. Of all his duties as viceroy, the one Antonio Bucareli most disliked was presiding over Mexico's highest court, the *audiencia*. There was always the risk of handing down decisions that made enemies. Sometimes very powerful ones.

He had learned, however, that with persistence and imagination, enemies could be managed. Not so his robes of state, the source of much painful humiliation. The billowing mantle, made in Paris at shocking cost, was a disaster. The crimson color accented the broken veins in his cheeks and the Russian ermine made him sneeze. The enormous weight of the garments, together with the gold chains, jeweled sword and coronet, as often as not sent him staggering drunkenly at affairs of state when he should be striding regally. His early intention of using pageboys to carry the train had to be abandoned; four husky footmen were employed instead. They stood now in readiness on either side of the portal leading to the court chamber.

The viceroy's chief magistrate entered through a side door, approached and bowed. "All is in readiness, Excellency."

"What about Verro?"

"He will testify today," said the magistrate. "The bailiff guarantees it."

The viceroy's expression was pained. "In September, the bailiff guaranteed the Figuroa relatives would be here from Spain. They were not. In October, he guaranteed the trial would proceed on the charge of forgery in addition to fraud and embezzlement. It did not. In November, he again guaranteed that all parties would be on hand but at the last minute, the defendant was too sick to testify. This time, I don't care what the charge is or who is here to press it. I don't care if Federico Verro is on his deathbed. I want this matter settled today, is that clear?"

"Yes, Excellency," said the magistrate.

At the viceroy's signal, the footmen came forward to carry the heavy mantle of state. Another pair of footmen opened the great double doors leading to the court chamber. Preceded by the magistrate, to the flourish of trumpets, the viceroy grimly paced off the distance to his place of honor on the dais with its fringed canopy.

The *audiencia* got underway with its usual ceremony, the magistrate presiding at his massive bench. A succession of petitioners appeared in the stalls accompanied by their witnesses. Evidence was presented by a merchant to prove that a shipping master from Vera Cruz had cheated him out of several hundred gold ounces. A captain of the militia was charged with the murder of a prominent Palace official whom the captain had caught making love to his wife. And once again, the family and friends of Avila Flores de Figuroa charged the former steward, Federico Verro, with gulling his master out of his fortune.

Earlier, the viceroy's sympathies had been with the steward, though the Figuroa connections in Spain made a verdict in Verro's favor unthinkable. Don Avila was a drunken fool, thought Bucareli, and deserved his fate. As for Verro, he at first seemed more sinned against than sinning, especially in the matter of the meddlesome orphan, the one Font claimed so convincingly was a witch.

And then out of nowhere had come the equally meddlesome Costanza family. On what ground, wondered Bucareli, was the Costanza agent, Ernán Haros, giving evidence against Federico Verro?

"My *patron* Don Eduardo and his lady were close friends of the Figuroa family in Spain over thirty years ago, Excellency," testified Haros. "Don Avila is godfather to the eldest son of Don Eduardo and Doña Teresa Costanza, which can be verified in the cathedral at Seville. I submit a notarized copy of the cathedral record."

Ah, thought the viceroy, the eldest son. That would be Gómez, the one who later disgraced himself and disappeared.

"Indeed," continued Haros, "it is the Costanza family's correspondence from Don Avila which I place at the disposal of the court. A comparison of the signatures by experts shows beyond question that the hand signing the deed that conveyed Buena Suerte to Federico Verro was not that of Don Avila. We maintain that the deed is a forgery and that legal title to Buena Suerte remains with Don Avila and his heir."

Verro, in the prisoner's stall, turned white as chalk.

The magistrate examined the signatures and the statement of the experts. "What say you to this charge, Señor Verro?"

"I deny it!" shouted the prisoner. "False evidence has been contrived against me. I can produce a witness who saw Don Avila sign that deed you hold in your hand. She saw him with her own eyes! And she will so swear before God!"

The magistrate thoughtfully drummed his fingers on the bench. "Hm. And is this witness the same one you produced in October? The old servent who testified she was present when Don Avila made you a gift of a valuable emerald ring and other jewels?"

Verro tossed his head. "Well, perhaps her memory betrayed her in that case. But not in this. She was present when the deed was signed. The servant Pepita. She is nearby. I can send for her."

The magistrate glanced inquiringly at the viceroy who dismissed the offer with a barely perceptible shake of his head. The magistrate passed the papers to the clerk at his elbow and turned again to the prisoner. "Señor Verro, a final charge against you, as you know, has to do with mistreatment of a personal servant of Don Avila's household, one Señora Márquez, born Gabriella María Salgado."

Verro's lip curled. "The witch? My mistreatment of Gabriella Salgado has been exaggerated. But exaggerated or not, what of it? A witch deserves worse than what she received at my hand! I should have chained her to a stake, whipped her senseless and thrown her out."

"Has it been proved in a court of church law that the girl was a witch?"

"The proof was there at Buena Suerte, every day!" cried Verro. "The cats, her influence over the family, Señorita Bonita and her seizures! What more evidence is needed?"

The magistrate turned inquiringly to Haros, who had risen to his feet. "I respectfully ask permission to question two witnesses, Sire."

On his dais, the viceroy shifted impatiently. It was nearing dinnertime. Ernán Haros was as aware of the late hour as the viceroy. Haros was hungry, too. "Excellency, I shall be as brief as possible with these witnesses. First I wish to present Monsignor Raoul Mero, cousin of Augusta Christina Valderia, abbess of the convent of Santa Clara de Asís. Will you please come forward, Monsignor Mero?"

An ecclesiastic of great dignity came forward and took his place in the witness stall.

"Please explain how you happened to know Gabriella Salgado," said Haros.

"She was an orphan raised in the convent of Santa Clara de Asís. Madre Valderia — my cousin, the abbess — requested that I take charge of the child, hear her confession regularly, advise her. I was glad to oblige. I supervised Gabriella's religious instruction and knew her inmost thoughts for fifteen years. I can promise you, the child is no witch."

"One question further," Haros continued. "There is some question as to the extent of the injury inflicted on Gabriella Salgado by Federico Verro. The accused admits beating her but says the injury he inflicted was insignificant."

"I would have to disagree," said Monsignor Mero. "I was summoned to Buena Suerte immediately after the incident. I saw her myself, and later discussed her condition with the physician who attended her. Her face was unrecognizable, covered with cuts and swollen with bruises. She had been kicked in the face, you see. The physician was startled at the violence of the attack. He said there was scarcely a limb or a muscle undamaged. Ribs were broken, an ankle fractured. The physician suspected internal injuries. She coughed up blood for several days afterward."

"Thank you, Monsignor," said Haros. "That will be all. And now, I would like to summon Ana Lucero, if you please."

A tall, neat woman of low rank stood and approached the witness stall. Obviously nervous, she nevertheless held her head high. Federico Verro, recognizing her, uttered an angry cry and clenched his fists. Startled, she looked to Haros for guidance.

Haros reassured her, "Don't be afraid. You are perfectly safe. Ana, please tell the magistrate and the viceroy what your position was at Buena Suerte."

"I was personal maid to Señorita Bonita, if you please, Señor."

"Did you see Gabriella Salgado the morning she was beaten by Federico Verro?

"Yes, Señor."

"Would you agree with what you have heard Monsignor Mero say as to the severity of the beating?"

"Yes, Señor. She was very bad, with blood all over. I helped lift her up and I could feel her ribs scrape together, they was broke that bad."

"Thank you. Now, you have heard the charge that Gabriella Salgado is a witch."

"Yes, but that's not true. Gabriella Salgado's no witch, Señor."

"How can you be so sure?"

"There wasn't no witch at Buena Suerte, ever. You see, the lord who built Buena Suerte long ago, he was special scared of witches. And the way to stop a witch, well, like everybody knows, you put a cross under the door sill. And then there can't no witch cross that threshold. Maybe the witch can come in the window or down the chimney but not through the door."

"Yes, go on."

"So when the palace was built, the workmen put a cross under every threshold of every door in the whole palace, even the storerooms and stables. I seen one once. It was a pretty little cross carved in the marble. On the under side. There's not no door sill at Buena Suerte that hasn't got a cross under it. So all the time we lived there, no one was ever scared on account of witches. But anyway, Gabriella Salgado wasn't no witch. Least, I never heard of a witch that shamed you into saying your prayers every night like she did. Made you get up and say them twice if you forgot."

"Did Federico Verro know about the crosses under the door sills?"

"Oh, yes, Señor. Everybody did."

"Thank you, Ana. That will be all."

The Expedition West to Laguna de Santa Oyala
December 1775

Like all the expedition people, even the commander, Gabriella had ridden an assortment of saddle horses and mules, some more agreeable than others. Between Alamos and Horcasitas, Miguel had assigned her the same little chestnut mare she had ridden from Mexico, an amiable animal who read her mind and moods more accurately than any mirror.

North to Tubac, she alternated between a shifty-eyed, knock-kneed matri-arch of a horse named Tipa and a giant tireless mule known as Ruffio. On Ruffio's broad back she could, and often did, spread out her blankets and play endless games of solitaire.

Tipa developed a chronic cough, feigned according to Rita, and was perma-nently assigned to the *remuda* at the rear of the column. Miguel decided Ruffio's size and dependability were more badly needed elsewhere and took the brute for cargo duty. To Gabriella fell a restless, priggish mare, Lina, who demanded constant attention.

At the river crossing, Gabriella asked for Ruffio and got him. She gambled that her restored role of *enfermera* would allow her to keep the mount of her choice and made no secret of her wishes. They were respected.

Respected, too, was Gabriella's request that her little household not be harrassed by Vasco Bellis, although as Ramona foresaw, she met with resistance. Padre Font stirred from his illness long enough to urge a marriage with Colonel Anza. "The widow's thinking on the matter is too distorted to see that her best interest is in marriage with the children's father," lectured the priest. "Look at the facts: She proved herself a witch before leaving Mexico. No man of quality will have her anyway, since she's a bastard. Vasco needs a wife and will make a nuisance of himself until he finds one. What better solution to a difficult problem than to join the two in holy wedlock?"

But the commander disagreed and warned Bellis once again to stop pestering the expedition women.

By the second week in December, the colonists had come to the last of the native settlements and also the last of the dependable water supplies — a lake of trapped floodwater from the river known as Laguna de Santa Oyala. On the western horizon, the travelers glimpsed the great sand dunes and rocky deserts that lay ahead.

There being fewer natives about, and a month having passed since the two naked Pima warriors fled from her in terror, Gabriella had grown careless. She still bound up her hair, but often visited the sick in their shelters with no escort other than tiny José, dozing in his sling over her shoulder.

In the late afternoon, thinking herself safe, Gabriella went alone to the lakeshore to clean and refill the water bottles she and Ramona had used for the last few days of travel.

The colonists were preoccupied — children at their games, adults at their evening tasks — and the lakeshore was deserted. Laden down with the heavy containers, she failed to notice a group of Yuma men, none much older than herself, until they suddenly blocked her path.

She whirled to retreat but they quickly surrounded her, stonefaced and threatening. Her stomach tightened with fear and mounting acid burned the back of her throat. Hiding her terror, she scowled angrily at one who seemed to be the leader. "Go!" she told him firmly. "Go away!" and she pointed up the path toward the camp. "Go away! Leave me alone!"

"Go!" they sneered as they crowded closer. "Go! Go!" Without warning, she felt the *rebozo* snatched from her shoulders. The snugly-tied kerchief was ripped from her head and her flame-colored hair tumbled down her back.

She dropped the empty containers and plunged to get around them but the effort was hopeless. Before she could speak further or cry out, the leader clamped over her mouth a hand as tough as saddle leather. Clearly they were enjoying their sport, jabbering gaily and chuckling at her resistance. She felt herself bodily lifted, and twisted and writhed to get free. Scratching and kicking, she broke loose, only to be caught once more.

Along the shore of the lake grew a dense mesquite thicket. Toward this underbrush, the warriors carried her. When she glimpsed where she was being taken, she shouted again, "No! Leave me alone! Go away!" Her hair was yanked back roughly and again the pungent palm filled her mouth. She bit as hard as she could and was rewarded with a piercing scream that originated somewhere behind her head. The moment her mouth was free, she shrieked, "Miguel! Martín! Help me — !"

But her cry was interrupted abruptly. Bronze arms, an angry painted face, flying black locks and then the green of the mesquite branches filled her vision. Terror rekindled her strength and she fought more frantically than ever, kicking, stamping, pinching, struggling. The needle-sharp thorns of the mesquite limbs tore cruelly at her face and arms but she was too frightened to feel the pain. Striking with her fists and kicking in every direction, she twice broke free, screaming, but the young men overcame her and at last drew her into the dim light of the screening trees.

Quickly one of them gripped her head as in a vise, his hand clamped over her mouth. Others pinned her flailing legs, arms and fists to the ground. First one, then another blade flashed. They were going to scalp her! *Santa Madre, have pity!* she prayed. Death from hemorrhaging was a certain result. Her breath came in rasping gulps of fear. Her raging pulse pounded in her ears.

She was totally immobilized, unable to move. Then suddenly she felt her head jerked back and forth in a nightmarish rhythm. She braced for the sting of the knife against her skin — but it never came. A crazed minute passed of being twitched about before she realized they weren't scalping her at all, they were cutting off her long hair! Great handfuls of it! And shouting triumphantly, brandishing it about like war trophies!

"Señora! Señora Márquez!" At first, the sound came faintly over the cries of the Indian braves, but the second time Gabriella recognized Tómas' distant shout. Her attackers heard it too and as she renewed her struggles, the savage hand over her mouth tightened.

"Señora Márquez!" Tómas was nearer this time, his booted footsteps audible on the pebbled trail nearby.

With an irresistible jerk, Gabriella pulled free of the restraining hand, and with the last of her strength, shrieked, "Tómas! Help! Help me!"

The young warriors muttered among themselves and then, moving silently as a breath of air, melted away among the tangled branches, their mission accomplished. Gabriella, left alone behind them, wailed like a frightened child and clawed at her rumpled clothing.

Guided by her cries, Tómas quickly found her. He stared, horrified, at her shorn head, then collected his wits. "It's all right, Señora," he soothed her, awkwardly patting her on the shoulder. "They've gone. You're safe now."

"Tómas!" she cried. "Thank God you came when you did! I thought they were going to scalp me!"

Tómas held aside the clutching branches as she painfully crawled from the thicket on hands and knees. Her face and arms were scratched and bruised, her hair and clothing torn.

At the edge of the undergrowth, she fell to one side, sobbing. "Tómas," she sobbed, "The Madonna sent you. Oh, how I prayed for someone to help me!"

Tómas tried to avoid staring. Señora Márquez' head looked like a harvested wheat field, with the shorn stalks at odd lengths. Gabriella's hands flew to her head. As she comprehended her disfigurement, her eyes widened in dismay. "*Santa Padre*," she whispered. Then, like a rumbling, boiling tide, rage overwhelmed her. "Those fiends from hell!" she shrieked. "Those butchers! What have they done to me?"

"Sh-sh." Tómas tried to quiet her. On the ground nearby, he located her *rebozo* and found the scarf that the savages had ripped from her head. He offered what help he could as her fumbling hands tried to cover her ugliness. Gently, he pointed out to her, "With the others in camp, Señora, you always wore a scarf around your head anyway. With your scarf and *rebozo* in place, no one will ever know anything has happened."

Gabriella's lunatic stare drove him back several steps. "I'll know what happened!" she screamed. "And so will you! And so will those heathen savages!"

Nearby colonists had heard her screams and were already running toward the lakeshore. Early arrivals overheard her words and assumed the worst.

Emerging on hands and knees from the mesquite thicket, Gabriella's face had been pale as paper but now two bright coins of angry color tinged her cheeks. Her headcovering was in place, though askew. She tugged sharply at her rumpled skirts, glared at Tómas and snapped, "Now help me up! Carefully, please. I think I may have sprained something."

CHAPTER 25

Laguna de Santa Oyala
December 1775

No news ever traveled so swiftly or so inaccurately through the camp as word of the Indian braves' attack on Gabriella Márquez. Ramona Bellis, sobbing with anxiety, came running with the baby to meet her. So did Miguel, beside himself with fury.

Listening to his charges, Gabriella's indignation grew. "You yourself are the one who warned me they'd passed the word ahead of us along the trail — you! Why did they do it? It was revenge for frightening those two Pima men a month ago in the headquarters tent."

"They could have scalped her, Miguel," Tómas pointed out, "but they didn't. They knew better than to kill her. They — "

"You stay out of this!" screamed Miguel. "The bastards violated her! They as good as raped her!"

"Don't you think I'd know if I'd been raped?!" Gabriella tried to shout him down. "I was not raped, Miguel! Nor scalped! Given a haircut, yes. Manhandled, yes, and I'd like to give those men a good punch in the nose. But raped, no!" She longed for Martín to come take charge.

"Did they wrestle you to the ground and hold you against your will?" cried Miguel.

"Yes, they did." *Martín, where are you?!*

"Then you have been violated, and stop defending the villains!" yelled Miguel, and off he stumped to notify the commander.

Rita and Rosa Grijalva had been setting the headquarters tent to rights after the officers' dinner when Miguel and Tómas returned to camp with Gabriella, limping, scratched and torn. Following them to Miguel's shelter were angry colonists shaking their fists.

Rosa fetched ointment and bandages from the dispensary. While Tómas dispersed the crowd, the two women began doctoring Gabriella's hurts and untangling mesquite twigs from her clothing. Rosa examined the cropped hair. "You'll look best if I trim it the way I trim my boys' hair," and she set to work with a comb and shears.

Safe with her friends, Gabriella was glad to be pampered. Why hasn't Martín come? Once her anger and fear died away, she found herself weakened and sore in a dozen spots.

"You warned me not to go anywhere alone, Rosa," she said, contrition in her voice. "What happened was partly my fault."

"Still, those men should be punished!" said Rosa grimly. "They can't be allowed to get by with that! Not a woman in the expedition will be safe!"

"But they weren't after 'any woman in the expedition'," protested Gabriella. "They were after me."

Me, she thought, the only widow and everywhere known as such, even to the natives. Ramona had been right after all. Only a church-wedded husband would give her the protection she needed, a husband living with her in the same shelter. Whether she loved Martín no longer mattered. Her mind was made up. She would seduce or trick him into marriage.

And soon. At present, the colonists' anger was directed against the natives who had attacked her. But no one knew better than Gabriella how quickly sentiment could change, especially where a lone woman was concerned and a widow at that. "She was hungry for male attention," they would say. "She encouraged the warriors and deserved the abuse she got."

"Everyone's angry now," she sighed to Rita, "but a month from now, the camp could just as easily be laughing about Señora Márquez and her haircut."

"I won't be laughing!" snapped Rita.

Martín shouted outside the shelter, "Gabriella!"

Her hands flew to her hair. Thanks to Rosa's skill, it was at least uniform in length, and neat. Martín had always admired her rich, shining hair. Would he be revolted at the sight of her? "Yes, Martín?" she called.

"Are you dressed? Colonel Anza is coming to talk to you!"

Hastily Rita handed her a robe. Colonel Anza entered the shelter, followed by Martín. Both men stared, then turned away out of delicacy. The commander cleared his throat. "I regret that you were subjected to such treatment, Señora."

"It's all right, Colonel Anza," said Gabriella. "It's a shock for you, I know, seeing me like this but you need to see what everyone is so angry about. There's no damage that time won't correct. The Yuma braves humiliated me to avenge their friends, that's all."

"A technicality," said the colonel. "The men of the expedition were told weeks ago that the sentence for molesting the native women would be fifty lashes on the bare back. The punishment for Indians who molest Spanish women is the same. I have already sent a detail of men to apprehend your attackers."

A pause. "With all respect, Colonel Anza, those men don't deserve fifty lashes because of what they did to me."

"There is more at stake here than what happened to you. If other expeditions are to come through these lands, it must be made clear to the native men that such behavior will not be tolerated."

Before dark the five guilty youths had been tracked down and placed under guard to await their punishment the following morning. Rosa Grijalva took Ramona and the baby to spend the night with her. "After what Gabriella's been through, she needs a night of uninterrupted sleep," she said.

Miguel was at the headquarters tent with the officers. The shelter, protected from the night breeze by a screen of blankets, was snug and warm. Rita sat near the fire shelling dried beans for dinner the next day. At last Gabriella murmured stubbornly, "They don't deserve it."

"A funny way for you to talk," muttered Rita. "Those devils deserve a hundred lashes, not fifty!"

"Colonel Anza thinks he's going to teach the Indians a lesson. The lesson he'll teach is that an expedition of Spanish colonists passing through their land means trouble. They aren't going to forget how their young men were tracked down and whipped over nothing."

"That's Colonel's concern, not yours."

"Colonel Anza's in a terrible spot, don't you see, Rita? Every man in the expedition feels his womenfolk are threatened and they're looking to him to take action. The colonel has a choice: punish the natives who attacked me or turn his own colonists against him." A pause. "And that puts me in a terrible spot."

Rita gazed at Gabriella. Her hands slowed at their work. "Why do I have the feeling there's a plot brewing in that busy brain of yours?"

"Somebody has to do something!"

Rita nodded knowingly. "And you're the 'somebody'." She gathered the bean husks in her apron, set aside her bowl and rose to go to bed. "Good luck."

"Rita, wait," begged Gabriella. "You've got to help me."

"Not me!" said Rita. "Toss your slops into the wind if you like. But leave me out of it."

"Rita, listen," insisted Gabriella. "From the first month on the trail, you've had little use for the colonists. One time you said they're ignorant yokels for the most part and you dreaded having them for neighbors. D'you remember saying that?"

"So?"

"I promise you, if this punishment tomorrow morning takes place, the Indians will never forget it. We will be the only colonists who will ever go to California. There will never be any more. No merchants, no people to weave cloth and make glassware, no cobblers or milliners, no bishops or noblemen and their ladies for you to please with your cooking. Salvador Palma won't let them pass. They can't go by sea; they'll be blown away as hundreds have been in the past. So these paisanos and their families camped here tonight are the only people you'll ever have for neighbors. The only ones, Rita."

It was a telling point. More than once, Rita had thought of her future as a California farmer's wife and loathed it. "But there'll be others," she had always reassured herself. She shifted uneasily. At last, reluctantly, she sat down and folded her hands in her lap. "What do you want me to do?"

A half-hour later, Miguel returned to the shelter. "Martín says tell you he'll see you tomorrow after you've rested." he reported to Gabriella. "He's ready to go flay him a Yuma warrior or two, Martín is."

Gabriella tossed her head. "How silly!"

Miguel thrust his angry face within an inch of hers and shouted, "My girl, it's not silly! What kind of fool are you, anyway? Every man here knows it could just as easily have been his own woman that got roughed up."

"Then they're the fools, not me! I was the one who got roughed up because I was the one they mistook for a ghost."

But the fire in Miguel's eyes blazed up hotter than ever. His furious whisper cut the air. "Protect those scoundrels all you want, Gabriella Márquez, but listen to me. If those triflin' Injuns live through the night without a dagger stuck between their ribs, it'll be the biggest miracle since the Virgin Birth."

Viciously he kicked off his boots, bundled himself up, threw himself down on his pallet and after several minutes of thrashing from side to side, went to sleep. Gabriella waited for the assurance of his snoring, then crept to Rita's pallet and touched her shoulder. Outside by the fire, their shadows mingled for several minutes before they set off together.

The night was very cold; a million frigid stars glittered across the winter sky. At Padre Font's tent, Gabriella softly scratched the edge of the canvas beyond which, she knew, Tómas lay wrapped in his blankets. A moment later he joined them rubbing sleep from his eyes.

Gabriella whispered, "Tómas, I'm about to ask you to do something that's very important."

"What?" he asked warily.

"If Colonel Anza has those men whipped tomorrow, the native tribes and the Spaniards will be enemies forever. You know that, don't you?"

"Yes."

"There will never be another expedition through the land of Salvador Palma. He won't allow it. What you must do, Tómas, is help the prisoners escape."

"Escape? Me?"

"You must tell them to go as far as they can into the mountains and hide until the expedition has gone. When Colonel Anza finds they've disappeared, he can't waste several days looking for them. He says we've been delayed too long already. He'll have to leave without punishing the men, don't you see? And then no one will be angry. That's why it's important for you to set them free."

"Miguel could do it better than me," protested Tómas.

"No. Miguel is too angry. You're more careful than Miguel anyway. Rita and I stuffed some dried figs and dates with laudanum for the guards. Rita is going to offer them a little midnight refreshment. Let a half-hour go by. By then, the guards will be sleeping. Then you must go inside the shelter and untie them."

"But if I'm caught, they'll whip the prisoners and me, too!" Tómas's frightened eyes shone in the dark.

Rita grunted in disgust. "What did I tell you! He's a chickenhearted nothing, this one!"

Gabriella pressed on. "Tómas, do you remember asking me to exorcise the *mal ojo* for Flora Jiménez? Amanda's baby sister?"

"She's no baby," said Tómas. "She's two years old."

"If you do this thing for us, then I will conduct the ritual for Flora Jiménez."

"You will? You promise you will?"

"I'll do my best."

"When? When will you do it?"

Gabriella hesitated. The expedition had another day of preparation before leaving for the dreaded sand dunes.

"Tomorrow?" urged Tómas. "You can do it tomorrow morning. Will you do it tomorrow?"

"Yes. But we're talking about a bargain here, Tómas. If you find ponies for the Indians and make sure they escape tonight, I'll do the ceremony in the morning. They must get away to the mountains."

"Yes, I'll see to it. I know what to do."

They had talked too long already. From Tómas they borrowed a lantern and found the prisoners' shelter. Gabriella kept to the shadows while Rita greeted the sentries and sympathized with them for their thankless vigil. As she departed, both guards were greedily wolfing the confections.

Martín was on Gabriella's mind when she woke next morning.

What would he think when he learned the Indians had escaped? Elias had always been easy to persuade, but Martín had a mind of his own. Would it occur to him to blame her? She needed his support, needed it desperately!

With every muscle aching, she dressed, bound her head closely and helped Rita and Miguel with the officers' breakfast.

Martín stood waiting for her at the headquarters tent and her pulse quickened. He searched her scratched face. "I see you put up a fight," he said grimly.

"I was terrified. I didn't know what they intended to do. Miguel delivered your message last night."

"We'll talk later," he said. Gabriella read a special meaning in his eyes and her hopes soared.

The officers had barely seated themselves when one of the shamefaced guards arrived to report the escape.

"Damnation!" thundered Anza. He shot to his feet, nearly upsetting the breakfast table, and went to investigate. A quarter-hour later, he had organized a mounted search party with an expert tracker and sent the men on their way.

At Miguel's shelter, Rita whispered, "They left six hours ago. Have they made it to the mountains, do you think?"

Gabriella nodded. "Easily."

"I'd hate for Tómas to get in trouble over this."

"He won't," murmured Gabriella.

She was relieved when everyone, including Colonel Anza, assumed the captives had been released by members of their own tribe. But she was sorry on the guards' account. As punishment for sleeping at their post, the commander banished them to duty with the cattle for the remainder of the journey.

Only Martín was skeptical. After breakfast, he found Gabriella at her own shelter with the baby. Her eyes brightened at the sight of him but his words were sharp.

"Those guards were the best freight handlers I had, you know," he told her with a suggestive stare. "They'll be missed."

She busied herself with the baby. "I'm sorry to hear that, Martín."

"Rita brought them a little supper around midnight, they said."

"Yes. It was awfully cold and she thought they might like something to eat."

Martín's gaze didn't waver. "And it was right after she left that they dropped off to sleep."

"You seem to be blaming Rita. If your men were so tired, they would have gone to sleep whether Rita brought them food or not, wouldn't they?" She laid José in his little bed and exchanged a few words with Ramona, who was tending the fire.

To Martín, she said brightly, "I've borrowed a raw hen's egg from Rita. I'm going to perform a cleansing ritual for Señora Jiménez' little girl, Flora. Would you like to come watch?"

Martín scowled. "For weeks, you've been saying you wouldn't do it. What changed your mind?"

"The camp needs something new to talk about," said Gabriella airily. "Maybe watching a *curandera* at work will get their minds off the Indians."

"You fraud!" charged Martín. "You're no *curandera!*"

"Of course not." Coolly, Gabriella arranged a wool *rebozo* over her head. She picked up a small basket and smiled flirtatiously at Martín over her shoulder. "Coming?"

Martín lagged a few steps behind, liking the turn of events less and less. What was this crazy girl up to now?

No doubts bothered Gabriella. Señora Jiménez had already announced to all that Señora Márquez had agreed to remove the *mal ojo* from her little girl and a crowd had gathered. She found Tómas and Amanda inside the Jiménez shelter, preparing the child for the ceremony. Martín positioned himself just inside the entrance while Señora and her leatherjacket husband, tense with expectation, seated themselves on low stools along the wall. Relatives and close friends crowded in as space allowed.

Flora lay motionless on a pallet in the middle of the small room. Amanda had already undressed her as Gabriella had instructed and covered her with a light blanket. Gabriella began by lighting incense at the tiny shrine in one corner. She crossed herself and whispered a short prayer.

From a napkin, she then took twin packets of herbs and placed one in each of the child's outstretched hands. She closed the small fingers over the packets to form hard little fists. "You must hold tight to these," she murmured to the little girl. "Do you understand?" Flora's black eyes stared back. Slowly the child nodded. Then Gabriella gently straightened the little girl's legs and crossed her fists over her breast. Softly chanting the Credo, Gabriella then lit two votive candles and placed one at the child's head and another at her feet.

Still chanting, she knelt on a pillow at Flora's side. She poured scented oil from a flagon into her palms, held them together briefly to warm it, and with her fingers began to stroke the substance into the child's long hair. More oil. Gabriella's stroking fingers massaged the child's face, neck, shoulders, breast.

"*...et in spiritum sanctum, dominum et vivicantem, qui ex patre filio que procedit...*" The hushed chanting never faltered.

By now, working the oil through the child's black hair, Gabriella had begun to fan it like a dark halo around her head, over her shoulders, over her breast. "*...et expecto resurrectionem mortuorum, et vitam venturi saeculi. Amen.*" Arriving at the end of the Credo, she commenced again. "*...Credo in unum Deum, Patrem Omnipotentem, et in unum Deum, Jesum Christum, filium Dei unigenitum...*"

The murmured chanting, the soothing motions, the fragrance of the oil mingling with the odor of the incense all had a hypnotic effect. Martín was moved, more than he cared to admit, as Gabriella swayed back and forth, massaging the child's abdomen, her arms, then her legs. With Amanda's assistance, Gabriella turned her over and annointed her back, so that the scented oil covered every inch and crevice of her body. Again Amanda helped lift the child, and again Gabriella massaged chest, abdomen and loins.

Only then did she replace the stopper in the flagon and pause, briefly, in her chanting. With a smile, she gently opened the little fists, removed the herbs and replaced the fingers of both hands around the hen's egg which Rita had supplied. Chanting, Gabriella massaged legs, abdomen, arms, shoulders, neck, face and scalp one last time.

Satisfied at last, she took the egg from the child. Martín saw her pause as though startled. Resuming her chanting, she rubbed the egg over the child's forehead, cheeks, chest, arms and legs. Then, with great care, she traced the perimeter of the child with the egg as though she were marking off a pattern of some kind. Having been completely through the Credo several times, she came to the end. Holding the egg lightly in her hand, she made the sign of the cross over the child — head, feet, both shoulders — and brought the egg to rest in the child's navel.

Rousing himself, Martín estimated this massaging had been going on for nearly an hour. Gabriella was tired and looked it. She raised her eyes to Señora Jiménez. "Do you have the container of water ready?"

"Yes, Señora." The older woman reached to a shelf and handed down a metal tankard filled to the brim with water.

With uncertainty in her heart, Gabriella set the tankard on the ground beside the child's pallet. The *curandera* in Mexico had warned that sometimes the egg was as raw as when it came from the hen, signifying that no evil spirits had left the patient. Was the healing ceremony ineffective? Perhaps, but there could be another reason. Though the patient might be ill, the illness could be due to some other cause, not to the *mal ojo*.

What happened most often was that the egg appeared partially cooked, indicating that at least most of the evil spirits had been drawn from the patient. In Gabriella's hand, the egg felt heavy and she hoped for the latter result. She took care that her movements over the tankard were visible to the child's parents and to the child herself. She tapped the egg sharply against the metal rim, breaking the shell. To her amazement, the shell's contents slid out, whole, from the two halves, and sank like a firm white moon in the tankard, forcing an overflow of water over the brim.

No one was more astonished than Gabriella. She'd not been at all sure she could duplicate the *curandera's* performance that she had witnessed in Mexico. Her success dumbfounded her.

Not so the Jiménez family. "I knew it!" shrieked Señora. "I knew it! Oh, my baby! My sweet *pobrecito!* Oh, *Santissima Madre* be thanked!" She threw her arms around her husband in a frenzy of joy and relief.

Señor Jiménez, eyes streaming and his voice broken, patted her awkwardly. "You were right," he said. "God is good. You were right. Our daughter, she is safe now."

Outside the shelter arose a clamor of excited voices as those watching at the entrance reported to those behind them what they had witnessed. "It's a miracle!" "It came out whole! The egg came out whole!" "Whoever heard of such a thing?"

Within moments, excited voices were shouting the news from one side of the camp to the other. Those busy with other tasks dropped them to come see the miracle.

Martín was stunned. All his life he had discounted tales of amazing feats performed by the "white witches." But he could not discount what he had seen with his own eyes.

Outside the Jiménez shelter, the press of excited onlookers threatened to collapse the flimsy structure of blankets and mesquite branches, and Martín warned them off. Inside, Amanda and her sobbing mother wrapped the child in warm clothing while Tómas gathered Gabriella's belongings and helped her to her feet. She had been kneeling for nearly an hour on muscles overtaxed by her experience of the day before. Neither he nor Gabriella were surprised when she swayed, unable to stand alone.

"Lieutenant Neve could get a litter for you," suggested Tómas.

"It would be better if I walked," Gabriella answered. "But I'll need help."

The Jiménez family was too excited for goodbys. Little Flora cried and laughed by turns, along with her parents. Only Amanda tearfully grasped Gabriella's hand, kissed it, and murmured, "Thank you, Señora. Oh, thank you!"

Outside the Jiménez shelter, laughter, shouts and questions met Gabriella and Tómas. Gabriella, too weak to respond, let Tómas deal with the questions. "Yes, she learned the ceremony in Mexico." "This is the first time she ever performed it." "It was a raw hen's egg that she used. I tested it first. I shook it and could feel the yolk move."

With Tómas supporting her on one side and Martín on the other, they made their way slowly toward Gabriella's shelter.

Martín was clearly disturbed by what he had witnessed. If Gabriella wanted to distract him from the Indian escape, she succeeded. After the crowd dispersed, he could suppress his questions no longer. "How did Señora Jiménez know you could do that?"

"She didn't," said Gabriella. "Neither did I."

"What made the egg change the way it did?" asked Martín.

"I don't know," answered Gabriella truthfully.

"But in the middle of the ceremony, when you took the egg from Flora, you knew it had changed, didn't you? You paused, and there was a puzzled look on your face."

"Yes. It felt different. More — dense. I was surprised. I didn't think I could make the ritual work."

"What was wrong with Flora?" Martín asked. "Really, I mean."

"I don't know."

Martín had duties to attend to and left soon afterwards, his questions unanswered.

Tómas smiled. "It went well. Amanda was happy. Thank you."

"The treatment isn't over, you know. After a result like that, when the egg is so hard, a real *curandera* would repeat the ritual to make sure no further evil influences are left to bother the patient. She wouldn't consider the patient cured after what happened today. She'd keep on with extra treatments until the egg looked — well, raw."

Tómas frowned. "You mean you'll keep repeating the ritual you did today?"

Gabriella's head drooped with weariness. She had given the colonists something new to think about, but was no more sure of her chances with Martín than before. She ventured hopefully, "Maybe Señora Jiménez doesn't know about the extra rituals."

"I've never heard her say anything about extra rituals."

Silence.

"If you don't tell her and I don't tell her, maybe she'll never find out."

Tómas' boy's face took on a look of wicked innocence. "Never find out what?"

CHAPTER 26   Beyond the Settlements
                                                              December 1775

The day's travel through sagebrush, cactus, mesquite and dry, sandy streambeds had been hard on Gilbert Sandoval's big family, harder still on the pack animals. And in the days to come, the *tordeada* through the sand dunes would be most fatiguing of all. But at least they had left the natives behind!

Sandoval lifted family cargo from the last of his pack animals and gave the mule a sympathetic slap on the flanks. "Take him to the *arriero*," he ordered eleven-year-old Jorgé.

"Can Pedro come too?"

"Yes. And take Felipé. Make sure he doesn't wander off. We'll eat soon."

The afternoon sun already touched the western horizon. Ricardo had finished erecting the shelter and sat nearby winding surplus cargo rope into a coil for use next morning. Squashes lay roasting in the coals. Rina Sandoval tested them for doneness. Their tender skin gave at her touch, and with tongs she removed them to a large bowl.

Sandoval sniffed warily. "No buzzard meat tonight, I hope."

Rina shook her head. "No one would eat it," she said. "The Yumas fed it to their dogs."

Sandoval speculated thoughtfully, "Beef from a steer dead of exhaustion smells funny. It tastes funny, even looks funny. The grain of the meat's different. Why?"

"Ask the buzzards," Rina replied absently. "They're the experts." She wiped her hands on her apron. "We'll have beef tomorrow. Grijalva says they'll slaughter a steer to divide up for the *tordeada*."

Ynez emerged from the shelter holding the fretting infant Aurelia. Trailing behind Ynez were the twins, toddlers just learning to walk. "The baby's hungry," Ynez announced to her mother.

"She's also wet," replied Rina. "Change her for me while I finish with dinner."

"I always have to change the baby," argued Ynez. "Why can't Richardo change her sometimes?"

Sandoval, who adored his feisty eldest daughter, raised his eyebrows. "Aha! We have the little *condessa* with us today! Well, *Condessa*, — "

"No need to tell me," interrupted Ynez, bored. "Big strong Ricardo puts up the shelter every afternoon. And fine wonderful Jorgé takes it down every morning. And sweet darling Pedro gets all our water for us. I'm nothing but a girl so I have to change the baby's pants."

"Such an attitude!" chided her father, feigning shock. "Be a good girl and mind your mother or you'll end up like Gabriella Márquez. The Yumas will give you a haircut."

"Gilbert!" cried his wife, shocked and angry. "That's not funny!"

Instantly contrite, Gilbert agreed. "Forget what I said about the Yumas, *pobrecita*," he said to Ynez. "Go change the baby's pants. For your papa, eh?"

Ynez obeyed with a martyred air. Ricardo followed her into the shelter to stow the extra rope. Their mother began placing bowls and platters of hot food along the makeshift trestle table. "Gabriella needs a husband," she muttered. "Anza should make Lieutenant Neve marry her."

"If God wills a marriage in that direction, my dove, God will attend to it. One reason our colonel is so successful is his refusal to meddle in his colonists' personal affairs."

The children gathered. From Ynez, Señora Sandoval took the fretting infant and put it to her breast. Before long, Ramona would arrive with José, also to be fed. Only afterwards would Rina be free to enjoy her own meal.

Sandoval bowed his head and the family, in unison, softly said grace and crossed themselves. Though sanctified with prayer, the food drew suspicious looks from the children.

Rations were short, and the expedition families had come to rely on the store of bland fruits and vegetables left them by the natives. For their meal, Señora Sandoval had fried a generous platter of the small, hand-sized "sardines" netted by the expedition boys from the nearby lakes.

Ynez gingerly lifted a fish from the platter and ventured an experimental bite. The corners of her mouth turned down. "Phew!!" she cried and tossed it back on the platter.

Señora Sandoval, nursing the baby, turned upon her husband a glance of weary despair. Sandoval noted it and scowled at Ynez. "EAT IT!!" he roared.

Gabriella returned to her shelter after visiting her patients and reporting to the commander. Tómas approached, his long shanks and knobby elbows, as usual, too prominent for the frayed habit Padre Font had bequeathed to him. Scarcely containing his pride, he held out to Gabriella an armload of soft fur. Ramona drew close, staring.

"What's this?" Gabriella exclaimed.

"It's a present for you," explained Tómas. "A buffalo robe, to keep you warm at night. It's to thank you for teaching us to read and write." Tómas lowered his eyes. "And for making Flora Jiménez well again."

"Oh, Tómas, it's beautiful!" breathed Gabriella, overcome. She buried her fingers in the lustrous pelt, fumbled for the edges of the robe and began to unfold it. "— And it's so big!"

Tómas explained, "The nearest buffalo herds are two, three hundred miles away, so a buffalo skin is rare. The fur is very warm."

"But your own family needs it, Tómas! You shouldn't be giving it to me!"

"Mama and Papa said you should have it. Many in the expedition would be dead but for you. You've worked hard for all of us."

"You traded for it, didn't you?"

"Yes," and again Tómas lowered his eyes, for his answer was true in one sense only. The robe had been a thank-you gift to Tómas from the family of one of the Yuma braves he had freed. He was glad for Gabriella to have it, knowing that otherwise it could easily end up as the chaplain's property instead of his own.

"Padre is feeling better," Tómas changed the subject. "Amanda has been giving him fresh-squeezed melon juice. Five cups a day. She tells him it is a special tea brewed from medicinal grasses. He eats more now. He is stronger."

Indeed, the chaplain had become strong enough to renew his criticisms of the commander. That evening, Colonel Anza canceled the march for the following day. He wanted to refresh the spirits of the colonists and restore the animals before the *tordeada*. His plan to issue a ration of brandy the following afternoon became known around the camp and inevitably came to the ears of Padre Font.

The chaplain left his bed and confronted the commander at headquarters. "Drunkenness is a sin!" he charged crisply. "And a person in authority commits a sin when he issues brandy knowing drunkenness will result!"

"I do not give the colonists brandy in order for them to get drunk," replied the colonel stiffly.

"Then why?"

"The lot of the colonists has been hard. They have suffered much without complaining, and in the next few days they will suffer still more. They are guilty of no sin if they laugh and sing and enjoy themselves."

"A drunken orgy is a sin!" insisted the chaplain.

"I promise you, Padre, order will be maintained. There will be no drunken orgy."

"There is only one way to insure that sin will not be committed," insisted Padre Font. "Do not issue the brandy!"

But he failed to sway the commander.

Colonel Anza's patience had already been tried that morning. He early announced which families and military escorts would travel with which section of the *tordeada* and was instantly besieged by a chorus of pleas to change the rosters. "There will be no substitutions!" he thundered.

The *enfermera* and her patients were scheduled to travel with the commander. So were the chaplain and his servants. Lieutenant Neve would lead the third and final section, meaning that ten days would elapse before Gabriella would see Martín again.

Gabriella avoided Padre Font but no one realized better than she that the expedition without a priest would be a disaster. She indirectly monitored his welfare with great care. The chaplain suffered from advanced malnutrition as well as malaria which had plagued him periodically for years. Fresh melons had improved his health temporarily but Amanda would quickly run out of fresh melons traveling through the ocean of sand that lay ahead of them. Then what of her decision about Martín? Would the chaplain be strong enough to conduct a marriage service after traveling ten days through the worst of the desert? Would he even be alive?

Her heart thudding against her ribs and her knees turned to jelly, Gabriella made up her mind. She must see Martín alone, and soon. Perhaps she had already procrastinated too long.

Early morning at her shelter had found Ynez with her books, waiting for Gabriella who was dressing José in fresh clothing for the day. It was her favorite time with her adopted infant son, when Ramona had just brought him from his wetnurse. He was bright-eyed and sprightly, crowing, waving tiny fists and feet with exuberance. Already his eyes were changing, from the newborn dark blue to a muddy brown.

Gabriella planted a tender farewell kiss on the baby's forehead, replaced him in his basket and told Ramona, "If you need me, I'll spend an hour reading with the children. Then I'll see the patients and finish some work at the dispensary."

Later in the morning at the headquarters tent, she was busy with mortar and pestle. Sergeant Grijalva, leading the second section, and Martín, leading the third, would each need an emergency kit of remedies. She was including powders for headaches, burn ointments, and bandages for accidental cuts and scrapes.

She had never before encountered injury from cold. She was uneasy about treatment and went to Colonel Anza. "High in the mountains," he told her, "soldiers' toes, fingers and noses will sometimes turn white with frostbite. Warm the frozen areas gently till feeling returns, otherwise injury might be permanent."

"Is a hot posset helpful?"

"Warm tea or chocolate, yes. No brandy. Spirits only inflame the blood vessels and make the injury worse."

Shortly after noon, she finished her work. She was hungry but too excited to eat. Martín, she knew, would be with his men a half-mile away, readying the mounts for the commander's first section to leave next day. She would seek him out, deliver his kit personally, and — and, well, ask him.

But she was losing her nerve. She had waited too late. No sensible man would agree to the rushed-up plan she had in mind. Martín's slow, lazy eyes sometimes took in more than she realized. She was using him. Surely he would know it and resent it. Or, more likely, hold his sides laughing at her presumption and send her away.

Leatherjackets with their jugs and pitchers began to gather in the headquarters tent for their brandy ration. Sergeant Grijalva arrived to supervise the distribution. As she closed the dispensary, he approached with a brandy keg under each arm and set them on the counter. "For medicinal purposes on the *tordeada*," he announced with a wink. "One for my section and one for Martín's. Good for fighting the cold."

He gave each fat little keg a good-natured thump and returned to his distribution. Gabriella thought of the commander's frostbite advice. The sergeant's glib self-assurance made her uncomfortable, but she said nothing. She would tell Martín, who could pick up his own keg of brandy if he wanted it.

She stopped by the shelter. Ramona had taken José to Rina Sandoval for his noon feeding. From her packing case, she brought out her three outer petticoats, all of which had been turned at least once to hide the stains of travel. She decided on the brightest-colored of the three, of deep red fabric, carefully mended after she had stepped through the hem dismounting, and patched when singed by sparks from a cookfire.

If she wore the skirt with the patch over her hip, it suggested a pocket, less demeaning than a patch.

Shivering in the cold of the shelter, she put aside the ragged but warm shoulder-to-ankle homespun chemise that she wore traveling each day for the cherished embroidered linen she had worn when she and Elias were married. She gave her best velvet basque a good brushing, noting with concern how thin the nap had become. Her hands trembled as she threw her cloak about her shoulders and arranged the wimple that hid her cropped hair. Any other man would refuse to wed a woman with hair cut short like a boy's. Even Elias might have hesitated — what would people think? But Martín had pride enough for ten men, and except for explicit orders from the commander, he made up his own mind and did what he pleased.

She touched her wrists with scent, shouldered the heavy pouch of medical supplies and set out for the corrals, relieved that there were no longer any natives to worry about.

On the way, she rehearsed what she would say. The expedition had allowed many improvisations due to expediency; for a widow to ask an unmarried gentleman to be godfather to her adopted child, for example, was slightly irregular but allowable. But for that same woman to ask the single gentleman to marry her was an unheard-of effrontery. Yet she must somehow find the right words. But she was no better prepared when she arrived at Martín's field tent than when she left her own shelter.

She found the lieutenant writing reports. More animals were dying every night, and the reports left him depressed and shaken with worry. Fatigue added years to his appearance; his shoulders slumped like those of an old man. His eyes were dull from lack of sleep and the dark locks were carelessly tied back with a soiled ribbon. For the first time, she noticed a sprinkling of gray at his temples and caught her breath. Martín was too young for gray hair!

She wanted to gather him in her arms and kiss away his worries. Guilt sucked at her resolve; he had a mountain of troubles already without shouldering additional troubles of hers. Maybe she shouldn't — .

But no. She had plotted with Tómas, talked to the sergeant. Everything was arranged. The time was now, and she must seize it.

She straightened, lifted her head. "I brought your medical supplies, Martín," she said gently, and presented him with the heavy kit. She repeated the commander's advice about frostbite and told him about the sergeant's keg of spirits waiting at headquarters.

"Anything else?" he asked. He was preoccupied, worried about the muddy water he was having to supply his animals, and he wanted to get on with his work.

"Martín, you know Padre Font has been very sick."

"Yes."

"Tomorrow we're starting on the hardest part of the journey. The natives have told Colonel Anza all along that this is the coldest winter they ever experienced. If the cold keeps up, Padre Font could die before we reach California. Maybe you didn't realize that."

Unbeliever though he was, Martín understood the gravity of her words. He kneaded his hands, stiff from the cold. "No, I didn't realize it," he said. "But it's

Anza's problem. Why are you telling me?"

"Because of us. Because of you and me." She faced him. "Martín, for you there will never be another woman like Bonita, just as for me there will never be anyone to replace Elias. But those days in Mexico and Alamos, they're gone. And I've been wondering — . Well, do you think we like each other well enough to marry? To marry each other, I mean."

Martín's gloom evaporated like fog before the sun on a mountain lake. *She needs me,* he thought triumphantly. *She put off admitting it till the last minute, but the little fox has discovered she needs me!* Was he glad? Undoubtedly. Gabriella Márquez had demanded more of him than any woman had ever done before, even his martinet of a mother. Bonita was a porcelain doll for whom, even yet, he felt passion; but passion was not enough. Gabriella had reached far beyond and inward to touch and hold his character and his will.

Would he ever adore her as he had adored Bonita? No, though the thought of the little widow in bed made him tremble like an aspen. Was he likely to find in California a farmer's daughter who commanded respect, of himself and others, as did Gabriella? Not in his lifetime, he wouldn't. Not ever.

Gabriella stood waiting, hands gripped together, knuckles white.

Determined to control his trembling voice, Martín said, "Yes, Gabriella, I think probably we like each other well enough to be married."

At his reply, such radiant happiness suffused her features that he had to smile. She lowered her eyes. "As your wife, I'll try not to be so ill-tempered, Martín."

"I would appreciate the effort," he replied. "And now," noticing that her skirt was one she wore only at special fiestas, "if I know you as well as I think I do, you have already made plans of some sort."

She nodded.

"Let's see," he said sardonically. "The colonel says the first section of the *tordeada* will leave tomorrow morning. — Accompanied by your ailing priest who may die along the way, but then again he might not."

She bristled at his implication. "He is really sick, Martín! I didn't make that up to trick you into an early marriage!"

"Of course, you didn't," he soothed her. "Has the disordered chaplain been notified he is to perform a marriage? At his bedside, perhaps?"

"Well, Tómas — "

"Ah, the invaluable Tómas, ever available in any emergency! Emergencies with weddings, emergencies with natives who are to receive punishment — ." Gabriella studied her fingernails. "Quite so. Then do I understand all is in readiness for the wedding to take place? Tonight, perhaps?"

"I think so," said Gabriella, reddening. Everything was arranged except the wedding ring. She remembered the plaited gold ring Martín had ordered made for Bonita before they left Mexico. But perhaps it conjured up unhappy memories; since Alamos, he might have sold, traded or even given it away. "A wedding ring would be nice," she added, "but a twist of wire would do temporarily."

Martín glanced at her hand. "What about the ring you already wear? Would you mind if we used it, for now?"

She minded very much. As it was, she felt she was betraying Elias — . But she thrust the thought aside. "No, I wouldn't mind." She brightened. "When I left headquarters, the sergeant was issuing brandy. Everyone is celebrating."

"Aha! Now I see! And our wedding is one of the things to be celebrated! Of course! Then our wedding is to be tonight?"

"There are still two hours of daylight left," she pushed on, afraid he might change his mind. "How about right now?"

Scheming vixen! he thought with amusement. *In California, she will keep me busy.* A silence. "Gabriella?"

"Yes?"

"What if I said no?"

The joy drained from her face, replaced by desolation so bleak he almost winced. Then it was no girlish whim, this marriage. She had taken her time deciding, but Gabriella Márquez had finally made up her mind that she desperately wanted and needed a husband. And she wanted him, Martín Felipé Mendoza de Neve Ortega!

He touched her face. "I didn't mean to cause you pain, Gabriella. I was joking, but it was a bad joke." He caught her hand and solemnly kissed it. "I would be ten times a fool to say no to your suggestion. You have honored me." Gently he drew her to him. She found herself melting against his hard frame with an emotion more profound than sexual desire. Safe in his arms, it was as if a dire and threatening world had been shut out and she was safe, safe against all its ills and mockeries, injuries and hungers. He whispered in her ear, "I'll be proud to be your husband."

"Oh, Martín, we'll be happy together," she breathed. "I know we will be." And she lifted eager lips to his.

By candlelight, Padre Font had just finished his evening prayers. He was enormously gratified when Tómas told him that Lieutenant Neve and the redheaded trickster Señora Márquez were ready to be joined in the holy bonds of matrimony.

Not so gratified at the timing, however. "This is without precedent of any kind," fumed the chaplain. "No bans, no preparation, no counseling — which these two of all people need the worst!" Yet no one knew better than Padre Font that the redhead was unpredictable as a grasshopper and the officer, headstrong. If the chaplain wished to see them married, he must purse his lips, waive the formalities and perform the ritual immediately.

He left his sickbed, donned his finest robes, crept to the chapel and before a score of smiling, hastily-gathered witnesses mumbled the ceremony. The old man longed to deliver a lambasting sermon as well, but frailty cut him short and he released the assembly with a whispered benediction.

Gabriella wordlessly examined Elias' wedding ring, which she had removed before the ceremony so that Martín could put it on again, pretending it was his. Memories flooded back in spite of her determination to keep them at bay. For her and Elias, marriage had been shared laughter, shared love, and then, most delightful of all, the shared expectation of the child. No second marriage, not even to the man she once idolized, would ever be like the one she had known.

They left the chapel amid the cheers and ribald jibes of the witnesses. Night had fallen, and a beautiful evening it was. The cold desert air was clear as a prism, the stars breathtaking in their loveliness and so bright that no torches were needed for the wedding party to find its way among the shelters. The aroma of beef roasting over pits of glowing embers floated through the far-flung encampment. Real beef, slaughtered especially for the celebration. Several days before, Sergeant Grijalva had tried to interest the expeditioners in the slaughtered flesh of animals that had dropped dead of exhaustion. But the meat was sour and stringy and his offer found no takers. This was the real thing.

Gabriella suddenly remembered neither she nor Martín had eaten since breakfast. Her mouth watered at the smell of the roasting meat. "Rita and Miguel have been cooking all day for the fiesta!" she reminded Martín hopefully.

"Later!" cried Sergeant Grijalva, pressing mugs of brandy on them both. "The expedition has waited three months for this wedding, isn't that right, Rosa? To Martín and Gabriella! Drink up, everyone!"

"The best thing to happen since we left Alamos!" shouted Señora Jiménez. "To Lieutenant and his new missus!"

Some thirty-odd mugs, bowls, bottles and pitchers were raised. "Long life and a big family!" "Salud!" "To Lieutenant and Gabriella!" "Health and happiness!"

A corporal appeared at Martín's elbow. "The item you asked for," he whispered, "we can't find it."

At Alamos, Don Alesandro in his haste had left behind a few rather valuable Figuroa possessions. One of them was Bonita's beautiful sidesaddle, covered with crimson velvet and richly ornamented with silver-gilt. It was found several days later in a cupboard. The sight of it and the memories it brought pained Martín intensely, but he hated to leave such a valuable article behind. In California, a Filipino trader might give a pretty price for it. So he had packed it among his personal effects and decided only this afternoon to present it to Gabriella as a wedding gift.

But the blundering corporal upset his plans. To Gabriella he announced, "I have a surprise for you. Will the bride excuse her new husband while he executes an important commission? I won't be gone long."

Rita was not among the witnesses at the ceremony, nor was Amanda. Lieutenant had asked them to clean and decorate his field tent to receive the newlyweds later in the evening. Some two hours later, their task was completed. They followed the sound of music and merrymaking to a cleared area on the far side of the encampment. Blazing pine knots furnished light for the revelers. Violins wailed a lively duet, a guitar thrummed and castanets rattled. The colonists and soldiers formed a clapping, cheering circle, many standing on crates and saddles to get a better view.

Inside the circle, Tómas Sandoval was teaching the new bride some intricate dance steps involving much snapping of fingers and flipping of skirts, revealing ankles and even knees. The laughing bride's *rebozo* had slipped to her shoulders and the shame of her cropped hair was bared for all to see. Señora Gabriella Neve, relieved but unnerved at her sudden marriage, was drinking and dancing away her apprehensions!

Rita's startled eyes searched for Martín and easily found him among the cheering, laughing onlookers, holding under his arm what appeared to be a red ladies' saddle. Martín was not cheering and laughing. He was glaring. Miguel stood at Martín's elbow, clearly nervous.

The music stopped with much applause. Miguel pushed his way to Gabriella's side. "Here now, my girl," he urged. "The women have laid out food on trestle tables in front of the headquarters tent. Your husband is waiting for you to come share your wedding feast."

Gabriella made to follow Miguel but Grijalva and others closed in about her. To Rita's alarm, the new bride was offered a mug of brandy and accepted it.

"She shouldn't be drinking like that!" grumbled Rita.

"She will get sick," said Amanda.

"Not sick, drunk!" snapped Rita. "Others take wine and ale with their meals and have no trouble holding their liquor. Gabriella never touches the stuff. I've seen her get tipsy at Mass."

Amanda gasped.

"A song!" cried an onlooker. "Gabriella, sing for us!"

The demand was taken up by others. "'King Solomon,' Gabriella! Give us 'King Solomon'!"

Admiring hands pulled her, laughing, to the center of the circle. "King Solomon!" The violins began to whine, introducing the tune. And the bride, twirling and flirting, merry as a brook, snapped her fingers in time to the music as she sang one of the songs Elias had taught her.

> King Solomon and King David
> Led merry, merry lives
> With their many, many sweethearts
> And their many, many wives.
>
> But when at last they both grew old
> With many, many qualms
> King Solomon wrote the Proverbs
> And David wrote the Psalms.

Miguel was stunned that Gabriella knew words and the tune to a naughty song like "King Solomon" usually sung only by men and only in taverns at that! Never had he seen her so deliciously provocative. Every male in the crowd watched with glistening eyes as she pranced and tossed her head. When she finished with a wicked flourish, they cheered uproariously.

Quite suddenly, three things happened, all at once and all unexpected. Lieutenant Neve thrust the saddle into Miguel's arms, then shouldered his way roughly through the dancers, seized his bride by the arm and dragged her struggling away.

Nearby appeared Padre Font, brandishing his staff. Tufts of white hair waved furiously above his ears. Frail as he was, the cold night air should have left him speechless with coughing but instead he reacted with awesome vigor to the lieutenant's behavior. "At last!" he shrilled. "At last the hussy has a husband to give her the discipline she needs! Beat her, Lieutenant! She needs a good beating! Beat her, I say!"

At virtually the same moment, a short distance in front of Lieutenant Neve, there materialized Colonel Anza himself, brows bristling and the great nose lifted high with displeasure.

Martín froze. Gabriella's struggles ceased. A hush fell over the gathering. The music screeched to a stop.

In a firm voice that carried to every ear, the commander announced, "As long as I am in charge of this expedition, no woman will be beaten by her husband or by anyone else. If a crime of some kind is involved, the matter will be settled in the privacy of my office at headquarters. There will be no more talk of beating women."

Sighting Miguel in the crowd, the colonel beckoned him aside and spoke quietly. Then without a glance, he turned and strode back through the crowd toward the headquarters tent.

Lieutenant Neve faced his new wife. On his features was a look of purest venom. Violently he threw her arm from him. He had moved to follow the commander when Padre Font stepped squarely in his path. "You should beat her!" he squalled again. "As her husband, it is your duty! That is the only way you will ever subdue her unruly nature! Beat her, I tell you!"

"You meddling bastard," sneered Martín, "find a wife of your own to beat. My wife is no concern of yours. Now get out of my way."

"What?" Padre Font blinked, bewildered.

Martín shouldered past, jostling the priest who tottered and would have fallen but for onlookers who caught and righted him.

Miguel would gladly have forfeited several weeks of his life to witness this confrontation between Lieutenant Neve and the chaplain, but he was twenty feet away confronting the bride.

"Of all the stupid creatures on God's earth, Gabriella Márquez, you got to be the dumbest!" he snarled angrily into Gabriella's ear. "Colonel ordered me to take you to your shelter and see that you stay there! He says he don't want a drunk woman wandering around camp troubling people. I hope to hell you've had enough fun for one day and come quietly without a scuffle.

But if it's a scuffle you want, by God, woman, I'll oblige you if I have to. D'you understand me?"

In all the time that Gabriella and Miguel had known one another, he had never spoken to her so roughly. What had she done? Married women at fiestas danced and sang all the time. What was so bad about that? Thoroughly confused, she averted her eyes and nodded. "Yes, Miguel, I understand," she said, though she didn't.

At the shelter, Ramona looked up in surprise when Miguel shoved Gabriella, disheveled and weaving, through the entrance. Ramona touched a finger to her lips for silence. The baby was asleep.

Miguel whispered, "Señora Neve is to stay here and not go wandering around. Colonel's orders." He abruptly turned and left.

Gabriella tried to explain to Ramona but her thoughts were so jumbled and the explanation so humiliating, she was at a loss. She stood swaying.

Ramona was wary. "What's wrong? This is your wedding night. You're supposed to be at the field tent with the lieutenant." And then the familiar smell of liquor met her nostrils, explaining everything. Her features twisted with disgust. "You're drunk!" she charged. "You're no better'n Pa!"

She reached for her heavy *rebozo*, threw it around her shoulders, tucked an extra blanket over the baby's basket and picked it up. "If you need tending, Miguel can do it himself, not me! The baby and me, we'll see you in the morning when you're sobered up."

Having taken an unaccustomed amount of spirits on an empty stomach, Gabriella was really inebriated for the first time in her life. She scarcely knew what to make of the tricks her senses were playing on her. Their lean-to stood against one wall of Miguel's shelter, and the murmur of his familiar but indistinct voice swelled and faded like waves on a beach. The flame from the tiny lamp become two flames, then one flame, then two flames again. The earthen floor tilted gently.

She began to shiver. Everyone was angry at her, Martín angriest of all. But why? Where was he? They had said their vows before a priest but was Martín still her husband? Or would he refuse to acknowledge her as his wife? Could he do that?

Her eyes came to rest on the lone pallet with the hastily-disturbed buffalo robe. Woozily she smiled, understanding at least a part of Ramona's anger. The girl had planned a cozy night's sleep in the folds of Tómas' sumptuous gift.

Oh, well.

She fell more than sat on the pallet and with a vast effort, pulled off her boots. True to the habit of years, she turned and knelt to pray, couldn't remember the words, fell forward, pulled the robe about her, and dropped off to sleep.

A short time later, she roused to find herself perspiring. Perspiring? Who would have thought the buffalo robe would be so warm? By lamplight she shrugged and twisted out of her clothes, tossing each item aside, until she lay naked, stretching voluptuously, completely enfolded by the sensuous fur.

She had no idea how much time elapsed before she awakened again. The lamp had gone out. Restless, she lunged to change her position — and came in contact with someone bending over her in the dark. Her terrified gasp brought a gentling hand upon her arm. "Sh-sh-sh," the figure breathed. "You'll wake Rita and Miguel."

Martín!! she thought, her glad heart leaping.

"I brought something for you," breathed the figure, and placed in her palm a wedding ring. Gabriella's groping fingers detected the smooth, braided pattern.

Bonita's ring!

"Oh, Martín!" she sobbed, and threw her arms around him. Truly, then, they would be man and wife — no reservations, no holding back. Glad tears erupted, choking her. "I'm so sorry I made you angry!"

"The ring," he breathed. "Put it on."

Trembling, she placed the patterned ring on her finger with Elias' narrow gold band. An unexpected wave of passion overtook her, the desperate hunger she had felt since Elias' death.

Suddenly she was in his arms, in the arms of the white vision she had first seen across the ballroom at the National Palace. Her instincts had not played her false then — and she knew, as his dear naked length pressed close, that they were not playing her false now.

There was no fumbling, no awkwardness. Borne up on stormy wings, she became whole again, a wife, a woman!

Later, as her breathing slowed, Gabriella realized once again, as she had so surely with Elias, that for her, marriage was life's true blessing. The disturbing dream of her childhood had borne a message. A woman of her nature was never destined for religious orders. She hadn't the temperament of Madre Valderia, who could channel her passion, who could protect and cherish the convent and all those whom it nourished and served. No, the convent orphan would instead protect and cherish this forgiving husband, the intended love of her life, who would from this day forward grace her bed, sire her offspring, and head her household.

She ran adoring fingers through Martín's curls, and at their touch, her subconcious stirred uneasily. Martín's hair had a soft, fly-away quality. But her lover pulled away, tossing a thick, spikey shock of hair away from his face.

Martín was perhaps three inches taller than she was. Yet now, under the buffalo robe, the tips of Gabriella's toes touched her lover's shins while the top of her head rested against his chin. In his embrace, she became rigid as marble.

Only three men in the expedition were so tall. One was Colonel Anza; another was a rangy leatherjacket from Tubac. Both were married men with wives awaiting them at home.

....And then there was Tómas.

Tómas!

He slipped like a shadow from her side. She heard the rustle of clothing, followed by the soft slap as the rawhide closure over the shelter's entrance fell back in place. And then silence.

CHAPTER 27

The *Tordeada*
December 1775

Before dawn next morning, fevered, unable to sleep, head throbbing, Gabriella ladled water from the olla and washed. Her shame at betraying her marriage vow was almost more than she could bear. — Martín who had protected her, who had held her in his arms and told her how proud he would be to be her husband. She buried her flaming face in her hands. Wed not twelve hours and already an adultress! She wished for Padre Garcés, and on the heels of the wish thanked the Holy Mother that Padre Garcés was miles away, for surely he would most severely condemn her drunken behavior, her shame.

— Condemn her more severely than she condemned herself? No.

Suddenly she gritted her teeth in anger. What of Tómas and his shame? How spiteful of him to take advantage of her at such a time! — Tómas the acolyte, her pupil, whom she had trusted as she would trust her own brother! — More, even, than she trusted Martín! What a villain he was, to treat her so!

Rinsing her hands, she noticed the braided ring and jerked it off. Bonita's ring! What mockery! But mockery of whom? Martín? Gabriella herself? She had believed the bearer to be her husband! What was that devil Tómas doing with Bonita's ring?

She'd worry about it later, she decided. Taking care not to unsettle her throbbing head, she quickly dried her hands. The commander's first section would be leaving soon and there was work to do. Martín must never know she possessed Bonita's ring. From her leather case of valuables, she took Elias' turquoise stone and slipped the ring beside it into the same embroidered pouch.

She dressed warmly and organized her belongings into a pack for transport. As she shook out and folded the buffalo robe, remembered moments assailed her and she found her breath coming quickly. *None of that!* Her meeting with Tómas later in the morning would be as icy as she could make it, the blackguard!

And when she met Martín? Surely they were still married. Or were they? And Colonel Anza. *Santa Madre!* She remembered the commander's anger in the glare of the torches but couldn't remember a word he'd said.

But she must find medicine at the dispensary for her splitting headache, else her thoughts would continue all day buzzing in her head like angry bees.

Along the eastern horizon, a band of dull gray indicated another cloudy day ahead. This early in the morning, Martín would be with his men, but others would soon be arriving at headquarters to wink and smirk about her misdirected wedding celebration. Fervently she wished herself a desert creature, to disappear in a cactus thicket without a trace!

Chinks of lamplight showed at Rita and Miguel's shelter. From the chaplain's dark quarters, Padre Font's voice, rusty with sleep called, "Tómas! Bring a light, Tómas!"

Quietly she slipped into the headquarters tent and busied herself at the dispensary cabinet. The supply of laudanum was nearly gone. Instead, she prepared a mixture of sauz, powdered willow bark. She swallowed her draft and gasped at the bitter taste.

"Señora Neve?" Anza called. "Is that you?"

"Yes, Colonel, I needed to check my supplies," she lied glibly. "I'm going to visit the patients now."

"Where's Tómas?" he asked, materializing from around the partition as he adjusted his uniform belt. "Font woke us up calling for him. Did you see him outside?"

"No, Colonel, I didn't. Should I summon Amanda?"

"Tómas is needed, not Amanda," he said. "Last night, Font was determined to say Mass this morning before we leave. But the man's so frail he can scarcely dress himself, let alone conduct a service."

Sergeant Grijalva appeared at the entrance. "The chaplain is calling for Tómas," he said.

"I know," replied the commander. "Where could he be?"

"I'll look in on the chaplain," the sergeant volunteered. From the headquarters lantern he lit a spare, and with it ducked out the entrance.

Anza frowned. "It's not like Tómas to disappear like this. I hope he hasn't met with an accident of some kind. If he's lying unconscious somewhere in this cold — ." Suddenly resolved, he turned to Gabriella. "Summon Amanda. Stop by the Sandovals' shelter. Tell Ricardo we need him until Tómas can be found. I'll organize a search."

At the crowded Sandoval shelter, Gabriella unexpectedly found Ramona with the baby. From Ramona, Rina and Gilbert Sandoval knew already that something was amiss with the newlyweds. But Señora Márquez — now Señora Neve — seemed as self-contained as ever so their curiosity went unsatisfied. Learning that his oldest son Tómas had disappeared, Gilbert Sandoval was puzzled, but not disturbed. "He's around the camp somewhere," he said. "Tell the commander not to worry. Tómas can take care of himself."

Gabriella clamped her teeth together and said nothing. Take care of himself, indeed!

Meanwhile, in Tómas' absence, Gilbert Sandoval was willing for his son Ricardo to help out in the chaplain's tent. "But I won't know what to do!" protested Ricardo.

"I know," Ramona volunteered, her pale eyes shining with eagerness to be rid of her boring role as nursemaid. "I've helped Amanda lots of times. Tómas, too. Come on."

She thrust her baby brother into Ynez' surprised arms, threw her heavy cloak about her shoulders and marched out to join Amanda.

One by one, Gabriella saw her patients. She accepted the new-bride jokes with feeble grace, dosed fevers and dressed wounds. Most of all she helped to improvise warm clothing for the journey ahead.

Afterwards she paused briefly at the chaplain's tent for Mass. Ricardo Sandoval made a competent acolyte — better than Tómas. Tómas' head sometimes brushed the tent roof and set the altar hangings a-jiggle, amusing the worshipers and trying the chaplain's patience.

Gabriella expected a few sniffs and snubs for her excessive celebration, but the colonists were too busy with their own preparations — or felt guilty for having celebrated excessively themselves — and Padre Font was too sick.

At dawn, a suggestion of sunlight had filtered through the cobweb clouds, warming and cheering the travelers. The day before, Colonel Anza had told the sergeant, "Forage will be meager for a few days. Have each family prepare grain and gather bundles of grass to take along for their animals." Every child had shucked dried corn kernels into bags and tied vast bundles of grass together to be loaded on the pack animals. Many of the mules, when loaded, looked like immense porcupines propped on slender legs.

By mid-morning, Tómas was still missing and Colonel Anza recalled his search party. If Tómas turned up, he was to join Sergeant Grijalva's second section or Lieutenant Neve's third section, but the commander could wait no longer.

Gabriella was far more worried about Martín's absence than about Tómas'. Curious glances darted her way. Surely it was unusual for a new bride to depart alone after her wedding night.

The party mounted and Gabriella made a last-minute check of her patients with unsteady hands on her reins and a smile that was not quite convincing. Her desolation was almost unbearable. Was Martín so angry he wouldn't appear to say goodby? Wasn't she even to have a chance to implore his forgiveness?

At a signal from the commander, the bugler sounded the call to march and the train moved out amid parting cries from the colonists who were to follow later.

Martín, my dearest, where are you? Gabriella twisted and twisted the simple wedding band that two husbands had placed on her finger, and resolutely blinked back her tears.

During the next five days, Colonel Anza's party traveled north by northwest, covering nearly a hundred miles of barren terrain. They journeyed across ancient seabeds with drifts of tiny seashells underfoot. Sometimes sand dunes blocked the trail, and the commander skirted them to spare the horses. Water would be hard to find. Everyone knew it. But the first night out, the *pozos* were opened and animals watered with no trouble.

The milky sunlight that had cheered the colonists at dawn the first day quickly faded. Cold winds bit into their lungs and snatched words from their mouths. Few of the colonists had ever known any climate other than semi-tropical Sonora with its palms and cactus. But they made the best of things and bore their discomfort without grumbling. Everything wearable was worn. Many of the children, bundled up, looked like fat sausages.

Fuel was as scarce as water, and as badly needed due to the cold. When the caravan happened by a wooded arroyo, Colonel Anza chose it as the second night's campsite, though the party had traveled only fifteen miles. The ground beneath the mesquite trees was quickly picked clean of fallen branches and twigs, and all night long the air rang with the sound of axes.

Ricardo Sandoval remembered that on their farm in Sonora, poverty had forced them to use every scrap of fuel, including manure from their livestock. "I'll get some of the other boys to help me," Ricardo told his father. "Each morning we can stay behind and shovel up after the mules and cattle. It won't take long. With no rain, the manure will be dry enough to burn by the next day."

But it did rain. Then it snowed. Gilbert Sandoval organized a few fathers to improvise waterproof containers, but still, waste from the animals was of little use.

The third day's march to Santa Rosa de las Lajas — thirty miles — made up for the distance lost the second day. The sandy trail, tiring for the animals, soon changed to rubble, which was more tiring still. Along the way, pauses were frequent. Exhausted beasts were retired to the rear and replaced with fresh mounts. First one mule and then a second dropped, could not be coaxed up again and had to be abandoned. Many colonists now went on foot, jealously hoarding what little strength their animals had remaining.

Gabriella was so distraught over Martín that her throat threatened to close with fear whenever she thought of him. To maintain her composure, she stayed busy. As they traveled, she fondled and played with the baby, crooning and talking softly to him. During the encampments in the late afternoons, she showed the mothers how to muffle the children's faces, ears and hands against frostbite and to recognize the slick white marble appearance of freezing flesh. She bullied older brothers and sisters to hold in their mouths, and thus thaw, their younger siblings' frostbitten fingers to prevent gangrene from developing. With Ramona to help her, she improvised ways of draping blankets across the mothers' laps as they rode, mingling and conserving body heat of both horse and rider.

When some of the exhausted travelers grew careless, Gabriella could be impatient and quarrelsome. Ramona grumbled at her ill temper, but was silenced by Rina Sandoval: "Have pity on the poor Señora! You'd be cross too if your husband deserted you three hours after the wedding!" Colonel Anza heard the complaints but ignored them. His *enferme*ra was saving lives, and a discourtesy or two was a small price to pay.

Night was falling when the travelers made camp at Santa Rosa. Low, barren hills surrounded what had once been an Indian settlement but was now deserted. Anza had sent a detail of soldiers ahead to commence work clearing the *pozos,* but water was slow seeping into them. That night the commander threw off his coat and worked beside his men, deepening the wells to as much as six feet. All night long the digging continued. As water appeared, baskets waterproofed with pitch were lowered for the thirsty animals.

The threat of yet more rain led Colonel Anza to cut short the march on the fourth day. He dared not risk exposing his people to the cruel elements. Food was skimpy. Clothing was threadbare, shoes and boots were worn through, patched with leather from the soldiers' coats or with wood chips if the travelers were not so lucky as to possess one of the fabulous coats. Muffs of rags and cast-off clothing were improvised for even the youngest children to keep their hands warm. The commander upbraided men who shaved; they needed beards on their faces for warmth.

Again, the travelers made camp at a thinly-wooded *barranca* with sparse grazing for the animals. The men began immediately shoveling wells in the dry streambed below, and by two in the morning, they were running full and clear. At sunrise, a strong frigid wind arose and the women and children hovered in their shelters. But the men, knowing water might not be so plentiful farther on, continued watering the animals until all were satisfied.

The *tordeada's* final day took the first-section travelers across a treacherous mile honeycombed by underground burrows and nests apparently inhabited by huge rats. At the commander's order, the horses proceeded slowly to avoid injury. That afternoon, he halted the party near San Sebastian, site of a brakish spring. Moisture oozing from the ground was warm, forming a steaming marsh with no outlet. The surrounding earth was white with salt but good water was available nearby.

Again, the colonel and his men worked throughout most of the night, shoveling the *pozos* ever deeper and hauling up salt-free water for the animals.

For patience, competence and energy, Ricardo was no match for the rangy Tómas, but together with Ramona, he nevertheless gave Padre Font what passed for a replacement. Ricardo even developed pride in his work. A request in Padre Font's name, anywhere in the small camp, was an order no one refused and Ricardo lorded it a bit over the few other boys his age.

After the first night's encampment, Colonel Anza saw for himself how ill his chaplain actually was and moved him to more comfortable accommodations in the headquarters tent. "The old buzzard still won't take medicine or eat solid food," Ramona reported to Gabriella. "For cussedness, he's in a class with Pa. He wants his own fire in his own tent but there's not enough fuel. It's so cold his slops freeze in that fancy close-stool he makes us set up for him every night. He wants to say Mass but can't. He'd fall on his face if he tried."

"He's even too weak to pick fights with Colonel Anza," remarked Ricardo. "Every night, we wrap him in blankets and settle him on a cot before the fire. I sleep there too, in case he wakes in the night, but he never does."

Ramona often erected Gabriella's shelter, then shared the warmth of the buffalo robe with Gabriella and Ynez Sandoval. Even without Tómas and Ricardo, the Sandoval shelter was crowded and Ynez had become a permanent resident. Ramona welcomed Ynez; the younger girl gladly helped with José and besides, Gabriella was more cheerful when Ynez was with them. By hovering together, the three were probably the warmest of all the colonists. —Except possibly the baby, who had his own basket and coverlet lined with rabbit fur.

At dawn of the fifth day of the *tordeada*, the leather-jackets were still clearing the San Sebastian *pozos* and watering the animals when Ynez, with the baby, returned to Gabriella's shelter after his feeding. "Colonel Anza says we'll camp here for a few days and wait for the other sections," she told Gabriella as she replaced José in his basket. "The colonel's worried because the weather is so bad." She curled up beside Gabriella to be hugged.

Ramona had taken over many duties as servant to the ailing chaplain and to Ynez, ten years old, had fallen the total responsibility for the baby. She had not slept well the night before and her thin shoulders sagged with fatigue. She was slightly built; yet caring for the baby, she often worked as hard as Ramona who was older and much stronger.

Tears of gratitude and compassion stung Gabriella's eyes and she folded the child close. "Traveling like this is so hard on you children," she whispered against Ynez's soft cheek. "All of us need rest, but you children most of all. What would Padre Font do without Ricardo to help out? And what would the invalid families do without the other boys to help them with fuel to keep warm? You've all been so brave and strong!"

Ashamed for Ramona to see her tears, Ynez cried softly as Gabriella gently rocked and soothed her.

Later they left the shelter together. Steam rose from the alkali bog several hundred yards away. Above them, the iron-gray clouds rode higher in the sky, giving a clear view of the barren valley and above it the mountains, range upon range, into the far distance. Every mountain peak, every pinnacle, crag and valley was completely covered with snow. Like Gabriella and Ynez, others in their threadbare rags stood about the small camp, mutely staring, their eyes dull, their features pinched and ashen. They were natives of a land of date palms and orchids growing wild in the treetops, and had never seen snow.

Ynez said, "Yesterday I asked Colonel Anza what California would be like." She paused. "He said we've already come to California. This is California." The desolation in the child's voice wrung Gabriella's heart. She held Ynez close and blinked back the unshed tears behind her eyes.

All day, the travelers expected Sergeant Grijalva's section to arrive. But the day passed with snow, then rain, then more snow. To conserve scarce fuel, Gabriella's little household merged its shelter with that of Rita and Miguel.

The sun set behind clouds which later cleared; the white, frozen earth reflected the starlight, making lanterns outdoors unnecessary. The commander had counted sixteen mounts and cargo animals lost on the way from the Yuma villages. That night two more mules froze to death.

The second day at San Sebastian dawned colder than ever. At noon, Ricardo and his friends were gathering frozen manure chips at the livestock corrals and trying to dry them over a slow fire. Suddenly they abandoned their work and raced toward the silent camp shouting, "They're coming! Sergeant Grijalva's section! They're coming!"

The shelters boiled over with excitement, with running soldiers throwing on their jackets, with campers hastily wrapping themselves in blankets. "Bring fresh mounts!" Colonel Anza shouted to his soldiers, "Get horses saddled and down the trail. You, Ricardo, get more boys and build up the fires in all the shelters. Hurry!"

Turning, he pointed and shouted again, "You, Gilbert Sandoval! Organize the men to help unload the pack animals and erect the shelters for people coming in this new section. Where's Gabriella?"

"Here, Colonel!"

"Tell Miguel to fill two big ollas with water. Put them to warm beside the headquarters fire. For frostbitten hands, toes, elbows. Unpack the fleece we've kept with the medical supplies. We'll need it for warm water poultices on cheeks and noses."

The headquarters tent began filling up with the newcomers. Rita and Miguel served warm broth and chocolate while Gabriella and Colonel Anza examined for frostbite and other injuries.

"What about the lieutenant's section?" the commander asked Sergeant

Grijalva. "When the weather delayed you in the rat fields, he should have caught up with you."

"We expected him, Colonel. But the snow was so thick we could barely see those in our own section. Martín's party may have been close behind, but we didn't see him!"

"Was there enough water?" asked Anza.

"Plenty!" exclaimed the sergeant gratefully. "Maybe Martín's been held up by the snow, but he won't have a problem with water."

Rosa Grijalva fell joyfully into the welcoming arms, first of Rita and then of Gabriella. To Gabriella she murmured, "Bad news. I reminded Juan what you said about the brandy but he passed it around anyway. We have two cases of frostbite that went bad. The soldier tossed and groaned all night long. His foot's turned black."

Colonel Anza didn't need to be told. His sensitive nose had already picked up the distinctive odor of decaying flesh. With Gabriella at his elbow, he examined the now-useless left thumb and forefinger of a grizzled farmer, father of seven children, and the rotting flesh on a young leatherjacket's toes.

The colonel was severe. "Soldier, this farmer never experienced cold like this before, but in the military, you've been taught the dangers of frostbite. You've injured yourself through carelessness. Any pain you feel is your own fault."

He turned away and said to Gabriella, "We'll amputate now, otherwise the gangrene will spread and kill them both. Have you a surgeon's saw?"

Gabriella blanched. "No, Colonel. I've never done surgery."

"Then we'll improvise. For closing the wound, we have gut in the dispensary cabinet. I've seen it. Scalpel? Needles?"

"Yes. We have both."

"Tell Miguel to sharpen that saw we use for butchering the cattle. The small one. We'll work in Miguel's shelter. There's a solid table and a good fire."

The surgery candidates were offered more brandy for anesthesia and within half an hour, the operating room was ready. Miguel volunteered to attend but the stench drove him from the shelter, heaving. The lucky farmer, unaccustomed to liquor and its effects, was unconscious when Colonel Anza cut away half his hand and the expedition nurse stitched the wound closed, cleaned the blood away and applied a bandage. The man was still sleeping soundly when Miguel and Ramona returned him, on a litter, to the headquarters tent where he slowly awoke to the anxious weeping of his wife and children.

The young soldier was drunk but conscious. "This will hurt," the colonel said coldly. "It will help to have something to clamp your teeth against." He placed a short length of folded harness between the soldier's unwilling jaws. Four leatherjackets were placed at the corners of the table to hold him while the blackened flesh was cut away.

Colonel Anza arranged a tourniquet around the patient's ankle and tightened it slightly. He said to Gabriella, pointing, "In making the cut, it's important to avoid the main blood vessels, here and here. But there will be blood anyway. Keep it wiped away so I can see what I'm doing."

At the first bite of the saw, the soldier jerked uncontrollably. Gabriella dutifully sponged the blood away but her hands shook and the room began to spin. Anza sensed her distress. "Breathe deeply through your mouth," he ordered.

Halfway through the amputation, the groaning, thrashing soldier vomited violently. The leather bit flew from his mouth, and with a swift intake of breath, he appeared to be choking. The colonel laid the saw aside and tightened the tourniquet. "Turn him over and drop his head off the edge of the table," he ordered the soldiers. Several hard slaps upon the patient's back cleared his air passages. He began to howl and writhe more violently than before.

Gabriella held the patient's foot rigid but even with the tightened tourniquet, blood spurted alarmingly. The patient's lunging had caused the very thing the colonel wanted to avoid.

"Grijalva!" thundered the colonel, scarcely heard over the agonized screams of the soldier.

The sergeant's white face appeared at the entrance. "Yes, Colonel?"

"We'll have to cauterize. Get a broad knife from Miguel. Be sure it's clean. Put it in the coals until it's white hot. Hurry! Gabriella, bring laudanum."

She fetched the bottle from the headquarters dispensary and administered a stiff dose, but the soldier's crazed writhing continued for several minutes before the drug took effect. By the time Grijalva brought the glowing knife, the colonel had completed his work with the saw.

Anza protected his hand with a thickness of leather before taking the knife handle. He nodded at the patient and warned, "He'll jerk." At his signal, Gabriella gave up her place beside the table and two of the men held the patient's leg. "Ready?"

The commander, careful to cauterize an area no larger than necessary, applied the flat of the glowing blade with a rocking motion. The sound and smell of searing flesh filled the room. The soldier threw himself wildly about, filling the air with curses. Colonel Anza withdrew the smoking knife.

The raw flesh had turned white, and the pumping flow of blood had miraculously stopped. Gabriella's stomach surged into her throat but she clenched her teeth, compelling herself to watch. In the California settlements, after Anza returned to Mexico, the time might come when she would need to perform an amputation to save a life. And next time, unless the mission fathers or one of the packet boats could resupply her dispensary, there would be no laudanum to dull the pain. The dose she had just administered was the last.

The room was cold but Colonel Anza's face glistened with perspiration. He stood back, concentrating on the wound. Blood began to ooze. He signaled the soldiers to once more hold the patient's limb rigid, and again he applied the searingly hot knife. This time the cautery held.

Anza put the blade aside and carefully examined the wound. "Now watch," he ordered Gabriella. He loosened the tourniquet and after a few seconds, re-tightened it. "Leave the tourniquet too tight for too long and gangrene will take the whole foot," he explained. "Loosen it too soon and the heavy blood flow will break through the cauterization. For the next 24 hours, have someone to do every few minutes what you just watched me do. Line up several of the older children. Your Ramona has the makings of a good drill sergeant. Put her in charge. Now bandage him."

As he left the shelter, wiping his hands, the colonel stared coldly at Grijalva. "Liquor's no good for frostbite," he said. "Next time give your people chocolate or tea."

Gabriella's anxiety mounted as the evening and the next morning passed with no sign of Martín's section. For different reasons, Anza was anxious too. Tentative early-morning snowflakes turned to sleet and the wind rose. Finally Anza would wait no longer. At noon he sent two leatherjackets with twenty fresh mounts back along the trail. They had not far to go. By midafternoon, the encampment heard the whoops of the colonists approaching through the storm.

Amanda Jiménez, sobbing with relief, ran to greet the travelers. She had feared her family was lost. Lagging behind Amanda was Ramona whose father was also in the third section. Far down the approaching line of march, she located him and nudged Gabriella. "Look there at Pa."

Vasco Bellis, amply hooded and scarfed in primitively-sewn furs, rode comfortably on the broad back of a cargo mule. Leading the animal on foot was a Yuma woman of mature years, apparently comfortable in a deerskin shift and a thin cotton blanket thrown over her head to ward off the sleet.

Amanda embraced her mother, weeping. Noticing Gabriella among the welcomers, Señora Jiménez shrieked, "He saved us, Señora! Your husband, he saved us all! We would not be here if it were not for Lieutenant Neve!"

"Where is he?" Gabriella called after Señora Jiménez, but her question was lost in the tumult. Her concern mounted as the travelers and their exhausted animals straggled into camp. Families were helped to warmth and food. The pack animals were relieved of their burdens and led to forage and water.

At last all were accounted for but Martín. Gabriella was frantic with worry when she saw approaching, far down the trail, a little knot of men, three riders and one soldier on foot. Ignoring the storm, Gabriella started to run. As she drew closer, she saw that the leatherjackets had wrapped the lieutenant in blankets and lashed him to a fresh mount. One of the soldiers walked alongside to support him in the saddle.

Colonel Anza, as apprehensive as Gabriella, also saw the stragglers approaching. He caught up the reins of the nearest saddle horse and raced to meet them. As they drew nearer, Gabriella could see for herself that Martín was drowsy and limp with exhaustion.

"This man's clothes are soaking wet!" Anza was shouting, angry eyebrows bristling. "What's he doing riding in this weather in wet clothes?"

"A colonist said he fell into one of the *pozos*, Colonel," answered a cavalrymen.

Anza's jaw clenched. "Time enough later for explanations. In the meantime, he's dying." He turned in the saddle. "Señora!" he bellowed.

"Yes, Colonel?"

"Is that buffalo robe of yours in Miguel's shelter?"

"Yes, Colonel."

"Good. Run ahead and build up the fire. Tell Rita to bring hot broth."

At the entrance of Miguel's shelter, Martín had to be lifted inside. His complexion was the color of porridge. His sightless eyes stared out of darkened sockets. Anza flipped open the soft fur robe beside the hooded fire. "Strip off all his clothes and wrap him in this," he told the cavelrymen.

Rita brought a large mug of steaming broth. "Leave it," Anza ordered.

Martín lay heaped under the fur like a lifeless collection of bones. The colonel waved the men out. He ordered Gabriella, "Take off your clothes. All of them."

Gabriella stared.

"Don't just stand there, woman! You heard me! Strip! Then lie down naked beside your husband under the robe. Get him warm. Get some of that soup down him if you can."

"But —"

Anza was losing patience. "You're married to him, aren't you?"

"Yes, Colonel."

"Then unless you have some particular affinity with the widowed estate, I'd advise you to use every feminine wile possible to get the blood flowing in this man's veins. It's up to you. Do you want him alive or do you want him dead?"

He turned abruptly and disappeared through the entrance.

Gabriella whipped off her garments as though they were on fire. Within seconds, she had moved the mug of steaming broth within reach and crawled into the pallet alongside her husband. It was like stretching out full length, naked, beside a frozen corpse.

CHAPTER 28   To Mission San Gabriel
                                        December 1775-January 1776

The third section refugees crowded into the headquarters tent like wet rabbits into a warm burrow. The kitchen crew served hot food and drink while Colonel Anza examined for injuries and frostbite. As the shock of cold and hardship eased, the colonists began to talk of their adventures. — Of clearing acres of snow from the ground so the starving animals could get at the meager forage beneath; of the injuries of cold-numbed children tumbling from the backs of exhausted, stumbling mounts; of hacking meat from frozen mule carcasses along the way when food ran short. *"Santa Madre!"* breathed Miguel, "such tales to tell their grandchildren!"

Meanwhile, the section's most severely stricken victim, Lieutenant Neve, lay against one wall of Miguel's kitchen shelter, too weak to talk and too sick to eat. Particles of ice clung to his hair; his skin had the clammy feel of raw fish.

Lying naked beside the victim under the buffalo robe, Gabriella shivered as much with apprehension as with cold. She went through the motions of chaffing her husband's face, his arms, his hands, though she was scarcely conscious of what she was doing. The commander's words nearly paralyzed her with fear.

Twice a widow and not yet seventeen? She had loved Elias with all her heart; the shock of his death had been even more traumatic than her treatment at the hands of Federico Verro. — And now though she loved Martín less, she needed his strength, his pride, far more than she had ever needed Elias. From the bottom of her soul, she prayed, *Santissima Madre, please don't let me lose Martín too!*

The prayer steadied her and she began to massage her patient with method. Grimly, she scrubbed and kneaded at the cold flesh to stimulate blood circulation. She reflected that Elias, of *paisano* stock, would have been more respectful of nature's unforgiving ways; had Elias commanded the section, he would never have jeopardized himself so carelessly. But then Martín was a courtier, more proficient at intrigue than at battling the elements.

The kitchen people came and went — Miguel, Rita, Amanda, Ricardo and Ramona — stepping over and dodging around the victim and his wife. As the day waned, so did the moaning wind; in its place came the whisper of sleet. Gabriella left off massaging and fit herself closer to Martín's curves; to her alarm, his body felt colder than before. She laid her fingertips along the blood vessel in his throat and felt scarcely any pulse at all.

"Help me, Rita!" she cried. "Martín's dying! Send one of the children for rocks. Heat them in the coals to put around his feet!" Again she massaged his back and arms, briskly rubbing upward to encourage the flow of blood to his heart.

Within seconds, Rita had put fist-sized stones to heat and brought random scraps of rawhide from which she cut off strips to fashion into pockets. She wrinkled her nose in displeasure. "This was left over from one of the shelters on the trail last night. The soldiers skinned the animals that died along the way, skinned them quickly before they froze. Used the hides against the wind and rain. A smelly business but better than freezing."

"Sounds like something Elias might think of."

"'Think of' maybe, but not mention till later," muttered Rita, busy with her knife. "Elias was never one to bring work on himself." She noticed Gabriella's indignant frown and apologized. "Shouldn't have said that, I guess. Your Elias was a good man. Never had an enemy." She jerked her head toward Martín. "But you got the better one here. There's no quit to this one. You'll see."

Gabriella dismissed her words. Rita was quick to find fault with the low-born and to praise aristocrats. Mostly she was wrong about Elias, though indeed he had always been better at beginnings than he was at seeing projects through to the end. She'd noticed that about him.

With Rita, she arranged the leather-covered stones around the lieutenant's feet and legs. He roused but his eyes refused to focus. Gabriella offered the warm broth, which he sipped, then gulped thirstily. She set aside the empty mug and gathered him close in her arms, his head on her shoulder. "Martín?"

But he feebly pushed her away. His dull gaze surveyed the enclosure, pausing on Rita as though trying to recall who she was. His sodden trousers, boots and heavy leather jacket had been hung nearby to dry. As soon as he located them, he grunted, shifted to a more comfortable position and was soon asleep and faintly snoring.

Gabriella shrugged off her hurt feelings with sarcasm. "It's probably normal for a man in bed with his wife for the first time to fall asleep and snore."

"I'd say so," replied Rita absently, "especially if he's half-frozen. To him, you're just another warm rock." After a pause, she continued. "One of the third section youngsters wandered off in the snowstorm and fell in a *pozo*. No one told you that, did they? Lieutenant jumped in and pulled him out!"

"What?!" Martín endangering himself to save a child was a thought that took getting used to. "Is that how his clothes got wet? I thought it was the snow."

"His pack horse with his dry clothes was a half-day behind with the other livestock. Rather than hold up the section, he threw a blanket over his shoulders and rode on as he was."

"What a stupid thing to do!" muttered Gabriella. "He could have borrowed dry clothes from someone."

"Not likely. Everyone was damp from the snow. And anyway, wet or dry, everyone was wearing all their clothes on account of the cold. Layers and layers! Remember the Yumas saying this was their coldest winter ever? We were lucky, my girl. The first section, coming through, we had snow and a bit of sleet. Lieutenant's section had blizzards. One yesterday and another this morning! They lost twenty-one head of livestock."

Gabriella's massaging hands slowed at their work. Twenty-one more dead animals meant nearly a fourth of the expedition's original livestock was gone. The third section was lucky to have gotten through at all, and Mission San Gabriel on the coast was more than two weeks away. Two more weeks? Wasted and weary as they all were, could the expedition survive two more weeks? Fear left her mouth dry as sand.

Rita put more stones to heat in the fire, then gazed with a speculative eye at Martín's sleeping form. Stealthily, she stood and fingered the lieutenant's sodden coat, especially noting the lining and the seams.

"What are you doing?" Gabriella asked.

"When he roused up, he looked for his clothes first thing," Rita whispered. "I wonder why."

Taking care to make no sound, she lifted down the trousers from their peg and ran probing fingers around the waistband.

Gabriella was bewildered to see a series of lumps ranging from the size of a pea to that of a cat's eye.

Rita smiled slyly and replaced the trousers. "Diamonds?" she muttered. "Rubies to trade with the Filipinos? That's why he rode in his wet uniform. He must have figured it was worth the risk." She waved away Gabriella's question. "Lieutenant's no different from the rest of us. Half the colonists have treasure put away somewhere. Sewed in their clothes. In their saddles. Sealed inside the Madonnas in their shrines." She lifted her petticoats. Suspended on a stout cord from her waist was a small bag holding what appeared to be coins. "Our life savings in gold," Rita whispered. "Miguel's and mine."

Gabriella snapped, "But if it was your life you were risking, you'd be thinking of Miguel's welfare, not that bag of gold coins!"

"Yes, I would," Rita admitted fondly. "But Miguel? He'd be thinking of the gold. That's the way men are, whether we like it or not."

Gabriella didn't like it. —Which was silly, she admitted, since there was nothing she could do about it. She scowled at her slumbering husband, doubled up her fist, gave him a stout punch on the shoulder and shouted into his unhearing ear, "I am not just another warm rock, Lieutenant! I am your wife!"

Rita whooped with derisive laughter. "You want tender thoughts from him, but what about you? You married him for the same reason a *paisana* builds a coop for her hens. But you like him better than you admit."

"I like him," Gabriella agreed, glad that Rita never knew how her heart knocked against her ribs that night at the National Palace. "Not the same as Elias, maybe, but well enough."

Rita heard the stubborn pride and marveled at the way of the world. With Gabriella's fresh good looks, her energy, her quick mind and convent upbringing, she had only to choose the lucky candidate and crook her finger. But Rita remembered her own bitter years as her father's aging dough-faced daughter. Among the farming community where Rita grew up, a young woman who couldn't attract a husband was as bad as a feebleminded child, both a tragedy and a joke. In those days, Rita would have married anyone, even a villain like Vasco Bellis. It was her good fortune that Miguel was there, and willing.

And now, in this remote place, it was Gabriella's good fortune that Martín was there, and willing. If the lieutenant betrayed more concern over his hidden wealth than about his bride, well, that was a reality Gabriella could learn to live with, especially since the gems would someday sparkle on her own fingers, or pay to build the hacienda she would rule as mistress.

It was full dark outside and a fiesta of sorts was taking place next door at the headquarters tent. Rita brought warm food for Gabriella and for the lieutenant, should he wake. She changed the rocks at Martín's feet, then slipped out the entrance and Gabriella was left alone with her husband.

Husband? In her turn, Gabriella, like Rita, marveled at the way of the world. "Be careful of your wishes," she had heard as a child at the convent, "for they might come true." She had wished for Martín — a haughty, domineering popinjay — and gotten him. — Gotten him because she needed "a coop for her chickens," a protector, a father for her children, a male relative without which a woman lacked authority of any kind, no matter how beautiful or how clever she might be. There had been a time when she had loved Martín, had suffered a desperate sickness of heart because he was pledged to another. Could she love him again? His frigid body roused no responding warmth in hers, her breasts against his bare back could as well have been flattened against a stone wall.

Martín shifted his position under the fur coverlet and Gabriella moved with him, pressing herself against his curves, massaging his shoulders and chest, stroking the smooth skin of his naked thighs and buttocks with her legs. At last she became aware that he was recovering. His skin was warmer, more plastic; the muscles moved smoothly.

Not long afterwards, he moved again, and she found his hand on her waist.

Feebly, his arms sought her and his lips found hers. A wave of joyful relief swept over Gabriella at the loving touch of his soft mouth. He accepted her, forgave her!

Sick as he was, he had quickened with desire, and to her surprise she felt in her loins an answering hunger.

It was quickly over. The lieutenant fell back, exhausted, but fulfilled. His even breathing told her he had drifted off to sleep. "Oh, Martín," she whispered in his unhearing ear, "My beloved, I was so wrong. I always loved you and I always will!"

His features were barely discernible in the dim lamplight but she stared at him, half in wonder and half in shame. Comparing, as lovers, the men she had known seemed wicked and her face grew hot. Yet there it was! During the brief weeks of her married life with Elias, he had always been tender, gentle, thoughtful of her. Very different had been Tómas, the treacherous rascal, scratching and bruising her, setting her afire with his passion.

But Martín, ah, Martín! Weakened though he was, he seemed instinctively to know every fold of her body, every nerve. When he was well again, the nights would never be long enough to satisfy their joy in one another. She collapsed against his shoulder, hot tears of happiness splashing against his bare skin, thanking from the depths of her heart the Holy Virgin and all the saints for the blessing of such a husband.

A rustling noise interrupted her reverie. Amanda had slipped through the shelter's entrance to make Padre Font's bedtime toast and tea. Behind her came Ramona with José, freshly fed and changed. Gabriella wondered if they had listened outside the door and waited to enter until all was still. If so, she silently blessed them for their tact.

She welcomed the baby, and snuggled him under the robe — another "warm rock" to keep Martín warm.

Colonel Anza returned to check on his officer. He held the lantern close. "His color's better," he said, then felt his forehead and shoulders. "Body temperature is still too low but he's out of danger. We'll remain here in camp tomorrow. He'll be well enough to ride the day after." He stood. "You'll have an invalid on your hands for a week or two, Señora. Stay with him as much as possible. Rosa is caring for the other patients."

He turned to go. "Actually," he added, "the invalids we brought from San Sebastian have nearly all recovered. There is very little for Rosa to do." There was surprise in his voice, as if he could not quite believe that something good could happen after so much had gone wrong.

Gabriella heard his words from a rosy aura of happiness. Nothing seemed quite real to her, nothing but her husband asleep by her side and the baby in her arms. She moved little José to the warmth of his fur-lined basket and returned to her husband. The lieutenant roused, yawned and stretched. Gabriella checked his pulse and found it normal but his sunken eyes and trembling hands betrayed his infirmity. *It was too much for him, what we did,* she reproached herself. *We should have waited.*

Soon after the commander left, the noise level rose even higher in the headquarters tent next door. Someone fingered quick chords on a guitar and a fiddler sawed out a lively dance tune.

The lieutenant accepted a few spoonfuls from the bowl of stew Rita had left warming by the fire and lay back, marshalling his meager strength. His hand came to rest against his five-day growth of beard and he fingered it.

"If you like, I'll shave you tomorrow," Gabriella said softly. Then she smiled. "But you'd look very distinguished with a beard."

He gazed at her in the soft light. The indolent look that she knew so well returned to his eyes. "Señora Neve?"

"Yes, Lieutenant?"

"Is that a party I hear next door?"

"Yes. They must be celebrating because the expedition is reunited." She smiled and snuggled within the curve of his shoulder. "And please don't ask me if I'd like to go join the party. If it's all the same with you, I'd rather stay where I am. The last time there was a party, I woke up next morning without a husband."

After a pause, he whispered softly, "It's our first night together."

She drew closer beside him, her cheek against his. "I'm afraid I tired you out."

"You did," he confirmed weakly. "You tired me out completely. I haven't enjoyed anything so much in years."

She caught up his hand, kissed it and uncurled his fingers along her cheek. But he had already dropped off to sleep.

The native boy tending the mission's cows stared at the two soldiers approaching on horseback through the wooded hills. Leaving the herd to take care of itself, he raced in terror toward the stockaded mission below. "Soldiers!" he screamed. "Run! Hide! The soldiers are coming!"

Indian workers in the fields beside the road straightened. Seeing the cavalrymen for themselves, they dropped their tools and fled.

The frightened boy entered the stockade gate where he nearly collided with a colossus in Franciscan habit and sandals. "Fray Zalvidea! Look! On the trail coming down from the hills! See them? The soldiers are coming. I ran fast to warn everyone!"

The young friar shaded his eyes against the noon sunlight and smiled. "Soldiers indeed, Pico. But we haven't much to fear, I think. What I see are two weary fellows dressed in rags riding on two starving nags. With a pair of mallets, we could play tunes on those skinny ribs. I'll go meet them while you notify Father Paterna. Oh, and Pico! Tell Fray Gómez the soldiers have come. He's at the winery."

Father Paterna was an elderly, ruggedly-built man with open, benevolent features. His cropped gray hair riffled in the warm midday breeze as he welcomed the cavalrymen. "You're Anza's men, aren't you?" he called. "We've been expecting you for a month! What kept you so long?"

The soldiers Luis and Ramón dismounted and knelt for Father's blessing while Fray Zalvidea led away their exhausted mounts to grain and fresh hay in the mission stable.

"We've been held up by a little of everything, Father," said Luis, the older of the two soldiers. "Christmas Eve a baby was born, so there was no travel on Christmas Day. Then coming through the mountains, we had to stop when an earthquake frightened the livestock."

"An earthquake!" laughed Father Paterna. "Well, here that's nothing. We have earthquakes all the time. The horses race about the pasture a bit but no harm's done. What message do you have from Colonel Anza?"

"First he asks for fresh mounts, if you have them to spare. Many of our colonists are afoot, to save the few horses we have left."

"Yes, we can provide horses. Not as many as he needs, I'm sure. But we can send fifteen. Perhaps as many as twenty. Would that help?"

"Yes, Father, it would," said Luis.

"What else?"

"He says you can expect the expedition within three days. We left the colonists camped beside the Santa Ana River."

"Then we'll have time to prepare!" cried Father Paterna. "But come. I see you're exhausted. We can talk after you have refreshed yourselves a bit."

Riding down from the hills, Luis and Ramón had been impressed by the mission's far-flung meadows, vineyards and irrigated winter crops. They wondered who tended them, as there were no workers in sight. Inside the mission compound, they found a primitive chapel, workshops and living quarters for some fifty people, all with walls and beams of willow roofed with thatch.

"You have room here for many people," Luis remarked, his voice echoing in the big refectory. "Where are they?"

"There are four of us," said Father Paterna. "Fray Sanchez, Fray Cruzado and Fray Zalvidea. Right now, we have a fifth brother, an assistant who has only been here a few weeks, Fray Gómez."

"And you five men tend those fields out there? And herd the livestock?"

"No. Our workers saw the soldiers coming and ran away." Father Paterna's amiable features grew solemn. "When the first garrison was stationed here a few years ago, one of the soldiers molested the wife of the chief. The Indians retaliated angrily and the chief was killed. The military commander, not knowing the cause of their attack, cut off the chief's head and mounted it on a pole as a warning to the others. For years, the natives wouldn't come near the mission." He sighed. "Gradually we have won their trust, but as you see, they are still terrified of the military."

"Colonel Anza will be surprised to hear this," said Ramón.

"He already knows about it," Father Paterna said. "The Colonel was here last year, remember. He will explain to your men and warn them."

A few of the wary servants were lured back to prepare a hot meal for Father Paterna and his guests. Fray Sanchez and Fray Cruzado joined them. Soon a redheaded monk ran up the steps two at a time, habit flying, and entered the refectory. He was a man of middle age and medium height; impetuous, loose-jointed, with big feet and the deeply weathered skin of an outdoorsman. He brought with him two bottles of honey-colored wine.

"Welcome! Welcome!" cried the stranger, gripping the soldiers' hands till they cracked. "I brought along a sample of our best vintage from the mission at Sinaloa! In a few years, we will have wine of this quality from our vineyards here. We must drink a toast to the Anza expedition!"

Father Paterna explained, "Fray Gómez is our vintner. He has been looking forward to the coming of the expedition for a particular reason."

The Franciscan calmed himself with an effort. "Is — Is there an *enfermera* with you?" he asked. "A young woman with auburn hair? Like mine, you see."

Ramón smiled. "You mean Gabriella? Yes, of course. She married one of our officers. She's now Señora Gabriella de Neve."

"She delivered the baby Christmas Eve!" added Luis. "A fine baby boy."

"Gabriella is a close relative of Fray Gómez," explained Father Paterna.

Gómez cried, "She's all right, then? She's in good health? She's safe?"

"Yes," replied Ramón.

"Let me go back with the soldiers, Father," pleaded Gómez. "We should send supplies. I can help —"

Father Paterna gently shook his head. "They need horses. We're sending as many as we can spare. If you go along, you would take a mount badly needed by some mother with a child or two."

"I don't need to ride, Father!" urged Gómez. "I can walk. I'm strong for a man my age. Please let me — "

Father Paterna was patient but firm. "It's best that you wait here for the expedition, Gómez."

The friar bowed his head. "Forgive me, Father. It's just that I've waited so long to see her." His voice wavered under the strain of emotion, and Ramón wondered if the vintner had been sampling his own wine.

Several days' travel behind the cavalrymen, the expedition had reached the mountains at last. After weeks of cold weather, the long column had climbed through barren foothills and negotiated a pass through the mountains. Within a day's march, the land through which they traveled was transformed from wasteland to sweet green hills of live oaks and sycamores warmed by the wind from the sea. Sparkling brooks offered water for bathing and laundry. Fish darted in the deep pools, and along the banks grew mint, watercress, dandelions and mushrooms. Wild grapevines twined in the thickets; yellow blossoms of wild mustard, deep blue brodiaea, and pink and purple lupine carpeted the hills.

Padre Font was reminded of his homeland in Spain, and collected ingredients for Amanda to prepare salads and cooling drinks. His disposition improved. He no longer brooded testily that during the entire expedition, no one had come to him for confession. Lured by the old man's unexpected smiles, a few began, warily, to seek him out.

The native Indians, so different from the Pimas, were ever present but shy as chipmunks. The expedition children had been the first to see them, even before the *tordeada* — mere dots high among the faraway crags. They looked like mountain sheep or antelope, leaping by twos or threes among the rocks. Were they following the expedition? It appeared so.

The one who had seen these new natives more closely than anyone else was Gabriella. Most of Christmas Eve, she had sat up with the young mother in labor. The baby arrived at daybreak, and the mother was safely asleep. Gabriella drew her heavy cloak about her shoulders and left the shelter for a breath of fresh air. Along the eastern horizon glowed a band of intense orange beneath a heavy mantle of dark cloud.

She thought of Martín, now well recovered and alone in his tent at the corrals a half-mile away. Since the *tordeada,* they had enjoyed a honeymoon of sorts, poorly appointed but lacking nothing in bliss. It was their first night apart and she missed him. She had loved Elias, had cherished their intimate secrets and private jokes. That would never change. But this new and unexpected fervor where Martín was concerned was a heady aberration that encompassed her every thought. They were as one, she and Martín, reading one another's thoughts and feelings as though they shared the same blood, bones and nerves. That, too, would never change.

In the early dawn, she strolled farther than she intended. At the outskirts of the camp, she happened on a half-dozen semi-human creatures silently rifling a pile of cargo left untended beside one of the shelters. Upon Gabriella's approach, the thieves clutched their loot and leaped to the safety of some nearby boulders. They turned and barked defiantly, like dogs, then one by one, silently scaled the rocks.

Gabriella watched them, dark silhouettes barely visible as they scampered up the uneven cliff face. And then her eye caught and held. High above, standing alone on a projecting ledge, was a tall, hooded figure that she at first mistook for part of the rock formation.

It was Tómas!

He was at least a hundred yards away and the dawn light was uncertain, but there was no mistaking his presence. They stared at one another across a distance that seemed to grow as the moments passed. Neither spoke. Neither moved. At last he merged into the boulders behind him and disappeared.

From Martín, she had learned that Gilbert Sandoval, not Tómas, had bought Bonita's wedding ring. It was to be a wedding gift for Tómas and Amanda. Gilbert and Rina had never stopped believing their son would rejoin the expedition. Neither had Amanda. Perhaps there had been secret messages. Whatever the outcome of Tómas' disappearance, Gabriella fervently hoped their future paths would never cross.

Tears and shouts of joy welcomed the cavalrymen who brought the extra horses from the mission. Days before, Gabriella and Ramona had given up their mules for the children, but even with the fresh stock, the expedition was short of needed mounts. The pack animals were so weakened they could carry only partial loads. Some of the men shouldered heavy packs themselves rather than abandon their household goods beside the trail.

News of Friar Gómez was relayed to Gabriella through Martín. "Does the name sound familiar?" he asked.

Mystified, she shook her head. "Maybe someone who visited the convent years ago," she suggested.

"Would your abbess have sent him with a message?" asked Martín. "Perhaps she's dying."

Gabriella's face clouded. "I'd be grieved to hear it, but I'm not going back. — Not for Reverend Mother, much as I love her. — Not for Monsignor Mero, dear as he has always been to me. — Not even for the archbishop."

"How about the pope?"

They laughed uproariously, fell into one another's arms and went to bed.

The final morning, when the expedition wound its way down through the hills, Martín was with his men at the rear, urging along the emaciated livestock. Gabriella was in her usual place with the headquarters contingent near the front of the train. She was afoot, leading her big saddle mule on whose back rode the Sandoval twins and Ynez supporting José in his sling.

In their nostrils was the sharp smell of the sea. Spread out at their feet was the golden valley with the mission buildings in the distance.

Three Fransciscan brothers — one a titan well over six feet tall — strode to meet the expedition as it crept along the road between the valley's deserted fields. The colonists had been told to expect as much. What they did not expect were the heads that began to rise like black bubbles among the fields of waist-high grain. By twos and threes, the heads converged and shoulders began to rise also, with arms pointing out this and that curiosity passing before their astonished eyes. The natives drew closer, whispering and staring at the unending line of gaunt pack animals with their sagging cargo and plodding nags with exhausted riders. On foot, rawboned men and women with hollow eyes struggled to keep up.

Hunger was no stranger to the natives; before the padres came and taught them husbandry, hunger and adversity were their constant companions. But they had thought the pale-skinned padres and their kind immune to such hardship. To see hundreds of these aliens so ravaged filled them with amazement.

The Franciscans greeted Colonel Anza and Padre Font with appropriate ceremony and escorted them on to the mission stockade. But the tall one, Fray Zalvidea, searched for Gabriella. When he found her, he was as astonished as the natives. Her copper-colored hair was chopped off below her ears like a boy's. Covering it and shading her face was a broad-brimmed soldier's hat. (*Soldier's hat?!!*). He stared at her bare suntanned arms and low-cut chemise, at the enormous mule she led with its burden of solemn, dull-eyed children; at Ramona following close behind, barefoot and in rags, leading a limping cargo mule and the spunky little donkey with the dispensary strapped to its back. "You have walked all morning, Señora?" he asked, incredulous.

"I have walked most of the last fifty miles, Señor," Gabriella replied shortly. "As you must surely see, our people need rest. I hope the mission is ready to receive us."

"Yes-yes," stammered Fray Zalvidea. "I am sent to tell you, Señora, that Fray Gómez is eagerly waiting to see you in the chapel. The soldiers told you about Fray Gómez, did they not?"

"My husband told me. I don't know anyone by that name."

The friar reddened. "He knows you, Señora. He has known you for many years, and is eager to see you."

"Both my husband and I have duties to discharge. I'm afraid your gentleman will have to wait."

"He wishes to see you alone."

Gabriella's brown eyes hardened as she appraised the friar. "My husband will accompany me when I meet Fray Gómez."

"But, Señora —"

They had reached the stockade gates. "You must excuse me now," said Gabriella. "Colonel Anza will want his dispensary set up in the headquarters tent. There will be patients I must care for. Please tell Fray Gómez that my husband and I will see him as soon as possible."

Two hours later — a longer time than usually required — the expedition's familiar village of shelters had materialized on both sides of the main road leading into the mission stockade. Leatherjackets and their wives moved languidly about unpacking cargo, but a curious lassitude had overtaken the travelers. Even the children seemed content to sit in the sun and gaze unbelieving at the whitecapped mountains to the east through which they had come, or to the sparkling blue of the Western Sea, a barely visible line along the opposite horizon.

Gabriella was near the last of her strength and hoped the meeting with the stranger would not take long. With Martín at her side, she walked to the chapel. The interior was dim, lit only by shallow windows near the thatched roof. Along a side wall was a long bench, from which eagerly leaped a balding, breathless Franciscan. In the shadows, his hair appeared brown but a low-slanting ray of sunlight showed it to be auburn.

The man seemed scarcely in control of himself and Gabriella edged closer to Martín. "Señora?" he gasped, clutching at her hands. "Yes, you are Gabriella Salgado. I would recognize you anywhere. You look so much like your mother you could be her twin. Except, of course, that your mother's hair was black. And such a beautiful, lustrous black! She was indeed a beautiful —"

Gabriella firmly withdrew her hands. "You have made a mistake, Señor," she interrupted. "My mother Carmen Salgado had hair the same color as mine."

Nonplussed, the friar shook his head. "They told you that. Padre Mero and the others. For your own protection. My dear child, you have your hair color from me. I am your father."

Despairing, Gabriella looked to Martín for help. "There is a misunderstanding of some kind," Martín said quietly. "On what evidence do you claim that my wife is your daughter?"

"She — she just is!" the friar exclaimed. "I am Gómez Costanza, her father. My mother has written to me regularly, for years, about Gabriella. She sent Padre Mero every month to make certain she was all right. He is our household chaplain, you see, Padre Mero. Monsignor Mero now — I correct myself. My mother paid Gabriella's fees to keep her enrolled in the convent school."

Gabriella's head was swimming from shock and exhaustion. She held tight to Martín and jumped when the giddy friar cried, "Ah! I know what will convince you!"

He dug into a pouch at his waist and withdrew a knot of cloth. With trembling fingers, he untied it and produced a magnificent emerald ring. Enormously pleased with himself, he placed it in Gabriella's palm and said, "There now. My mother says I am to give you this. It is a present. For you."

"It's Don Avila's emerald ring!" Gabriella exclaimed to Martín.

"My mother says you are to have it," said Fray Gómez. "She said you were loyal and kind to Don Avila's family. She wanted you to have something of his."

"But it's a fake!" Gabriella exclaimed. "Federico Verro stole the original and had a copy made. The stone is nothing but glass."

"Federico Verro was convicted of embezzlement. Maybe you didn't know that. Don Avila's family jewels were retrieved and sent to him in Madrid. All but this emerald ring. Mother kept it for you."

Martín interrupted. "This mother of yours, again — ?"

"Doña Teresa de Costanza. Carmen — my Carmen, Gabriella's mother — was a maid in our household. Doña Teresa is Gabriella's grandmother."

Gómez looked from one to the other in silence. "There is much to tell you," he plunged on. "My father died and left most of the family properties to my mother. I am the oldest son but I have told her if she leaves any mines or plantations to me, I shall give them all to the church. I never liked that life in Mexico. Half the time I felt like a dunce and the other half like a galley slave. I was an embarrassment to my father because I fell in love with Carmen, the most beautiful, virtuous woman who ever —. Well, I wish you had known your mother, Gabriella. My father and I had a fight over her. A real fight, you know. With rapiers. Here, I'll show you."

Like a small boy parading his trophies, he lifted the hem of his habit and displayed a long white scar along the calf of his leg.

"It was a terrible scandal, you see, for me to want to marry a servant in our household. In Mexico, people don't do such things. When I ran away, after the fight with my father, I didn't know that Carmen carried my child. I didn't know of it until years later. By then, she — she had died."

Fray Gómez shuffled to the door, turned and faced them. "About my father's properties, I want no part of them. But my mother says I must think of my grandchildren — the children my daughter will have someday. They are the proper heirs."

This strange man with his incredible news, coming to Gabriella already traumatized from four exhausting months of primitive travel, was almost more than her consciousness could absorb. She found herself silently offering a prayer of fervent thanksgiving to the Holy Virgin that her husband Martín sat beside her, protecting her with his moral strength, his authority.

She was surprised to discover that the thought uppermost in her mind was not of the friar — this awkward stranger who claimed her as his daughter — nor of Padre Mero nor of the mysterious Doña Teresa, who claimed her as grand-daughter. Instead she said softly, "Tell me about my mother."

Gómez' gnarled face folded into a smile. He returned and sat beside her on the bench. He traced a delicate finger over Gabriella's knuckles. "She had strong, square hands like yours. Wonderful hands. She could do anything — sew, weave, make lace. Eyes like yours, too. Dark brown, nearly black. Slanted, like the Filipinos we sometimes see here on the coast. She was a quiet, gentle person, so soft." He gazed, unseeing, into the distance. "I was big and awkward, always falling over my feet, never finding the right words to say what I meant. Carmen was the only one who never laughed at me. I loved her more than life itself. I will always love her."

And for all her weariness, Gabriella realized she could come to cherish this earnest, bumbling man. Her mother, Carmen, had cherished and, strange though it seemed, protected him. He would look to his daughter for that same protection. Well, later when she was alone with Martín, she would see what he had to say.

After an embarrassed pause, Fray Gómez cleared the unshed tears from his throat. "Well," he said. "What are your plans? Will you take up land and stay here? Or will you go north with Anza to establish a presidio at San Francisco? Or — or perhaps you will return to Mexico and drive through the Alameda every afternoon showing off your silks and satins."

Gabriella and Martín looked at one another. Through the minds of both paraded the memories of the beautiful city and its many advantages. Their children could have the proper schooling there; they could maintain ties with the monarch and his court in Spain; theirs would be a life of social distinction and honor.

But no. Without further hesitation, Martín spoke for them both: "That life has meaning for some, but Gabriella and I came to California to stay. Perhaps for the same reasons you did."

The question of his daughter's future had obviously lain heavily on Friar Gómez' thoughts, for now he beamed. "I like the decision you have made. My mother will like it too. She believes California will someday be more important than Mexico!"

Martín asked, "And what about you?"

The friar said gaily, "I will continue with my work, showing the Franciscan brothers how to make good wine. In my youth, I drank enough wine for a lifetime. So I know good wine from bad, you see. It's interesting, being a vintner. And I'm good at it. I'll spend another five years here, getting the vineyards established and a proper winery built. Then perhaps Father Paterna will send me to Monterey, who knows?"

Gabriella smiled. "Martín and I plan to have many children. You must visit us as often as possible."

"My mother and sisters in Mexico will be eager for news of their family in California. Of course I will write a long letter. Maybe you will give me a note to enclose with it. Sooner or later, there will be a packet boat to deliver it by way of San Blas. If not, I will send it back to Mexico with Colonel Anza. It's easy keeping in touch with those you love. Easier than most people think."

Epilogue   Convent of Santa Clara de Asís
                                                              March 1781

Doña María Teresa Gracés de Costanza appeared at the office door. "You've been
at those ledgers long enough!" she cried. "Come share a pot of chocolate with
Consuelo and me. The orchard's in bloom and it's heavenly on the terrace."

The abbess straightened reluctantly. She felt the cold nowadays and was
more comfortable at her office desk near the glowing grate. But her eyes had
begun to sting. And indeed, this past week, the fruit trees had provided more than
their usual festival of blossom. And Sister Consuelo, serene as the Madonna
herself, was a refreshment to the spirit no matter what season of the year. Madre
Valderia reached for her cane.

Reverend Mother had scarcely settled her gnarled figure against a pil-
lowed chair on the terrace when the young nun swiftly descended the stone
staircase to join them. "I can't stay long," she said, slightly out of breath. "The
novices are decorating the chapel for Palm Sunday. With so many guests coming
this year — "

" — So many that you've taken it upon yourself to supervise every tack and
tendril," nodded Doña Teresa with a knowing smile. "And the effect will be
breathtaking, as usual."

"Guests!" grunted the abbess, accepting a steaming cup. "How I used to dread
them! But Santa Clara today isn't the gutted old quarry it used to be."

And indeed it was not. The marble fountain beside which they sat had been
restored to its original splendor. The buildings' many cracks had been mended;
stucco ornaments and moldings had been replaced. All about them grew exotic
trees and flowering shrubs imported from Ceylon and Madagascar at the insis-
tence of the natural science teacher lured from a convent school in Salamanca.

Sister Consuelo touched Reverend Mother's arm with affection. "Doña
Teresa has made a big difference, hasn't she, Madre?"

"The money made the difference," Doña Teresa interrupted. "For that, you
have Gabriella to thank. And Gómez."

"Yes," Reverend Mother admitted. Her eyes began to smolder. "And there
would have been more money if the archbishop hadn't diddled you out of a
hundred ounces for the privilege of living here! You should have made him
negotiate, talked him down."

"I did talk him down!" replied Doña Teresa indignantly. "In the beginning,
the greedy fox wanted five hundred!"

Sister Consuelo stared and Madre Valderia's withered lips formed a ragged

O of wonder. "Five hundred ounces of gold!? The man's mad!"

"Not mad," replied Doña Teresa reassuringly. "A bit senile, perhaps. He thinks if he amasses enough wealth for Mother Church, God will look the other way and let him bring it with him when he dies. Fortunately, I'd had word from Gómez and was ready with a plan. The governor — you remember, Martín's uncle, Felipé de Neve — makes land grants from time to time. Two years ago, he granted the Costanza family a generous tract in the foothills behind San Gabriel mission."

"I remember," said Madre Valderia. "Gabriella and Martín are building their hacienda there."

"I told the archbishop of Gómez' work developing the winery and vineyards. I said we intended to supply wine to settlements and haciendas up and down the coast, which of course, we did. — There are so many of them now, you know, and more all the time! — I told him that out of gratitude for Gómez' assistance, I had thought of signing over the wine revenues to the Diocese. But since the fee he demanded was so much more than the hundred ounces I had expected to pay — " She sipped daintily.

" — And after the old miser thought it over, he —?" inquired Madre Valderia.

"After thinking it over, he reconsidered the fee."

Madre Valderia clacked her walking stick on the flags at her feet, more incensed than before. "And this is what you call negotiation?" she shouted. "You're as mad as he is!"

Doña Teresa raised a restraining hand. "Let me finish. Gómez had become increasingly disappointed in the grapes. The wine was drinkable, but —. He had tried olive trees with far greater success. Of course, it will take the trees a few years to develop their full commercial potential. But he is already experimenting, searching for the best way to convert the presses to produce olive oil instead of wine."

Sister Consuelo divined what was coming and hid a discreet smile behind her hand.

Not Reverend Mother, who trembled with indignation. "You're arranging matters so the greedy pirate will get more revenue, not less! Even a doddering idiot like the archbishop knows good olive oil is worth more than bad wine!"

"But my dear Luz," Doña Teresa protested mildly, "the agreement I signed with him said nothing about olive oil. Oh, I shan't deceive the old dear! All considered, he has been very kind to me over the years. He'll be paid every penny of revenue from the wine; Gómez will see to that. But after a few dwindling years, there will be no more wine. And since the archbishop is so advanced in age, there may soon be a new archbishop. The new man will have so many local properties to oversee he won't worry about the California vineyard that didn't turn out well."

The abbess drew a long breath and exchanged looks with Consuelo. "Everyone says Gabriella's changed," said the young nun. "Left to herself, would she have thought of such a scheme, do you think?"

Doña Teresa answered tartly, "Probably. But in California, there's no need. The padres aren't so greedy. They are dedicated missionaries with work to do. Mother Church will benefit, never fear. But the benefits will stay in California where they will do the most good. They won't buy statuary for the Vatican or tapestries for the archbishop's palace in Mexico."

A pause while Reverend Mother enjoyed a smile of transcendent satisfaction. She selected and tasted a macaroon. "It means a lot to us, Teresa, having you here," she confessed at last. "You almost compensate for losing Gabriella."

"But you're still not reconciled, are you, Luz? Not after five years?"

"Um," grunted Madre. "Nearly killed me, losing her."

Doña Teresa said quietly, "She's happier in California. I realize you don't agree, but she needed to live her own life."

"I think it was the suddenness of it all," said Consuelo, troubled. "In the wink of an eye, Don Avila was gone, Poof! How could the viceroy get by with such a thing, sending the family to an outpost like Alamos, to the wilderness! Doña Dolores is a cousin of the queen, after all!"

Doña Teresa murmured, "That's precisely why Bucareli sent him there, my dear. It was better than publicly booting him out. I had several conversations with the viceroy — "

Madre turned suspiciously to her friend. "You had conversations? You suggested Alamos?" A pause.

"Well, — "

"You did, didn't you, Teresa? Gómez was aboard ship headed for California and you wanted Gabriella there too! You wanted her in Alamos where she was certain to meet Colonel Anza, certain to be invited to join the expedition."

"You make it sound like a plot," protested Doña Teresa. "I can't help it, can I, if things turned out that way?"

Madre Valderia's voice was hard. "Things didn't just 'turn out that way', Teresa. You took her away. Her rightful home was here at the convent. You took her away!"

"And now you have Consuelo, who wanted to be here all along and is happy here."

"Consuelo is a saint but we are not talking about your niece Consuelo. We are talking about your granddaughter Gabriella. You took her away!"

Sister Consuelo raised her hand as if to speak.

Doña Teresa set down her cup with a rattle. "Luz, be realistic. Consuelo envied Gabriella because she thought Gabriella would become a nun and she wouldn't. Please don't try to tell me Gabriella was happy here. She had no family to acknowledge and support her. She was illegitimate, born out of wedlock! In the Spanish world a girl in that position is looked upon as a whore! Gabriella loved the convent, yes, but for the same reason a rat loves its hole: it was a safe place to hide!"

"You planned it all!" Madre pressed on. "Buena Suerte with the faltering aristocrat. The move to Alamos. Even Alesandro! When Gómez was growing up, he and Alesandro Figuroa were inseparable. You plotted with Alesandro to kidnap his parents and leave Gabriella stranded at Alamos. That way, she'd have no choice but to go to California." Silence. "Didn't you, Teresa?"

Sister Consuelo silently rose and replaced her empty cup on the table.

Doña Teresa protested, "'Kidnap', Luz? That's too strong a word. Avila was no longer able to control his affairs or even himself. — According to Carlos, he wasn't, anyway. And Alesandro could hardly ignore the monarch, could he? Carlos wanted Avila and Dolores returned to Madrid. He insisted."

"Insisted at whose prompting, Teresa? Yours?"

Sister Consuelo rolled her eyes, turned and soundlessly tiptoed away.

"No. The Costanzas have never been close to the royal family. You know that, Luz."

"Whose, then? The archbishop's?"

"Well, Avila did promise those two maguey plantations in Havana, you'll remember, but they never materialized. The archbishop was indignant about that. He returned to Spain for a visit about that time. He mentioned to Eduardo that he might bring the matter up with the king while he was there."

Madre said crisply, "You're a meddler, Teresa. You know that? What else did you arrange? For the Apaches to murder Elias? For Gabriella's miscarriage? For Martín?"

Doña Teresa shook her head. "No. No."

"Those things just happened, I suppose. You left something for God to do. How thoughtful of you! I know He appreciated your forebearance." After a grim silence, Madre said, "I was taken in. I can see it now. You set your chaplain on me, my own cousin."

"Don't blame Raoul. The worst disagreement Raoul and I ever had was over Alamos. He was terrified at the thought of Gabriella in Apache country."

"But you weren't!" Madre angrily pointed an arthritic finger at Doña Teresa. "You! Loving grandmother that you are, you abandoned her there!"

"That's ridiculous, Luz!" cried Doña Teresa. "How could she be 'abandoned' with Colonel Anza and 250 people of the expedition to turn to. Anyway, Gabriella's no pampered infant in a christening dress. She's tough! You raised her to be tough, as I knew you would! The same way you taught my daughters to be tough. Why do you think I had Raoul bring poor Carmen all the way out here to this Godforsaken ruin? Yes, that's what Santa Clara de Asís was twenty years ago, a ruin! There were half-a-dozen better places I could have sent her without leaving the city. But I wanted my grandchild to learn perseverance and dependability. I knew that's the training she'd get here with you. She did, too!" She flipped her *rebozo* out of the way over her shoulder. "Gabriella's no ninny. Quite a number of those decisions could have been hers and not mine at all; had you bothered to think about that?!"

Madre rose with the help of her cane. "Where's Consuelo?"

"She went indoors. She always hates it when we quarrel."

Madre Valderia repositioned her cane and stood for a moment to make sure of her balance.

"I'm sorry I've made you angry, Luz," pleaded Doña Teresa. "Don't you go in, too. The sunshine's good for you, puts color in your cheeks."

"I wasn't going in," grumbled the abbess. "Just moving about to keep my joints from going stiff."

She took a few steps, then turned frowning. "I can't believe you'd take such liberties with a person's life! Meddler!"

Doña Teresa tossed her head in exasperation. "'Such liberties'? My dear Luz, what of the liberties you take, every week, every day, with hundreds of lives! But that's your duty, to supervise these people, to guide and help them. If you think 'meddling' is a more appropriate word — " She sighed. "Luz, listen to me. While Gabriella was growing up here at the convent, Raoul used to hear her confessions and afterwards he'd be so sad. I knew why. The child was an orphan. — But you still don't understand. For example, if she'd had relatives among the expedition people, Font and Bucareli could never have called her a witch, could they? But today, she's in California where people care only about the future. Gabriella belongs to the future."

They descended the stone steps to the orchard. Doña Teresa murmured, "She's like you, you know."

But Madre shook her head. "More like you than me. When you were her age, you wanted to get away too, remember?" She breathed deeply of the perfumed air. "Maybe it was right, what you did. The girl's gone, anyway. I should stop brooding, stop complaining."

"People our age have earned the right to complain. Grouse all you like."

Madre smiled. "It was a blessing for all of us when you came to Santa Clara, Teresa. Before, we were like a colony of mindless ants — bustle-bustle, hurry-hurry. Today we're all more relaxed, more open with one another."

"I hope I haven't interfered with anyone's spiritual devotion."

"Your own devotion sets a good example and you know it. You spend so much time on your knees, I'm surprised they still work properly."

Silence. "Luz?"

"Um?"

"Have you always told your confessor everything? — I mean, — you know, everything?"

"Of course not! I'd frighten the poor man to death!"

Madre waited. "Come-come. What is it you should have told your confessor but didn't? I'm no confessor but I'll express indignation, wrath, pity, whatever will oblige you."

Doña Teresa gazed at her companion. A mutual affection welled up in their eyes. Madre shrugged. "What are friends for?"

Doña Teresa bit her lip and looked away. Madre smelled a secret and waited, spider-like, for the morsel she knew was coming. She even knew — now — what the secret was about.

"It's hard to talk about it — "

"Then perhaps I can help," said Madre. "By arranging for Gabriella to go to Buena Suerte, you made certain she would get to know her real grandfather, didn't you, Teresa?"

Doña Teresa's discomfiture confirmed her guess.

" — and that's what you never got around to mentioning in the confessional. That your husband was not the father of your first child."

They walked another ten yards before Doña Teresa replied. "I made it up to Eduardo, I think."

"Two more sons and four daughters. Yes, I think you made it up to him."

"That's not what I meant."

"You always seemed a happily married couple. I think I can imagine what you meant. You and Eduardo knew the Figuroa family rather well before you left Spain. What happened?"

A pause. "We hoped to marry, Avila and I. But his father wouldn't hear of it. Dolores was the queen's cousin and Avila was ordered to marry her." She shrugged. "So he did. It broke his heart and mine too."

"But Gómez — . Did it come as a surprise when you found you were pregnant?"

"I was surprised it didn't happen earlier." Doña Teresa covered her face with her hand. "I shouldn't be telling this."

"Come now, don't be coy. Pre-nuptial sex isn't all that rare."

"By then it was adultery."

Madre leaned forward to catch the faint words. "By then'? By when? I'm not getting the time straight."

"What Avila and I felt for one another, Luz, it was more than love. It was a craziness, like two people with only one heart to share. It couldn't go on. I kept insisting to Eduardo that we should come to Mexico, to the New World. It was on the journey coming here that I realized I was pregnant." She paused.

" — and then the unexpected," murmured the abbess. "Papa Figuroa sent Avila and his family to Mexico, too. A pretty kettle of eels!"

"When — when Avila saw Gómez for the first time, he was devastated. Both of them with that fiery auburn hair! We wept in one another's arms, Avila and I. From that day, he was never without a periwig, sometimes white, sometimes dark brown. He told everyone it was to conceal his baldness. Soon most people had forgotten Avila de Figuroa ever had red hair." She closed her eyes. "What a shameful thing!"

"Teresa," Luz said firmly. "There is a well-kept secret that you need to know: Your sin is not all that spectacular. The gratifying thing, to me, is that Gabriella got to know her real grandfather. You told her, of course."

Doña Teresa recoiled at the thought. "No!" she cried.

Surprised, Luz said, "Then Gómez — "

"Gómez doesn't know either! He must never know!"

"But you went to so much trouble to save the Figuroa properties. I thought you sent Raoul — . Well, of course not, now I think about it. The California missions are primitive, aren't they? They need someone like Monsignor Mero, so good with ritual."

Doña Teresa arched an eyebrow at her friend but was ignored.

Madre smiled with contentment. "I always hoped Raoul would bring enlightenment to the heathen. He could have done so much with his life but threw away his opportunities."

Doña Teresa squirmed. "The reason I sent your cousin Raoul to California,

Luz, was to make certain my great-grandchildren are taught proper social
decorum — how to meet people of quality, how to entertain their friends. Gómez
is there with them, of course, but Gómez is hopeless at that kind of thing. I haven't
gone to this much trouble for my heirs to have them grow up like barbarians."

"*Santa Madre*," breathed the abbess in wonder. "You've kept a close eye on
these heirs of yours, haven't you?"

"Of course! That's why I sent Ana to Buena Suerte, to watch out for Gabriella
and protect her if she could. Raoul disapproved of Ana, said she was a slattern.
I told him Gabriella would straighten her out. She did, too."

"Who's this? Ana? Ana who?"

"Bonita's maid, Ana. She reported to me every week. Not even Avila knew
about Ana. She would have saved Gabriella from that monster, too, but — "

Silence.

"What monster? Saved her from whom?"

"That was another secret. I shouldn't have given it away. Luz, there's no need
for you to be upset now that it's all in the past."

Madre Valderia came to a halt, leaned on her cane. "What monster?"

"Federico Verro."

"The steward?"

Doña Teresa nodded. "I warned Avila. I'd heard of the man and didn't trust
him, but Avila hired him anyway. Well, this Verro person resented Gabriella,
treated her like a common servant. Demanded most of the salary Avila paid her.
As you remember, it was rather generous."

"He defrauded her of her salary. That's all?"

"He — "

"He what?!"

"Luz, I know you're going to be angry. This Federico Verro sent for Gabriella
in the middle of the night and beat her senseless."

The abbess tensed. Growling with suppressed fury, she rose to her full height
and shook her walking cane at the heavens. "Why wasn't I told about this?" she
shouted.

"Now, Luz. Luz, calm yourself. Raoul said not to tell you and I agreed. He said
you'd come to Buena Suerte and tear the man limb from limb."

"He's right! I would have! I will yet! What happened to the scoundrel? Where
is he today?"

"Dead."

The abbess sagged. "Dead?"

"He was charged with fraud and embezzlement in the management of the
Figuroa properties — "

"I know that!" Madre barked.

"Bucareli sentenced him to hang but he escaped. Stowed away on a packet
ship out of Vera Cruz."

"Then how do you know he's dead?"

"Ernán hired men to track him down. They found him in Boston." She cleared
her throat. "He happened to run into a rapier. The blade lodged in his chest and

killed him."

"My compliments to the owner of the rapier," said Madre with satisfaction. "You know he's dead? You're certain?"

"The men brought back an affidavit from the constable. And an emerald ring he'd stolen. It was Avila's. I recognized it."

"You're positive it was the same ring?"

" — And not a fake stone? Ernán had it certified. And yes, I'm positive it's the same ring. I gave it to Avila the night before he married."

They strolled in silence. Madre exclaimed, "Incredible!" Then putting the incident behind her, she remarked, "Raoul is enjoying himself in California, isn't he? Hah! The ruling prelate, Monsignor Mero! Everyone smothering him with favors. He will have some good stories for us when he returns. I'll be glad to see him."

"He won't return."

"He said he'd be back in a few months."

Doña Teresa shrugged. "Gabriella and Martín need him. He's a wonderful chaplain, Luz. So sweet with children. Comforting. Punctilious. He's a perfect addition to their household."

"Pah! He likes his luxuries too well. Before long, the novelty will wear off and he'll be back home again."

"How? By land? With the Indians slitting every Spanish throat within hundreds of miles?"

"What are you saying, Teresa? He went to California by sea and he can come home by sea. It's risky, of course, but not all ships are wrecked on the rocks or blown halfway to Hawaii. Believe me, I know Raoul Mero. If he truly wants to return to Mexico, he will return."

"No, Luz, he won't. Since I'm not on the spot, I can't tell you the exact reason. But there will be one. Perhaps the ship in port will have no room for a passenger. Or perhaps Monsignor Mero will be detained at the last moment on important military business. Or — animal hides smell dreadful, you know — maybe the cargo will be so repugnant he will decide not to return after all. Something will happen, never fear. He will never return."

"You're very sure of yourself."

"Of course, Luz. You forget. I own all the ships."

Madre's eyes widened. *Who whould have thought the old girl could possibly be as wealthy as all that?* she marveled, glowing happily at the prospect of endowments.

Silently the two women strolled contentedly among the trees. A draft of warm air stirred Madre's veil and a wry twist of amusement lifted the corner of her mouth as she reflected with pride how well Gabriella had done on her own, with no help frm either of them. "God must find us altogether ridiculoud," she said, lips primly closed against the unseemly giggle rising in her throat.

Doña Teresa sighed by way of agreement, but the sigh emerged as a musical titter. "We tried very hard, didn't we?"

Before either of them knew or intended, their genteel simpering grew to chortling, then to cackling, and at last to very unladylike whoops and explosions of laughter.

It was an unusual but thoroughly wholesome sound for the convent of Santa Clara de Asís. Peal upon joyous peal, it floated above the petaled fruit trees where it roused the birds and sent them soaring, challenged the cicadas and silenced their droning. It echoed against the towers of the convent's lovely chapel overlooking the orchard.

From a chapel window, Sister Consuelo gazed down in smiling wonder.

END

THE CALIFORNIA EXPEDITION 1775-1776
ROSTER BY FAMILIES

From enlistment and church records, census and military reports, historians have compiled names of those who actually participated in the 1775-76 California expedition. Multiple spelling of names was common; the spellings given below are those usually found in the records.

ACEVES,
Antonio Quiterio, age 36, recruit
*María Feliciana Cortés, his wife
María Petra, age 13
José Cipriano, age 11
María Gertrudis, age 6
Juan Gregorio, age 5
Juan Pablo, age 3
José Antonio, age 2

ALTAMIRANO,
Justo Roberto, age 31,
presidio soldier
María Loreta Delfin, his wife
José Antonio
José Matias

ALVAREZ DE ACEVEDO,
Luis Joaquín, age 36, recruit
María Nicolasa Ortiz, his wife
Juan Francisco
María Francisca

ALVISO,
Corporal Domingo, presidio
soldier
María Angela Chumasero,
his wife, known in California
as María Angela Trejo
Francisco Xavier, age 10,
generally called Xavier
in California
Xavier, age 9, also known
as Francisco Xavier but
generally called Francisco
in California.
María Loreto, age 5
Juan Ygnacio, age 3

AMEZQUITA,
Juan Antonio, age 37,
presidio soldier.
Juana María de Gaona, his wife
Salvador Manuel, age 23.
Also known in California
as Manuel Domingo
Amezquita and Manuel
Francisco Amezquita.
Rosalía Zamora, his wife
María Josépha, age 20
María Dolores, age 10
María Matilde
María Gertrudis, age 3
María de los Reyes,
infant

ANZA,
Don Juan Bautista de,
Lieutenant-colonel, commander

ARBALLO,
María Feliciana, widow of José
Gutierrez
* María Tómasa
GUTIERREZ, age 6
* María Estaquia
GUTIERREZ, age 4

ARELLANO
(See RAMIREZ ARELLANO)

BERNAL,
Juan Francisco, age 39, recruit
María Josefa de Soto (sister of
Ignacio de SOTO)
José Joaquin, age 13
Juan Francisco, age 12

José Dionisio, age 10
José Apolonario, age 9
Ana María, age 5
María Teresa de Jesus,
    age 3
Tómas Januario

BERREYESA,
  Nicolás Antonio, age 15,
    settler accompanied by his
    unmarried sister, María Ysabel,
    age 22

BOJORQUES,
  José Ramón, age 39, presidio
    soldier
  María Francisca Romero, his wife
    * María Antonia, age 15,
      married en route.
      (See VASQUEZ)
    * María Micaela, age 13,
      married en route.
      (See HIGUERA)
    María Gertrudis, age 12

BOJORQUES,
  Pedro Antonio, age 22, recruit
  María Francisca de Lara,
    his wife
    María Agustina, age 4

*CARDENAS,
  Ygnacio, adopted son.
  (See SANCHEZ)

CASTRO,
  Joaquin Ysidro, age 44, recruit
  María Martína Botillér, his wife
    Ygnacio Clemente, age 20
    María Ana Josefa, age 18
    María de la Encarnacíon,
      age 12
    María Martína, age 10.
      Listed thus by Bolton;
      may be the same as María
      del Carmen Castro listed
      by Eldredge.
    José Maríano, age 9
    José Joaquín, age 6
    Francisco María, age 2
    Francisco Antonio
    Carlos Antonio

*CORTEO, María Feliciana.
  (See ACEVES)

EIXARCH,
  Fray Tomás, missionary who (with
    Garcés) joined the expedition
    at Tumacacacori and accom-
    panied the colonists as far as
    the Colorado River.

FELIX,
  José Vicente, age 35, recruit
  María Ygnacia Manuela Piñuelas,
    his wife. (Died in childbirth at
    La Canoa en route. She was
    buried at Mission San Xavier
    del Bac on 25 October 1775 in
    services conducted by Padre
    Francisco Garcés. No trace of
    her grave remains at the
    mission today.)
    José Francisco
    José Doroteo
    José de Jesús
    José Antonio de Capistrano,
      surviving infant son born
      at La Canoa on 23 October
      1775. He was baptized at
      Mission San Xavier del Bac
      two days later by Padre
      Tómas Eixarch.
    María Loreta
    María Antonia
    María Marcela

FONT,
  Fray Pedro, O.F.M. official
    chaplain. Joined the expedition
    at Horcasitas, accompanied
    Anza to California and returned.

FUENTE
  (see PÉREZ DE LA FUENTE)

GALINDO,
  Nicolás, age 33, settler
  María Teresa Pinto, his wife
    Juan Venancio, age 1 year

GALLEGOS,
Carlos, presidio soldier
María Josefa Espinosa, his wife.
Gallegos and his wife were
granted permission to return
to Sonora and left with Anza
and Padre Font from Monterey
on 14 April 1776.

GARCÉS,
Fray Francisco, missionary who
(with Eixarch) joined the
expedition at Tumacacori and
accompanied the colonists as
far as the Colorado River.

GARCÍA,
José Antonio, recruit
Petronila Josefa de Acuña, his
wife, more commonly known
in California as María Josefa
de Acuña.
María Josefa
José Francisco
Juan Guillermo
Also accompanying the GARCÍA
family were two children from
the mother's first marriage to
Dionisio HERNÁNDEZ,
*María Graciana and
*José Vicente Antonio.

GONZALES,
José Manuel, settler
María Micaela Ruiz, his wife.
Sometimes known in California
as María Micaela Bojórques.
Juan José
Ramón
Francisco
María Gregoria

GRIJALVA,
Sergeant Juan Pablo, age 34,
presidio soldier
María Dolores Valencia, his wife
María Josefa, age 9
María del Carmen, age 4
Claudio, infant

*GUTIERREZ,
María Estaquia, age 4
(See ARBALLO)

*GUTIERREZ,
María Tómasa, age 6
(See ARBALLO)

GUTIERREZ,
Ygnacio María, recruit
Ana María de Osuna, his wife
María Petronila, age 10
María de los Santos, age 7
Diego Pasqual, infant born
on the Gila River, en route,
at Cerro de Pasqual
18 November 1775, and
baptized the next day by
Padre Font.

*HERNÁNDEZ,
José Vicente Antonio
(See GARCÍA)

*HERNÁNDEZ,
María Graciana (See GARCÍA)

HIGUERA,
Ygnacio Anastacio
*María Micaela BOJORQUES,
age 13, his wife. Married en route
26 October 1775 at Mission
San Xavier del Bac by Padre
Pedro Font.

LINARES,
Ygnacio, age 31, presidio soldier
María Gertrudis Rivas, his wife
María Gertrudis, age 7
Juan José Ramón, age 5
María Juliana, age 4
Salvador Ygnacio, infant born
en route, at the upper end
of Coyote Canyon on
Christmas Eve, 1775, and
baptized on Christmas Day
by Padre Font.

LOPEZ,
  Sebastian Antonio, recruit
  Felipa Neri, his wife. Also known
    as Felipa Zermana Sebastian
      María Tómasa
      María Justa

MESA,
  Corporal José Valerio, age 42,
    presidio soldier
  María Leonor Barboa, his wife
      José Joaquin, age 12
      José Ygnacio, age 9
      José Dolores, age 8. Known
        as Ygnacio Dolores Mesa
        in California
      María Manuela, age 7
      José Antonio, age 3
      Juan, age 3

MORAGA,
  Lieutenant Don José Joaquin,
    age 35, presidio soldier. Came
    alone because of the illness of
    his wife. Family joined him
    later in California.

MUÑOZ,
  Don Francisco, unmarried recruit

PACHECO,
  Juan Salvio, recruit
  María del Carmen del Valle,
    his wife
      Miguel, age 20
      Ygnacio, age 15
      Ygnacio Gertrudis, age 15
      Bartolome Ygnacio, age 10
      María Barbara, age 10

PERALTA,
  Corporal Gabriel, age 45,
    presidio soldier
  Francisca Manuela Valenzuela,
    his wife, known in California
    as Francisca Xaviera
    Valenzuela
      Juan José, age 18
      Luis María, age 17
      Pedro Regalado, age 11
      María Gertrudis, age 9

PEREZ DE LA FUENTE,
  Pedro, unmarried recruit

PICO,
  Santiago de la Cruz, age 43,
    recruit
  María Jacinta Bastida, his wife
      José Dolores, age 12
      José María, age 11
      José Miguel, age 7
      Francisco Xavier, age 6
      Patricio, age 5
      María Antonia Tómasa
      María Josefa

PINTO,
  Pablo, age 44, recruit
  Francixca Xavier Ruelas, his wife
      Juan María, age 17
      *Juana Santos (See VARELA)
      Juana Francisca
      José Marcelo

RAMIREZ ARELLANO,
  Manuel, age 34, recruit. Manuel
    Ramírez Arellano's surname
    evolved to Arellanes in
    California.
  María Agueda Lopez de Haro,
    his wife
      José Maríano
      *Matías VEGA (adopted)

SANCHEZ,
  José Antonio, age 25, recruit
  María de los Dolores Morales,
    his wife
      María Josefa, age 7
      José Antonio, age 2
      *Ignacio CARDENAS
        (adopted)

254 ✤ FAIR LAUGHS THE MORN

SANDOVAL,
Cristobal, settler. Bolton lists
"Cristóbal Sandoval" but the
name given at the time of
his marriage at San Xavier
Mission was "Gregario
Antonio Sandoval."

María Dolores Ontiveros, his wife.
Married 26 October 1775 at
San Xavier by Padre Font.
See also HIGUERA and
VASQUEZ two other young
couples married on this same
date.

SOTELO,
José Antonio, recruit
Gertrudis Peralta, his wife.
Sometimes known in California
as Manuela Gertrudis Buelna.
Ramón (only child)

SOTO,
Ygnacio de, age 27, recruit
María Barbara Espinosa, his wife
María Francisca, age 2
José Antonio, age 1

TAPIA,
Felipé Santiago, age 31, recruit
Juana María Cardenas, his wife.
Sometimes known in Califor-
nia as Juana María Filomena
Hernándes.
María Rosa, age 15
María Antonia, age 10
José Bartolome
Juan José
José Cristobal
María Manuela, age 10
José Francisco
María Ysadora, age 4
José Victor

VALENCIA,
José Manuel, age 27, recruit
María de la Luz Munos, his wife
María Gertrudis, age 15
Francisco María, age 8
Ygnacio María, age 3

VALENZUELA,
Juan Agustin, age 26, recruit
Petra Ygnacia de Ochoa
María Zeferina

VARELA,
Casimiro
*Juana Santos PINTO, his wife

VASQUEZ,
Juan Atanasio, age 41, recruit
Gertrudis Castelo, his wife
José Tiburcio, age 20
*María Antonia
BOJORQUES, his wife.
Married en route 26
October 1775, by Padre
Pedro Font at Mission San
Xavier del Bac.
José Antonio, age 10
Pedro José

*VEGA,
Matías, adopted son (See
RAMIREZ ARELLANO)

VIDAL,
Don Maríano, commissary

VILLELA,
Marcos, unmarried recruit

_____

*Listed under more than one name

In addition to the individuals named above, there were thirty muleteers, vaqueros, servants and Indian interpreters whose names appear seldom if at all in the documents.

Twelve of Colonel Anza's families remained in the San Gabriel area (now part of greater Los Angeles) and established themselves as ranchers and farmers. Anza escorted the remaining colonists north to San Francisco Bay, where he dedicated the presidio in September 1776. The following year, several enterprising pioneers established a settlement at San José, on the bay's southern shore. The community was made up of soldiers brought to California by Anza, colonists from the territorial capital at Monterey and from the new presidio at San Francisco.

During the five years after Anza, as many as three hundred more settlers followed his overland route to California. In the summer, blistering heat made the trail impassable. At all times, it was impassable without the natives' assistance, which eroded after 1776 until the overland route had to be abandoned altogether.

As for Colonel Anza, in recognition of his service to the crown and his skill in establishing order on the frontier, he was appointed governor of New Mexico in 1777. He served in this post until his death in 1788. Many of his most enthusiastic admirers, this author among them, feel that Juan Bautista de Anza has never received the acclaim he deserves.